BY TERRY BROOKS

SHANNARA
First King of Shannara
The Sword of Shannara
The Elfstones of Shannara
The Wishsong of Shannara

THE HERITAGE OF SHANNARA
The Scions of Shannara
The Druid of Shannara
The Elf Queen of Shannara
The Talismans of Shannara

THE VOYAGE OF THE *JERLE SHANNARA*
Ilse Witch
Antrax
Morgawr

HIGH DRUID OF SHANNARA
Jarka Ruus
Tanequil
Straken

GENESIS OF SHANNARA
Armageddon's Children
The Elves of Cintra
The Gypsy Morph

LEGENDS OF SHANNARA
Bearers of the Black Staff
The Measure of the Magic

The World of Shannara

THE MAGIC KINGDOM OF LANDOVER
Magic Kingdom for Sale—Sold!
The Black Unicorn
Wizard at Large
The Tangle Box
Witches' Brew
A Princess of Landover

THE WORD AND THE VOID
Running with the Demon
A Knight of the Word
Angel Fire East

Sometimes the Magic Works: Lessons from a Writing Life

LEGENDS OF SHANNARA

THE
MEASURE
OF THE
MAGIC

LEGENDS OF SHANNARA

THE
Measure
OF THE
Magic

TERRY BROOKS

BALLANTINE BOOKS

NEW YORK

Published in the United States by Del Rey, an imprint of The Random House Publishing Group, a division of Random House, Inc., New York.

DEL REY is a registered trademark and the Del Rey colophon is a trademark of Random House, Inc.

Library of Congress Cataloging-in-Publication Data
Brooks, Terry.
The measure of the magic : legends of Shannara / Terry Brooks.
p. cm.
ISBN 978-0-345-48420-8 (hardcover : alk paper) —
ISBN 978-0-345-52921-3 (ebk.)
1. Shannara (Imaginary place)—Fiction.   I. Title.
PS3552.R6596M43 2011
813'.54—dc22   2011014440

Printed in the United States of America on acid-free paper

www.delreybooks.com

2 4 6 8 9 7 5 3 1

First Edition

FOR BETSY MITCHELL

A good editor, a better friend

LEGENDS OF SHANNARA

THE
MEASURE
OF THE
MAGIC

ONE

HUMMING TUNELESSLY, THE RAGPICKER WALKED the barren, empty wasteland in the aftermath of a rainstorm. The skies were still dark with clouds and the earth was sodden and slick with surface water, but none of that mattered to him. Others might prefer the sun and blue skies and the feel of hard, dry earth beneath their feet, might revel in the brightness and the warmth. But life was created in the darkness and damp of the womb, and the ragpicker took considerable comfort in knowing that procreation was instinctual and needed nothing of the face of nature's disposition that he liked the least.

He was an odd-looking fellow, an unprepossessing, almost comical figure. He was tall and whipcord-thin, and he walked like a long-legged waterbird. Dressed in dark clothes that had seen much better days, he tended to blend in nicely with the mostly colorless landscape he traveled. He carried his rags and scraps of cloth in a frayed patchwork bag slung over one shoulder, the bag looking very much as if it would rip apart completely with each fresh step its bearer took. A pair of scuffed leather boots completed the ensemble, scavenged from a dead man some years back, but still holding up quite nicely.

Everything about the ragpicker suggested that he was harmless. Everything marked him as easy prey in a world where predators dominated the remnants of a decimated population. He knew how he looked to the things that were always hunting, what they thought when they saw him coming. But that was all right. He had stayed alive this long by keeping his head down and staying out of harm's way. People like him, they didn't get noticed. The trick was in not doing anything to call attention to yourself.

So he tried hard to give the impression that he was nothing but a poor wanderer who wanted to be left alone, but you didn't always get what you wanted in this world. Even now, other eyes were sizing him up. He could feel them doing so, several pairs in several different places. Those that belonged to the animals—the things that the poisons and chemicals had turned into mutants—were already turning away. Their instincts were sharper, more finely tuned, and they could sense when something wasn't right. Given the choice, they would almost always back away.

It was the eyes of the human predators that stayed fixed on him, eyes that lacked the awareness necessary to judge him properly. Two men were studying him now, deciding whether or not to confront him. He would try to avoid them, of course. He would try to make himself seem not worth the trouble. But, again, you didn't always get what you wanted.

He breathed in the cool, damp air, absorbing the taste of the rain's aftermath on his tongue, of the stirring of stagnation and sickness generated by the pounding of the sudden storm, of the smells of raw earth and decay, the whole of it marvelously welcome. Sometimes, when he was alone, he could pretend he was the only one left in the world. He could think of it all as his private preserve, his special place, and imagine everything belonged to him.

He could pretend that nothing would ever bother him again.

His humming dropped away, changing to a little song:

Ragpicker, ragpicker, what you gonna do
When the hunters are hunting and they're hunting for you.

Ragpicker, ragpicker, just stay low.
If you don't draw attention they might let you go.

He hummed a few more bars, wondering if he had gotten past the predators. He was thinking it was almost time to stop and have something to drink and eat. But that would have to wait. He sighed, his lean, sharp-featured face wreathed in a tight smile that caused the muscles of his jaw to stand out like cords.

Ragpicker, ragpicker, you're all alone.
The hunters that are hunting want to pick your bones.
Ragpicker, ragpicker, just walk on.
If you wait them out they will soon be gone.

He crossed a meadow, a small stream filled with muddy water, a rocky flat in which tiny purple flowers were blooming, and a withered woods in which a handful of poplars grew sparse and separate as if strangers to one another. Ahead, there was movement in a rugged mass of boulders that formed the threshold to foothills leading up to the next chain of mountains, a high and wild and dominant presence. He registered the movement, ignored it. Those who had been watching him were still there and growing restless; he must skirt their hiding place and hope they were distracted by other possibilities. But there didn't appear to be anyone else out here other than himself, and he was afraid that they would come after him just because they were bored.

He continued on furtively, still humming softly.

Daylight leached away as the clouds began to thicken anew. It might actually rain some more, he decided. He glanced at the skies in all four directions, noting the movement of the clouds and the shifting of their shadows against the earth. Yes, more rain coming. Better find shelter soon.

He stalked up the slope into the rocks, his long, thin legs stretching out, meandering here and there as if searching for the best way through. He headed away from the watchers, pretending he was heedless of them, that he knew nothing of them and they, in turn, should not want to bother with him.

But suddenly his worst fears were realized and just like that they were upon him.

They emerged from the rocks, two shaggy-haired, ragged men, carrying blades and clubs. One was blind in one eye, and the other limped badly. They had seen hard times, the ragpicker thought, and they would not be likely to have seen much charity and therefore not much inclined to dispense any. He stood where he was and waited on them patiently, knowing that flight was useless.

"You," One-eye said, pointing a knife at him. "What you got in that bag of yours?"

The ragpicker shrugged. "Rags. I collect them and barter for food and drink. It's what I do."

"You got something more than that, I'd guess," said the second man, the larger of the two. "Better show us what it is."

The ragpicker hesitated, and then dumped everything on the ground, his entire collection of brightly colored scarves and bits of cloth, a few whole pieces of shirts and coats, a hat or two, some boots. Everything he had managed to find in his travels of late that he hadn't bargained away with the Trolls or such.

"That's crap!" snarled One-eye, thrusting his knife at the ragpicker. "You got to do better than that! You got to give us something of worth!"

"You got coin?" demanded the other.

Hopeless, the ragpicker thought. No one had coin anymore and even if they did it was valueless. Gold or silver, maybe. A good weapon, especially one of the old automatics from the days of the Great Wars, would have meant something, would have been barter material. But no one had coins.

"Don't have any," he said, backing away a step. "Can I pick up my rags?"

One-eye stepped forward and ground the colored cloth into the dirt with the heel of his boot. "That's what I think of your rags. Now watch and see what I'm gonna do to you!"

The ragpicker backed away another step. "Please, I don't have anything to give you. I just want you to let me pass. I'm not worth your trouble. Really."

"You ain't worth much, that's for sure," said the one who limped.

"But that don't mean you get to go through here free. This is our territory and no one passes without they make some payment to us!"

The two men came forward again, a step at a time, spreading out just a little to hem the ragpicker in, to keep him from making an attempt to get around them. As if such a thing were possible, the ragpicker thought, given his age and condition and clear lack of athletic ability. Did he look like he could get past them if he tried? Did he look like he could do anything?

"I don't think this is a good idea," he said suddenly, stopping short in his retreat. "You might not fully understand what you're doing."

The predators stopped and stared at him. "You don't think it's a good idea?" said the one who limped. "Is that what you said, you skinny old rat?"

The ragpicker shook his head. "It always comes down to this. I don't understand it. Let me ask you something. Do you know of a man who carries a black staff?"

The two exchanged a quick look. "Who is he?" asked One-eye. "Why would we know him?"

The ragpicker sighed. "I don't know that you do. Probably you don't. But he would be someone who had real coin on him, should you know where to find him. You don't, do you?"

"Naw, don't know anyone like that," snarled One-eye. He glanced at his companion. "C'mon, let's see what he's hiding."

They came at the ragpicker with their blades held ready, stuffing the clubs in their belts. They were hunched forward slightly in preparation for getting past whatever defenses the scarecrow intended to offer, the blades held out in front of them. The ragpicker stood his ground, no longer backing up, no longer looking as if he intended escape. In fact, he didn't look quite the same man at all. The change was subtle and hard to identify, but it was evident that something was different about him. It was in his eyes as much as anywhere, in a gleam of madness that was bright and certain. But it was in his stance, as well. Before, he had looked like a frightened victim, someone who knew that he stood no chance at all against men like these. Now he had the appearance of someone who had taken control of matters in spite of his apparent inability to do so, and his two attackers didn't like it.

That didn't stop them, of course. Men of this sort were never stopped by what they couldn't understand, only by what was bigger and stronger and better armed. The ragpicker was none of these. He was just an unlucky fool trying to be something he wasn't, making a last-ditch effort to hang on to his life.

One-eye struck first, his blade coming in low and swift toward the ragpicker's belly. The second man was only a step behind, striking out in a wild slash aimed at his victim's exposed neck. Neither blow reached its intended mark. The ragpicker never seemed to move, but suddenly he had hold of both wrists, bony fingers locking on flesh and bone and squeezing until his attackers cried out in pain, dropped their weapons, and sank to their knees in shock, struggling to break free. The ragpicker had no intention of releasing them. He just held them as they moaned and writhed, studying their agonized expressions.

"You shouldn't make assumptions about people," he lectured them, bending close enough that they could see the crimson glow in his eyes, a gleam of bloodlust and rage. "You shouldn't do that."

His hands tightened further, and smoke rose through his fingers where they gripped the men's wrists. Now the men were howling and screaming as their imprisoned wrists and hands turned black and charred, burned from the inside out.

The ragpicker released them then and let them drop to the ground in huddled balls of quaking, blubbering despair, cradling their damaged arms. "You've ruined such a lovely day, too," he admonished. "All I wanted was to be left alone to enjoy it, and now this. You are pigs of the worst sort, and pigs deserve to be roasted and eaten!"

At this they cried out anew and attempted to crawl away, but the ragpicker was on them much too quickly, seizing their heads and holding them fast. Smoke rose from between his clutching fingers and the men jerked and writhed in response.

"How does that feel?" the ragpicker wanted to know. "Can you tell what's happening to you? I'm cooking your brains, in case you've failed to recognize what you are experiencing. Doesn't feel very good, does it?"

It was a rhetorical question, which was just as well because neither man could manage any kind of intelligible answer. All they could do was hang suspended from the ragpicker's killing fingers until their brains were turned to mush and they were dead.

The ragpicker let them drop. He thought about eating them, but the idea was distasteful. They were vermin, and he didn't eat vermin. So he stripped them of their clothing, taking small items for his collection, scraps of cloth from each man that would remind him later of who they had been, and left the bodies for scavengers he knew would not be picky. He gathered up his soiled rags from the earth into which they had been ground, brushed them off as best he could, and returned them to his carry bag. When everything was in place, he gave the dead men a final glance and started off once more.

> Bones of the dead left lying on the ground.
> One more day and they will never be found.
> Ragpicker, ragpicker, you never know
> There are rags to be found wherever you go.

He sang it softly, repeated it a few times for emphasis, rearranging the words, and then went quiet. An interesting diversion, but massively unproductive. He had hoped the two creatures might have information about the man with the black staff, but they had disappointed him. So he would have to continue the search without any useful information to aid him. All he knew was what he sensed, and what he sensed would have to be enough for now.

The man he sought was somewhere close, probably somewhere up in those mountains ahead. So eventually he would find him.

Eventually.

The ragpicker allowed himself a small smile. There was no hurry. Time was something he had as much of as he needed.

Time didn't really matter when you were a demon.

TWO

WHEN SHE HEARD THE EXPLOSION RIP THROUGH the steady patter of the rain, Prue Liss knew at once what had happened. Deladion Inch, her rescuer and protector, had done exactly what she had feared when he sent her on ahead of him: sacrificed himself so that she might have a chance at safety. She had seen it in his eyes and heard it in his voice when he had told her he would catch up to her when he could. He was too badly injured to keep up with her; they were still too far away from safety for him to have any real hope. He had recognized the truth of things, accepted the inevitable, and given up his life for hers.

She was standing just outside the locked door that led to the entry of his fortress when the end came. She closed her eyes for a minute, listening as the sound of the explosion reverberated and died away. She wondered how many Trolls he had taken with him, whether he had experienced any sense of satisfaction.

She wondered if she was worth it.

She was only a girl, after all. He hadn't even really known her. He had rescued her from Taureq Siq and his Trolls as a favor to Sider Ament, and whatever promise he had made surely didn't include dying in the bargain. It was a choice he had made on the spur of the moment, an indication of how seriously he took his word and the kind of man he was.

She brushed away her tears, cleared her eyes, and set to work releasing the lock on the door. If she didn't escape now, his sacrifice would have been for nothing. She would not allow that to happen. She busied herself with her work, pushing aside everything else. The locks were right where he had said they would be, hidden in the crevices of the stone blocks. She worked the levers until she heard the locks release and then pulled down on the big iron handle. The door swung open with a squealing of hinges, and she stepped inside out of the rain and looked around. The solar-powered torches Inch had promised were standing upright on a shelf; she grabbed two, stuffing one into her belt and switching on the other.

Then she pulled the heavy door closed and locked it anew.

She stood staring at it for a moment afterward, wondering if it would keep out whatever Drouj remained. She looked around to see if there was anything else she could do to stop them, but it appeared she had done all she could. It was better than she had expected, and it gave her the chance she needed.

Her plan now was simple. Inch had told her to work her way back through the corridors and rooms of the complex to the rear exit, which would take her higher up on the slopes where she could see if anyone was following. He had sketched a map in the dirt to show her the way, giving her signs she should look for to keep her on the right path. There were doors all through the complex, heavy barriers with locks. She could close them off behind her as an added precaution. Nothing could follow her. She would be safe. He suggested she hide out in the fortress for at least a day or two before trying to venture out. That way there was a better-than-even chance the Trolls would grow tired of waiting for her to reappear and abandon their efforts, and then the possibility of slipping past them and finding her way home would be even greater.

Home. How long had she been gone from it now? Two weeks, three, more? She had lost all track of time. She thought about Pan for a minute, wondering where he was and how he was managing without her. He would be worried sick, of course. But perhaps Sider had told him that Deladion Inch had promised to help her, so that he would know she hadn't been abandoned entirely. She only hoped he wouldn't make the mistake of trying to come for her himself. The fate of Deladion Inch was an object lesson in how dangerous such an endeavor could be.

She wondered, too, if anyone had discovered the duplicity of the treacherous Arik Siq. He had fooled them all in the beginning, even Sider, but his luck couldn't last forever. There was every reason to think that he had been found out and dealt with by now. But if he had escaped, then the valley was at risk. He would lead the Drouj into the passes and flood the valley with Trolls bent on taking everything away from them and either killing or casting them out. How could they possibly stop something like that from happening, even with help from Sider Ament?

She was still standing there, thinking about it, when she heard voices on the other side of the door, low and guttural in the silence. Trolls. Some of her Drouj pursuers still lived. She found herself hoping that Grosha was not among them, but what difference did it make who it was? She flicked off the handheld solar light and stood motionless in the dark, listening. The Trolls stood outside for a long time, trying the handle, pushing on the door, talking among themselves. She waited, not knowing what to do.

Eventually, all the sounds disappeared as the Trolls moved away.

She stayed where she was for a long time afterward, waiting on their return. But finally she realized they weren't coming back right away and decided to venture deeper into the fortress compound. Turning the solar light back on, she started down the darkened corridors, following the path Deladion Inch had laid out, intent on reaching his personal quarters, where she had been told she could find something to eat and a place to sleep.

It took her forever. Or at least, it seemed that way. Part of the problem was in the directions, which required that she follow a series of painted red arrows. There were painted arrows of all sorts, and sometimes they overlapped and sometimes they disappeared for long distances. As a result, she was forced to retrace her steps repeatedly to stay on the prescribed path. She didn't blame Inch for this; after all, he probably never once thought that someone would have to find the way without him. It wouldn't have occurred to him to improve on the markings or to develop a more comprehensive map.

She was tired by the time she reached her goal and found herself in the kitchen where he kept his foodstuffs, cold storage, dishes, and utensils. She set about making herself something to eat and sat at the wooden table he must have used for himself many times over. She thought on him at length, imagining what his life must have been like, saddened all over again that it had ended because of her. She had liked him and now wished she had been given a chance to know him better. But chances were few and far between in their world, and mostly you had to settle for what you were given and be grateful.

When she had finished eating, she climbed some steps to an overlook and crept forward to its edge, scanning the darkness. Far away—perhaps a mile distant, but directly in front of the entrance to the ruins through which she had fled to reach the compound—a fire burned bright and steady in the blackness. The Trolls had not left after all, only retreated a short distance to wait out the night. In the morning, they would likely come looking again. She wished she knew what the odds were, but there was no way of telling. Better than before, but still too great.

Then she remembered the automatic weapon Inch had given her, still stuck in a pocket of her coat. She reached down and drew it out. It was a short-barreled, stubby black killing tool, one that used metal projectiles like they had during the Great Wars. The name on the barrel, raised in tiny letters, said FLANGE 350. Inch had called it an automatic. Twelve shots. Just pull the trigger and it would fire them one at a time or all at once. She studied it dubiously. She had never seen a weapon of this sort, never held one before, and certainly never fired one. She supposed she could use it if she had to, but she found herself hoping it wouldn't come to that. She would be happier with a bow and arrows, if she could find them. The metal weapon felt uncomfortable, as if it were as much a danger to her as to anyone she might try to use it against.

It gave her no sense of satisfaction at all to know she had it. She stuffed it back in her pocket and went back downstairs to sleep.

⁂

WHEN SHE WOKE, she was heavy-eyed and disoriented, brought out of her sleep mostly by a sense that something wasn't right. For a moment, she couldn't remember where she was. She pushed herself upright and peered about in a darkness lit only by gray light seeping through a ventilation opening high up on the wall behind her. She remembered then she was in Deladion Inch's fortress lair, cocooned away from the rest of the world, sealed off from the Drouj.

She rose and yawned, stretching her arms over her head. She had slept, but felt as if she hadn't gotten much rest. She switched on the torch, scanned the room in a perfunctory way, and then climbed the steps to the exterior overlook.

This time when she emerged, she did so much more cautiously, crouching down so that she couldn't be seen from below. The sun was overhead; it must have been somewhere close to midday. She slipped through the door and made her way on hands and knees to the edge of the overlook, keeping the wall between herself and whatever or whoever might be looking up. She found a split in the stone blocks and peered out, searching the landscape below.

She didn't see anyone.

She kept looking anyway, then shifted her position, moving to one of the sidewalls. This time when she peered over the edge, she saw a Troll moving up through the rocks, scanning the walls of the keep.

They were still hunting her.

She slid down against the wall, putting her back against it and staring at the mist-shrouded peaks of the distant mountains. If Grosha was still alive, he wouldn't give up. She could feel it in her bones. He would keep looking, and eventually he would find a way inside. She needed to get out of there before that happened. She needed to be far away and leave no trail that he could follow.

She moved in a crouch back across the overlook and through the door leading to the stairs. She passed rooms filled with old furniture and large paper boxes that were battered and broken and stacked against the walls. Pieces of metal and types of materials she didn't recognize littered the floors of those rooms, which seemed not ever to have been used by Inch. Strange black boxes with shattered glass screens and hundreds of silver disks lay scattered about one room, and in another beds filled huge spaces that reminded her of healing wards, all of their bedding torn and soiled and ruined. Remnants of the old world, once useful, now discarded and forgotten, they were a mystery to her. She glimpsed them fleetingly, dismissed them, and hurried on.

Once in the kitchen, she packed up enough food and drink to sustain her for three days, strapped her supplies across her back, and started away.

She had just reached the hallway leading deeper into the complex when she saw the big cabinet with its doors not quite closed and caught sight of the weapons.

She stopped where she was, debating, and then walked over and opened the doors all the way. There were all kinds of old-world guns, explosives like the ones Deladion Inch had carried, knives, swords, and bows and arrows. She smiled in spite of herself, taking a set of the latter and adding a long knife in the bargain.

She almost left the Flange 350 behind, but at the last minute changed her mind and kept it in her pocket.

The light was poor at best within the corridors she followed, making it no easier to read the sign markings during the day than it had been at night. But she persevered, using the torch when no light penetrated from ventilation shafts, taking her time. Because the rear of the compound was elevated, there were stairs to be climbed, and as long as she was going up she could be certain she was headed in the right direction. It wasn't like tracking out in the open, where you could see the sky and the sun and the way ahead was clear. But her sense of direction was strong enough that even without those indicators to rely on, she could find her way.

Still, she got lost and was forced to retrace her steps more often than she would have liked. It was oppressive being closed in like this, buried under tons of stone and shut away from the light. She thought about how people had lived like this before the Great Wars, and she wondered how they had endured it. If she had lived then, how would she have managed? She expected she would have lived her life much as she was living it now, even given the differences. She couldn't imagine living it any other way.

At one point, she sat down and rested; the complex was so much bigger than she had expected, and the constant back and forth of her efforts was draining her strength. If Pan were there, this wouldn't be so difficult. Pan could read sign and intuit trails much better than she could. He would have had them out by now. Back in the light. Back in the fresh air.

Thinking of his absence depressed her, and she got back to her feet and continued on.

It took better than an hour, but finally she found an exterior wall and a huge pair of metal doors. Light seeped through the seams of the doors, and their size and shape and the presence of huge iron latch bars marked them clearly for what they were. She studied them for a moment and then decided that opening something this big and closing it again was too risky.

She moved right along the wall, searching for a smaller portal. She found one another fifty feet and several storage bays farther on, tightly sealed with a drop bar and slide latch. She stood at the door and listened, but heard nothing. Carefully, she lifted the drop bar, slid back the latch, and opened the door, just a crack.

The daylight was hazy, but visibility was good, and she could see hundreds of yards in front of her where the foothills climbed toward the distant mountains. She opened the door a bit farther, looked right and left, and didn't find anything that looked out of place. It should be all right, she thought. The Drouj were still out front. She could slip away before they knew she was gone.

She pulled the door open all the way and stepped outside—right in front of a Troll as it came lumbering around a corner of the outside wall.

She froze, stunned by her bad luck. What were the odds that a Troll would appear just now? It was moving parallel to the wall perhaps twenty yards away, studying the ground, glancing up toward the hillside as it did so, clearly believing she had already gotten clear. Against all odds, it hadn't noticed her.

She backed toward the open doorway, slowly and carefully. She took one step after another, eyes fixed on the Troll.

Then her foot slipped on the loose rock, and the Troll's dark eyes found her.

She had but a moment to escape back inside; the Troll was coming much too fast for anything else. It carried a war club studded with spikes, a killing weapon she could not defend against. She was quick, but too small to stop a creature like this without help. The bow and arrows were slung across one shoulder—no time to get them free. She had the long knife out, but she didn't think it would do much good. She would have to run, but there was no time to go anywhere but back inside.

It took her only seconds to gain the opening and rush back into the building. Once there, she began to run. The Troll came after her without slowing, undeterred by the darkness. It was faster than she had thought it would be, picking up speed as it pounded down the corridors. She would have to hide or outmaneuver it. But she didn't know her way. Where would she go? She began to panic, searching the shadows for a way out, for an escape. But there were only other corridors and locked doors and hundreds of feet of stone floors and walls.

I should have stayed inside, she thought despairingly. *I should have stayed hidden. I should have waited.*

The Drouj had almost caught up to her when she remembered the Flange 350. She fumbled for it, yanked it from her pocket, released the safety as Deladion Inch had instructed her, wheeled as the Troll flung itself at her, and fired six times as fast as she could. She heard the sound of the metal projectiles striking her attacker and threw herself aside as it lurched past her, tumbling head-over-heels into the corridor wall.

She came back to her feet at once, swinging her weapon about, searching the gloom.

The Drouj lay folded over in a motionless heap, blood running from the wounds to its body. She looked away quickly, fighting not to vomit. She'd never killed anyone, she realized—as if it were a revelation. Only animals for food and once a wolf that tried to attack her. She didn't like how it made her feel. Even though it was a Drouj intent on doing her harm. Even so. She looked back, forcing herself to make certain of it. She stared at it for a long moment, but it didn't move.

Taking a deep, steadying breath, she slid down against the wall. A shiver passed through her slender body, and she closed her eyes. She tried to think of what she needed to do. She must retrace her steps quickly and close and lock the door. She could not chance going out again now. She was too frightened, too unsure of herself. She would wait, as she should have done in the first place. If Pan were here, he would approve. He would tell her she was doing the right thing.

She stared at the body of the dead Troll a final time and realized suddenly that she was crying.

THE HOURS PASSED and dusk approached in a webbing of shadows and ground mist crawling down off the heights. In the vast expanse of the wastelands surrounding the complex, the Trolls were still at work, searching for a way in, trying to find a weak spot in the mix of stone and steel. The ragpicker counted five of them—big, hulking brutes with tree-bark skin and hunched shoulders. He didn't like Trolls much. They were all the same, using their size and their strength to intimidate and, if need be, to overpower. Reasoning with Trolls was of little value. Trolls had a different mind-set about creatures like himself. Why reason with things so much smaller and weaker, they asked themselves, when you could simply crush them like eggs?

His ragged, scrawny figure was hidden by the glare of the fading sunlight as he approached them, barely more than a blurred image. The Trolls hadn't noticed him at all, even though he had gotten to within a quarter mile of them and was traveling over ground that was mostly flat and bare. He had no wish to engage them, and so he was moving away, heading north toward the darkness, when he sensed the magic.

He stopped where he was, surprised.

Where was magic coming from in a place like this? Not from those Trolls, surely. From someone else, then? Someone inside the buildings that the Trolls were trying to penetrate?

He considered the possibility that it might be the man with the black staff, but couldn't quite bring himself to believe that he was that lucky. For one thing, the magic he sensed did not appear strong enough. Nor did it appear to be of the right type. The ragpicker could parse degrees of magic; he could intuit their shapes. Over time, during his travels, he had encountered it often enough that he recognized its differences. This magic that he was sensing now was not that of a talisman, but of a living creature—a magic that was personal and innate.

Still, one thing usually led to another. A source here could lead to a source elsewhere and eventually to the one he was seeking. Baby steps, he reminded himself. Small successes.

He sighed. Pursuing this would mean confronting the Trolls. He would have to walk over there to determine what it was they were trying so hard to reach. He was not fond of the idea, but what was he to do? He couldn't walk away if there was a chance that the origin of the magic he was sensing was one of the missing black staffs.

He stood looking at the Trolls, debating. Then, out of the corner of his eye, he caught sight of shadows moving like quicksilver on the air, so thin they were virtually transparent. He didn't bother looking at them. He didn't need to; he knew what they were. He knew, as well, that trying to look directly at them wouldn't work. You couldn't see them that way. You could only glimpse them as bits of motion.

Feeders.

Once, they had been clearly visible to those who had use of magic. Humans and Elves and their ilk couldn't see them, not unless they had magic at their command. But demons could. And Knights of the Word. But something had changed all that with the destruction of the old world, and in the aftermath of the Great Wars, feeders had evolved into something that was almost entirely devoid of substance. They still fed on human emotions, still savaged those consumed by their darker instincts. But they had become as empty as wind.

What mattered here, however, was that there were feeders present at all. Their appearance signaled the presence of magic; it was the possibility of feeding that had attracted them. Use of magic expended the sort of dark emotion that feeders craved. They were drawn to it like flies to garbage and Men to evil. He smiled. You couldn't find a better indicator than that, could you?

Decided, he switched directions and walked slowly toward the Trolls, the now distinct possibility that his search was over a guiding light.

THREE

HE TROLLS DIDN'T NOTICE HIM AT FIRST, AB-
sorbed in their efforts to find a way into the complex, working to pry loose the locks and hinges on massive iron doors
that sealed the exterior walls. One Troll had found a ladder and
climbed to a second level, where he was poking about at windows that
were barred and shuttered, having not much better success than his
fellows. The ragpicker approached slowly, so as not to alarm them un-
necessarily. If he could just speak to them, he might be able to discover
whether or not what he was looking for was inside the complex and
could then determine if any further action was necessary. It was a risky
business; Trolls were unpredictable. But they didn't usually attack you
without reason, so it was possible to believe they might listen to him
first.

Not that the ragpicker cared if they didn't. But it would be a nuisance to dispose of them.

He glanced at the sky, noting the expanse of darkness that had
crept steadily westward as twilight faded and night closed in. A cluster

of whip-thin clouds formed purple streaks across the encroaching blackness, momentarily lit by the last of the sunlight. It would be a mostly clear night, and the moon, three-quarters full, was already a bright presence on the eastern horizon.

He was only two dozen feet from the closest Troll when the one climbing about on the upper levels noticed him and called out to his companions in warning. All heads turned; all eyes fixed on the ragpicker. The latter stopped where he was, relying on his unthreatening appearance to keep them from attacking him, looking from one face to the next with a benign expression. He had his bag of scraps slung over one thin shoulder, and as the seconds passed and no one moved he lowered it carefully to the ground and straightened up.

"I'm looking for someone," he said, speaking in the Troll tongue. He could speak perfectly in any language, an ability he had acquired early on in his life, when he had made the choice to abandon his humanity for something more permanent. "A man who carries a black staff. Do you happen to know where I can find him?"

One of the Trolls, a short, mean-faced individual with thick barkskin that gave him the look of something sculpted from a block of wood with a chisel and hammer, walked over and stood in front of the ragpicker. "Why should we tell you?"

The ragpicker shrugged. "Common courtesy?"

The other snorted. "Why shouldn't I just kill you? Then the man with the black staff won't be a problem for you."

The other Trolls exchanged glances and said nothing. Even the one atop the exterior wall came over to listen. The ragpicker had the distinct impression that the speaker was the leader.

He cleared his throat and looked down at his feet. "I could give you something valuable for that information," he offered.

The Troll stared at him. "What could you give us that we would want, *chilpun?*"

Chilpun. Troll for "fool." A decided lack of respect was not helping matters, the ragpicker decided. But he had to play along for the moment. "I could show you a way into those buildings."

The Troll looked at him with sudden interest, as if killing him was no longer of interest. Not that the option was completely off the table, of course. The ragpicker nodded encouragingly. "What do you say to that?"

"How do you know a way in?" the Troll asked. "That's what I say. Do you know the man who lived here?"

Lived here. Past tense. That meant dead or fled. "No. But I can find a way into anything. It's a skill I learned awhile back. If you want to get inside these buildings, I can help you." He paused, tried out a smile. "Do you have a name?"

"Do you?" The Troll sounded newly belligerent. "Tell me yours first."

The ragpicker smiled some more. "My name doesn't matter. Call me 'ragpicker.' That will do."

The Troll smirked. "Well, *ragpicker*, I am Grosha, son of Taureq, Maturen of the Drouj. Have you heard of me?"

The ragpicker hadn't, but he said, "Of course. Everyone speaks of you. They are afraid of you."

Grosha nodded. "They are right to be afraid. Now tell me how to get into that complex, and I will spare your life." He drew out a long knife and gestured toward the other's throat. "Do it now, old man, or we are finished here."

The last of the sunlight had faded and night had closed down around them. Moonlight gleamed off the knife's razor-sharp edge. Everything had gone still in the wake of Grosha's threat; the other Trolls stood motionless, waiting.

"First, you must tell me of the man with the black staff," the rag-picker insisted. "Then I will help you get inside the complex."

"You will help us anyway, if you don't want your throat cut," the Troll replied softly. "Or should I feed you to my hounds?"

He whistled, and a pair of dark shapes materialized out of the night, their faces long and lean and bristling with dark hair that stuck out in clumps. Wolves, the ragpicker guessed, though not like any he had encountered before. When their jaws opened and their tongues lolled out, he saw rows of sharp teeth. They sidled up to Grosha and rubbed against him like pets. Or spoiled children anxious for attention.

"What's it to be?" Grosha demanded, reaching down with his free hand to stroke one of the animals on its grizzled head.

The ragpicker thought about it for a few moments and then shrugged. "It seems you leave me no choice. But I am very disappointed. Tell me the truth. You don't know anything of a man who carries a black staff, do you?"

Grosha laughed. "That's a legend for superstitious fools, ragpicker. Do you take me for such? Those who carried the black staff are long since dead and gone. No one has seen one since the time of the Great Wars!"

"I have," the ragpicker said softly.

There was a long moment when everything went silent and everyone motionless. A strange hush descended, and even time itself seemed to stop moving.

"In a dream," the ragpicker finished.

Grosha's face changed just enough to reveal the hint of fear that had suddenly uncoiled deep in his belly. The wolf dogs must have felt it, too; their much stronger response was mirrored in their yellow eyes. Both of them backed away suddenly, going into a crouch and whimpering.

Grosha looked down at them, confused. Then he wheeled back on the ragpicker. "What are you doing to my hounds, you skinny old . . . ?"

He didn't finish. His knife swept up in an attack meant to disembowel the ragpicker with a single stroke. But the latter caught the Troll's wrist with one hand and held it fast, pinning it to the air in front of him, his grip as strong and unbreakable as an iron cuff.

"Were you speaking to me?" the ragpicker asked, bending close. "What was it you called me? Say those words again."

Grosha spit at him in fury, yanking on his wrist, trying to break free. But the ragpicker only smiled and held him tighter. The other Trolls started forward, but a single glance from the ragpicker stopped them in their tracks. They saw in his eyes what he was, and they wanted no part of him. Not even to save the son of their Maturen. Instead, they backed away, as cowed as the Skaith Hounds, which had retreated all the way into the rocks, still whining and snapping at the air.

The ragpicker forced Grosha to his knees. The Troll's mouth was opening and closing like a fish gulping for air. His scream was high and piercing. He groped at his belt with his free hand for another weapon, but he couldn't seem to find one, even though there was a dagger not three inches away.

"Speak my name!" the ragpicker hissed at him.

"Ragpicker!" the hapless Troll gasped.

"My real name! Whisper it to me!"

Grosha was crying and sobbing. "Demon!" he moaned.

"Am I your master and you my servant?" The ragpicker put his face so close to the other he could see the veins in the Troll's eyes throb. "Or are you detritus to be tossed aside?"

"Anything! I'll do anything you ask of me!" Grosha was slobbering and drooling, and his hand and wrist were turning black. "Please!"

The ragpicker released him. When Grosha sank down all the way, cradling his damaged hand, the ragpicker put a foot against his chest and pinned him to the earth.

"Now tell me what I want to know. Everything I want to know. What are you doing here? What are you looking for? What is inside this fortress that you want so badly?" He looked up at the rest of the Trolls, hunched down amid rocks and debris and on the point of fleeing. "Don't try to run from me! Get down here with your friend!"

He shifted his gaze to Grosha once more, his eyes gleaming. "You were about to say?"

Grosha shook his head, eyes squeezed shut against the pain, body shaking. "Nothing, nothing!"

The ragpicker reached down and tilted the Troll's chin upward. "Look at me. What are you doing here? Where is the master of this keep?"

"Dead. Last night. Blew himself up with explosives and killed seven Drouj . . ." He trailed off, shaking his head. "Seven of us dead. He stole . . . something. Something that was ours!"

"Something you stole from someone else, maybe? Something he's hidden in his lair?"

"Yes, yes! That's right!"

"Gold coins, maybe? Silver?"

"Yes, yes! Gold and silver!"

"And then, once he had it safely hidden, he blew himself up?"

"Yes! He blew himself . . ." Grosha trailed off, realizing that he had been tricked. "No, I don't mean . . ."

The ragpicker shook his head. "You really are worthless. A liar, and a bad one at that. A coward. A piece of . . ." He looked over suddenly at the other Drouj, clustered together on the edges of his vision. Hopeless, as well. He reached down and seized Grosha's injured hand anew, squeezing. "This is your last chance, Grosha, son of Taureq, Maturen of the Drouj. What are you looking for? And don't lie to me!"

"A girl," the other answered quickly, gasping in agony. "A hostage from the valley beyond the mountains. There!" He pointed east, his arm jerking spasmodically. "But she escaped! Let me go!"

The ragpicker experienced a sudden rush of adrenaline. "A girl. From where? A valley, you say? Does she carry a black staff?" He squeezed the wrist savagely. "Does she wield magic?"

Grosha screamed and shook his head, fighting to free himself. "Stop, please! My chest! Exploding! Listen to me! She's just a girl, but the boy thinks . . . Arik says . . . Please! I can't . . ."

The ragpicker squeezed harder. *Useless. Nothing more to be learned from this one.* He fastened the fingers of his other hand about the Troll's thick neck and added more pressure, an intense and killing tightness.

Grosha screamed. His neck snapped, his body sagged, and his eyes rolled back in his head. The ragpicker released his lifeless weight and let him drop to the ground.

"A girl," he whispered to himself, wondering if it meant anything, if it could help him in his search.

He shifted his gaze to the walls of the complex, searching high up where the buildings were stacked like blocks, one on top of the other, and caught a sudden, momentary whiff of the magic he had been tracking.

That was all it took. A demon with his talent could sense the presence of magic with much less to work with than that, and he sensed it now. Real magic, the kind he was looking for. The girl—or whoever was in there with her—had use of it. After all his searching, after all the roads he had traveled and disappointments he had endured, all the false leads and dead ends, he had found the real thing. He clapped his hands like an excited boy and smiled.

He kicked Grosha's body aside and started for the nearest door. He would have to be careful here. He didn't want to lose her. He had to make certain she didn't elude him. He glanced around. The Skaith

Hounds had fled, disappeared into the rocks. But the Trolls were still there, cringing away from him as he went past. The demon's lean form was hunched within his ragged disguise, his eyes as bright and hungry as a predator's as he beckoned for the Trolls to follow him.

"You'll search this place with me, once we're inside," he said, his voice hard-edged and laced with venom. "All of you. No one comes out until I do. We stay there until we find this girl. But she is not to be harmed if you find her. She is to be brought to me."

The reluctant Drouj fell into line behind him, being careful not to get too close. In a knot they converged on the main doors to the complex.

The ragpicker's bundled cloth scraps lay where he had dumped them, as rumpled and forgotten as the shattered form of Grosha Siq.

*   *   *

ATOP THE RUINS, high up on the overlook where she had witnessed most of what had taken place between Grosha and the ragpicker, Prue Liss hunched down behind the concealing wall so that the old man couldn't see her. What sort of creature was he, she wondered, that he could subdue Grosha and cause Skaith Hounds to slink away like beaten puppies? What kind of power did he possess? Now Grosha lay sprawled on the ground below, and from all appearances he was dead. And that ragged old man, together with the Drouj who were now at his beck and call, were coming for her.

Stupid, she chided herself, to have believed he couldn't smell her out. It had happened so fast. One moment he had been questioning Grosha, all of his attention on the Drouj, and the next he was looking right at her hiding place. He couldn't have seen her—probably couldn't even know who she was—but her fate was determined nevertheless. He was at the doors to the keep, and she had a feeling that what had kept the Trolls out would not be enough to stop that old man.

What should she do?

She made up her mind at once to escape before they locked her in. That they would think to do so was questionable, but she couldn't take the chance. Some sixth sense—perhaps her warning instincts—told her that they were going to get inside the fortress, iron doors and locks notwithstanding, and that once they did it would not take them long to find out where she was hiding.

She left the overlook, moving away from the wall in a crouch, easing herself back through the door and descending the stairs. She had returned from her previous attempt at escape by following the same corridors that had taken her to the rear of the building, shaken by her ordeal and haunted by the killing of the Troll that had discovered her. She had made several wrong turns, fought to remember how the signs worked, and eventually made it all the way back. Unable to think of anything else to do and needing to know what was happening with the Drouj, she had gone back up onto the overlook. Watching the Trolls move about the walls without seeming to find a way in had calmed her, and after a time she had believed herself safe again. With the doors securely locked, it didn't appear that anyone could reach her.

But then that old man had appeared to confront Grosha, and now everything had changed.

Her backpack was still sitting on the kitchen table where she had left it. She shrugged into it once again, stuck the long knife back in her belt, and slung the bow and arrows over her shoulder. After taking a last look around the room, making sure she hadn't forgotten anything, she set out once more.

Too much time had been wasted already, she knew. She should have kept her head after her encounter with the Troll and gone back outside and made a run for it. The Trolls were all back around the front of the complex by then, engaged with that old man. She would have been able to make a clean break. By now, she would be high into the foothills and safely on her way to the mountain passes. They wouldn't have even known she was gone.

But that's how it was with hindsight. If she went far enough back in time, she could argue that she should have stood her ground when Phryne Amarantyne had cajoled Pan into creeping up on that night-time campfire for a closer look. She would have squelched that suggestion and they would all still be safe inside the valley and Arik Siq would never have gotten in.

She shook her head in disgust, picking her way along the stone corridors. Or something else would have happened and she might be in an even worse situation. Who could know? She studied the signs on the walls, the array of different-colored arrows and the strange language she couldn't read, trying to remember. It wasn't as easy as she had thought it would be. All at once it seemed so confusing.

She slowed when she heard the sound of metal clanging and hinges squealing with the weight of a door opening from somewhere behind her. The old man and the Drouj were inside. She knew it at once. She didn't think they would come straight for her; they would have to search the front rooms first, all the way up to the overlook, and that could take time. On the other hand, if that old man could dispatch the locks on those iron doors, then he might have a few other skills, as well. One of them might have something to do with finding her.

Adjusting the backpack so that it rested higher up on her shoulders, she continued on, choosing what she believed was the right way to go. She hurried a little more now, walked a little faster, a twinge of genuine fear seeping through her. It wasn't like her to panic, but she could feel the urge to give way to it. Something about that old man. Something about how he had looked at her, even from that far away.

Pan, I wish you were here with me.

But he wasn't, and she didn't know where he was. Hopefully, he was back inside the valley and doing what he could to help Sider find her. She believed that he would come for her, but she wanted to reach him first. She didn't want him to venture outside the valley again. She didn't want that old man to find him, too.

No, I wouldn't want that. Not for him or anyone.

She found herself in a hall that didn't look familiar, even though the arrows had pointed her that way. Had she taken a wrong turn somewhere farther back? She didn't think so, but then she had been dwelling on things other than the arrows, things having to do with the danger she was in. That old man. The Drouj. The growing sensation of isolation, of walls closing in and darkness descending. She still had the solar torch, and its beam was still strong, but she had no way of knowing how long its power would last.

Sounds of doors opening and closing, of boots thudding and of furniture and supplies being moved about echoed through the stillness. It all felt far too close, as if the searching had progressed much more swiftly than she had expected. Voices lifted out of a subsequent silence, a mix of soft whispers and gruff mutterings. Heavy armored bodies scraped against rough walls.

She hurried ahead, abandoning her plan to try to get back to the exit she had found before, concentrating now on reaching any opening at the rear of the complex where she might find a way out. All she wanted was to escape, to get clear of a place that was beginning to feel like a tomb.

While she floundered like a rat in a maze, sunshine and fresh air waited outside. She would recognize features in the wall of the distant mountain peaks, and then forests and hills and trails she knew well would guide her home. Somehow she would find her way. She kept that thought foremost as she searched for an exit. But the corridors ran on, twisting and turning, the arrows pointing this way and that, and eventually she realized she no longer knew which way she was going.

She stopped then, took a deep breath, and tried to think clearly. She was lost, but she could still find her way if she kept her head. The sounds of pursuit were still audible, but they didn't seem to be quite as close as before. Maybe she was wrong about where she was. Maybe she was farther back in the complex than she had thought.

"Where do you think you are running to?" said a voice in the darkness just ahead of her.

She started so badly that she dropped the bow and arrows. Snatching them up again, she backed away from the voice, terrified. She had reason to be. The old man was standing there looking at her, tall and lean and bent, ragged clothing hanging off his skeletal frame, narrow head cocked to one side, obsidian eyes fixed on her.

"Get away from me," she whispered.

"Well, I can't do that until we've talked. But I can stand right where I am, if it will make you feel any better. All you have to do is answer my questions."

She took a deep breath, steadying herself. "What kind of questions?"

He gave her a tight smile. "Nothing much. Like what sort of magic you possess, for instance?"

"None. I don't have any magic. I'm a Tracker."

"Oh, you have magic, all right. I can sense it. I don't make mistakes about that sort of thing. What can you do that no one else can? Tell me."

She swallowed against her fear. One hand snaked into her pocket and her fingers closed about the automatic weapon. "I can sense danger. I can tell when it's close to me."

The old man nodded. "Really? Do you sense it now, from me, when I am close?"

She shook her head no. "It doesn't always work."

"What an unreliable gift! Sometimes it helps and sometimes it leaves you hung out to dry. Like now." His smile returned, colder. "You really shouldn't think about trying to use that weapon on me. It won't work. Those sorts of things can't hurt me."

She was trying to think what to do, how to get away. She could run, but what was the point if she didn't know where she was going? "I only have your word for that. I don't think I should take your word about anything. I don't think you can be trusted."

"Oh, but I can. I will tell you exactly what I am going to do before I do it. Just so long as you don't attack me. Fair enough?" He glanced around. "Why don't we go back upstairs and outside? It would be much more comfortable out there. We could talk just as easily. You might feel better about things. Trackers live outside, don't they? You must feel trapped down here under all these tons of stone. Don't you?"

"I'm fine where I am."

"I doubt it, but it's up to you."

"Why don't you just let me go?"

"Questions, remember? Do you know a man who carries a black staff? Ah, your face gives you away. You *do* know such a man, don't you? Tell me where he is. Tell me how to find him. Then you can go on your way."

Sider Ament. He was looking for the Gray Man. Prue was furious with herself for giving anything away, but she imagined that where this old man was concerned it didn't take much to reveal yourself. "He's dead," she said quickly. "Killed a month ago."

The old man shook his head admonishingly. "You're lying, young lady. How unbecoming. I can tell when people lie to me. It's a waste of time to try doing so. The man who carries the black staff is alive and you know where he is. So now you had better tell me or things will quickly become very unpleasant for you."

She hesitated only a moment, and then she jerked the automatic weapon from her pocket and fired it at the old man until it clicked on empty. She was running by then, tearing back down the corridors, racing for a freedom she had no idea how to find. She threw away the weapon and began struggling with the bow and arrows—although if the Flange 350 wasn't enough to stop the old man, she had no reason to think the bow and arrows would work any better.

Risking all, she glanced back to see if her pursuer was anywhere in sight. Her heart sank. A shadowy form was cleaving the darkness, keeping pace with her, coming much more quickly than should have been possible for someone so bent and old.

She pounded ahead, running faster, her stamina already waning, her breathing uneven. The old man continued to draw closer. She could not outdistance him.

She notched an arrow to the bowstring as she ran, swung about abruptly, and fired the steel-tipped missile directly at him. The arrow struck his chest and bounced away. The old man didn't even slow.

Then he was right on top of her, so close she could hear his breathing. She heard his voice in her mind, screaming at her. *Stop running! Running is pointless! You cannot escape me!*

She refused to give up. She ran on even faster. But she was beginning to labor. Ahead, she could hear the sounds of the Trolls. She was running right toward them. She flashed on a corridor that would take her another way and turned down it without thinking.

She had run more than a dozen yards before she realized she had chosen a dead end.

She wheeled back, frantic now. The old man was slowing to a walk, not twenty paces away, blocking her escape. His smile was slow and mocking, as if he had known all along that this was how it would end. She notched another arrow to her bow and held the weapon in front of her, pointing it at the old man. He shook his head, a clear admonishment. But he didn't say anything this time. He just kept walking toward her.

She cast aside the bow and arrows, knowing they were useless, and was reaching for her long knife, determined to die fighting rather than let him take her, when the light appeared behind her, sudden and intense. It came out of the darkness, out of nowhere, growing swiftly to fill the whole of the corridor. She risked a quick glance over her shoulder, but the light blinded her to whatever was there. She turned back to the old man, saw the perplexed look on his face, the sudden flicker of concern that changed quickly to rage.

Then the light closed about her and everything vanished.

IN THE AFTERMATH of the girl's disappearance, his equanimity recovered, the ragpicker stood quietly in the darkness, thinking it through. She hadn't gotten away from him by herself; of that much, he was certain. She had magic, but she didn't have magic powerful enough for this. If she had that kind of magic, he would have sensed it immediately. No, another magic had been brought to bear; someone had intervened to aid her, to remove her from his grasp.

He sniffed, able to smell the magic's residue even now, pungent and raw. He stared off into the darkness. Even without light, he could see perfectly well—but of course there was nothing to be seen. He was alone, back where he had started when he stumbled on the Trolls trying to break into this aged fortress.

He licked out with his tongue, tasting the stale air. What should he do about the girl? What should he do about finding the one who carried the black staff, the one he had come to find? He shook his head, mulling his choices.

Grosha had said something about a valley. This was where the girl had come from. Which meant that the bearer of the black staff might come from there, as well. He nodded to himself. He had his starting point.

Turning around, he began retracing his steps, intent on retrieving the collection of scraps he had dropped outside. It wouldn't do to leave his memories. The dead needed their due. Yes, he was impatient, but good things come to those who wait.

As he walked, he hummed and then began to sing.

Ragpicker, ragpicker, take your time.
There are plains to walk and mountains to climb.
Ragpicker, ragpicker, find your way.
The black staff's bearer comes closer each day.

He smiled eagerly as he disappeared into the darkness, anxious to resume his long search for the one he had come to kill.

FOUR

PANTERRA QU KNELT BESIDE SIDER AMENT, ONE hand resting on the dead man's chest, looking off toward the pass at Declan Reach. Time didn't have meaning for him. Time had come to a standstill, the world stopped where it was, everything as still and immutable as the mountains and the sun in the sky.

Take the staff.

Sider's words echoed in his mind, the last spoken by the Gray Man before he died, a plea to Pan to accept responsibility for what needed doing. A bearer for the black staff must be found—a protector for the people of the valley, a wielder of magic who could withstand the demands that would be laid upon him. It was easy to forget, in the crush of things that had transpired since the agenahls had broken through Sider's wards and come into the valley to kill Bayleen and Rausha, that five centuries of knowing their world was safely locked away from the devastation of the Great Wars had come to an end.

Take the staff.

A bird cried out from somewhere high up in the mountain peaks, and Pan's eyes shifted skyward. A sleek winged predator was hunting, sweeping in wide circles across the open skies. Pan watched its flight, suddenly fascinated. A hawk, he thought. Maybe it was an omen. Maybe it was the spirit form of the boy who had saved them all those years ago, looking down on them.

Looking down on him.

He shook his head. Nonsense. The old days and all those who had lived them were dead and gone. There was only the present and those alive now. Himself and Prue and the people of Glensk Wood and the Elves of Arborlon and all the others who called the valley home.

What was he to do?

He took a deep breath and exhaled, looking down at Sider's face for the first time since his final words. He had died saving Pan and trying to prevent Arik Siq from reaching the Drouj with information on the passes leading into the valley. But now Sider was gone, and the threat from the Troll army remained. Worse, Arik Siq had escaped back into the valley, where he might cause further trouble.

Something had to be done; Pan knew this. He knew, as well, that he was the only one who could act, the only one who knew that Arik Siq had not yet managed to get word of what he had learned to the Drouj. All those who had come with the Maturen's sons lay dead. Arik alone remained. If he were stopped . . .

But did that mean that Panterra must do what Sider had asked of him? Did it mean he must become the Gray Man's successor, the next bearer of the black staff, the next servant of the Word? Could he not simply go after Arik Siq, using the skills he had already mastered as a Tracker? He could, he told himself. He could hunt down the treacherous Drouj and finish the job Sider had started. He could return to Glensk Wood and then Arborlon and tell everyone what had happened. Then others could step forward and act in Sider's place, men and women older and more experienced than he was. It would be better that way, wouldn't it?

He shook his head at the enormity of what Sider had asked of him. He could admit to himself, if to no one else, what he knew was true. He was still only a boy. He was just seventeen.

He experienced a sudden wave of shame. By thinking like this, he was making excuses he had never made before. He was saying to himself that he was not equal to the task. If Prue were there, she would order him to stop. She would tell him that he could do anything he set his mind to. But of course Prue wasn't there—nor anyone else who could tell him what to do.

He took his hands away from Sider's body and clasped them in his lap, unwilling to let them stray too close to the black staff. He couldn't leave it, but what would happen if he touched it? Would it hurt him just to pick it up and carry it somewhere safe? Would he be accepting use of it by doing so? Would he be taking on a larger commitment by conveying it elsewhere with no intention of using it himself?

He didn't know. The truth was, he didn't know anything about how the staff would react. He didn't even know if he could summon its magic, if he was capable of wielding it. He was painfully ignorant of everything that mattered about the staff.

Except what he knew in his heart and could not deny—that Sider Ament had wanted him to take it for his own.

He stood up slowly and looked around the vista of the plains west and the mountains east, searching the landscape. He sought signs of movement, looking for Drouj in the direction their army was encamped and for Arik Siq in the dark mouth of the pass. But there was nothing that attracted his attention in either direction. His gaze shifted skyward and he tried to locate the hawk he had seen flying through the peaks earlier, but it was gone.

He was alone with the dead and his thoughts on what their dying had meant.

Because that was the final measure of all of his choices. It wasn't only Sider, but the men of Glensk Wood, too, who had given their lives attempting to hold the pass. What did he owe them for doing this? What obligation did he have? He could argue that he owed them nothing because he hadn't asked that they give their lives. But when men die in your company, sharing their last moments with you, surely you incur an obligation of some sort.

It did not stop there, either. Eventually, the Trolls would find their way into the valley, and many more would die. Did he owe something to those people as well? In his heart, he knew the answer. If he could do something to help them, perhaps even to save them, he must act. It was an oath he had sworn long before this day. It was a

Tracker's oath to his people: he must serve and protect them to the best of his ability, using his training and skills and determination. Nothing that had happened here changed the fact of that commitment.

He shifted his gaze once more, looking down again at the black staff. He might not like it, but that was the way things stood. The people within the valley depended on him. Prue depended on him. He was obligated to them all, bound to them as much as if they were his charges and he their guardian. He could not forsake them because he was afraid for himself. He could not allow doubts and uncertainties to rule his choices or to undermine his determination.

Without thinking about it further, he reached down and took the black staff from Sider Ament's dead hands.

"Do with me what you will," he whispered, eyes locked on the smooth black surface of the wood, scanning the sweep of intricately carved runes, searching for something that would reveal the magic hidden within.

But nothing happened.

Nothing at all.

He stood in the shadow of the mountains, the skies beginning to cloud with the approach of rain, and wondered what more he needed to do.

WHEN ENOUGH TIME HAD PASSED and still the staff had not reacted in any noticeable way to his handling of it, he propped it up against a cluster of rocks and set about burying Sider Ament. The ground was hard and rocky, and he lacked any sort of digging tool, so he had to settle for building a cairn. He lifted stones and carried them over to where he had laid out the Gray Man, then piled them about him until the body could no longer be seen. He tried to fit the stones as closely together as possible to prevent animals from digging their way in. He used the heaviest stones he could manage, aware that the larger creatures residing in the outside world—the agenahls, for instance—would not be deterred. But most scavengers would likely let the cairn be. The remains of the Drouj were an easier choice for satisfying their hunger. The Gray Man's body should be safe enough until he could come back for it.

When he did that, something he promised himself he would do as soon as it was possible, he would uncover his friend and carry him back inside the valley to be buried in the country where he had been born and which had served for his entire life as his home. A marker would be placed and words would be spoken over his remains. Those who had known and cared for him would come together to remember him.

But that would have to wait. Panterra would not take the Gray Man back with him now.

Instead, he would go after Arik Siq.

He had choices in the matter, and they were all compelling. Going to Glensk Wood to warn the villagers of what had happened in the pass and from there to the Elven city of Arborlon would be necessary at some point. It could be argued that this was a Tracker's first duty and should be carried out now. Going in search of Prue was equally necessary; he still had no idea if she had been rescued from the Drouj. She was the most significant person in his life, his best friend since childhood, and he was responsible for her. Every fiber of his being screamed at him to forget everything else and save her.

But more important than both of these was tracking down the Drouj traitor whose continued freedom imperiled them all. If Arik Siq managed to escape the valley, there would be no more concealing the secret location of the passes and nothing to protect any of them. If he escaped, Sider Ament's death would have been for nothing. Panterra Qu could not allow that to happen. He could not justify any other choice than going after the Drouj.

In part, he knew, he would be testing himself against a very dangerous adversary. The Troll was skillful and experienced. He would not be easily tracked and even less easily caught or killed. But Panterra had made his choice when he had picked up the staff, and whether or not he could use it, whether or not he could summon and employ its magic did not alter in any way the extent of his obligation to exercise a responsibility that was his and his alone.

Still, he thought, glancing over at the black staff for the first time since he had laid it down, it was important to discover if the magic that had belonged to Sider Ament now belonged to him.

He picked up the talisman once more and stood looking at it.

What would it take to make it respond? What must he do to bring the magic alive? He ran his hands up and down its length, feeling the indentation of the runes beneath his fingertips. Perhaps there was a secret to the way it was held or in how the runes were touched. But wouldn't Sider have told him so? Even dying, wouldn't he have said something about how to engage it?

He held it a few moments longer, trying to find something in the touch of his fingers on the runes, in the staff's weight or its balance, anything at all that might indicate what was required.

But no matter what he did, nothing happened.

Finally, his patience exhausted and his concern growing over the increasing distance Arik Siq was putting between them, he shouldered the staff and set out.

Reentering the pass, he walked quickly, but paid close attention to his surroundings. It wouldn't be out of the question for Arik Siq to wait in ambush or to set traps to snare him. He found the Troll's tracks quickly enough, deep gouges where the rock gave way to soft earth. The Troll was running, not bothering to mask his passing. It appeared that he was afraid and wanted only to get away. Panterra didn't think the Troll feared him. He must be concerned that the poison from the blowgun wasn't doing what was needed and that Sider Ament might still be alive.

He remembered suddenly how disturbed Arik Siq had been when he first saw the Gray Man all those weeks ago, coming out of the camp with Pan on the pretext of being his friend. He had thought the bearers of the black staff were all dead; he had looked decidedly uncomfortable to find out otherwise. Apparently he knew something of the old Knights of the Word, and he was frightened by that knowledge. It made Pan wonder how much of what the Troll had told him about Hawk and the Ghosts was the truth. How much of that whole story was real, and how had he known it in the first place?

He skirted the bodies of the dead, the Trolls and the men from Glensk Wood, as he wound his way ahead through the defile's twists and turns. The rock walls loomed high to either side, all but shutting out the sky, and as the sun worked its way west, the shadows continued to deepen. He would get clear of the pass before nightfall, but tracking anyone after that might prove impossible. If the moon clouded over, he might have to wait until morning to resume his hunt.

When he reached the barricade the men from Glensk Wood had constructed to defend the pass, he found the few bodies of the Trolls killed coming over the wall lying undisturbed. Climbing to the other side, he took a moment to study the killing field below, but nothing seemed changed there, either. He descended a second ladder and picked his way through the dead. No one had come up from the village yet. They would all be thinking that the pass was defended and they were safe from a surprise attack, lulled into a false sense of security.

Until he told them otherwise, of course—something he would have to do sooner rather than later.

He considered rethinking his priorities and going to Glensk Wood first, if only to alert everyone in the valley about the danger they were in. He did not want to abandon tracking Arik Siq, but if he couldn't pick up the trail outside the pass, wouldn't it make sense to go on to Glensk Wood, to travel through the night and reach the village by dawn? He could always resume tracking the Drouj afterward, couldn't he?

But he hated the idea. He needed to respond directly to Sider's death, and the only way he could do so was by catching up to Arik Siq. Letting him slip away now, no matter the reason, felt like a betrayal. He didn't think he could live with himself if he let the Drouj get away, possibly for good.

At the far end of the approach to the pass, still walking among the dead, he felt a sudden surge of warmth from the black staff. It caught him by surprise, and he drew up quickly, stopping where he was. He stood looking at the staff in surprise, noticing that the runes were beginning to glow softly, to pulsate.

What was happening?

It took him a moment to decide. The staff was warning him. It was responding to something that he had not detected; it was telling him that something was wrong.

He looked around, taking in his surroundings, peering off into the shadow-laced trees and the wide rocky stretches of the hillside that led up to the pass. He studied everything carefully, searching for anything that seemed to be out of place. But everything looked as it should. Out of habit, he dropped into a crouch, making himself a smaller target, no longer silhouetted against the fading light.

He looked at the staff. It continued to pulse.

Then he saw it. Not three yards away, all but invisible in the darkness, a trip cord stretched across the trail leading downhill. He followed its length both ways until the ends disappeared into the gloom. Dropping flat against the ground, he crawled forward just far enough that he could reach the cord with the end of the staff, and he gave it a sharp poke.

Instantly a handful of black objects flew through the darkness right in front of him, their passage so swift he only caught a glimpse of movement. He heard the missiles ping as they bounced off rocks some distance away, steel striking against stone. Then everything was quiet again.

He poked the trip cord once more, just to be sure, but nothing happened. He stood, walked up to the wire, and followed it in the direction the black objects had gone. He found several some distance away, lying on the ground. Darts, the tips laced with poison, their butts notched to fit a bowstring. He walked the other way and found the bow, cleverly wedged in the rocks so that it would not shift, its bowstring hanging limp from guy wires where the trip cord had released it.

So he had been right to be cautious. Arik Siq was setting traps, intent on putting an end to any attempt at pursuit. He wasn't running blindly, after all. He had taken time to stop and construct this ambush, knowing it would be dark before anyone following got this far.

Pan looked down at the black staff. The more important revelation was here. That the staff's magic had warned him of the danger was a complete surprise. Pan hadn't summoned the magic or even thought to do so. He had never considered the possibility that the staff might be able to act unilaterally. He had assumed all along it only responded to the commands of the user. But the unbidden warning he had been given demonstrated clearly how wrong he was.

Perhaps, he thought suddenly, summoning the magic wasn't even necessary. Perhaps the magic responded to something more complex and personal. To the user itself? To the user's immediate circumstances?

He took a deep breath and exhaled.

Was the staff in some way sentient?

He didn't know. He couldn't be sure. Not yet, not on the strength of a single event. But the possibility was there, right in front of him. The staff might be more than a tool of magic. It might be an extension of the bearer himself.

The way forward made safe, he started off again, more slowly now, watching for traps. He descended from the pass and into the foothills, passing out of the snow line and entering the forests below. Once or twice, he found footprints left by a Troll going in the same direction and knew them to be fresh—made within the last few hours. He followed them by staying off to one side, keeping close enough to read them but not so close as to put himself directly on top of them. There had been one trap set; he would likely find more.

Less than an hour had passed when he realized suddenly that even though it was fully dark, he could see the ground ahead clearly. The moon, almost full and rising in the east, was a dim presence in a heavily clouded sky. He should be having trouble tracking on a night like this. Yet he could see Arik Siq's tracks. How could that be? He scanned the sky and the horizons for some sign of ambient light and found nothing. It was his own vision that was providing the light; he could read sign ten times better than he had ever been able to before.

The staff, he thought at once. It was the magic of the black staff that was doing this.

Yet the staff's runes were dark, and the heat that had emanated from its wood earlier was gone. Still, something was happening. His instincts, always good, were unusually sharp and he was attuned to everything around him. The staff was enhancing his natural abilities so that even in almost total darkness, he would find what he was looking for.

He felt a sudden rush of elation. The magic was responding to him after all, just not in the way he had imagined it would. Taking up the staff as Sider Ament had asked was all that was necessary to make the magic his. He felt relief mixed with caution. He had formed a connection with the magic, but he must not take for granted that he knew all there was to know about what it could do or how it would respond.

Time and experience would teach him more. For now, he needed to re-member he was new at this and did not fully understand the magic's nuances and intricacies.

But maybe he understood enough to track down Arik Siq.

He picked up his pace, determined to find out.

FIVE

PAN HUNTED FOR ARIK SIQ ALL THE REST OF THE night, tracking him steadily through the enveloping darkness and the curtains of mist that rose off the valley floor. For a time, it seemed he would not catch him, his efforts hampered by the latter's skill at hiding his passing, at concealing his tracks by using tricks well known to Pan but difficult to unmask nevertheless. The Drouj clearly had experience and talent in this area, something that Pan found increasingly troubling. He had envisioned a quick end to his pursuit once he discovered he had the staff's magic to enhance his abilities and instincts. He had not believed that his adversary would prove to be much of a problem.

The chase wore on past midnight as Arik Siq descended out of the high country toward the upper rim of the valley floor. He stayed well away from the villages and towns, skirting places where he might be seen, keeping to the woods and less traveled paths. He was working his way east again, an indication that he intended to try making his escape a different way, perhaps through Aphalion. Pan found this odd, given he must at least suspect the Elves knew of his deception by now and would be guarding the pass. But the Troll's steady progress in that direction seemed a clear indication of his intentions.

Until, abruptly, his trail disappeared altogether.

It happened right at the beginning of a particularly rocky stretch where tracks would have been hard to locate under the best of circumstances. Panterra walked out onto the flats, searched the ground carefully, and found nothing. He crossed all the way to the far side, a distance of several hundred yards, and still found nothing. Even in the softer earth that lay beyond, there were no marks. He walked back again, hoping to sense something with the aid of the staff's magic.

Still nothing.

Standing once more where he had lost the trail, he tried to think his way through his confusion. He knew he must have missed something. Arik Siq could not have simply disappeared. He had to have used a trick to disguise his trail, one that Pan simply hadn't recognized. The trail led right up to the rocky stretch. Where had Arik Siq gone from there that would leave no further tracks at all?

Pan knelt to take a closer look at the footprints that ended at the flats, and a moment later he had his answer.

The tracks were deeper than they should have been and on close examination revealed that they had been stepped in twice. The Troll, taking no chances with anyone who might be following, had walked backward in the same tracks to leave the impression he had disappeared into thin air.

Pan retraced his quarry's footprints for almost a hundred feet, at last finding the place were the Drouj had stepped sideways onto a patch of loose rock and then followed it north until he was safely away from his own trail. Pan, still following the first set of tracks, had walked right past without noticing the second. He took his time now, working with little more than traces of dust disturbed and rocks nudged from one side to the other. When he was finished crossing the hardpan, navigating both stretches of flat rock and beds of crushed gravel, he found the other's trail once more.

To his surprise, the trail abruptly swung west again.

Pan followed it for a time, wanting to make sure of what he was seeing. But there was no mistake. Arik Siq had reversed direction and was returning the way he had come. He was heading back toward Declan Reach.

It made sense. He would have trouble getting past the Elves at Aphalion. But there were only dead men at Declan Reach, and that scenario was not likely to change for a few more days. Even if his deadly snare hadn't put an end to any pursuit, anyone hunting him would think he was going east to Aphalion and would not suspect he intended to double back. By the time they had figured it out, he would be outside the valley and well away from any danger.

Panterra knelt and examined the rediscovered trail carefully. How much of a lead did Arik Siq have? How much time did Pan have left to catch him before he was outside the valley? He couldn't be sure. Enough that there was a chance. Enough that he had to give it a try.

He set out at once. This was his valley, his country, and he knew it better than the man he was chasing. Arik Siq might have learned some things about the valley in the time he had been there, but he wouldn't yet know enough to identify shortcuts and places where his passage could be eased. Nor was he as driven as Pan was. It was enough of an edge that Pan had already made up his mind he could win this race.

He climbed high onto the slopes where the woods opened into meadows and grassy hillsides, and he began a slow, steady trot west toward Declan Reach. He was young and in excellent condition; he could run twenty miles at a steady speed. It would have been better if he'd had some sleep beforehand, but he wouldn't use that as an excuse. At least, he didn't have to bother with following tracks anymore. He needed only to concentrate on putting one foot in front of the other and not burning himself out before he reached the pass.

The hours passed, the sun rose and began its familiar journey west, and in the haze of weary determination that enveloped him Panterra Qu began to think of Prue. He still knew nothing of what had happened to her. She might still be in the hands of the Drouj, a possibility that made it even more imperative he catch up to Arik Siq. Holding the latter captive would give him something to bargain with for Prue's safe return. A father, any father, even Taureq Siq, would not give up the life of his son for no better reason than spite.

Pan visualized Prue in his mind. He found an image of her face that pleased him, pasted it on the air in front of his eyes, and ran faster.

It was almost sunset when he found himself approaching Declan Reach once more. He slowed automatically, coming up on the pass and its killing field soundlessly, a shadowy figure in the growing darkness. He searched for signs of Arik Siq's presence and found nothing. He tested the air with his senses—listening, tasting, smelling, and watching.

Still nothing.

He had gotten there first.

He stopped where he was, just in view of the sprawled forms of the dead, high up on the slopes but to the right of the pass, out of view. His breath clouded the air before him, the cold bone-chilling. He had to choose a place to wait for the other man. He had to find a way to catch him off guard. Arik Siq would be cautious of a trap, wary of being tricked in the same way he had tried to trick Pan. He was no fool. Any chance of capturing him alive would require some thought.

He felt an odd calm settle over him; everything became slow and easy. Nothing was beyond him now.

Odd, he thought suddenly, that he had abandoned so readily his intention of killing Arik Siq to avenge Sider. Arik's death had been the driving force behind his choosing to take the black staff, enraged and bitter beyond words. But now all that was gone, bled out of him during his pursuit, left behind in the wake of his determination that the man would not escape him and replaced by his need to save Prue. Sider would not mind, he thought. Sider would not only understand, but also approve. It was the right thing to do.

He studied the dead men where they lay before the defensive wall, the positioning of the single ladder that remained upright against the ramparts and the way the uneven terrain rolled and shifted beneath all of it. Finally, he walked over to where Trow Ravenlock lay sprawled in death, propped him upright so that he was facing back the way Arik Siq would come, calculated the way things would work when the Drouj made his cautious way toward freedom, and nodded in satisfaction when he was certain of what would happen.

Then he took up a position at the base of the wall, stretching out on the ground close by where he had left Trow, his body partially obscured by that of a dead Troll, and began his vigil.

It was a short wait. He had arrived ahead of Arik Siq by no more than thirty minutes, the latter traveling almost as fast as he had in an attempt to get there ahead of any pursuit. He probably still worried it was Sider Ament who was coming after him, an inexorable force of nature somehow able to fight off the killing effects of the poison. That he was wrong made the moment that much sweeter. Pan saw his quarry out of the corner of one eye, watched him appear out of the trees, silhouetted against the horizon as he approached with slow, careful steps.

When he was perhaps twenty feet from Trow's body, Arik Siq drew up short, troubled by the dead man's strange position. After hesitating a moment, he came forward, dropping into a crouch, a long knife in one hand, his blowgun in the other. From his posture, it was clear he suspected a trap of some sort, which was exactly what Pan wanted. The Drouj stopped not six feet on the other side of the Troll corpse behind which Panterra lay, studied the dead leader of the Trackers, looked around for trip wires, and then started cautiously for the wall.

Pan came to his feet soundlessly, right behind the other, gripping his black staff in both hands. Arik Siq sensed something at the last minute, his own instincts sharp enough to warn him, and turned. But Pan was already swinging the staff with as much force as he could muster, striking the other on his raised forearms with numbing force. Both weapons went flying. The Drouj screamed in pain and stumbled backward, trying desperately to flee the unexpected attack. But he had no chance; Panterra was on top of him instantly. The black staff made a strange whistling noise as he swung it a second time, catching Arik Siq on the side of his head.

The Drouj dropped like a stone.

◦ ◦ ◦

BY THE TIME his prisoner began to stir, Panterra had built a fire, made himself a meal from food scrounged from the remains of the dead men's supplies, and eaten and drunk his fill. He had dragged Arik Siq down the mountainside far enough that they were in the shelter of a clump of rocks surrounded by alpines and scrub, well away from the pass at Declan Reach and its dead.

Pan sat with his back against the flat side of a large boulder, facing uphill toward the dark entrance to the pass so he could see if anyone appeared from that direction. At his feet, the fire had burned down to red embers and ash. Arik Siq was propped up across from him, slumped forward and leaning sideways against a stack of blankets Pan had retrieved.

The Drouj woke with a start, wincing at pain that Pan could only imagine, but in which he took quiet satisfaction. His prisoner tried to stretch and then paused as he discovered that his hands and upper arms were bound tightly with cord and his ankles chained to a heavy set of roots.

"Don't bother trying to move," Pan offered when the other looked over at him. "Just sit still."

The Drouj lowered his eyes to his shackles and gave them a cursory appraisal. There was a deep bruise and some blood along the side of his head where he had been struck by the staff. He looked ragged and dirty, a fugitive not only from the people in the valley but from anything resembling soap and water. Yet his eyes were sharp and calculating, and there was no sign of defeat mirrored there.

"You should have let me go when you had the chance," he said finally. He lifted his head, his blunt features wrinkling unpleasantly. "It was the only way you'd ever see your little friend alive again."

Pan shook his head, giving the other a long, steady look that pinned him against the darkness. "You had better hope that's not true. Getting her back is all that's keeping you alive. Your life for hers—I think your father will be happy to make the trade."

Arik Siq laughed. "My father won't spare her for me. He will kill her outright the moment he knows the arrangement you made with him is a sham. You don't know him. He doesn't care about anyone but himself."

Pan ignored him and went back to working on a repair he was making to one boot. The binding had broken near the sole, and he was stringing new leather through the sole. He let the silence build.

"Where are you taking me?" His prisoner sounded bored, irritated. "Back to my father, so that you can make this exchange that won't happen? Back to the Drouj so that you can be killed, too?"

Pan didn't respond.

"To the Elves, then? They will want to see me dead, as well."

Pan shrugged.

"The old man died, didn't he? The poison was too much for him. He should have left me alone. Coming after me like he did was foolish. One man, bearer of a black staff or not, is no match for so many." He leaned forward. "I knew he was coming, you know. I left someone on watch in the pass, just in case. The old man walked right into the trap I set for him."

He stopped talking, looking down at his hands. "It was all for nothing. He died for nothing."

Pan kept his gaze lowered. "He kept you from escaping, didn't he?"

Arik Siq raised his hands to his face and wiped away a streak of dirt mixed with blood. "To what end? Another of the Drouj went on without me to give my report. My father already knows everything about the valley. He probably marches on the pass at Aphalion right now. Stopping me accomplished nothing. You are as stupid as you look."

Pan finished tying off the leather binding and held it up for the Drouj to examine. "There you are. As good as new." He pulled the boot back on, testing his weight on the sole, walking around a few paces before reseating himself. He gave Arik Siq a smile. "Your father doesn't know anything. No one made it out to tell him. Your companions all died at the head of the pass. I saw it all; I was watching."

The Troll went silent, looking off into the dark. "Others will come looking for me. You don't have that old man to protect you now. How will you save yourself when they catch up to you?"

Pan studied him a moment, and then he reached down for the staff and held it up for the other to examine. "With this," he said.

He caught a glimpse of surprise in the other's yellow eyes, a surprise that was reflected in his blunt features, as well. It was only there for an instant, but Pan didn't miss it.

"Those others you think might be coming to rescue you," he said, "had better hope they don't catch up to me."

Arik Siq's features hardened. "You're a boy! How old are you? Fifteen, maybe? How well do you think you can control the magic of that staff? You don't even know how to use it, do you? That old man didn't teach you anything. You know just enough to get yourself killed. Which is what will happen, soon enough."

Pan nodded. "Not soon enough to save you, however. Your father will come for you or come for whatever he thinks is inside this valley or come because he can't help himself. But we will be waiting for him. All of us who live in this valley—we will be waiting for him. We will trap him in the passes or on the open slopes or wherever we find him, and we will cut him and all those with him to pieces."

He pointed at the Drouj with the tip of his staff. "And you'll be right there to watch it all if anything happens to Prue."

"Boy, I will skin you alive myself!" Arik Siq sneered. "You will beg for me to kill you before I am finished!"

Panterra Qu climbed to his feet, tossing aside the remains of his repair work. "Get up. We're going for a long walk, so you better save your strength. You might be the one begging before we get to where we're going."

They set out for the valley floor, Panterra leading the Drouj by the length of chain, which he had removed from the other's ankles and tightened in a rough slipknot about his neck. The boy walked just fast enough that his prisoner, encumbered by the chain and the ropes about his wrists and shoulders, had to struggle to keep up. Arik Siq trudged along with his head lowered and his eyes on the path, forced to keep close watch on where he put his feet so he wouldn't trip. Dawn had not yet broken, and the land lay under a gloomy shroud of clouds and mist. Morning was only a thin silver line, jagged and washed out, behind the craggy summits of the mountain peaks east, and the air was thick with cold and damp. Panterra was used to it; his life as a Tracker had trained him to tolerate the cold. But his prisoner, for all that he had the armor of his bark-like skin to protect him, did not seem happy.

"Swing those arms while you walk," Pan offered cheerfully. "It will help keep you warm."

The other man did not reply, and the boy immediately regretted saying anything to him. Taunting him was not going to do anything to help the situation; there was more at stake here than taking pleasure from making the Drouj feel as miserable as possible. In the end, he might need Arik Siq's help in making an exchange for Prue. He was already thinking ahead to how that might happen, but the details remained fuzzy and uncertain in his mind.

"If you set me free, I give you my word that the girl will be returned safely," his prisoner said suddenly.

Pan shook his head. "I don't think so."

"How will you free her otherwise? You can't simply walk out of the valley and ask my father to do it, can you? If you take me, he'll just kill us both. You don't know him. You don't know what he's like. Remember that story I told you about the Karriak being my people? About how I was the son of their Maturen given in exchange for Taureq's eldest? You know now that it was a lie, that I made it up to gain your trust. But this much isn't a lie. The Karriak were all killed by my father, annihilated in retaliation for their refusal to accept him as their leader. Even their Maturen, who was his cousin." He paused. "Just so you understand. He won't bargain. He won't even trouble himself to hear you out. He won't waste the time. He'll simply kill us both and be done with it."

"He won't kill you. It would be pointless."

"Not to his way of thinking. He'll kill me because I've failed him."

They were silent for a time, walking ahead toward the dawn, watching the light in the east grow brighter and the shadows begin to fade. Ahead, the trees of the forest that filled the west end of the valley slowly took on definition through the gloom, strange sentries in the wash of the morning's misty damp.

"How much of the rest of that story was true?" Pan asked finally.

For a moment, the other man didn't say anything. "All of it. Except that it wasn't about my people—it was about theirs, the Karriak. They were the descendants of the ones called Panther and Cat, the boy and girl who came east with the Hawk to escape the aftermath of the Great Wars. I heard the story from the Karriak when I was visiting with them. They were proud of it, of their heritage. Little good that it did them."

Panterra thought about it, saying nothing. "What do you care?" Arik Siq asked. "Who your people were matters hardly at all. Who they are now is what matters. Who *you* are."

"Your history is sometimes a way of understanding your present," Pan replied. "You are your history."

The other snorted. "No wonder I was able to trick you so easily. You don't understand anything. The past is nothing. The past is a world that's dead and gone. All those tales about the one called Hawk and his Ghosts, all that nonsense about the valley and the chosen—it doesn't mean anything." He stopped suddenly, causing Pan to turn. "Your people will go the way of the Karriak. The Drouj will wipe you out. That is what the past has to teach you, boy. You aren't strong enough to survive us. You don't deserve to live."

Panterra yanked on the chain in irritation. "You don't get to make that decision. Not you or your father or any of the Drouj. Now shut your mouth and keep walking."

Arik Siq lowered his head and went silent. For the remainder of the time left to them before reaching their destination, neither spoke again.

SIX

IT WAS WELL INTO THE AFTERNOON BY THE TIME PAN-
terra Qu reached the outskirts of Glensk Wood, his reluctant prisoner in tow. The day was unusually bright and sunny, the skies
clear even where they were brushed by the peaks of the surrounding
mountains, swept clean of clouds and mist by a north-bearing wind infused with unusual warmth. The people of the village who saw him
coming stopped whatever they were doing and stared in surprise. He
understood it was as much because of his ragged and worn appearance
as it was the Troll he was leading on a chain. Some of those who
watched him pass waved and greeted him uncertainly, and he responded with whatever small gesture or word he could manage.

By now, he had gone almost two days without sleep, and the combination of physical and mental stress expended in capturing Arik Siq
had left him exhausted. He was functioning on instincts and muscle
memory, unable to see or think as clearly as he otherwise might, but
unwilling to stop and rest until this business was finished. Whatever
his own deficiencies, whatever his needs, they would have to wait until
he had settled the matter of what to do with the Drouj.

He marched Arik Siq through the center of the village to the building that housed the council chambers and inside.

There was no one there.

He stood for a moment wondering what to do next. Then he shoved his prisoner onto a bench and called out for someone to come.

No response.

"Maybe they don't want to see you, boy," the Drouj taunted. "Maybe they have less use for you than you realize."

Pan ignored him. He walked to the door and flagged down the first person he saw. As it happened, it was Collwyn, a friend from the old days and someone he knew he could depend upon.

"Collwyn!" he called. "Can you help me?"

The other boy, the same age as Pan, though considerably smaller, hurried up the steps to embrace him. "What's happened to you, Pan? You look a wreck!"

Pan nodded, managed a small smile. "I need you to find Pogue Kray and the Seraphic and bring them to me. Can you do that? It's important that they come right away."

Collwyn nodded wordlessly and dashed off. To his credit, no questions were asked and no objections raised. Pan watched him go, glanced over his shoulder to where Arik Siq sat slumped on the bench, and stepped back inside, taking a position by a window where he could watch who was passing by without losing sight of his prisoner. The Drouj might look tired, but given the opportunity he would be gone in a second. Pan was not underestimating the other's cunning.

His weariness washed over him suddenly in a massive wave that threatened to knock him off his feet. It had taken everything he had just to get this far, and he still hadn't resolved what he was going to do now that he was here. He had brought back Arik Siq, but he needed to find a way to exchange Taureq's son for Prue. What help did he think he could expect from Pogue Kray or Skeal Eile? Why would they want to help him at all? They had already pronounced him a nuisance and would have preferred it if he simply went somewhere else and stayed there. He knew this. Yet here he was, back in a place where he wasn't wanted.

He exhaled slowly, watching the road. He supposed he was here because there was nowhere else for him to go. He couldn't get any farther without sleep. This was his home; he should be allowed to rest here. He knew it was possible that he wasn't seeing things clearly. But so much had happened so quickly. Without Prue to advise him, to act as his conscience and be his friend, he was adrift. Aislinne would help if she could. Yet he did not care to take the man who had killed Sider Ament into her presence. No, he would not do that.

But what would he do?

The enormity of his situation reared in front of him. He was the new bearer of the black staff, the successor to the Gray Man, and he was only seventeen years old. How could he possibly expect anyone to take him seriously? Why would anyone listen to him? They would brush him aside as a boy who had been in the right place at the right time and so had inherited the staff. But he had no stature that would justify it as right and proper. He lacked any credentials, any evidence that would suggest he could wield the magic. They would not accept him for who he had become, or believe he could do what he claimed.

How could he prove them wrong? How could he convince them they should listen?

Movement near the front of the building caught his attention. Collwyn was approaching with Pogue Kray following, the latter's burly form striding ahead with clear determination and purpose. Pogue's bearded face was dark with emotion and the big fists were clenched. Not an auspicious beginning to things, Pan thought.

He stepped away from the window as boots clomped up the steps to the veranda and slowed. "Leave," Pan heard Pogue Kray order Collwyn.

Then Collwyn was gone, and the big man shouldered through the door and stopped dead, staring first at Panterra, then at Arik Siq, and then back again at Pan. "Boy, what's happened to you?" he whispered.

There was genuine concern in the query, and it took Pan by surprise. He had expected to be attacked straight off; he hadn't expected this softer response. For a moment, he was speechless.

"Who is this?" Pogue asked, nodding toward Arik Siq, who was now sitting up straight and watching carefully.

"Someone who would betray us all," Pan answered, meeting his prisoner's dark gaze. "Someone who pretended to be my friend so I would bring him into the valley." He paused. "Even worse, only a day ago he killed Sider Ament."

Pogue Kray's face went white. "The Gray Man is dead?"

"Killed at the far end of the pass at Declan Reach. Poisoned by darts from a blowgun. He was caught unawares. The poison was too strong for him to fight off, even with his magic to aid him."

"Sider Ament is dead?" a voice demanded. "You're certain?"

Skeal Eile stood in the doorway, staring at him. The way he asked the question did not suggest it was voiced out of concern, but out of a need to make certain the deed was done and no mistake.

"I was there when it happened," Panterra answered him, trying to keep his voice from shaking, suddenly dismayed by the presence of the other man. "I held him in my arms while he died."

"Then we don't have the magic of his staff to help us against the Trolls," the Seraphic declared, directing his remarks now to Pogue Kray. "Do you see what that means? We have to make peace with these invaders. We have to use this prisoner as a tool for negotiation."

Arik Siq was on his feet instantly. "I have been telling this to the boy, but he refuses to listen. I see you have more sense than he does. If you let me act as emissary, I will negotiate—"

Panterra didn't stop to think. He simply charged Arik Siq and struck him so hard across the head with his staff that the Drouj went down and did not move again. Then he wheeled back to face Skeal Eile.

"You had better listen to me before you start deciding what needs doing. I'm the one who's been out there, outside the valley where the real danger lies. I'm the one who knows about the Drouj—this one especially." He thrust the staff out in front of him, hands clasping it tightly. The runes blazed with white fire. "Do you see? I'm the one who carries the black staff now, the one to whom Sider Ament entrusted it, the one who now wields its magic and must exercise the responsibility that goes with it. Not you! Not either of you!"

He saw a flicker of fear in the Seraphic's lean face, and he was emboldened. "I tracked down this killer of men, this betrayer. I caught up to him and I captured him and I brought him here. But not so you could decide what needs doing! It is not your place to do that!"

His gaze shifted to find Pogue Kray's features twisted with confusion. "But it is yours, Pogue. Will you hear me out?"

"No one has to listen to you, little pup!" Skeal Eile screamed at him. He had recovered himself enough to remember who it was that was chastising him, and he was immediately enraged. "You are a boy with no talent or ability beyond your Tracker skills! You know nothing of that staff, and we have no reason to think that you didn't steal it from a dying—"

"Hold your tongue, Seraphic!" Pan advanced on him swiftly, stopping him midsentence. "Another word from you, another baseless accusation, and I will lay you out alongside the Drouj!'" He leaned forward, close to the other. "I didn't come all the way back for this! You are here because I asked for you to be here—not because you have any right to be here. Nor any right to slander me!"

"I will not be lectured to by a foolish boy who—"

Pan swung the black staff around and held it up in front of him, so angry by now he had forgotten to be afraid or even cautious. "Be careful of what you say next, Seraphic."

But it was Pogue Kray who spoke instead. "Enough. I am council leader of this village. The safety of its people and their homes is my responsibility. I will decide who speaks. Skeal Eile, you will allow the boy to tell us what he knows. Is that clear?"

The Seraphic managed a small nod, the venom in his eyes unmistakable as he shot a quick glance at Pan.

"Panterra," the big man said, turning to him, "don't waste our time. Get right to the point."

Pan slumped against the wall, his exhaustion overtaking him anew. He wanted so badly to sleep. But first he must deal with this. Choosing his words carefully, he related everything that had happened since they had last met at Pogue's house with Aislinne and Sider Ament. He told them of the attack on the defenders at Declan Reach and their annihilation by the Drouj. He told them of his own escape and how he had hidden just out of reach of his pursuers, of Sider's coming to his rescue and of the ensuing battle and the deaths of all but Arik Siq and himself. He said nothing of Prue. To do so would have given Skeal Eile leverage to use against him, something he dared not do until this matter was resolved. He knew he must not lose control of the situation if he was to save her.

"This man is the son of the Maturen of the Trolls who seek to invade the valley?" Pogue asked in surprise. "Then isn't Skeal Eile correct? Don't we need to use him to bargain for our safety?"

"It might seem so," Pan replied, searching for a reason to dismiss this line of thinking. "But Arik Siq himself has told me repeatedly that his father would kill him before he made a bargain with us. Taureq Siq is a brutal man. He has destroyed whole tribes of Trolls who resisted him. He would kill his son as quick as thought if it suited his purposes."

"But you cannot know this," Pogue persisted. "Not for sure. Not without testing it in some way."

"I know. What I haven't figured out yet is how to do that without compromising our safety in the process. I can't simply march the Maturen's son out there and try to make a trade; we would both be dead in an instant."

"You also risk giving away the location of the passes leading into the valley," Skeal Eile added, his voice soft again, but still tinged with anger. "As you have already done. You and your Elf friends, both."

"Sooner or later, the Drouj are going to find their way in anyway," Pan pointed out. "We can't pretend it won't happen. Which is why Sider thought it so important to fortify the passes at Aphalion and Declan Reach. The Elves have done their part, but Declan Reach is unprotected with its defenders all dead. More have to be sent, Pogue. Right away."

The big man nodded. "I don't need you to tell me that. But what about the help we were promised from those who live south? No one has come to stand with us. Not even Esselline. We cannot be expected to do this alone. Perhaps the Seraphic is right: some sort of accord with the invaders is required, if only to stall them until we get help."

"They will not bargain, and they cannot be trusted to keep their word even if they do." Pan looked down at the slumped form of Arik Siq. "They have built a reputation for treachery. If we even think of trusting them, we are fools. We need to wait for Esselline. He will come. Sider was sure of it."

"The Gray Man is dead," Skeal Eile snapped.

Panterra held his temper in check. "So it is left to us to be as selfless and strong-minded as he was." He turned to Pogue Kray, an idea suddenly taking shape. "What of this? What if you keep Taureq Siq's son a prisoner, locked away and not allowed out for any reason? The stronger the prison, the better; he is clever and dangerous. While you hold him, I will travel south to meet with Esselline and be certain he is coming. After that, we can discuss how best to deal with the Drouj."

Panterra was telling them a dreadful lie, and he felt no small amount of guilt in doing so. But he couldn't stop to worry about that. Desperate circumstances demanded desperate measures. He might indeed go to Esselline, as he had said, but first he intended to go after Prue. Somehow he must find a way to reach her and, if he could, rescue her. Failing that, he would bargain for her life in exchange for Arik Siq's. He still did not believe the Maturen would kill his own son; he had made that determination some time back, in spite of what Arik said. The latter would say anything if he thought it might gain him his freedom.

As for protecting the secret of the passes, he would find a way to do that, too. But he would not abandon Prue.

"Also," he added, "someone should go to the Elves and let them know what's happened. They guard Aphalion, and we must work with them if we are to keep the Drouj out of the valley."

"I will go," Skeal Eile volunteered quickly, speaking directly to Pogue Kray, ignoring Pan. "I promised Sider Ament I would stand with him in this, and I keep my promises. Even though I think this boy should not have been given the staff or be listened to just because he carries it, I know we are all agreed on the danger that threatens. I will speak to Oparion Amarantyne and his Queen on our behalf and make certain we are united."

Pan could not object without looking foolish, and so he kept still. Pogue was enthusiastic, clasping the Seraphic by his shoulders and telling him how much this meant. Pan thought he caught the latter casting a veiled glance in his direction, but impaired by his exhaustion he couldn't be certain. He wondered momentarily if there wasn't something else at work here, something he didn't know about. But the moment passed, and Pogue was speaking again.

"I will gather a fresh detachment of men from the village to clear Declan Reach of the dead and to occupy the defenses until further help comes. I will go with them myself. The council can act for me in my absence. But you need to travel quickly, Panterra. Find Esselline and any who might be coming with him and tell them we are at great risk and to hurry."

Pan straightened. "I will leave at once."

"Don't be stupid," Skeal Eile snapped. "Look at you. Any fool can see you wouldn't get five miles in your condition. You need to sleep for at least twelve hours. Rested, you might have a chance of getting the job done."

"He is right, Panterra," Pogue agreed immediately. "You've been through a lot. Go to bed. Sleep as long as you need to and leave when you wake."

"You'll make sure Arik Siq is locked away and guarded well?" he asked, glancing down one final time at his prisoner.

Pogue nodded. "You have my word."

Pan leaned on the black staff momentarily, wondering if there was anything left undone, anything forgotten. He could think of nothing.

"I'm going, then," he said, and went out the door and into the brightness of the new day.

HE HAD TOLD THEM he was going, but he hadn't told them where. Sleep was necessary, but it would have to wait. Instead, he went straight to Aislinne Kray to tell her about Sider. He wasn't looking forward to doing this and would have preferred that someone else carry the news. But he didn't feel right leaving it up to Pogue, who would at least in some measure be relieved that the Gray Man was out of her life forever.

So he walked the familiar roadways and paths of the village—this new bearer of the black staff every bit as tattered and spectral as Sider Ament had ever looked, no better in appearance than the poorest beggar—until he had reached Aislinne's home and was standing at her door.

He took a deep breath, exhaled, and knocked softly.

"Panterra," she gasped when she opened the door and saw him. She took in the wreckage of his appearance, and then her eyes found the black staff he was holding and she sagged visibly. "He's dead, isn't he," she whispered.

He nodded. "Two days ago, at Declan Reach. Poisoned darts from a blowgun. He was caught by surprise and he couldn't . . ."

She held up one hand quickly. "Stop. Don't say anything more. It's enough to know that he's gone."

He looked down at his feet, embarrassed. "I'm sorry."

"I know. But let it alone."

"Your name was the last word he spoke."

She was crying now, not bothering to hide it. "Look at you. What did you have to go through to get back here?" She took his arm and led him inside, closing the door behind him. She led him over to a chair and sat him down. "Wait here."

She disappeared for a few minutes and then was back with clean cloths, hot water, and bandages. She knelt in front of him and cleaned his wounds and bound them up, not saying anything as she did so, absorbed in her task. Panterra let her be. He knew enough to keep quiet while she struggled to come to terms with the news.

"Does Pogue know?" she asked as she was finishing up, getting ready to take away the bloodied water and cloths.

"I went to him first. Skeal Eile was there, too."

She said nothing more as she picked up the water and cloths and carried them out of the room. She was gone for several minutes this time, and he sat thinking on what he had said he would do to find Esselline and how all along he had intended to do something else completely. He wondered if he should tell Aislinne. What would she think of him?

When she came back into the room, she took a seat across from him, hands folded in her lap. "I see that he did not keep his word to me. Even at the end, he failed."

"What do you mean?"

She gestured at the staff. "He persuaded you to take that. I begged him not to. I told him your life was your own and not his to manipulate. But it didn't matter. He had made up his mind about you. Now you will carry the staff and do his work."

"I made the choice. He didn't have any hold on me when he asked it of me. It was at the end of things. He was dying, and he needed someone to take the staff from him. I took it because I knew what it would mean to refuse when so much threatens the valley and our people. I couldn't just walk away, Aislinne. I can't pretend the need isn't there when I know it is."

She sighed. "No, I suppose not. I think it was like that for him, too." She shook her head. "I just know what it means when you carry the staff, Panterra. I know what it will do to you, to any plans you might have for your life. It becomes the reason for everything. You give up so much."

He knew it was so. He supposed he had always known. It was why he had been so reticent even to consider the idea. He might have managed to avoid taking on the responsibility for it if the Gray Man hadn't been dying right in front of him—and if his own guilt for his part in it hadn't been so strong. Not only about Sider, who had died defending him, but about Prue, as well. Leaving her behind, coming back without her, doing nothing as yet to save her—it was too much for him to bear. He knew that. He understood what he had done and what he must now do.

"I have something else to tell you, Aislinne," he said finally. "Something you won't like. I brought back the man who killed Sider. His name is Arik Siq. He is the son of the Drouj Maturen whose army threatens the valley. Pogue has agreed to hold him prisoner so that we can use him to bargain with. I think Pogue will do the right thing, but I am not sure about the Seraphic. Will you do what you can to make sure Pogue doesn't go back on his promise to me?"

She nodded slowly. "It won't be easy, but I will try. Pogue's word is usually good, but he is heavily under the influence of Skeal Eile. The council might intervene, as well. Where will you be if this happens?"

He hesitated. "I said I would find out if Hadrian Esselline is coming to help us as he promised. Pogue worries that the people of Glensk Wood are not strong enough by themselves to stop an attack at Declan Reach if it comes. He is right to worry. I have seen the size of the Drouj army."

She gave him a hard look. "You would go in search of Esselline before seeking out Prue Liss? Why do I find that so difficult to believe? I think maybe you are telling me what you told Pogue, but not what you intend."

"Maybe I am." He blushed at the admission. "You know me too well. I can't leave Prue out there. You haven't heard anything more of her, have you? Nothing since I left to go up to Declan Reach?"

She shook her head. "Not a word. I don't fault you for making her your primary concern. I would do the same." She leaned forward in her chair. "But I must add a fresh complication to your plans. And you won't like hearing this any more than I liked hearing that you have brought Sider's killer to Glensk Wood. Oparion Amarantyne is dead. He was killed several days ago, murdered. His daughter, Phryne, stands accused of the killing. The Queen has locked her away and charged her with patricide. In all likelihood, if nothing happens to change things, she will be tried, convicted, and put to death in the Elven Way."

Panterra didn't know what the *Elven Way* was and didn't want to find out. "Phryne wouldn't kill her father. Something is wrong. Someone else must be responsible."

"That may be so. There are whispers about the Queen and the first minister. She was quick to assume the throne once her husband was dead, and the first minister was quick to support her right to do so. So far, no one has dared to stand up to them. One or two spoke out, but their voices were quickly silenced. They were *reasoned with*, I think you would say."

"Do you believe I should go there first?" he asked.

"I do. I think you should go there while on your way to find Prue. Maybe you can do something to help the Princess. I know you like her. I know she meant something to you. Not as much as Prue, of course. But enough so that you should not abandon her entirely."

He hesitated. What *did* Phryne mean to him? He should help her if he could, but was it right to do so if it cost him time he could have spent searching for Prue? How much could he sacrifice for her before the cost became too great?

"I can't make a decision on this," he admitted, looking away. He was tired, so tired. All he wanted was to lie down and close his eyes.

She rose and came over to him. "Go to your home and sleep, Panterra. A decision on what to do will wait that long. Come back and talk to me, if you want. Whatever you decide, you know I will support you. That said, I can do this much to help you. I can send Brickey to find out what has happened to Esselline. Brickey comes from that country and should be able to find out easily if the King intends to honor his promise to aid us in our fight against the Drouj."

She helped him to his feet, guided him to the door and back outside. He stood with her for a moment, searching for something to say in parting. But words failed him. He started across the porch and down the steps and then suddenly turned. "I'm so sorry about Sider," he said. "I wish I could have done something more to help him."

She smiled. "You're doing something now. I think that's what he would have wanted. Go home."

He turned once more and walked away.

● ● ●

SKEAL EILE WAITED until Panterra Qu was safely gone from the council chambers before making his excuses and leaving Pogue to deal with his prisoner. He had better things to do than stand around lamenting his lost chances, although he could not stop thinking of them. Still seething from his confrontation with the boy, he set out for the deep woods. He chose a path that took him in the opposite direction, even though it lengthened his journey, not wishing to chance meeting the boy somewhere on the way. He was wary of Panterra Qu, much more so now that he carried the black staff, although the staff wasn't the reason for his caution. Before today's meeting, the boy would have been intimidated by him. He would have deferred to him in the matter of the Troll prisoner; he wouldn't have dared to question him or even consider standing up to him as he had.

But the boy was changed. It might be the staff had contributed to this, but Skeal Eile thought it more likely had to do with the time he had spent with Sider Ament. He might still be a boy, but his self-confidence and determination were a man's.

Panterra Qu had been a nuisance before, but now he was something much worse. He was dangerous.

Fortunately, there was a cure for that.

The Seraphic worked his way through the village, following little-used paths and trails that would help him avoid prying eyes and annoying questions. Not that many chose to speak to him when they saw him like this, but now and then someone who followed the teachings of the Hawk would insist. As their spiritual leader, he could hardly refuse conversation with the faithful.

His thoughts turned momentarily from Panterra Qu to the matter of the Drouj prisoner and the threat from the army encamped outside the valley. Somehow he must find a way to meet with the Maturen of these people so that he could discuss their mutual interests in the fate of the valley. The Drouj would not believe there were such interests, of course, but Skeal Eile would persuade him otherwise. There was something for everyone in this; it just had to be explained in terms they could understand.

For that, he might need the aid of the Maturen's son, which meant finding a way to spirit him out of Glensk Wood without being discovered. Or at least keeping him close enough that he could make use of him when it was necessary.

Skeal Eile had been thinking about his future long and hard ever since the boy had brought word to the village council of the collapse of the protective wall. The world was changing, and there was no going back to the way things had been. Life in the valley would change, and those who survived it would have to start over. Those inside and outside, whatever species they were, would be joined in the search for a harmonious relationship. The consequences of doing that could be brutal, but there was no escaping the inevitable. What was needed was a way of avoiding the worst of it, and he had already determined that strength of arms on the battlefield, in whatever form, would not be enough to protect the faithful.

Or himself.

What was needed was something else entirely. Something that only he, with his considerable skills and special talents, could manage.

He reached the old cabin while it was still light, the forest surrounding the dilapidated structure thick with biting insects and deep layers of seething heat. It was not a place for the faint of heart or the unwary, but Skeal Eile was neither of these. He cloaked himself in scents to repel the insects and a lifetime of steely resolve to ward off the heat, then walked to the porch and stood waiting.

This time, the old man did not appear. Instead, Bonnasaint walked out of the house and stood looking down at the Seraphic, his young face beatific and shining with an inner light. *I am innocent of all crimes*, it seemed to say. *I am at peace with who I am.*

Which he probably was, Skeal Eile realized. Madness took many different forms.

"Your Eminence," the boy greeted him, bowing low at the waist, extending his arms. "What service can I perform for you?"

"Do you remember the boy and girl whom I sent you to find in the city of Arborlon some weeks back?"

"Of course."

"You failed in your efforts on that occasion, but chance and circumstance present a fresh opportunity. What do you say?"

The boy smiled, his smooth face wrinkling only slightly. "I welcome fresh opportunity. In which direction does it point?"

Skeal Eile hated looking up at the boy like this, but he didn't want to let him know that this was a problem. Nevertheless, he climbed the steps and stood next to the other, addressing him at eye level. "It points in the same direction as before. But time is your ally on this occasion, if you make good use of it. The boy sleeps this night. You can track him when he wakes and slip ahead to set an ambush. He says he goes one way, but I am not sure he can be trusted. So you will have to discover the truth of things. Can you do that?"

"If it pleases you, I can do anything." Bonnasaint paused. "The task given me is the same? Both the boy and the girl are a problem?"

"The girl is no longer with the boy," the Seraphic advised, wondering as he did why that was so. It was his impression that the two were inseparable. He wondered momentarily what had happened to the girl, and then brushed the matter aside. "The boy is who I am interested in. I don't want to see him anymore. Not here or anywhere. I don't want anyone to see him ever again, and I don't want any part of him ever found."

Bonnasaint cocked his head. "Not even the smallest bit of fingernail or sliver of skin? Not even the whisper of his last scream or the smell of his warm blood as it drains from his body?" When he saw there was to be no reaction from the Seraphic, he shrugged. "Consider it done."

"I considered it done the last time I sent you out. This time I will reserve judgment on your success until I hear it from you firsthand."

"Fair enough, Your Eminence."

The boy bowed low, but Skeal Eile stopped him midway with a soft touch on one shoulder.

"Bonnasaint," he whispered, and waited for the other to look up at him. "Don't fail me."

WHEN PANTERRA QU FINALLY CAME AWAKE in the slow, dream-time hours that precede dawn, he was so disoriented that for a moment he couldn't remember where he was. But then he recognized the feel of his bed and knew he was in his own home for the first time in weeks. He lay where he was, pulling together the tattered threads of his memories of the past three days. It took time and effort to do so. Nothing came easily; each step was slow and painful. Even Sider Ament's death was a reality he could not seem to come to grips with, an event that had the consistency of smoke and lacked anything of substance.

Even what he had become, the new bearer of the black staff, had the feel of a dream.

Eventually, he sat up and looked around. The windows were curtained over, and where small gaps allowed hints of a lesser darkness without he could tell the moon and stars were clouded over. Even the lights of the village were so faint that they were almost not there. He waited for his eyes to adjust. He had no idea what time it was, but it didn't matter. What mattered was that he had slept, was rested, and could set out for whatever destination he chose.

And that was the problem, wasn't it? Where would he go, now that he had to make a choice?

He climbed from his bed and walked to the living area and kitchen, suddenly hungry. He had slept for at least twelve hours; he was certain of that much. Long enough that some of the aches and pains and most of the exhaustion had vanished. His body was still tender here and there, but whatever discomfort remained would dissipate once he had begun his journey. He could set out as soon as he had eaten.

And go where? To find Prue or help Phryne?

He could stall his decision by starting north toward Aphalion, since Phryne was imprisoned in Arborlon and Prue was likely somewhere on the other side of the pass. Once upon a time, he had hoped Sider might bring Prue back to him by way of Declan Reach. But he had waited in vain for that to happen, and now he couldn't be sure where she was or what had become of her. The difficult task of finding her himself lay ahead, and its resolution might well turn out to be unpleasant.

Carrying a candle, he sat himself down at the tiny kitchen table and made a meal of cold meat, bread, and fruit he had scavenged from the larder of the Tracker quarters on his way home. It was not nearly enough to sustain him for long, but all he could manage. He would find something else along the way, stopping at homes where people might feed him. It occurred to him Sider must have lived like this, seeking aid and sustenance when and where he could find it. It wasn't so different, really, from how he lived as a Tracker. There were supplies at the beginning of his long patrols, but sooner or later he always had to scavenge or hunt for what he needed. He knew how to do that. Every Tracker did.

He had finished eating, the remnants of his meal cleaned up and put away, his bed made for his leaving and his backpack and its contents laid out atop it, when he heard the front door open. He was standing in the bedroom and could not see who entered. He picked up the candle where he had placed it on the table by his bedside, reached for the black staff, and walked back out into the living area.

A solitary figure stood in the darkness of the open doorway facing him. He stared, a premonition rippling through him like a chill. For just an instant, he thought it was . . .

"Pan?"

He felt his throat tighten. It couldn't be. He advanced on the speaker quickly, needing to get closer, needing to be sure he was not mistaken.

He wasn't. In the dim glow of the candlelight, he could see her face clearly.

It was Prue.

She had come back to him.

But something about her was wrong. He held the candle higher, illuminating her face, and he saw what it was. Her eyes were a milky white, empty of light and color, fixed and staring.

She was blind.

SEVEN

WHEN THE LIGHT ENVELOPED PRUE LISS AND everything around her disappeared in its brilliant glow, she did not panic. She was fifteen, but she had been trained well enough as a Tracker to stay calm when faced with the unfamiliar and potentially dangerous. She couldn't know what was happening to her; nothing in her life experience had prepared her for this. But what she did know was that—whatever it was—it had saved her from that old man who had hunted her through Deladion Inch's fortress lair. That was good enough for her. It might be a different kind of dangerous, but it couldn't be worse than what she had just escaped.

If she *had* escaped, she added quickly. She didn't know for sure that she had. She didn't know where she was. She might even still be trapped somewhere in the complex.

But she didn't move, even when the light died and she was left in complete darkness. She sat very still on the hard surface on which she had been deposited, smelling the air, listening for sounds. Her intuition hadn't flared up in warning; apparently, no danger threatened her.

Though she couldn't be sure of that either—not after the way her instincts had failed her already during the past few weeks. Three times, at least, that she could count. She had been so sure of those instincts once. But that was a long time ago, and everything had changed. What was then so reliable was now tinged with uncertainty. Sometimes her instincts worked and sometimes they didn't, and she no longer knew if they would react to warn her or remain dormant.

On this occasion, there were no sounds, smells, tastes, or hints of movement in the blackness. She had only herself for company in an impenetrable void.

She forced herself to breathe slowly and evenly, to keep quiet and wait for the light's source to reveal itself. Sooner or later, she sensed, it would appear to her.

When it finally did, she was caught by surprise. A pinprick of light appeared in the distance, so impossibly far away that it felt to her as if it were miles off. Very slowly, it drew closer, working its way ahead steadily through the darkness, and her surroundings began to brighten in response. She saw that she was no longer in the fortress, but had been spirited away to somewhere else entirely. She was sitting on a patch of hard earth at the edge of gardens that spread away from her toward the approaching light, a vast rainbow of flowers that grew from bushes, beds, and vines amid carefully tended greenery of all shapes and sizes. The flowers seemed to bloom right in front of her as their petals were touched by the light, brightening as the intensity of the light grew, stretching out their slender stems in response.

She rose, wanting to be on her feet when whatever was coming reached her. She could feel her heart beating, and she felt oddly light-headed. A sense of wonder enveloped her, and she sensed that this was a transformative moment, life altering and wondrous in a way she had never experienced. She couldn't have said how she knew this, but it was irrefutable. Something important was about to happen, and she knew she would never again experience its like.

The light was very close now, and she could see that it emanated from one end of a strange metal cylinder gripped by the hand of its bearer. Yet even though the light was directed, it seemed diffuse and all-encompassing, spreading out in ways she had never witnessed, brightening a world that only moments before had been dark.

"Good day, Prue," the bearer of the light greeted her.

It was a man of indeterminate age, neither young nor old, but some part of both. His features were unremarkable, his size and build and weight average, his voice quiet and soft around the edges. He was wearing robes that were white and silver, garments meant not for common use but ceremonial occasions. It did not seem wrong or unusual to find him wearing such garments; instead, it felt perfectly natural, although Prue could not have said why.

"Hello," she said. And then added, "Are you the one who brought me here?"

"I am," he replied. "Do you like my gardens?"

"I do," she said. "They make me feel safe."

It made him smile, which in turn caused her to smile in response. "They are my home," he said. "I tend them, and in turn they tend me. Here, all is in balance, a harmony that is lacking in so many other places. Do you know who I am, Prue?"

Amazingly, she did. She knew it instinctively. "You're the King of the Silver River," she said. "The legend of the Hawk speaks of you. You are an ally of the Word and a child of the Land, they say. My mother told me of you."

"I am what they say, but mostly I am things that no one knows. Secret things. I was a Faerie creature once, in a time long ago. I was caretaker of the old world, of the world that disappeared when the Faerie folk gave way to the coming of Man and everything changed. My space has become much smaller since then, a fraction and no more of what once was given to me. I keep it hidden now from all, but it is still here, part of a better time and better world."

She looked past him to the gardens. "Your flowers are beautiful. They seem to grow everywhere, as if the gardens never end."

"In one sense, they don't. When you walk within them, there are no boundaries. You cannot leave or become lost or reach a point where you can see what lies beyond them. Would you like to visit them? Will you walk with me?"

He reached for her hand, which she gave to him willingly, and he led her away from where they had been talking and into the gardens. Once there, they strolled down pathways formed of flat stones here and crushed rock there, of mossy earth and deep grasses. Hedgerows bracketed their passage at one point; vines grown thick on trelliswork shadowed their quiet walk at another. All around, the vast sweep of the flower beds formed blankets of color that radiated in a sudden wash of sunlight, their myriad scents filling the air.

"This must take an awful lot of work," Prue said to him finally, unable to conceive of how he could manage.

"It takes everything I've got to offer, but not more than I wish to give." He pointed. "See the rainbows formed by the sunlight reflecting off the moisture from the dew? There, where the scarlet and gold meet? I cannot imagine life without gardens. Can you?"

The way he said it told her he already knew the answer. There were flower beds and gardens in her world, but nothing like this. Mostly there were only the forests, meadows, and rocky heights of the mountain peaks, and for her people beauty such as she saw here was solely the province of the imagination.

"The legends say you were alive at the beginning of things when the old world was born," she said. "That would make you very old. But you don't look old."

"I don't always look the same. This is how I look to you, but to others I look different."

She studied him a moment. "Am I safe here? Are you going to send me back?"

He seemed to consider. "You are safe for now, but I am going to have to send you back at some point. Although I won't send you back to where I found you."

"I'm not anywhere close to where I was, am I? Or even close to the same country?"

"You are nowhere anyone can reach you. The boy Hawk was here once, a long time ago. He walked these gardens, too. He talked with me as I am talking to you. He asked questions of me, and I gave him what answers I could." He glanced over at her. "Just as I will give you what answers I can."

They walked side by side for a few minutes, saying nothing, the man and the girl, surrounded by a profusion of colors and smells and a sense of peace. Birds flew past in bright bursts of color, and insects buzzed and hummed from within the cool, shadowed depths of the greenery.

"You saved me from that old man for a reason," she said, making it a statement of fact.

"That old man is a demon come out of the ruins of the Great Wars, a creature of vast and terrible appetite, a beast with a singular vision. It lives for only one reason—to destroy all those who bear the black staff. It thought for many years that it had done so, that all of them were gone. It wandered the wastelands of the old world, seeking out any it might have missed, without success. There were none to be found. Then, one day, not so long ago, it had a dream of such a bearer— a dream that came to it unbidden and was fostered by its preternatural instincts. It sensed the presence of the Word's magic and the nature of its source. A man who wielded such magic had ventured outside a valley that had once been hidden and no longer was. It caught a whiff of both, nothing more, but that was enough. The demon knew its hunt was not ended."

The King of the Silver River gestured toward a stone bench that was settled in a small circular clearing in the middle of the pathway. They walked to the bench and sat down together.

"There were others of its kind once, hunters of Knights of the Word. This demon may be the last. Do you know of the man it hunts? Have you met him?"

She nodded. "His name is Sider Ament. He bears a staff that was carried into my valley homeland five centuries ago by one of two Knights of the Word who came there with my ancestors."

"Do you know, as well, of your own heritage as a child of the Ghosts, one who was a companion of the boy Hawk and came with him into the valley?"

She shrugged. "It was a rumor in my family history, but I did not know for sure. So is it true? Am I a direct descendant, and has the magic come to me through the girl Candle?"

He spread his hands on his knees and studied her face. "All true. You have Candle's magic in your blood, passed down to you through the generations. Some of your ancestors had use of it, some didn't. You do. But it is a fragile gift, and it does not always serve its user success-fully. It is quite unpredictable. You must have noticed."

"It warns when danger threatens either me or those around me. It tells me when to be careful or turn back or do something to avoid what might otherwise happen." She paused. "But you're right. Sometimes it doesn't work. Sometimes it fails to warn me of anything. Then I am at risk—as are those who depend on me. Was it like that for Candle, too?"

The King of the Silver River nodded. "It was. Too much so. It almost killed her. Not only her, but others, too. The boy Hawk almost lost his life because of her inability to control the magic. But that is its nature. Magic works differently for different people, and there is no way of knowing how it will respond. Even those who have used it repeatedly and come to rely on it have found that it can abandon them."

She wrinkled her forehead in thought and brushed at her red hair. "Do you know why that happens?"

He shook his head. "Mostly, we have to accept it as it is." He paused. "But there is something I can do about your specific problem."

She looked at him hopefully. "Do you have that kind of power? Could you make it predictable? Could you make it do what it's supposed to do and warn me when I'm in danger? Or if Pan is in danger when he's with me? I can't help him otherwise, and I have to help him. He needs me to help him."

"Panterra Qu. Your best friend since you both were small. He's very important to you, isn't he?"

She nodded quickly. "More important than anything."

"Did you know that he now carries the black staff? That he has become the bearer whom the demon hunts and seeks to destroy?"

She went pale. "Why would Pan be carrying the black staff? It belongs to Sider."

"Sider Ament is dead, killed just outside the walls of your valley. He was hunting the Drouj who betrayed you, the one you believed was your friend."

Quickly he told her the truth about Arik Siq and what he had been seeking to do when he left her imprisoned in the Drouj camp and accompanied Panterra Qu back into the valley.

"Sider found out the truth and tried to stop him from leaving the valley to impart what he knew to the Drouj. He was successful, but it cost him his life. As he was dying, he persuaded your friend to take the black staff and become its new bearer. Your friend did so out of a strong sense of responsibility for the people of your valley. But also out of a sense of responsibility for you. By accepting the staff, he believed he might have a chance of freeing you from the Trolls who held you prisoner."

"Not knowing that Deladion Inch had already freed me," she added. "Oh, Pan."

"He searches for you now."

"And the demon searches for him." She got to her feet quickly. "I have to warn him. I have to help him."

The King of the Silver River did not move. He remained where he was, his face calm and his gaze steady upon her. "Do you really want to help him? Doing so may prove much more dangerous than you think. It might cost you something precious. It might take something away from you that you could never get back again. Would you still want to help him, knowing this?"

"Can you show me a way, if I say yes?"

He nodded, his eyes still fixed on her.

"I will do whatever it takes because he would do the same for me."

"Let me explain something," the other said quietly, his eyes shifting momentarily to his gardens before returning to meet hers. "You are a child of one of those who were called Ghosts. But so is Panterra Qu. Not a child of those who followed Hawk, but of the boy himself. He doesn't know this; no one does except me. Family members knew it once, but over time the family grew large enough that the connection lost importance. None of Hawk's descendants had the use of his magic, and none played a role in the events that followed. Eventually, the family died back again, and their memory of their lineage was lost to time and circumstance. But Panterra, while not the last of that family, is the one who matters."

He leaned forward slightly, as if in confidence. "If I tell you why, you must not tell him. Not of that or of anything else I confide in you. You must promise me. It is important that you know but equally important that he does not. Do you understand?"

She shook her head. "I'm not sure I do. But if that is what you require, I give you my word."

The King of the Silver River nodded. "Very well. Panterra Qu has a destiny to fulfill that is not altogether dissimilar from the one given to the boy Hawk. But Panterra is not imbued with magic like his ancestor was. What he has is the ability to wield magic in a way no other has since the Knights of the Word came into the valley to escape the Great Wars. What he also has is a task that would crush the soul and spirit of anyone who knew the truth of its demands. It is a task which he must assume nevertheless."

He paused, and then unexpectedly he smiled. "He is to lead the people of the valley back into the larger world, where they and their descendants will settle and multiply and eventually become dominant once again."

"Panterra?" she asked in disbelief.

He nodded. "Assuming the demon doesn't find him and kill him first."

"But I can prevent this from happening?"

"You can try. You are the only one who can. I cannot see the future, but I can sense its possibilities. I sense now that what I am telling you is the truth. But truth, like magic, can have different meanings. It is not an absolute. It does not always come about as we think it will. So I can tell you what I believe to be so, and you can act on that if you wish. But, as I said before, the price may be steep."

She stood looking down at him, thinking it through. "Can we walk some more while we talk about this? It helps me to think when I walk."

They set out once more through the gardens. Prue chose a grassy path that meandered through rows of clematis and broad stands of paintbrush and shooting stars. Such flowers should not have been able to grow together as they did, but somehow the King of the Silver River had found a way for them to do so. That he was a creature of magic—perhaps of very great magic—was undeniable. But could he do enough to help her accomplish what he was asking of her?

"What can you do to enable me to help Pan?" she asked him finally, looking over at him so that she could watch his face when he answered and perhaps judge the sincerity of his reply.

"I can restore your instincts so that they will never fail you again. I can give you back the power to know when danger threatens, from which direction it comes, and how it will manifest itself. I can restore your confidence in its reliability. When you stand beside Panterra Qu, you will always be able to tell what's needed."

She sensed there was a loophole of some sort in all this, but on the surface of things it seemed she was being given what she needed. "Can you give me the use of magic that will let me protect him?"

The King of the Silver River laughed softly. "Such a brave girl, such a fighter! I admire your courage, Prue Liss. But no, I cannot give you more than I have offered. Panterra will have to defend himself, if the need arises. But know this. The dangers he is likely to face come not so much from what he can see as from what he can't. Your instincts will warn him of what's hidden. That is the best use to which you can be put."

She mulled over his phrasing: *That is the best use to which you can be put.* As if she were a tool or a weapon. It suggested she was agreeing to serve as a pawn in the struggle ahead, and that she would become not so much Pan's friend and companion as his guard dog.

"But there will be a price exacted for this?" she queried. "You said it might be more than I was prepared to pay?"

He stopped and turned to face her. "There is always a price for tinkering with magic, especially in the way I am suggesting I tinker with yours. It will require that you become fundamentally changed from the way you are. The magic must become stronger, more dominant. It must increase sufficiently that it will not fall victim to the failings you have experienced in the past. It must be able to withstand not only exterior pressure, such as the demon's considerable magic, but your own interior obstructions, ones you might create without even realizing you are doing so."

His smooth brow wrinkled as if he had tasted something bitter. "Changes of that sort result in unexpected consequences. Increasing strength in one place requires decreasing it in another. But where and how that happens isn't something that can be foreseen and controlled. Its pathway cannot be chosen; the magic takes whatever route it chooses, and while the purpose can be determined, the overall results cannot."

"Then I might not end up as I am now?" she pressed. "I might end up altered in some way?"

"You almost certainly will. But what I cannot tell you is the form your differentness will take. Nor can I tell you for certain if the changes are permanent or temporary. Nor can I tell you if there will be a further price exacted somewhere down the line or if you will think the cost worth the sacrifice."

He paused, waiting on her. She shook her head. "But it will help Pan for me to do this?"

The King of the Silver River sighed. "Let me say it another way. The demon that hunts Panterra Qu will almost certainly find him. It might take a while for that to happen, but in the end it will. The demon is relentless and it is driven. Unless it is killed, it will not cease in its efforts to find any who are left of those who carry the black staff. Panterra might evade it, but he will not escape it. Not unless he has help. You might be able to give him that help with your ability to sense and avoid the danger that threatens him. Your help gives him a better chance at survival than if he is left on his own. He is young and new to the magic of the talisman he carries. He will need time to learn how to master that magic so that when he faces the demon—which I think he must—he will have a reasonable chance of defeating it."

"There will be a fight between them? You are certain of this?"

"Unless fate intervenes and one or the other is killed, yes."

Prue nodded without speaking, thinking it through. Panterra was a skilled Tracker, but that might not be enough against the old man. She could still remember how he had looked at her, how trapped and helpless he had made her feel. Pan was stronger than she was physically, but this demon had killed other bearers of the black staff, ones infinitely better equipped to defend themselves than he was, and it knew how to break down their defenses. It wasn't human; it probably wasn't even sane.

She looked down at her feet, watching their steady progression along the pathway as she walked. There was no one she was closer to than Pan, not even her parents. He was the big brother she didn't have. He was her mentor and best friend, the one she relied on to see her through the toughest of times, the one she turned to first when she was in need of advice or reassurance. There wasn't anything she couldn't tell him—hadn't told him, in point of fact. They were so close they were almost one person.

If something happened to him, it would be the same as if it had happened to her. Given that, was there anything that she wouldn't do for him? Was any sacrifice too great?

She stopped where she was and looked over at the King of the Silver River. "I want you to do it. I want you to make it possible for me to help Pan. I want my instincts back and I want them dependable. I'm willing to take my chances with what that means."

He studied her for a moment, as if to make sure that she meant what she was saying, and then he nodded. "We will walk a little more. It's a beautiful day and the gardens are especially lovely in the sunlight. Let's enjoy them while we can."

She didn't know what he meant exactly, but she was willing to spend more time in the gardens, so she did as he asked. They walked for a long time, much longer than she thought they would or even than she thought she'd feel comfortable with, given how anxious she was to find Pan. At the end of their walk, when they were back where they had started, she felt unexpectedly fresh and rested, even though she knew she should feel exactly the opposite.

"Look!" he said suddenly.

She turned to where he was pointing and saw what she had never seen—a dove that was all red, flying across the gardens, a brilliant flash of color against the brightness of the sun.

"Oh!" she gasped, and it was all she could manage as she watched it disappear into the distance.

When she turned back, the King of the Silver River had become an old, old man with white hair and beard, his face deeply lined and his eyes a pale blue set deep within the folds of skin surrounding them.

"Even for me, use of the magic diminishes who I am. Good-bye, Prue Liss. I wish you well."

Then she felt herself slipping toward the ground, suddenly too weak to stand. She collapsed gently, as if hands held and lowered her so that she would not be harmed. She had a moment of lucidity in which she saw an image of the scarlet dove flash before her eyes, flying swiftly away, but clearly visible to her.

Then she was asleep.

*   *   *

IN THE AFTERMATH of the girl's collapse back into slumber, the King of the Silver River knelt next to her, studying her young face. "Sleep, child," he whispered. "Dream of better days."

It broke his heart that so much sacrifice was needed to keep the magic in balance, to keep the war between the Word and Void from tilting the wrong way. He had great power at his disposal, power second only to the Word's, but he felt so helpless. To give her what she asked for, to give her what she needed, came at such a high price.

He had told her he didn't know what she would lose by helping Panterra Qu, but that was not entirely true. He knew more than he was telling her, but less than he would like. So he had told her just enough and let fate and circumstance take matters where they would.

After all, it was like that for all living things—they could never know everything they wished to know. That would never change.

He reached down, took her head in his hands, and placed his fingers on her temples. He closed his eyes and disappeared inside himself. With his eyes still closed, he moved his fingers and thumbs here and there about her face, touching this and that, giving and taking what was required, seeking the sources for her magic's wellspring. He found them easily, and he gave them bits and pieces of his own strength, his own deep insights, his own vast instincts. Then he took his hands away and rose.

He had given her what help he could. He had taken from her what was necessary. The future would reveal if the exchange had been worth it—a future that was only a droplet of water to him, but would seem like an ocean to her. She would wake and discover what had happened, and when she did her journey would truly begin.

He hoped she would be strong and brave enough to survive it.

With a wave of one hand, he sent her back into her own world to find out if she was.

EIGHT

WHEN PRUE LISS AWOKE, THE LIGHT WAS SO gray that it seemed as if all the color had been drained from the world. She blinked uncertainly as she emerged from a deep sleep that had left her lethargic and weak. She was lying on a grassy patch of ground somewhere in a forest where the trees canopied overhead and the air smelled of damp and rot. She could not tell the time or even if it was day or night. Everything had a twilight cast to it, as if the sun were down and night coming on.

She lay where she was for a time, waiting for her strength to return. Her meeting with the King of the Silver River was still fresh in her mind, although it seemed more a dream than real. She could see his face and hear his voice, but she lacked any sense of time and place. How long had she been with him, and where had their meeting occurred? None of it was clear, and there was no way of finding out now.

What she did know was that he had done something to her, just as she had asked him to, just as he had promised. To regain use of her instincts in a way that would allow her to trust them again, she had been irrevocably changed.

She took some deep, slow breaths—inhaling, exhaling—the simple act of breathing a reassurance that she was still alive and functioning. She looked down at herself to see if she was still all there, and she found to her relief that she was. Arms, legs, feet, and hands—all of her was of a piece and recognizable.

Yet something was different. She could feel the change, even without being able to discern its source.

When she felt strong enough to do so, she sat up and looked around. She was sitting in woods, the trees alive and well, their canopy thick and leafy and their limbs dark arms linked in the gray light. She could see birds darting here and there, as gray and colorless as the landscape itself. She caught glimpses of tiny creatures moving through the foliage and flitting through the trees. Sounds rose in tiny bursts, calls and cries that signaled hidden presences. In the distance, just barely visible through the screen of the forest, a wall of dark and craggy mountain peaks rose.

Where was she?

There was only one way to find out. She climbed to her feet, waited a few moments to see if there was any dizziness or weakness, and found none. She brushed pine needles and bits of grass and dirt from her pants, and looked around some more, trying to decide which way she should go. She was a skilled Tracker, and she could find her way even in darkness. But she could not do so now. Everything looked strange to her. Different. The shadings of shadows and light didn't look right; the casting of light and dark was skewed in some way.

Then suddenly a flash of bright scarlet appeared through the branches of the trees, skimming close to the ground, soaring to gain the open spaces between the dark trunks. It was the first bit of color she had seen, and it was so unexpected that for a moment she just stood there and watched it as it flew.

It was a bird of some sort.

It was a scarlet dove.

But there were no scarlet doves in her world, only in the world of the King of the Silver River. Why was she seeing one here? Unless she was still in the Faerie creature's world and hadn't returned to her own after all. But how could that be, when the whole reason for her agreeing to chance an infusion of deep magic was to come back and help Pan?

Then she realized something else, something so astonishing that it froze her in place. Forgetting for a moment the question of which world she was in or what she was supposed to be doing—why could she see the bright scarlet of the dove but not see colors anywhere else?

She blinked rapidly, closed her eyes tightly, and opened them again. The world around her was still washed of any color but gray and black, light and dark. Nothing else. She searched the landscape, trying to find something that would yield even a small dab of color.

Nothing. Anywhere.

The dove reappeared, streaking past, its sleek form revealed in bright scarlet hues, its feathers lustrous, its color so unimaginably vivid, so incomprehensibly intense, that it left her breathless. She peered around wildly, searching anew for something that would explain what was happening. But no matter where she looked or how long she spent searching, there was no other color to be found.

Frantic now, suddenly frightened of what was happening, she bolted away into the trees, running hard in the direction the dove had taken. It wasn't difficult to find, its scarlet body standing out clearly, and it did not seem to be trying to escape her. Rather, it flew away and then came back to her, repeating this act over and over until finally she realized it was beckoning her to follow. Why it was doing this and where it was leading her, she couldn't say. But the dove was a lifeline to the explanation she desperately needed, and so she followed it.

Finally it swooped down and perched on a low-hanging branch above a tiny pool of water, a pond that was little more than a depression in the earth through which a small stream meandered like a lost child. She walked over to the pool and knelt, looking down into its clear depths. There she was, Prue Liss, looking back, her image rippling slightly with the sluggish movement of the stream as it passed through, her features bending . . .

She peered closer. Something was wrong. She tightened her focus, trying to make certain.

Her eyes. There was something wrong with her eyes!

She bent closer still, almost to a point where she was touching the water with her face, almost to where she was kissing it with her lips, and she saw that her eyes no longer had definition. They didn't look like her eyes—or the eyes of anyone who could see. They looked like the eyes of a blind person.

Clouded and empty.

She jerked back in shock. What was going on? Her eyes made her look as if she were blind, but she could see! She looked around quickly, making sure. Yes, she could see. There was no mistaking it. What did it mean that her eyes were those of a blind person, but she could still see the world around her, even if it was all gray and colorless . . . ?

Oh, no! Oh, no! She screamed the words in the silence of her mind, unable to trust herself to speak them.

She could see the bright scarlet of the dove, but no other color anywhere. She could see a bird that didn't exist in her world, but was flying about in it anyway. She was in her world, she decided. Her instincts and her senses told her so. This wasn't the world of the King of the Silver River. The two were different enough that she would have known if that wasn't so. She was in her own world, and there was no color.

Except there was. She just couldn't see it. That was the point of the dove—a sign from the King of the Silver River to tell her what the use of his magic had cost, an indicator of what had been extracted from her in payment. She could still see, but only in black and white, in gray tones and shadows. All of the colors were gone.

She rocked back on her heels and tried not to cry. Her red hair—she would never see its brightness again. The green of the trees, the sky's assorted blues, Pan's hazel eyes, his sun-browned face—nothing, nothing, nothing of their color anywhere! She was crying now, realizing what that meant, grasping right away how much she would miss it, how terrible it would be to live in a world where all the colors were gone.

Forever.

But it was to help Pan that she had sacrificed herself, and she refused to regret it. The cost was clearly defined. She had given up seeing the world's brightness so that she could see what was hiding in its darkness—all the dangers that threatened the unwary, all the predators that would steal something infinitely more precious than color. Panterra needed her to save him so that he could do what the King of the Silver River had said he was fated to do—to save their people, to lead them out of the valley and into a new world.

Oh, but to a world in which there would be no color! Not for her. Not ever again! She could hardly bear it, and she started crying all over again, weeping into her sleeve, her small body shaking, her sobs audible in the stillness of the forest. She was only fifteen, she told herself, and she would never see color again!

It took her a long time to regain control of herself, much longer than she had expected. But when she had cried herself out and silently voiced all her bitter thoughts, she climbed back to her feet and stood staring off into the grayness that was now the measure of her future. She had to let go of what had been and embrace what would be. She had to accept the consequences of her decision to help Panterra Qu and remember that something good would come of this.

If she could manage to protect him. If she could stand with him for as long as he needed her.

When the scarlet dove reappeared, slipping like quicksilver through the branches of the trees, she took a deep, steadying breath and began to track its flight.

NOW SHE STOOD in the doorway of Pan's home, watching as he took in the damage she had suffered, gave an audible gasp, and moved quickly to embrace her.

"Your eyes!" he whispered into her hair, rocking her gently.

It seemed that he was the one who needed steadying, and so she managed to not give way to the tears that threatened to come. Instead, she breathed in his scent and hugged herself against his solid warmth.

"It's all right, Pan. It isn't as bad as it seems."

She could feel him shaking his head in denial. "But you're blind!"

It was so good to be held by him. It was the first time she had felt as if she were really home safe, and she didn't want the feeling to end too quickly. She had walked for two days to get here, coming up out of the wasteland beyond the valley and through Declan Reach where the bodies of the dead still lay uncovered, the scavengers beginning to feed by now. She had crossed the divide and descended the inner slopes through familiar forests until she had reached Glensk Wood and this moment. She had avoided being seen except at a distance and reached Pan's home without a direct encounter with anyone. She had traveled a landscape rendered gray and colorless by her change in vision, a condition that by now she realized would forever give rise to aching memories and dark emotions.

All the way here she had been thinking about what she was going to do. In the beginning of her journey, when she was still in the forest and confused about her direction, she had thought she might not be able to find her way back at all. But the scarlet dove had saved her. It was more than an indicator of her condition and a reminder of what was lost; it was also her personal guide, designed to bring her back to where she needed to be. She followed it out of the wastelands to the exterior slopes of the mountains that surrounded her valley and from there upward to Declan Reach. Then, quite suddenly, it had disappeared. She assumed it had done what it had been sent to do, and so it was gone for good. She didn't see it again, in any case. Once through the pass and inside the valley, she was on her own. Even though she looked for the dove repeatedly during the remainder of her trek, there was no sign of it. She would have welcomed even a momentary glimpse, would have treasured even a brief reminder of the brightness of its scarlet hue, but it did not return.

Already, she realized, she was forgetting the color of things. Already, her memories were fading, the colors she remembered washing out, their glow fading away.

"Pan," she said, forcing herself away from him, holding him at arm's length as she stared up at him with her cloudy eyes. "I can see, Pan. I'm not blind, even though I look as if I am. But there is a reason for this. I have to explain so you can understand."

"I don't need to understand," he replied quickly. "I'm just glad to have you back safe. I thought I might have lost you."

Then she really was crying, and they hugged each other anew, arms wrapped about each other, so grateful for the moment they couldn't speak.

Again, she pushed him away. "Pan, you have to listen to me. Come over here and sit down. Close the door."

He did so, and they sat together in front of the cold ashes of the fireplace. Panterra brought out blankets in which they wrapped themselves in order to fight off the night's chill. It was somewhere in the hours before sunrise by now—Prue couldn't be sure exactly when. She'd been walking a long time in the darkness, so she knew it was after midnight. She thought momentarily about eating because she was very hungry, but she decided it would have to wait.

Slowly, meticulously, she told him everything that had happened to her after he had gone off with Arik Siq, leaving her a captive of the Drouj. It took her a long time, and she stopped and started again repeatedly, choosing her words, not wanting to leave anything out or diminish its importance. She replayed the events of the ill-fated rescue attempt by Deladion Inch and of her efforts to hide in and ultimately escape from his fortress lair. She skimmed over the parts that were too scary to dwell on, especially those in which she had faced the demon that had pursued her. But she stressed the parts that involved the danger to him. She didn't want him to underestimate that old man. She didn't want him to think this was a hunt that he might escape if he were in the least way careless. The demon wanted his life and it wanted the black staff. If he valued both, he must begin to think now on what he was going to do.

She would help him, of course. That was why she had come back. That was the bargain she had made with the King of the Silver River, and the loss of her ability to see colors was the price she had paid. She didn't try to downplay how important that was, but she did insist that it was worth the trade to get the use of her instincts back again in a way she could depend upon. The King of the Silver River had been emphatic that if she did not come back to help Pan, the demon would find a way to kill him.

"You should have told him the price was too steep," Pan insisted, looking down at the floor between them. "You should have refused."

"Refused?" She almost laughed. "It was my idea, Pan! I insisted he help me. Neither of us knew what it would cost me. We only knew that I would be changed. But I would have given up more than I did if it meant helping you." She reached out for his chin and jerked his head up. "Look at me! What would you not do for me? If it were turned around, would you try to bargain down the price? I did what was necessary, and it's behind me. What we have to do now is find a way to help you."

She did not tell him all of it. She kept to herself that the price she had paid for that help might be steeper than he knew. She kept secret that the King of the Silver River had warned of the possibility that she might suffer further damage, something of a much more serious nature. She saw no reason to cause him additional worry.

Nor did she break her word to the King by telling Pan anything about either his heritage or his destiny. Telling him that he was a direct descendant of the boy Hawk would do nothing to help him in his efforts to stay alive. It would not aid him in his struggle to master the magic of the black staff. It was hard enough carrying the burden that Sider Ament had bequeathed him—to be the staff's bearer, to wield it in defense of the valley's inhabitants, to become the successor that the Gray Man had envisioned. For the same reasons, she said nothing of the future that the King of the Silver River had foreseen wherein he would lead the people of the valley into the larger world. It wasn't what he needed to think about now. She could not imagine how this exodus would come about in any case, but if it were indeed his destiny, it would have to find him without her help.

"I didn't think there were any demons left in the world," he said at one point. "I thought they were all destroyed in the cataclysm our ancestors escaped when they followed Hawk to this valley. I half thought they were a myth—that they weren't demons, but something else that the word *demons* fit and so that's what they were called."

Prue shook her head. "We heard stories about them often enough when we were children. Doesn't matter that no one has seen a demon since the valley was sealed up; there could still be others out there, some that escaped what happened to almost everything else."

"It's said they can shape-shift and make themselves look like someone else. That they are enormously strong and use magic we can't even begin to understand. Remember what Aislinne told us?" Pan said. "That they were the leaders of the once-men, humans who had been subverted and turned to predators? Almost nothing could kill them—although Elven magic was said to have destroyed the one that tracked the Hawk. Still, thinking that a demon is out there, hunting us . . . that he's real . . ."

"Oh, he's real enough. You can take my word for it. You should have seen his eyes. He made me feel helpless just by looking at me. If he had been a little quicker, I would be dead."

She trailed off, realizing she wasn't helping things. "Tell me what's happened in my absence, Pan. I know Sider is dead. I know Arik Siq lied. Is there more?"

There was, of course. Pan detailed the preparations that both the Elves and humans had begun to make to defend the valley from the

Drouj. He related the events that had taken Sider and himself south in search of allies and eventually brought him back to Declan Reach to witness the Gray Man's death. He told her how he had tracked down Arik Siq, captured him, and brought him here to Glensk Wood to be held as a prisoner until it could be determined if he were useful in bargaining with the Drouj. It had been his plan to go after her, to find and rescue her, until her unexpected reappearance.

"Oparion Amarantyne was killed several days ago," he added. "They have fixed the blame for this on Phryne. She is imprisoned and will likely be put on trial for her father's murder. I don't know all the details, but I know she couldn't have done it. Someone else must be responsible. Perhaps the Queen, according to Aislinne."

Prue nodded. "We should go to her. Phryne would never do anything to hurt her father."

"That was my intention, but not until I'd found you." He smiled. "I'm so happy you're here. I was so worried that I wouldn't see you again."

Prue reached out and again took his hands in hers. "Let's make a promise to each other, Pan. No matter what happens, we will not be separated again. Not for any reason. If I am to help you, as I was told by the King of the Silver River I should, we must stay close."

"We must," he agreed. "We shouldn't be apart. We are partners, you and me. As Trackers, friends, and family. We belong together."

"Do you give me your word we won't become separated? No matter what?"

He squeezed her hands. "No matter what."

She released his hands again and smiled. "That makes me feel much better. But we have to leave here. It's too dangerous to stay. The demon will be tracking you, and you can't wait around for it to find you. Besides, we have to discover if there is any way we can help Phryne. Do you have an idea how we might do that?"

"I don't. I just know we have to try. Pogue Kray wanted me to search for Hadrian Esselline to make sure he helps us defend Declan Reach, but Aislinne told me she would send Brickey instead. She said nothing I say or do will persuade somebody like Esselline to honor a promise to a dead man, but Brickey is from that country and might have better luck. I think what you and I should do is go to the Elves and speak before the High Council about what's happened with Phryne."

"Better start by speaking with the Orullians," she said. "They might be able to give us a better idea of what we're walking into. Even if we can't do anything about Phryne right away, we need to make sure the Queen listens to what we have to say about the Drouj. She won't ignore the threat of an invasion, no matter the extent of her complicity in the killing of the King. She's in as much danger as everyone else."

Pan nodded, rising. "Let's pack and leave."

They set about the task of preparing for their departure, stuffing their backpacks with clothes, tying on rolled-up blankets, and adding medicines and weapons from Panterra's locker. Preferring not to return to her own house, Prue selected clothes from the extras she always kept at Pan's cottage. Her parents might have returned from their travels by now, but as yet they knew nothing about what had happened to her. If they saw her eyes, their reaction would be much worse than Pan's. They would pull her from the Tracker ranks in a millisecond, no matter how hard she tried to explain things. Better that they remain ignorant of everything for a little while longer.

"I don't like doing this," Pan said at one point. "Deceiving your parents feels wrong." He paused. "Of course, telling them the truth doesn't feel like the right thing, either."

She stopped what she was doing and looked him in the eye. "I've been a Tracker long enough that I have the right to make that decision. So let's not talk about it."

They continued with their preparations in silence. Prue was glad for the excuse to keep busy, not wanting to think too hard about what lay ahead, still uncertain in her own mind that they were doing the right thing. Going to the Elves might create fresh complications since it meant getting involved with Phryne again. But abandoning her wasn't something that she was prepared to do, either. Even knowing that things were likely to be much more difficult than they expected, she was in agreement with Pan that they had to do something.

She worked quietly in her world of grays and shadows, trying not to think about how dreary it all was. She imagined the colors she wasn't seeing, tried to remember the intensity of hues when she began selecting from her clothes and pleased with herself when she could do

so and irritated when she couldn't. She pictured the colors of the furniture and wood moldings, of walls, floors, and ceiling, of the rendition
of the little painting of a woman at a well that Pan's mother had loved
so much and that he kept on the wall even after she was gone.
She tried to guess the color of his clothes, then of curtains and his old
comforter.

Stop it! she admonished herself finally. *Let it alone!*

She caught herself crying again and brushed the tears away
roughly. This was not the time or place. She'd had her cry. She was bigger than this, stronger. Pan shouldn't have to see her cry anymore.

When they were finished and had shouldered their packs, they
took a moment to look around the cottage, ostensibly to determine if
they had missed anything, but on a deeper level to consider the possibility that it might be the last time they would ever be here.

"Don't worry," Pan told her, as if needing to voice a response to
what they were both thinking. "Now that we're back together again,
we can handle anything that comes our way."

Prue nodded, smiled encouragingly. It was the right thing to say
and the right attitude to take. "Anything," she echoed.

Moments later, they were out the door and walking through the
predawn darkness.

HIDDEN DEEP within the trees where there was virtually no chance
of being discovered, Bonnasaint watched them depart the cottage.
They did not turn south toward Hold-Fast-Crossing and Hadrian Esselline, as Skeal Eile had insisted they would, but north toward Arborlon. Bonnasaint smiled. This was why you never put your trust in
others, not even someone who normally could be depended upon, but
only in yourself. If he had listened to the Seraphic, he would already be
miles away from where he should be if he was to carry out his assign-
ment, wasting his time looking for someone who was never coming.

The Seraphic hadn't been right about the boy being alone and the
girl being gone, either. It made him wonder what he *had* been right
about, but he left that question alone. What he had been right or
wrong about wouldn't affect how successful Bonnasaint would be
with the task he had been given.

It never was.

He stayed where he was, watching until the boy and the girl were well out of sight before leaving his cover. He would not attempt to shadow them, although that might be the easiest way. He knew something of their reputation as Trackers, and he respected their skills enough that he wouldn't risk getting caught following when he could just as easily and more safely wait for them to come to him. He knew they would go to Arborlon because that was where they would find their Elven friends. So he would go on ahead of them, taking a different route entirely, find a suitable place where they must pass, and wait.

Sooner or later, they would appear. When they did, he would put an end to them.

NINE

BECAUSE SHE WAS A PRINCESS AND DESERVED A measure of respect in spite of the accusations lodged against her, Phryne Amarantyne was not locked away in the prison that housed ordinary criminals. Instead, she was given a windowless room in the lower section of the buildings that contained the Council chambers, a room normally used for storing supplies. That way, it was reasoned, she would not be exposed to unnecessary dangers while she awaited her trial.

The room was of reasonable size, almost twelve feet by fourteen feet, but it felt so small because of boxes of records stacked floor-to-ceiling against two of the walls. She was given a pallet to sleep on, some bedding, a chamber pot, a small table and chair, and some writing materials. She had the use of candles for light, which was considerate as the sun never reached this room and so day and night were pretty much the same. A guard kept watch outside her door twenty-four hours a day, and the door was locked at all times save when a little serving girl brought her food on a tray. When the serving girl

appeared, the door was unlocked just long enough to allow for the tray
to be placed on the floor inside the opening and to replace the chamber pot—the serving girl was forbidden to go in any farther or to say
anything—and then it was sealed back up again.

All of the Home Guards assigned to watch her were men she did
not know. None of them was allowed to speak to her. When she tried
asking for things, they made her write out a request, which they
claimed they would take to those responsible for seeing to it that
she had what she needed. She wrote out several requests and there
was no response to any of them. When she asked one of her jailors
why she hadn't heard anything, he told her that such things take
time and to be patient. Something in the way he said this warned her
that patience would not be enough. She quit asking for anything soon
after.

She was allowed no visitors.

She was not permitted to write letters.

She was not told anything about what was happening outside the
walls of her cell.

She was not advised when her trial would be held.

When she asked to see her grandmother, Mistral Belloruus, a request that under any circumstances should not have been refused, she
was told that her grandmother didn't want to see her. It was such a
patently obvious lie, she accepted that nothing she really wanted was
ever going to be provided and that the best she could expect was that
they would do just enough to keep her alive and well.

She knew, of course, who was behind all this.

If it were possible to hate someone enough to kill them simply by
wishing for it, Isoeld Severine would already be dead. But since her
stepmother was still out there walking around, Phryne assumed she
needed to find another way.

She spent hours mourning for her father. The images of his final
moments were burned into her memory, and days after she had been
seized and locked away she could still see the shock and anguish in his
face as his assassin had stabbed him again and again with that knife.
She could hear him cry out, could recall the way his head had turned
and looked at her while Isoeld held her pinned to the floor, recognition
of what was happening reflected sharp and clear in his eyes. He knew

his wife had betrayed him. She could feel his pain as the dagger sheathed in his body withdrew, and his lifeblood drained away.

Phryne could see it all, even when she didn't want to.

The Home Guard had appeared shortly after, and they had hauled her away in spite of her protestations. The weapon that had killed the King was lying next to her. The real assassin was gone. Both Isoeld and First Minister Teonette pointed fingers at her, claiming to have witnessed the consummation of her vengeance, to have heard her cry out that her father would never mistreat her again, that she had endured enough. It must have had something to do with the terrible argument they had engaged in only days earlier, the one that everyone in the city had been talking about. Phryne had screamed at him even as she drove the knife home that he had humiliated her and could not be allowed to live. She had even accused him of letting her mother die all those years ago.

It got worse. Her accusers quickly suggested that she was suffering from delusions and other mental disorders, that her ability to reason and act rationally had been adversely affected. Isoeld had witnessed this behavior herself in the presence of the King, but had chosen to keep quiet about it and let her husband handle the matter. Phryne was not her daughter, after all—even though she loved her dearly—so it was left to her father. But she had always worried that sooner or later the girl would do something terrible, that her illness would overcome her in a way that would prove disastrous.

So they locked Phryne Amarantyne away in that storeroom and left her there to await her fate. She already knew what that fate would be. They would try her for her father's murder, convict her, and sentence her to death in the Elven Way. Everyone knew about that. It was an old punishment, seldom employed, reserved for the most heinous of crimes and criminals. She couldn't remember when it had last been used. Not in her lifetime, certainly. It was considered barbaric, monstrous.

But that was why it was utilized for killings like this one—a combination of patricide and regicide, the murder of a father and a King.

She tried over and over to tell anyone who came close that this was a mistake, that she was innocent of the crime, that she was not mentally ill or insane. But if she were sane, Isoeld told her on the one visit she and Teonette had paid shortly after her father's killing, then the murder must have been deliberate. That made things even worse, didn't it? But of course, as a dutiful stepmother, she would carry that message back to the members of the Elven High Council, who were charged with determining her fate, so that they could make up their own minds.

There was nothing she could do but wait for something to happen that got her out of this room and into the presence of other Elves. Then, and only then, would she have a chance to state her case to those who might stop long enough to listen carefully to what she had to say. In point of fact, she knew all of the members of the High Council, and she stood a reasonable chance of being able to persuade them that she was not guilty.

At least, that was what she told herself.

She thought all the time of ways she might get a message to the Orullians or to Panterra Qu. She kept hoping the brothers would find a way to come to see her, knowing they must have learned of her fate by now. Word might even have gotten as far south as Glensk Wood, so that Pan would know, too. If any of them had heard, surely they would come, wouldn't they?

But no one had appeared, and after a while her hopes had begun to dwindle. She started to think of ways to escape. When she wasn't thinking of her father, she was thinking of getting out of that storeroom. But she didn't have any weapons or tools or implements of any sort that might help her pry or loosen or break down the walls and doors that held back her freedom. She had no realistic hope of overcoming the guards. It seemed she was searching for something that didn't exist.

Things did not get any better when, a week into her imprisonment, her stepmother came for a second visit.

Phryne had no idea what time of day it was when Isoeld appeared. The locks released, the door opened, and her stepmother walked into the room in the company of Teonette. Phryne, who was seated at the tiny table, working on a drawing of some flowers in a meadow, closed her notebook and rose to face her visitors, unpleasantly surprised. A visit from Isoeld could not be good news.

"How are you, Phryne?" Isoeld asked, sounding genuinely interested. She smiled warmly and waited for the guard stationed outside to close the door before the smile left her face. "I don't imagine you're doing very well, locked away in this dark room. Maybe you would like to talk about what it would take to get you out?"

Phryne tightened her resolve. "I can't think of any reason you would want that, Isoeld. If I were let out, you would risk being locked in, wouldn't you? You and your consort. You would risk someone finding out who really murdered my father."

"Oh, I don't think there's any real danger of that. Everyone seems to have accepted my story about your relationship with your father. I tell them all the same thing. You are a delusional, marginally sane young girl who needs help with her afflictions. Of course, your insistence on refusing to accept responsibility for your actions makes it rather difficult for anyone to feel sorry for you. Some are beginning to consider the possibility that your acts were deliberate and you ought to suffer the consequences."

"We both know who ought to suffer the consequences of my father's murder," Phryne replied, eyes locked on the other. "Come close enough and I'll show you what I mean."

Isoeld laughed. "I think I'll stay where I am. I prefer to keep my distance from someone as disturbed as you obviously are."

Phryne actually considered the possibility of launching herself at her stepmother and tearing out her eyes. She measured the distance between them and decided that if Teonette weren't standing beside her, she might well try it.

"Why are you here?" she asked finally, turning away. "What do you want?"

Isoeld brushed back her long blond hair and shrugged. "I'll say it again. Would you like to get out of here? Do you want your life back? Because I can make that happen. I can arrange for you to be placed under house arrest. I can make your life a whole lot more comfortable, if I think there might be a good reason to do so."

"Yes, we've covered that ground. Assuming for the moment that you've lost your mind, what would it take for you to do this? I admit I am marginally curious. Is there someone else you want dead? Someone else for whose killing I am to take the blame?"

"No. Accepting responsibility for your father will suffice. You will admit you killed him in a moment of madness. You will tell the High Council that you acted out of an ungovernable rage, but that now you realize how wrong you were. You will show remorse. If you do that, I can keep you from being put to death. I can have you sentenced to something less final."

Phryne could not believe what she was hearing. "You actually think I might agree to accept the blame for my father's murder? That I might even consider for a single second removing all chance of seeing you pay for what you did." She laughed. "I'm not the one who's insane, Isoeld. Not so long as you talk like that!"

"Tell her the rest," Teonette snapped.

Isoeld clasped her hands behind her back like a satisfied little girl and leaned forward, clearly enjoying the moment. "You didn't ask me what I expected from you in payment for my generosity, Phryne. Don't you want to know?"

"I don't care what you want. It doesn't make any difference because I'm not doing what you want."

"Not even to save your grandmother's life?"

Phryne went pale with shock. *Mistral!* If she could have managed to move she would have attacked her stepmother on the spot, but she was frozen in place by the implied threat contained in the other's sly words. It took everything she had to stay calm, something she sensed instinctively she needed to do.

"What have you done with her, Isoeld? She's an old lady, and she has nothing to do with any of this. She barely spoke to my father after Mother died. You know that. What point is there in threatening her?"

"The point should be obvious. I want you to do what I ask."

"Well, I won't. Not even to save her. She wouldn't want it. She would hate me for it."

Her stepmother glanced at the first minister in a decidedly conspiratorial way. "If they should decide to put you to death in the Elven Way—an act I will try to prevent, but may not be able to—you will wish you had been less difficult. But what if they put Mistral Belloruus to death, as well? What if evidence were to surface that she conspired with you to kill the King? What if it became known that she encouraged it, and she did so knowing that you, only a step from madness already, would act on her suggestion? Her fate would be sealed. Think about it. Death in the Elven Way is not something you want to face at any age. Let me see. They bind you securely and then they bury you headfirst in the ground. But they construct an air pocket around your head so that you have sufficient time to contemplate your bad behavior before the air runs out or the insects start feeding on you. You and Mistral would be placed side by side. Perhaps you could hear each other's screams before your hearts gave out."

Phryne lost all control in that moment and flew across the room. She managed to reach Isoeld before Teonette could stop her. Screaming in fury, she raked her stepmother's beautiful face with her nails, leaving bloody furrows down both cheeks. She got in a few good punches, as well, and then Teonette hauled her away, stood her up, and backhanded her so hard she was knocked all the way across the room where she slammed up against a wall. She tried to rise, her head spinning, but he was on top of her again, hitting her over and over.

"Stop it!" she heard Isoeld scream at him. The words rolled and echoed behind a wall of pain and bright colors. "If you kill her, we'll never find them! We need her alive!"

The pummeling ceased, and she heard Teonette mutter something as he moved away. She tried to speak, to call them the names that were right on the tip of her tongue, but her mouth was full of blood. She lay where she was and listened as their footsteps receded and the storeroom door opened and closed again.

Then she was alone.

⁂

IT TOOK HER A LONG TIME to gain enough strength to sit up straight, bracing herself against the wall, her head still spinning, her body racked with pain. Everything hurt, especially her face, which Teonette had battered with both fists until she was barely conscious. She touched it experimentally and flinched. Wasn't a good idea to do that, she told herself. Shouldn't look in any mirrors for a while, either.

She desperately wanted something to drink, but the water pitcher had been toppled in the struggle and its contents spilled on the floor. She thought about lapping it up from the stones, but decided she wasn't quite ready for that. She would be soon, though. She could feel a sense of desperation creeping in, and it wasn't only about the water. Thoughts of her grandmother crowded her mind, and she imagined all sorts of terrible things that might have been done to the old woman. Mistral Belloruus was a tough old lady and a match for most, but sheer numbers and brute force might have been enough to overwhelm her.

What Phryne couldn't quite understand was why Isoeld thought that making her grandmother a prisoner would be worth the effort. Word of a seizure of this sort was bound to leak out—through those old men who were the old lady's consorts, in all likelihood—leading to rampant speculation. Mistral could hardly pose a threat to the Queen. She hadn't been all that fond of Oparion in the first place; his killing would affect her less than most. If he hadn't married her daughter, they probably wouldn't have had any relationship at all. So to lock her away out of fear of what she might do, an old woman living by herself on the outskirts of the city, what sort of sense did that make?

Holding her head in her hands, bent forward so that the pain seemed to lessen somewhat, Phryne pondered the question. Did Isoeld really think anyone would believe that wild story about her grandmother encouraging her to kill her father? It was patently ridiculous. Isoeld must have known that Phryne would never agree to take the blame for her father's death simply because of threats made to her grandmother. Doing any deliberate harm to someone of Mistral Belloruus's stature posed great risk in a tight-knit Elven community where everyone knew the history of the royal families.

No, something else was going on here. But what?

Phryne didn't know. She couldn't think straight. She wanted to lie down and go to sleep, but she knew that sleeping after a beating like the one she had taken was not wise. Concussions could kill you in your sleep. She needed to stay awake and wait for things to settle down. She thought about crawling over to the door to ask for water, but she had every expectation of being refused, and she didn't think she could bear that just now.

So instead, she stayed where she was, breathing slowly and deeply, searching for slight shifts of position that might help lessen the pain and slow the spinning.

She was still engaged in that endeavor when she heard the snick of the door lock. She raised her head high enough to watch the door open and a pair of young women enter the room carrying cloths and basins of water. They came over to where Phryne was sitting and knelt beside her. Saying nothing, working in silence, they cleaned her wounds and daubed at her bruises, using the cold water in the basin to bring down the swelling and warm water in the other to wash away dirt and blood. Phryne let them work on her, grateful for even this little bit of help. She didn't know these Elves and appreciated that in all probability they were under strict instructions not to make any attempt to converse with her. But at least someone was making an effort to keep her in one piece.

She wondered, though, who that someone might be.

When the young women were finished, they picked up the cloths and basins and disappeared out the door. Not one word had been exchanged.

Phryne went back to thinking about Isoeld's offer. Was there some way that Phryne could turn it to her advantage? Maybe she should pretend to accept, wait until she got clear of this room, and then make a run for it. But she knew it wouldn't work like that. Whatever sort of confession they extracted, they would put it on paper and have her sign it before they let her take a single step outside her prison. Besides, she knew she couldn't make herself confess to killing her father; the very thought of such a thing was revolting.

Still, why had Isoeld threatened her with compromising her grandmother's safety? What was it that she hoped to gain?

She thought back over the words her stepmother had spoken, trying to remember them exactly, hoping for a clue. But nothing revealed itself, nothing seemed out of place. It all fit together nicely.

Except . . .

At the very end, she remembered suddenly. When Teonette was beating her to within an inch of her life, when everything was so crazy for those few seconds, what was it Isoeld had said?

If you kill her, we'll never find them.

Them.

Phryne's triumphant smile would have been broader if it hadn't hurt her face so much to stretch her mouth. Them. Isoeld had to be talking about the blue Elfstones! Nothing else made any sense. She would have known about them, of course—a valuable talisman, a legacy from the time of Kirisin Belloruus. How she had found out they were in the hands of Mistral, Phryne couldn't imagine. But once her father was out of the way, her stepmother would have gone searching for them first thing.

Apparently, she hadn't found them. But she seemed to know that they were destined for Phryne and might now believe that they were in her possession. Hidden, perhaps, but waiting to be found. Isoeld would be intent on finding and gaining possession of them so that her hold on the throne was more than mere words; it was backed by the power of Elven magic.

All this reasoning was something of a leap of faith, a broad extrapolation of a conclusion drawn from a raft of possibilities. Yet Phryne could feel in her heart that she was right.

But what was she going to do about it? She had to get out of this room before she could do anything, and just at the moment that didn't seem like a very strong possibility. Or even a weak one, for that matter. Not unless someone outside the room chose to help her.

If she could just find a way to get word to her cousins!

She was considering various impossible ways to do that when dinner arrived. The storeroom door opened and the little serving girl entered with her tray, setting it down carefully just over the threshold before she backed out again and the door closed anew. Phryne stared at the tray and the food for several minutes, trying to decide if she was hungry. She wasn't, but she knew she had to eat.

She climbed to her feet gingerly and crossed the room to the tray. She sat down again, too weary even from that little effort to try to take the tray back across the room. She would eat on the floor and then maybe sleep. It had been long enough now that she no longer felt concussions were a worry.

The tray contained a hard roll, some cold meat and cheese, and a cup of water. Reasonable, if not very exciting.

She began to eat.

She had just finished pulling the hard roll apart and was about to take a bite of one section when she saw the folded slip of paper that was lodged inside.

Something was written on the paper—three words in large block letters.

HELP IS COMING

TEN

WHO HAD SENT THE NOTE?

It had been hours since she had split open that hard roll and found the slip of paper hidden inside, and she couldn't stop thinking about it. There were a limited number of possibilities that made sense, and she had gone over every one dozens of times. But none of them felt quite right.

The Orullian brothers, Tasha and Tenerife, were her first choice. Her cousins and friends, they would be the ones best able and most likely to try to help her. But they were stationed at Aphalion Pass as part of an Elven Hunter contingent charged with keeping the Drouj army from entering the valley. They had been up there for weeks, and while they must know by now what had happened to her there was no way they could return to Arborlon without permission. Because Isoeld knew of their close relationship, permission was likely to be a long time coming. They were the first ones she would think of when it came to making a list of friends and relatives who needed to be kept far away. So unless they had abandoned their post—something they were unlikely to do, in Phryne's estimation—they weren't the ones who had sent her the note.

Besides, even if they had come back into the city without permission, their absence in all likelihood would have been discovered by now and they were already being hunted. How much good could they do her in that case? How much, when they were at risk, too?

Her second choice was Mistral Belloruus. Isoeld's implied threat didn't necessarily mean that her grandmother actually was a prisoner. Phryne had jumped to that conclusion on her own. Now she was rethinking this assumption, especially in light of her belief that Isoeld was hunting for the blue Elfstones. Since Phryne didn't have them and Isoeld hadn't found them, it stood to reason that her grandmother still had possession of them. Didn't that mean she was still free and in hiding? If not, then why hadn't Isoeld extracted their location from Mistral? Certainly, she wasn't above using whatever means were available to her. Or did Isoeld know something about all this that Phryne didn't?

In any case, her grandmother might be out there trying to find a way to set her free. Those old men who worshipped the ground she walked on would do anything for her, including getting her granddaughter out of the clutches of the Queen.

But somehow that didn't feel right, either. While there was no reason to trust anything Isoeld told her, she didn't like the way the latter seemed so confident that the threat of harm to Mistral would make Phryne falsely confess to killing the King. In truth, she was afraid for her grandmother, and as much as she would like to believe that Mistral was safe, she just wasn't sure.

Who did that leave?

Only one other person. Panterra Qu.

It wasn't a stretch to think that the Tracker from Glensk Wood had heard the news of her imprisonment. Pan would never believe it was true; he would want to know what had really happened. He might have found Sider Ament and persuaded him to come looking for her. One of them or even both might already be on the way. The note could have come from them. Rescue might be at hand.

But she didn't think so. Panterra didn't have the skills or means to effect a rescue on his own, and Sider Ament would approach the High Council first and arrange a meeting. Even the Queen would have trouble keeping the Gray Man out if he insisted on speaking with her. But no one had come to see her but the Queen. The note suggested that this was someone else entirely.

So she lay on her pallet pondering the myriad options of being rescued, the candles burning in small bright spaces amid the shadows, until a darker possibility suggested itself.

What if Isoeld herself had written the note?

It was a decidedly chilling possibility and not one that could be dismissed out of hand. If she was right about Isoeld searching for the blue Elfstones, then she had to consider that her stepmother might be trying to trick her into revealing their location. If she thought Phryne knew where the Elfstones were, why not arrange for the girl to escape and lead her to them? After all, if you were a fugitive, wouldn't you try to reach the one thing that could protect you best or with which you could bargain for your life?

Isoeld was clever. She would not hesitate to use Phryne to get whatever she wanted, particularly if what she wanted was as valuable as the seeking-Stones.

Phryne took a deep breath and exhaled slowly. This business of the note was becoming increasingly complicated.

She was still mulling the matter over when the door to the storeroom opened and the little serving girl entered bearing her dinner tray. Was it really dinnertime again? How long had it been since she had last eaten? She couldn't be sure. It seemed it wasn't that long ago, but there was no way to know when day and night looked the same and time was a mystery. She watched as the serving girl set down the tray, straightened, and then—as if in defiance of the very explicit order given her—beckoned to Phryne. Phryne stared in surprise, hesitating. The serving girl beckoned again. Curious now, Phryne climbed to her feet and walked over.

When she got to within six or seven feet, the serving girl pulled back the hood of her cloak to reveal her face.

"Surprise," said Xac Wen.

"Xac!" she exclaimed rather too loudly, then quickly put a hand over her mouth. "What are you doing?"

"Getting you out of here. What does it look like? Hurry, Phryne, we haven't much time. The guard is sleeping, but the drug I put in his ale will wear off soon enough."

She nodded quickly. "So it was you who sent me—"

He ignored her, his attention focused on the storeroom door. "No talking until we're somewhere safe. Come on, hurry!"

They went out the storeroom door quickly, Phryne moving as fast as her battered body would let her. The Home Guard on watch was snoring loudly, slouched in one corner of the hall, his cup of ale spilled on the floor beside him.

Xac Wen reached back and closed the storeroom door. "No reason to announce that you're not here anymore," he whispered, his voice barely audible.

They hurried down the hallway to a set of stairs leading up to the back of the building, safely away from the main entry. They climbed slowly, listening for the sounds of other people, but everything was quiet. At the top of the stairs a short hallway led to a service door at the rear of the building. Xac reached for a hooded cloak hanging on a peg and handed it to her. She slipped it on wordlessly and pulled up the hood. When she nodded that she was ready, the boy opened the door.

Cold air rushed in, causing her to flinch. It was nighttime, everything dark save for where lamps and candles flickered in windows and from behind glass casings on poles and porches. The trees looked stark and bare, spectral giants looming over houses that had a squat, hunkered-down look. No sounds rose out of the darkness save the low wail of the wind come down off the mountains to the north.

It was early morning, Phryne decided, and most of the city was asleep. Hardly anyone would be up and about at this hour. Xac Wen—and the Orullians, she was guessing—had planned well.

The boy started off right away, motioning for her to follow. He hardly needed to bother; she was right on his heels, casting anxious glances left and right, hopeful they had gotten past the worst. She breathed in the cool, fresh air and felt her head spin with the sweetness of it. She concentrated on putting one foot in front of the other, still weak and a bit disoriented, still not quite believing she was free.

"Where are Tasha and Tenerife?" she asked, but he put his finger to his lips and silenced her. Questions would have to wait.

They made their way through the sleeping city, two more of night's shadows, following narrow trails that were seldom used, a roundabout way to wherever it was they were going. Phryne had no idea of their destination. Surely not the boy's home or the Orullians' cottage. Some safer place, but where would she be safe in this city?

She found out quickly enough when they arrived at the tree house that Tasha and Tenerife had been building some weeks earlier. Still unoccupied, it sat dark and silent, cradled in the bows of a huge cluster of spruce, barely visible in the darkness. A narrow wooden stairway wound upward through a series of platforms, and they climbed it as quickly as they could manage, gained the decking that surrounded the home, found the door leading in, and entered.

"No one will look for you here," Xac Wen advised, closing the door behind them. "It's empty. I'm acting as caretaker, keeping watch until Tasha and Tenerife return. I like it here, living on my own. My parents don't care."

Phryne took a quick look around, spying the vague shapes of cabinets and closets, but no furnishings or furniture save for a couple of sleeping pads pulled off to one side and stacked against a wall. The house had a nearly completed, but still not quite finished, look.

"That top one's mine," the boy announced, pointing to the sleeping pads. "But you can have one of the others."

Phryne nodded absently. "Where are the Orullians? Aren't they here?"

The boy shook his head. "They can't leave the pass. They're being watched. The Queen doesn't trust them. She's scary the way she thinks about things. So they made a plan, got word to me to come up with tools they claimed they needed, told me what to do, and sent me back down again. I did all the rest. Did it as fast as I could. And here we are. The plan worked just like they thought it would."

He grinned like the little madman the Orullians always called him. "Come sit, Phryne. Over here. You look a wreck."

He pulled off the top mattress and sat on it, looking back at her expectantly. She shook her head and joined him. Then abruptly, she took his face in her hands and kissed him on the forehead. "Thanks for getting me out of there," she told him.

She could feel him squirm, but saw his grin broaden. "That's all right." He looked down at his feet. "They didn't treat you very well, did they? It looks like someone hit you. Who did that?"

"It doesn't matter. All that matters is that I don't end up being caught and sent back. You know I didn't kill my father, don't you, Xac?"

He looked up again quickly. "Of course I know!" He sounded indignant. "You wouldn't do something like that! I don't care what anyone says! But who do you think did it?"

"I know who did it. Someone my stepmother hired. I was there when Father was killed, but I couldn't see the face of the man who did it because he was wearing a mask. But Isoeld and Teonette knew it was going to happen. They watched and didn't do anything to stop it. Isoeld attacked me and held me down so I couldn't do anything, either!"

There were tears in her eyes; they had appeared seemingly of their own volition, and she quickly wiped them away. Xac Wen looked horrified. "The first minister was part of this? He was helping the Queen? I've heard stories about them, but I didn't think they were true."

"I didn't, either. Not entirely, anyway. But Mistral insisted all along they were lovers." She took a deep, steadying breath and stopped crying. "Xac, I have to find my grandmother. Do you know where she is?"

The boy looked stricken. "No one knows. She disappeared from her house right after you were locked up in that storeroom. I went to look for her to ask if she could help you. Tasha said I should. But she wasn't there. The house was all torn apart and there was blood . . ."

He trailed off, unable to finish. "It was pretty bad."

Phryne stayed silent for a moment, fighting to keep her emotions in check. She was terrified now for her grandmother, no longer simply worried about what might happen, but devastated by what obviously had. Isoeld's threats hadn't been idle ones; she had gone after Mistral Belloruus.

She shifted her gaze to Xac once more. "I have to go to her house. I have to see for myself. Can we do that?"

"What? Tonight?" Xac was horrified. "But it's almost morning, Phryne! People will be waking up! You'll be seen!"

"I know the risks. But no one knows I've escaped yet, Xac. By morning, they will be looking for me. If I go now, maybe we can get to my grandmother's and back again before it's light."

She paused. "You don't have to go with me. You've done more than enough. This is too dangerous. You stay here. I'll go alone."

"You stay here, I'll go alone," he mimicked. "Why would you say that? I'm not afraid! Don't treat me like a child. If you go, I go."

She almost laughed at his efforts to sound tough and grown up. But that would have been a mistake, and she knew it. "All right," she said, "you win. We both go."

He gave a small yelp and was out the door and on his way down the stairs almost before she had finished speaking.

⸻

THEY WALKED BACK through the sleeping city, taking a more direct route this time because Xac was anxious to get this ill-advised visit over and done with and told her they would forgo the safer, but more circuitous route.

"Can't chance being caught out in the light once the sun comes up," he declared. "If something happens to you now, Tasha will skin me alive!"

"I wouldn't want that," she said, managing to keep a straight face.

"You know why they wanted you out of there, don't you?" He kept his voice low, talking rapidly as they walked. "Tasha and Tenerife? Why it was so important to free you?"

She shook her head. "You mean besides giving me a chance to prove I'm innocent of what I'm accused?"

He nodded vigorously. "Besides that. Most people don't really think you killed your father, anyway. They did at first because that's how things looked. But after they began to talk it over, they started asking questions. Why would she kill her father over an argument? Weren't they especially close? She wasn't like that before. She was a good person and she never hurt anyone. Stuff like that. Fingers were starting to point elsewhere. That's when Tasha and Tenerife really started to worry."

"What do you mean?"

"Think about it. If you don't get locked up for your father's murder, your stepmother doesn't get to take the throne. You do."

That stopped Phryne right where she was. She reached over and grabbed the boy by his arm. "What are you saying?"

He shook her off. "What do you think? I'm saying that keeping you in prison keeps you off the throne. You're next in line, you know. With your father dead, you should be Queen, not Isoeld."

She hadn't thought of that. In the rush of things, amid all the confusion and anger and despair, she had never once thought about being heir to the throne. It was such a ridiculous idea that she could hardly consider it. She had always thought her father would be King for years to come, and the prospect of having to rule in his place seemed ludicrous. But now she saw how wrong she had been.

"You still don't understand!" Xac snapped, frustrated by her inability to grasp what he was trying to say. "Keeping you locked up is only a temporary solution. It would be a lot better for Isoeld if you didn't *need* locking up. Now do you see?"

She did. "You mean if I were dead, the matter would be settled. Tasha thinks Isoeld might be intending to kill me, too."

He nodded. "But she would call it a suicide, Tasha says. In such despair over what you had done to your father, you took your own life. Something like that. Tasha sees these things a lot better than you do, Phryne."

She couldn't argue the point. It would make sense that Isoeld would dispose of her as quickly as possible. Especially if she viewed Phryne as a rival for the Elven throne. It was probably only her stepmother's desire to find the missing Elfstones that had kept her alive this long.

It was scary, but it was depressing, too. Things had not been good since her father married Isoeld, but she hadn't realized how bad they had gotten. She hadn't paid enough attention to what was happening. She had been too self-absorbed when she should have been thinking of her father and the possibility that Isoeld's intentions were more dangerous than he knew. Isoeld wouldn't have done this without having thought about it for a long time beforehand. An opportunity might have presented itself or desperation might have pushed her over the edge, but she had to have been planning this terrible thing long before that.

It made Phryne wonder anew about the fate of her grandmother and the Elfstones. Isoeld would not have stopped with her father if she thought it would cement her hold on the throne.

"Has there really been no word at all about Mistral?" she asked Xac. "She's just disappeared and no one's seen or heard anything?"

"I told you what I saw when I went to her house. I don't know anything else, Phryne."

They walked in silence for a time, approaching the eastern borders of Arborlon now, drawing closer to her grandmother's cottage. It was getting much darker as the lights of the city faded and the heavy woods loomed ahead, the pathway narrowing and twisting. Phryne found herself growing more uneasy, listening for every noise, searching the shadows.

"Why are we doing this?" Xac whispered suddenly. "I don't see what you think you'll find."

"I know. I don't, either." Phryne felt defeated. "I just have to go there and see for myself. I have to try to understand what happened."

She didn't say anything about the Elfstones. There wasn't any reason to discuss that part of things with Xac Wen. Although their fate was at the back of her mind, she wasn't sure what she would do even if she found them. Keep them from Isoeld, she guessed. Keep them out of her hands.

"I just think this is a mistake," Xac added unhelpfully.

She decided to change the subject. "How did you manage to get that note to me? How did you get into the kitchen long enough to hide it?"

"What note?" he said.

She stared at him. "The note you put in the hard roll that came with my dinner! The one that said HELP IS COMING."

He shrugged. "I don't know what you're talking about. I didn't send you any note."

She grabbed his arm and pulled him around to face her. "Wait a minute. Say that again."

"I didn't send you any note. Will you let go of my arm, Phryne? For cat's sake!"

The chill that ran through her now was much worse than anything she had experienced in the cold air of the high passes leading out of the valley. She had been so sure that it was Xac, after he had set her free, that she hadn't since considered the possibility that it might have been someone else.

And if it was someone else . . .

Quickly, she told the boy what had happened and how she had assumed the note must have been his. By the time she had finished, he was looking around wildly.

"It was her!" he hissed. "Isoeld! It must have been!"

"Probably," she agreed. "It makes sense. It was just coincidence that you showed up when you did. If you hadn't, I imagine I would have discovered the door was unlocked or something of that sort and been allowed to get free on my own, except that they would be waiting for me."

"So they could kill you," the boy finished. "They'd have an excuse."

Or follow me to see if I would lead them to the Elfstones and then kill me. She thought that the more likely possibility but didn't say so. She looked around at the darkness, half expecting someone to jump out of the shadows. But everything was quiet. Nothing moved.

"We have to forget this!" Xac Wen was saying. "We have to find somewhere to hide right now!"

Phryne put her hands on his shoulders, but gently this time and with no intention of trying to hold on to him. "Listen to me. I can't do that. I have to go to my grandmother's. I have to. There are reasons I can't talk about just yet. But I have to go. Isoeld doesn't know I've escaped. Not yet. That guard might still be sleeping. You closed the door, so even after he wakes he might not realize I'm gone. Not right away."

She paused, took her hands away. "I'm going. But you don't have to. You know that. You've done enough."

He stared at her as if she had lost her mind, and then abruptly shrugged. "Let's stop talking about this. Let's just go."

They entered the heavy woods, following the pathway that led to Mistral's cottage, working their way slowly through the darkness, aware now the danger they had supposed existed before was suddenly much greater. Phryne knew she should have insisted that the boy go back without her. There was nothing to connect him to her escape at this point, but if they caught him now he would be in as much trouble as she was. She knew he didn't want to go with her, but she also knew his pride and his loyalty to the Orullians would not let him turn back. He was not the sort to give in to his doubts and fears; he would face them down and overcome them. There was no point in suggesting he do anything else.

"I wish we had better weapons," he muttered. "All I have is a knife."

All I have is nothing, she thought. But weapons probably weren't going to be of much use at this point. If this was a trap, if Isoeld was waiting for them, she would have brought help to make sure that Phryne couldn't fight her way free. She shuddered to think of whom her stepmother might have found that would be willing to see her dead. Elves? Something or someone else? She was suddenly very scared.

But she kept going anyway, intent on reaching her grandmother's. It took awhile, the combination of darkness and forest slowing her sufficiently that she couldn't be sure exactly which of the many paths that crisscrossed the woods she was on. Then, all at once, the forest opened up ahead to reveal the clearing and the cottage.

She stopped just within the fringe of the trees. The cottage was dark and silent. The front door hung open, its hinges torn loose at the top. The windows were broken out, glass shards glinting in a shaft of moonlight on the porch decking. The house had an empty, dead feeling about it, even from where she stood.

She glanced over at Xac Wen, who shrugged. He couldn't detect anything, either.

"I'll go first," she whispered to him. "If something happens to me, you can go for help."

She didn't really think he would find any, but it was a way to keep him safely back from whatever was going to happen next. This way, he might have some small chance of escape. She didn't try to fool herself about how small that chance might be. It was the best she could offer.

He gave her a reluctant nod.

Taking a deep breath, she stepped out of the shelter of the trees and walked toward the house.

ELEVEN

PHRYNE HAD NOT GONE A DOZEN STEPS BEFORE she slowed, then stopped altogether. Suddenly she could not go on. Mistral's cottage was a malignant shell, empty and dark and so forbidding that it seemed impossible that anything good could come from going inside. The feeling was so intense that for a moment the girl considered turning back. Mistral was gone, but something else might be waiting.

But then she tightened her resolve and kept walking. She had come this far, and if Isoeld had set a trap for her it was already too late to back away. If whatever minions her stepmother employed to kill a King and husband had come for her, as well, she would not give them the satisfaction of seeing her attempt to flee. She might be terrified, but she would not back down.

Head up, she started forward once more.

She stepped onto the porch, eyes searching the shadows, ears pricked for any sounds. What she saw was an impenetrable blackness that obscured everything. What she heard was a deep and pervasive silence. The wooden steps and floorboards of the porch creaked softly beneath her feet. When she reached the open entry, the door splintered and hanging crookedly off its hinges mute evidence of the violence that had taken place, she stopped again. She could smell traces of things that testified to the nature of the emptiness that had claimed the house in her grandmother's absence. Dust, wilted flowers, and stale air mixed with the metallic scent of blood.

Turning sideways to avoid the edges of the collapsed door, she edged through the opening, taking each step carefully, trying not to make any noise. By now she was pretty sure that no one was lurking inside, waiting to strike her down. But while she felt certain the house was empty, bereft of its owner and her friends, there was something . . .

She stifled that line of thinking and moved into the darkness, letting it envelop her. She wasn't a particularly brave person; she knew that about herself. But she was brash and reckless in situations where sometimes that was enough to get you through. She felt it might be so now. She let her eyes adjust, all the while searching the shadows, listening for what might be hidden within their silent covering.

Nothing.

She took another step and suddenly dozens of dark shapes flew out of the blackness, wings beating madly all around her, swerving and diving, cries wild and shrill, before flying out the door and into the night. Phryne gathered up the shattered remnants of her resolve, so badly startled she had almost turned and fled. Birds. Just birds, roosting in the abandoned house, seeking food and shelter.

She had just managed to take a fresh step forward when a disembodied voice from almost right behind her said, "Phryne? What was that? Are you all right?"

She was startled all over again, instantly riddled with fear, but she held herself together when she realized it was Xac Wen speaking to her. Somehow he had managed to come up on her without her hearing. She wheeled on him angrily.

"I thought I told you to wait for me!" she hissed.

"You did, but I thought . . ."

"You thought you would creep up on me and give me the fright of my life, that's what you thought!"

She glared at him in the dark, realizing that he probably couldn't see the look on her face, but certainly couldn't mistake the tone of her voice. He took a step back and made a warding gesture.

"Just trying to help!" he snapped. "I thought you were in trouble or something! I didn't realize you were just fooling around with birds!"

She almost laughed, it sounded so ridiculous, but managed to keep a straight face. "Oh, never mind. Thanks for worrying about me. You just scared me, that's all."

"I know. But I didn't mean to." He looked past her into the darkened interior. "Find anything yet?"

"No. But I haven't started looking. I was making sure no one else was here but me." She brushed back a few strands of auburn hair from her eyes and instantly regretted it. Her battered face was not yet ready to be touched, and she winced in response to the gesture.

"Doesn't look to me like anyone's here," he said.

She appraised him critically. "I suppose now that you're here you want to help me look?"

The boy shrugged. "Depends. What am I looking for?"

"Anything that looks interesting. Any sort of clue that my grandmother might have left that would tell me what happened to her." She threw up her hands. "I don't know. Just look."

They prowled through the empty cottage, moving from room to room, searching the darkness, afraid to light a lamp or even a candle because anyone watching or passing by would know there was someone inside in an instant. Phryne moved cautiously but confidently, familiar with the layout of the cottage, pretty much knowing where things were. Xac Wen didn't seem bothered by unfamiliarity or darkness, slipping sure-footedly through the shadows, and Phryne found herself wondering if he had been here more often than he let on.

Their search was thorough, but there was nothing much to be found. Furniture was overturned, vases smashed, cabinets kicked in, and bedding thrown everywhere. Not only had Mistral been attacked, her cottage had been searched—which would suggest Isoeld was indeed looking for the blue Elfstones. Phryne knew Mistral had retained possession of them after their last meeting and apparently had hidden them again. Perhaps she had done so only as a precaution before the King's murder, but afterward she would have understood that she might be in danger, too. Mistral was no fool. If she had hidden the Elf-stones, it was unlikely that Isoeld would find them here.

Or that Phryne would, for that matter.

Still, she kept looking, taking time to study everything. Xac Wen trailed after her, searching the same places, examining the same things. But neither of them saw anything helpful.

"This is a waste of time," the boy said finally. They had reached the back porch and were staring out the window into the old woman's gardens. "We could search this cottage from now until doomsday and never find anything. Whatever it is you think you're looking for, I don't think you'll find it. Let's go. It will be light soon."

She knew he was right, but she was feeling stubborn about this. If her grandmother had felt threatened, she would have made preparations. She would have done something either to get word to Phryne or to leave her a clue as to where she had gone. She would have been prepared when Isoeld and her minions came calling. She wouldn't have been caught off guard.

"We'll look a little longer," she replied.

She had just decided to go back to Mistral's bedroom and start over when she spied the flowers. They were sitting in a vase by the open window, their petals caught in the faint starlight, radiating a soft crimson. Beautiful, she thought suddenly. But then she realized that flowers in a vase in an abandoned house should be wilted and dying, not fresh and new. She walked over to them, reached down and touched them experimentally.

To her surprise, they began to glow with a soft, steady light that suggested somehow they were lit from within.

"Um, Phryne," she heard Xac whisper.

When she turned to face him, she found him staring fixedly at something off to one side, his mouth hanging open. He tried to say something more and couldn't.

She followed his gaze and found herself face-to-face with Mistral Belloruus. Except that it wasn't her grandmother exactly—it was something that approximated her. This Mistral Belloruus was vaguely transparent and so washed of color she was reduced to various shades of gray. She stood in place facing Phryne, but not exactly seeing her, eyes staring at a point somewhere in between where they each stood.

Phryne, listen to me.

The voice was as pale and insubstantial as her image, and Phryne was certain in that moment that her grandmother was dead and this was her ghost. She sobbed audibly, and it was more than the night's chill that made her shiver. Her grandmother had always seemed so indestructible. That she was gone seemed impossible.

"Grandmother," she whispered.

This avatar will not last more than a few minutes, but I wanted you to be certain that it was I who was speaking to you. Isoeld and her creatures will come for me soon. It is inevitable. She knows about the Elfstones. Your father made the mistake of confiding in her. When she finds them missing from the palace, she will know who has them. With you imprisoned, there is no one to stand with me. My faithful will try, but they are old and lack even my strength. So the outcome is settled.

Phryne was confused anew. If this was not a ghost, but an avatar created by some form of magic, then there was a chance that her grandmother was still alive.

I regret I did not have a way of rescuing you. I have sent word to others who might. One way or another, you will be set free. When that happens, you will come here to look for me and for the Elfstones. But we will both be gone.

Xac Wen edged forward to stand closer to Phryne. His voice was a harsh whisper as he said, "I don't think that we should . . ."

But the avatar was already talking over him.

To keep the Elfstones safe for you, I am taking them to a place that I know even Isoeld will not think to find me. If I hide the Elfstones here, they will be found. If I choose to remain behind, I will be found. So I am leaving. When you find the cottage empty, you will touch the flowers, and this avatar will awaken. In departing, it will tell you where I am. Read it on the air. Come to me after you do, and I will give you the Elfstones. Your destiny is settled. It has arrived much sooner than either of us expected and comes cloaked in misfortune and grief. But it cannot be turned away; it cannot be denied. Embrace it, child.

Then she was gone, disappeared back into the night. Like smoke on a stiff breeze, the avatar shimmered and faded away. Phryne kept staring at the place it had last been, waiting for something more to appear. *Read it on the air.* She was trying, but there was only darkness and the memory of her grandmother's words.

Finally, Xac pulled at her arm. "We have to go, Phryne! I hear voices!"

Still, she lingered, unwilling to give up. If she left now, she would know exactly nothing of where her grandmother had gone. She would never find the Elfstones. Everything would be lost. *Read it on the air.* Shades! She was trying!

"Phryne!"

Xac Wen's voice had changed to a harsh whisper. She could hear the voices now, too. They were coming from outside the front of the cottage, soft and guarded. Men's voices—Elven Hunters or something much, much worse.

Then the gloom right in front of her blazed to life, filling the darkness with huge words written with flames in bright red letters that sizzled and popped as if the air itself were burning.

Phryne felt her breath catch as she read:

Go to the Ashenell beneath the Belloruusian Arch

With Xac Wen in tow, she went out the back door, across a small grassy open space, and into the gardens. Swiftly they gained the forest beyond, pausing there to crouch down and look back. Lights were moving inside the house, two or three, and she could hear the scrape and clump of heavy boots on the wooden floors. If she could have done so, she would have shuttered the house and trapped them inside. Buffeted by too many emotions to sort out all at once, she embraced the one that was strongest and made it her own.

Rage.

Someday, she would make Isoeld and those responsible for whatever had been done to her grandmother pay for their arrogance and their hateful disregard for any form of moral code. She would track them down and hurt them. She envisioned what she would do, but as she did so the anger leached away and tears filled her eyes. She brushed them away, not wanting the boy to see. When she looked over at him, though, he was looking back.

"Don't worry, Phryne, she'll be all right. Your grandmother, I mean. She got away from them."

He was trying to help, to make her feel better, and she gave him a smile for his effort. But she wasn't convinced that he was right. All she knew for sure was that her grandmother had created that avatar with magic Phryne hadn't even suspected she possessed and left it behind to let the girl know where she had gone.

To the Ashenell. To the tombs of the Elven people.

There were few places in the valley she wanted to go to less. The tombs were dark and haunted, a resting place for the dead, but a reservoir for wild magic, too. Specters and ghosts roamed its grounds, and it was said that an old city was buried deep beneath the earth in which the oldest of the dead were buried. Once, centuries ago, when Arborlon was still settled in the Cintra, Kirisin Belloruus and his sister, Simralin, had gone down into those tombs to recover the Elfstones from the matriarch of the Gotrin dead, a wraith presence still able to cross over from the other side. She knew a little of the story, enough to be wary of venturing anywhere near of her own volition. Yet here she was, faced with the need to do exactly that.

She would go, of course, her fears and doubts notwithstanding. She had no choice unless she wanted to ignore her grandmother's avatar and abandon her search. But she loved Mistral, and she knew she would not disobey her in this.

After all, she told herself, she would be aboveground in the cemetery. She would be among the dead, not beneath them as Kirisin and Simralin Belloruus had been all those years ago. She had no idea what she would do once she got there. She had no idea what to expect. Perhaps she would find nothing more than a clue indicating where she was supposed to go next. Or perhaps Mistral herself and not an avatar would be waiting this time.

She stared at her grandmother's cottage a moment longer, watching the lights bob and weave through the darkened interior, and then she rose and whispered for Xac Wen to follow her. She went back into the trees, safely out of view, and began to circle the cottage at a distance that would keep her hidden. The boy slipped along behind her, a silent presence. She would have to do something about him soon. She couldn't let him continue to follow her blindly. He had exposed himself to enough danger already, all to help her, and it was time for him to step aside.

"Are we going to the tombs?" he whispered once they were safely away from the cottage and walking back down the pathways toward the city.

She glanced back at him. "I should go alone, Xac."

"So I won't be in danger?" he guessed.

"That's right. So you won't be in danger. I know what you're going to say about the Orullians, but they can't expect you to do more than you've already done. You have to go home and let me carry on from here."

He stopped walking and looked at her. "I thought we already agreed on this. I thought I was staying with you until you were safe."

She took a deep breath and let it out slowly. "We did. But that was before I realized how long this might take and how dangerous it might be. I can't keep letting you risk yourself for me. Even Tasha and Tenerife would agree. There isn't anything more you can do."

The boy looked down at his feet, his young face a mask of disappointment. "Well, I don't agree."

She felt herself relenting, told herself not to, and then relented anyway. "Let's make a bargain. You come with me as far as the Ashenell. I wouldn't mind having someone with me when I go into that place. I don't like it there. But afterward, you leave me and go back home."

He looked up again quickly. "Agreed. Except that afterward, we talk about it some more."

She started to object, but he had already turned away, walking quickly up the path, not giving her the chance. She stared after him for a moment, and then gave it up. She could deal with it later, after they had found whatever it was they were going to find in the tombs.

Dawn had appeared as a faint brightening on the eastern horizon, its vague coloration making just enough of a difference in the darkness to reveal it was on its way. Time was shortening for what needed doing in the tombs, and while Phryne had no desire to go into the Ashenell while it was still dark she knew that it would be much more dangerous once the sun came up. She picked up the pace, passing Xac Wen, who glanced at her in surprise, then hurried to catch up.

Together they wound along the pathways until they had arrived at the edge of the city on the north side and come up to the near entrance to the tombs. As they reached the gates, they drew to a halt and stood looking at what lay beyond.

The Ashenell was huge. It had been transported along with the city when Kirisin Belloruus used the Loden Elfstone to rescue his people after the Great Wars. In it were hundreds of thousands of Elves who had died over the centuries, some buried in huge stone mausoleums that held as many as a hundred members of a single family, some buried in the earth in layers that ran twenty to thirty feet deep, and some even buried standing up beneath inscribed flagstones measuring no more than three feet square. There were hundreds of thousands more who had been cremated and had their ashes stored in urns, sometimes entire families, preferring that their remains be joined for all time. No one knew for sure how many Elves were buried here. Some markers had been shattered or their inscriptions damaged so badly they were unreadable, and those to whom they were dedicated had been lost. Some of the tombs had collapsed, and some of the grave sites had been rededicated. Keeping track after so much time in a city that had existed since the dawn of Faerie was impossible. There were records kept in the palace archives, but even these had not survived entirely intact.

But it wasn't this that made the Ashenell such a forbidding place for Phryne. It wasn't the dead or their tombs and markers.

It was the dark magic that resided in the earth.

Everyone had heard the stories. Elves who had disappeared without a trace while venturing into the tombs after sunset. Elves who had tinkered with the markers and the writings and been found burned to a crisp. Elves who had wandered in thinking to find their way out again and been lost. Elves who had encountered things so terrible that it had cost them their voices and their sanity. Elves who had been changed into something unrecognizable.

She did not necessarily believe all those stories. But she had witnessed at least one incident firsthand, and that was enough. When she was a little girl, she had gone into the Ashenell on a dare, leaving behind her two cousins, Pare and Freysen. Girls like her, though older, they had given her a dare and she had been stubborn enough to ignore common sense and her own instincts and accept it. She had gone in with the intention of touching the tomb that housed the most recent members of the Amarantyne family. Her word that she had done so would be good enough for them, her cousins had agreed.

Phryne would not have lied in any case—not about this or anything else that had to do with accepting a dare. She was still trying to find her place in the family, her mother recently dead, and her father already beginning to drift away. What confidence she possessed derived in part from her legacy as part Amarantyne and part Belloruus and from an iron resolve that got her through everything difficult. She employed that resolve on this night and went into the tombs and touched the one that belonged to her father's people.

She was on her way back again, feeling strong and steady as a result of her accomplishment when she encountered the dog, a creature fully six feet high at the shoulder and perhaps a dozen feet long. It came out of nowhere to confront her, blood dripping from its jaws and eyes burning like live coals. She froze where she was, unable to move, unable to do anything but stand there and wait to see what it intended. For a long time, it regarded her, as if measuring her value against its interest. But in the end, it turned away and vanished.

She came out of the Ashenell shaking in terror, unable to do anything but run home and cower under her sheets. When morning came she was herself again and decided it must have been an apparition.

But then she heard that a man engaged in breaking into one of the tombs had been killed that same night, his wounds indicating that he had been torn apart by a creature the like of which no one could even imagine.

So she did not discount the presence of magic and of things born of that magic. She did not think the Elven people brought such things to life intentionally, but she did think their use of magic left a residue and a legacy that allowed such things to come alive on their own.

"You should wait here," she told Xac Wen, looking at the dark shadows of the mix of trees and tombs and markers.

"You should stop talking and just follow me," he answered back.

Without waiting to see what she would do, he walked right through the gates and into the Ashenell. *That boy's got more courage than good sense,* she thought. But she hurried after him.

She caught up to him and took over the lead. She knew in what section of the cemetery the Belloruus family was buried; she had been there more than once, although always in daylight except for that one unfortunate time. She also knew about the Belloruusian Arch. Constructed not long after the city and its populace had been carried out of the Cintra and resituated in this valley, it was the monument that defined the section reserved for the whole of the family and its various members.

They reached it quickly enough—it wasn't that far from the southern gate—taking a direct path through the tombs in an effort to reach their destination while it was still dark. Phryne found herself searching the shadows the entire way, memories of her encounter with the ghost dog suddenly as fresh as the day it had happened. But they encountered nothing and no one, and arrived without incident.

That should have been the end of it. She was where she was supposed to be, where her grandmother had told her to come. But Mistral was nowhere to be found.

Phryne stood at a distance of perhaps twenty feet from the Belloruusian Arch, weighing her next move. But she quickly grew impatient. Dawn was approaching, and people would be out and about. Unwilling to just stand in place any longer and resigned to whatever fate awaited her, she decided to take a closer look.

XAC WEN WATCHED HER GO, hanging back and studying the arch as if it might hold some clue he could decipher. He kept thinking something would appear that would explain the message from Mistral Belloruus. Why had she summoned Phryne here? What was it she wanted? He thought of Phryne's grandmother the way most people did—a very peculiar, reclusive old lady who knew how to do things that other people didn't. Like how to do magic, some of it dangerous. He kept wondering if Phryne's insistence on finding her had something to do with that. After all, a little magic might be useful when you were dealing with people like Isoeld Severine.

Phryne was almost to the arch now, moving cautiously, taking her time. Xac didn't think this was a trap, but he couldn't be sure. He wished that Tasha were there. Big, strong Tasha, who was a match for anything. Or even clever Tenerife. But there was only Phryne and himself, and that seemed less than adequate given the extent of the danger they were in.

He started forward now, not wanting the girl to get too far ahead of him. He needed to be close if something happened, and he didn't want to have regrets about that later.

He no sooner completed the thought than Phryne Amarantyne walked beneath the arch and disappeared.

For a moment, he thought his eyes were playing tricks on him. There one minute, gone the next—that wasn't possible. Nothing had happened to cause it; she had just disappeared into thin air. He rushed ahead, blinking rapidly, trying to find her in the mix of gloom and shadows. But she wasn't there. She was gone.

"Phryne!" he called aloud, throwing caution aside.

He plunged through the space beneath the Belloruusian Arch, but nothing happened. He wheeled back and rushed through again. He turned back once more and placed himself directly beneath the arch. He tried every different approach he could imagine, trying to put himself on the path she had taken, at one point even standing in the faint prints of her boots.

Nothing.

He stared around in dismay. What was he supposed to do now? How could he find her? Would she come back on her own from wherever she had gone, or was she in trouble?

He stayed by the arch all that day, waiting for Phryne Amarantyne to return. When she didn't, he decided there was only one thing to do. He had to go back to Tasha and Tenerife and tell them everything that had happened. He had to get help.

At dawn the following day, a food sack and water skin slung over one shoulder, he set off for Aphalion Pass.

TWELVE

PANTERRA QU AND PRUE LISS TRAVELED NORTH out of Glensk Wood through the remainder of the night, following roads and paths that led toward Arborlon and the Elves. Prue was using a walking staff now, one cut from a hickory limb by Pan shortly after they had set out so that she could continue to give the impression that she was blind and needed help in making her way. They had agreed that even though she could see as well as any sighted person she would be better off not revealing the truth of this. It would lend others a false impression of how vulnerable she was and give her an advantage she might not otherwise have. Given the situation in which they found themselves, any advantage they could gain was not to be passed up.

Nevertheless, Prue continued to be decidedly unhappy about the price exacted. She was growing used to the idea that she could not discern colors, could only see shades of gray and white and black, but it did not ease the fresh pain that each new reminder of her disability created. She told herself that she should not let this bother her, that colors were lovely and sometimes even wondrous, but that being able to see, whether in colors or not, was what really mattered. And while this was true, it made the fact of it no easier to bear. There was a subtlety to the emotional pain she experienced that deepened as time passed and it became increasingly clear that not only was her ability to see colors forever gone but her inability to adapt to that loss was deepening.

She thought more than once to talk it out with Pan because she had always talked out everything with him. But she chose against doing so here because it would only remind him of the fact that he was the cause. Better that she suffer quietly and not make him share in her pain. In any case, he could never know the extent and nature of that pain, because it hadn't happened to him.

So they talked of other things.

"There are still a good many old-world weapons out there," she told him at one point. "Deladion Inch had some of them, all in good working order, all deadly. He had vehicles that ran on solar power and explosives that were no bigger than my hand but could destroy whole buildings. If he had them, others will have them, too."

"But not so many maybe." Pan was peering off into the forest, always paying attention to his surroundings. "Besides, they weren't enough to save him, were they?"

"They might have been, if he hadn't chosen to rescue me."

Pan nodded. "For which I will always be grateful. It says something about him that he decided to come at all. He didn't know you, didn't have any reason to make rescuing you his business. He did it for Sider."

"Oh, I think he did it for himself, too." She gave him a quick smile as he looked over. "No, it's true. He liked challenging himself. I think that's what made life worth something to him."

He nodded and looked away. She wondered if the look of her eyes troubled him. He didn't seem to want to focus on them. Maybe he found her ugly or a little less human now. She didn't like to think that he would be this way, but she would understand if he were. She didn't like it any better than he did. She didn't want to look at herself anymore, either.

"I want you to know . . ." He stopped midsentence, shook his head, and kept walking. For a minute, he didn't say anything more. Then he looked at her anew, and said, "I just want to say again how sorry I am that this happened."

She gave him a fresh smile. "I know. But I like hearing you say it. It makes it all a little easier."

"Do you think that what he did—the King of the Silver River— that it sharpened your instincts?"

She thought about it. In the time since she had returned from wherever the Faerie creature had taken her and resumed her trek home, she had been given ample opportunity to discover if she had been helped or not. It seemed to her that her instincts were fully restored. More than once, they had warned her of dangers she could not see, of creatures in hiding, sometimes directly in her path. When she changed course, the feelings would diminish.

"They are much stronger," she said finally. "I could tell coming back to Glensk Wood. Are they strong enough to warn me consistently and accurately? I can't be sure yet. I have to wait and see. I have to trust in what he told me. And I do trust him, Pan. I still think the exchange was a fair bargain."

She had noticed something else, too, although she didn't choose to talk about it just yet. As they walked, traveling through the gloom and shadows of the woods, alone amid the trees save for those things that lived there, she found she was able to detect, identify, and isolate almost everything that drew breath. She couldn't always tell exactly what she was sensing, but she could tell if it was big or little, safe or dangerous, lying in wait or sleeping, hunting or simply moving about. It was a subtle thing, filled with nuances she had not recognized before, and it gave her insights that filled her with unexpected confidence.

"How far do you want to travel today?" he asked.

She shook her head dismissively. "As far as you want."

"But you've already traveled several days just to reach me. You haven't had time to rest. You haven't slept in how long?"

"Not so long, Pan. I can keep going. I feel all right." She saw the way he was looking at her, and she could see the doubt in his eyes. Apparently doubt wasn't a color. "Really, I do."

They walked through the remainder of the morning, climbing out of the valley floor and onto the higher, more open expanses of the lower slopes while staying below the snow line. They passed isolated homes and farms, and once or twice they saw people and exchanged waves. The sun rose and the day brightened, and the heavy mists receded far enough up into the mountains that the air warmed and dampness of the dawn's dew faded. Hunting birds circled in the skies overhead, and patches of paintbrush and avalanche lilies appeared amid the rocks.

"It could almost be like it used to, couldn't it?" she asked him at one point, gesturing at the countryside. *It could,* she added to herself, *but not so long as I can't tell the colors of the flowers.*

"This is like it used to be," he said after a moment. "You and me, doing what we've always done."

You and me, she repeated to herself, and the words were comforting.

They stopped and ate a meal at midday, backed up against a moss-covered berm that shielded them from the chilly northern exposure and gave them a clear view of everything in all directions. Prue found herself eating more than she expected, strangely at peace in her cloudy world, unexpectedly happy. It didn't matter about her eyes; it didn't matter about the colors. In those few moments, it only mattered that her life was back on course.

But as soon as they started walking again, she was reminded of what it was they were trying to do, of the dangers that lay waiting at almost every turn and of the responsibility she had been given by the King of the Silver River, and all the good feelings vanished.

They traveled through the afternoon until the sun had begun to sink behind the mountains west and the light to dim. Pan chose to make camp before they climbed the escarpment that separated them from the meres and Arborlon, choosing a thin copse of alpine and fir amid a rough cluster of rocks that would shield them from prying eyes and warn them if there were unexpected visitors approaching. Pan was in full Tracker mode now, using all his skills and experience to keep them safe. He might hope they were able to rely on her instincts, but he wouldn't take any chances that they might unexpectedly fail her, even given the promises of the King of the Silver River.

He was like that, she knew. He always had been. The best defense was your own, and you should never rely on chance or other people.

Even her. This might have hurt her if she hadn't known him so well. He wasn't denigrating her abilities; he was simply putting his own to use, as well. Two sets of skills were always better than one, he was saying.

They ate their meal and went to sleep. She had thought she would be awakened at some point to share the watch, but when she finally opened her eyes the sun was just coming up over the rim of the mountains and the new day was beginning. Pan was fixing breakfast off to one side, and she couldn't tell if he had just come awake or been awake all night. When she asked if he had slept, he shrugged and didn't reply.

When they had finished eating, they packed up and set off toward the ridgeline on the far side of the escarpment, following the trail that would eventually lead them down into country west of the meres and from there to the Elves. The day was cool and clear, the mists again receding into the higher elevations where the peaks cradled them like woolly blankets. There was a maternal cast to their upswept, draped-over appearance, and Prue smiled in spite of herself as she imagined the baby they would swathe.

It was a bracing walk across the ridgeline and down through the rocks on the other side, the wind brisk and cold as it skidded down off the northern heights in sharp gusts. But the cold and the rush made Prue feel alive, and she lifted her face to the exciting sensation of it.

They were just coming off the ridge and descending toward the southern end of the meres and she was thinking idly of how pleasant their journey was turning out to be when she sensed the danger.

It was there all at once, not in a gradual way or in a rush of small tingles, but in a massive wave that threatened to knock her off her feet and flatten her against the ground. She gasped with the force of it and dropped to one knee. Pan was beside her at once, holding her up by her shoulders, whispering hurried words of reassurance.

"It's all right, Prue. I'm right here." His words came tumbling out. "Just take a deep breath and let it out slowly. Shades, you look like you've seen a ghost!"

She nodded and made a reassuring gesture. "More like I've felt one," she corrected him. "Something very bad, Pan. Something just ahead, waiting for us." She gulped and swallowed hard. "I don't know that I've ever felt anything as bad as this."

"Is it the old man? The demon?"

"I can't tell what it is. Only that it's ahead, probably hiding in those rocks below the path, waiting for us."

He was down on his knees beside her, holding her in his arms. "An ambush. This would be the right spot. If whatever's there is hiding down below, it could see us coming over the ridge. It could follow our descent. But how did it know to wait for us? How did it know we were coming?"

She looked up at him quickly. "We have to go another way. Can we circle past it?"

He looked up, still on his knees. "Wait here."

He inched forward until he found a spot that suited him and then raised himself carefully to peer between a cluster of rocks. He stayed there for a long time, studying the land ahead. When he had satisfied himself, he dropped down and crawled back to her.

"We can get past it without being seen but we'll have to go out of our way. We might even have to circle north above the meres—not the easiest route. Maybe we should just confront whatever's down there and get it over with."

She shook her head quickly. "No, we don't want that. Not if it's that old man. Let's try to sneak past. Once we're in Arborlon, we should be safe."

He gave her a dubious look, but nodded his agreement.

Crouched down far enough that they could keep the rocks between themselves and anything watching from below, they inched sideways across the slope, moving north toward the mountains. Prue understood that this effort might fail and they might have to face their stalker anyway. Their disappearance from the trail would send a clear signal to whatever was after them, and it would adjust its thinking accordingly. The best they could hope for was that it would guess wrong about which direction they had taken or that it would decide they hadn't moved and try to wait them out.

But she was able to live with the uncertainty if it meant they had even a chance of slipping past. Prue was not ready for a confrontation with whatever was down there. She knew it in her heart, knew it the moment she felt the weight of her instincts press down on her in warning. She might have thought she could do whatever was needed to help Pan, could act on his behalf as the King of the Silver River had intended she should do. But when she thought about what that meant, she realized she had no idea how she could protect him. Somehow, she hadn't understood that part of things when she had accepted the Faerie creature's bargain. She could sense Pan's danger and warn him, but she could do nothing to save him. He was the one with all the power, the bearer of the black staff, the inheritor of the Word's magic. She was only a fifteen-year-old girl who didn't want to see him die.

It was a bitter moment, the truth revealed in a way that left no doubt in her mind of the extent of her inadequacy. It shouldn't have been like that. There should have been something more that she could do to help him. But the truth was inescapable, and she must find a way to learn to live with it.

And with whatever strength and abilities she possessed, she must discover ways to help him learn to live with it, as well.

They worked their way north along the face of the slope, keeping carefully hidden within their rocky covering, moving soundlessly and smoothly in the way that Trackers were taught when they first signed on, listening and watching, alert to any movements and sounds. Only once did Pan stop and position himself so that he could take a quick look. He ducked back down again immediately, shook his head at Prue to indicate there wasn't anything to be seen, and they started off again.

At some point they turned downslope toward the northwest corner of the meres. By then, Prue's instincts had gone quiet and all the warning signs of the danger she had sensed earlier had dissipated. She was feeling better about things by then, hoping they had succeeded in deceiving their stalker into believing they were somewhere else—either still up in the rocks or gone another way. She touched Pan on his shoulder to signal as much, and he nodded his understanding.

But it was late by then, and they would have to decide whether to push on to reach Arborlon that night or stop to rest and go on in the morning. The meres were treacherous in places and difficult to navigate in darkness, but once across the distance to Arborlon was short.

Pan signaled that they would continue on.

They kept their cover until the slope leveled out and the rocks gave way to huge old cedars and willows that marked the northern boundary of the meres. They were still too far south and would have to skirt the edges until they reached the far north end if they wanted a clear, safe passage. Neither of them fancied trying to navigate the meres at night, so they resigned themselves to what needed doing and set out, keeping just within the shelter of the trees so that they could not be seen. It was slow going because the woods were thicker at the edges of the ponds and swamps that formed the meres and required angling in all directions to avoid ravines and drops. The trick was to keep moving. Once they had put enough distance between themselves and whatever was stalking them, they could slow their pace.

Prue had just finished estimating that they were still four or five hours away from the Elfitch and safety when her instincts kicked in anew, and she felt the familiar crushing wave start to close in on her.

"Pan!" she hissed, causing him to turn and come back to her immediately. "It's following us! It's figured out which way we've gone!"

He was quiet as he stared back into the growing darkness, his gaze fixed on something she couldn't see, but could easily imagine.

"We have to go faster," she urged.

He shook his head. "We have to stop and face it, but not here. Not out in the open where it will have an advantage over us."

She waited, already knowing what he was going to say.

Even so, the words were chilling when he spoke them. "We have to lead it into the meres."

*　　*　　*

IT WAS NEARING MIDNIGHT, the darkness illuminated by the light of stars that had appeared from behind broken cloud cover to filter down through the heavy canopy of the trees. Panterra Qu crouched within a thick stand of brush no more than six feet from where Prue was hiding, her slender body flattened against the ground at the base of an ancient willow, stretched out between tree roots that hid her completely from view. She was covered with leaves and all but buried in the earth, a good choice for concealment from someone hunting them. Pan's position was more vulnerable, but that was his intent. She had objected, but he had pointed out that her instincts would warn her when whatever tracked them got close and then he could employ his staff's magic to protect himself. To signal that approach, he had tied a length of string about his finger and given her the other end. When she sensed the danger to be close enough, she would give it a yank to let him know.

But he was counting on the straw men he had built with leaves and brush stuffed inside their extra clothing to draw their stalker's attention away from where they hid. Wrapped in blankets and placed back against the trees at the edge of a broad clearing fronted on the far side by the shores of a lake, the straw men appeared to be the boy and girl asleep. It was good enough that it would fool almost anyone, even in daylight.

Still, Pan wasn't taking any chances. He had his staff ready, and he was expecting to use it.

The minutes crawled by as they waited. An hour passed. Pan scanned the forest over and over, searching for movement. Prue was so still she might have been sleeping. But he knew she wasn't. She could lie silent like that for hours; he had seen her do it. Her patience was phenomenal, the kind that defied everyone's expectations. She told him once she had practiced it as a child when there was nothing better to do than sit and watch for birds to land in her backyard. She had been only three or four.

The yank of the string on his finger caught him by surprise, and he yanked back to let her know he was paying attention. He slipped the string from his finger and took a new position, crouched and ready. More time passed, and nothing happened. He scanned the lakeshore and the clearing, then the edges of the trees and back again, waiting. He glanced repeatedly at Prue, wanting to speak to her, to ask her what was happening. But it was so dark by then he could barely make out the tree roots between which she had settled herself, and he could not risk giving himself away.

He kept looking and listening, growing impatient. Their stalker still did not appear.

He had passed the point where he thought their plan had any real chance of working when Prue screamed. Her scream was high and piercing and filled with fear, and he reacted instinctively, rolling quickly to one side as he tried to bring the staff's magic to bear. The attack came from behind, a black-garbed figure catapulting out of the darkness in a soundless rush that told him at once what had happened.

Their stalker—a man, judging by his size—had figured out they had laid a trap, circled around through the meres, and come at them from behind. If not for Prue's scream . . .

The flash of a knife blade in the starlight banished all other thoughts. He caught the blade on his staff just as the magic flared to life, all of it happening in seconds. He blocked the strike and the magic exploded off the staff and threw his attacker away. But the latter was back on his feet almost immediately. Abandoning his attack on Pan, he turned on Prue who was scrambling up, wanting to help, revealing herself in a way that made the boy's heart lurch in dismay.

"Prue!" he screamed.

But the attacker was already on top of her, bearing her to the ground, knife rising and falling. Pan was running toward her, aware that he was too late to save her. But to his astonishment, she had somehow managed to roll out from beneath the attack and was back on her feet, her staff held ready. Her attacker was coming toward her once more, but she took his measure and swung her walking stick not at his head, but at his legs, taking them out from under him. He went down, thrashing wildly. Pan had summoned the magic and it flared at his fingertips and along the black length of the staff, but he could not bring it to bear when Prue and her attacker were so close together.

She seemed to sense this and dived to one side as the knife swept toward her. She went down in a hard rolling motion that took her out of reach, and Pan struck out with everything he could muster. His aim was true, and the magic hammered into their stalker with such force that it threw him twenty feet into a tree trunk where he went down in a heap and didn't move.

Pan stood gasping in mingled shock and relief, painfully aware in the aftermath of the attack how close they had come to being killed.

THEY APPROACHED the downed man cautiously, Pan a step ahead of Prue, ready to defend her should there be need. But their assailant was unconscious, and even when Pan prodded him with his boot, he did not move.

So they propped him up against the tree trunk, stripped him of his knife and every other weapon they could find, of which there were a considerable number. Certainly, there were more than any ordinary hunter would ever think to carry—hidden in his boots, sleeves, pockets, and slits cleverly sewn into the seams of his clothing, in his belt, and even in his wide gold bracelet. Some were unidentifiable, things that looked like throwing stars and curved blades, though tiny and barbed. In the end, Pan cut off his sleeves and pant legs and removed his belt and boots, taking no chances that there might still be weapons hidden on him that they hadn't found. Then they lashed him to the tree and removed the mask that was covering his head.

Neither of them had ever seen him before.

"He doesn't look like he belongs out here," Prue observed.

Pan agreed. He was young and rather pale, almost soft looking. His hands were smooth and free of calluses, and there were no visible scars. He was certainly no hunter or Tracker. There was nothing about him that suggested he spent much time outdoors or engaged in any sort of physical labor.

"He's an assassin," Pan said. "Sent to find us."

Prue shook her head. "By whom? Who would want to kill us?" She hesitated as Pan gave her a look. "Skeal Eile? I thought that was finished. I thought Sider put an end to that."

"Sider is dead." Pan backed away from the slumped figure and seated himself cross-legged on the ground. "When he wakes up, we'll see what he has to say about it."

Abruptly, Prue got to her feet, walked over to her pack, took out their cooking pan, carried it down to the lake, filled it with water, walked back to him, and threw the water in the unconscious man's face.

The man jerked awake immediately, shaking his head and sputtering. Blinking rapidly, he looked from one to the other. "Children," he muttered. "I've been taken prisoner by children."

"Who are you?" Pan asked, leaning forward, but staying out of reach. Prue had taken a seat next to him. "Why were you trying to kill us?"

The man smiled. "You'll forgive me, but I don't think I'm going to answer either of those questions."

"You won't give us your name?"

"I won't give you the time of day. Or night, in this case."

"Or who sent you?"

"Or who didn't."

They stared at one another in silence then. "What should we do with him?" Prue asked finally.

"Why don't you just let me go?" their prisoner asked. "I'll go straight home and not come back. You have my word."

"I'm sure your word is good, too," Pan answered. "The word of an assassin. I have a better idea. Why don't we just leave you tied up to this tree and see if anything interested in an easy meal finds you in— oh, I don't know, say the next two weeks. I don't know that anything will, but it might be better than starving. No one much comes into the meres, you know."

The young man smiled. "You won't do that. You won't leave me."

"I won't?"

"You do, and you'll never find out anything. Also, you're not built that way. You don't have it in you."

Pan almost contradicted him, but Prue cut him off. "You're right. We aren't like that. So we have to take you to someone who knows what to do with you."

She looked at Pan. "Since we are on our way to Arborlon, let's take him there. We can give him to Tasha and Tenerife to guard and if they don't want him they can give him to the Home Guard or even to the Queen."

A flash of uneasiness appeared in their prisoner's eyes.

"Tasha and Tenerife are all right, but the Queen?" Pan had seen the look in the other's eyes and was just talking now to see what would happen.

"All we want is to keep this creature locked away until we find out more about him." Prue cocked an eyebrow. "What does it matter where he's kept or who's doing the keeping?" She glanced over at their prisoner. "Tell you what, though. We can let Skeal Eile know what happened to you, if you like. Maybe he will decide to come see about getting you released."

The young man was looking down at his hands now, refusing to meet their eyes. "I suppose you have to do what you think is best. But I'm still not going to tell you anything."

Pan shrugged. "You don't have to. We don't care." He got to his feet. "Better get some sleep, though. You still have to walk to where we're going. Come on, Prue."

He helped her stand and then made a show of walking her back to where their packs were, picking them up, and carrying them to a place just a little distance off from the bound man. Neither said anything as they spread their blankets on the ground and prepared to go to sleep.

"One minute," their prisoner called out suddenly. "There is something you should know."

Pan exchanged a quick glance with Prue. On his nod, they walked over together and stood in front of the prisoner, waiting.

"If you take me to Arborlon, I'll be killed," he said. He paused. "You won't be safe, either."

Prue shook her head. "That's what you have to tell us?"

"No, there's more. But first I want your promise that if I tell you what I know, you won't take me to Arborlon."

"We have friends in Arborlon," Pan pointed out. "If someone wants to harm you, that's your problem. No one wants to harm us."

The young man looked disgusted. "You don't know anything. You don't even understand what's happening. I do. Make the promise, and I'll tell you."

Pan looked at Prue for guidance. She shrugged. "I don't believe him. Besides, we have to go to Arborlon. That's where Phryne is. What happens to this one isn't important."

"You heard her," Pan said to their prisoner. "Keep what you know to yourself."

He turned away, Prue going with him.

This time their prisoner didn't call them back.

◾ ◾ ◾

PAN SLEPT LATE the following morning, not coming awake until the sun had crested the mountains and daybreak was long past. It might have been his exhaustion from the previous day's flight and subsequent battle or the deep stillness of the meres or even the way the sunlight was absorbed by shadows and gloom as it tried to pass through the thick canopy of the trees that kept him sleeping longer than he normally would. But the result was the same—he was the last to wake and not at all unhappy about it.

He had kept watch while Prue slept deep into the night before waking her to take his place, and she was sitting where he had left her, eyes on their prisoner. The bound man was staring back.

· "You're blind," he was saying to Prue. "I didn't see that last night. But how can you be blind? You fought back like you could see me perfectly. You shouldn't have been able to get away from me, but you did. How?"

The girl ignored him. "Morning, Pan. Breakfast in a few minutes."

She set about pulling out bread, dried fruit, and a little cheese from her backpack, and then poured them cups of water from the pouch. Pan blinked awake as he sat watching her, yawning. "You should have woken me."

"I should have done nothing of the sort."

"You can see, can't you," their prisoner called out, unwilling to drop the subject. "You look like you can't, but you can. Who are you? You aren't what you seem, I know that much."

"You aren't, either," Prue called back to him. "Here you are," she said to Pan, handing him his food and water.

They sat side by side looking out at the lake while they ate, ignoring their prisoner, who continued on about her sight along with questions about his own meal and when he was going to get it. He seemed more agitated this morning, less patient with his captivity. There was an undercurrent of uneasiness that matched what they had seen in his eyes the night before when they had mentioned taking him to Arborlon.

When they had finished their breakfast, Prue took food and drink over to their prisoner and hand-fed him, refusing his requests that he be freed so that he could feed himself. In the end, he ate quietly and drank down his cup of water in one long series of gulps. He studied her face in a way that she found disconcerting, but she was careful to mask her emotions. With someone like this, you never wanted to reveal what you were thinking or feeling.

While she was engaged with their prisoner, Pan packed up their supplies and tied up their blankets in preparation for setting out. Even though he had slept longer than he had planned, they still had plenty of time to reach their destination before nightfall. He was already thinking about what they would do once they reached Arborlon and rid themselves of their prisoner. First they needed to find Tasha and Tenerife, and together they could figure out what to do about Phyrne.

They were almost ready to depart when their prisoner, still bound to the tree, called out. "I've changed my mind," he told them. "I'll tell you what you want to know. If that is what it takes to keep you from marching me off to Arborlon, why not? I have to do something to save you from yourselves."

Pan, kneeling beside his backpack, glanced over. "That's very kind of you."

"Kinder than you know." He sighed and shook his head, much as if he were dealing with small children. "All right, then. Listen. You were right about me. I have special skills, talents that are of use at times to others. I am for hire to those who have the coin. But mostly only to one man."

"Skeal Eile?" Pan suggested.

"I would appreciate it if you would come close enough to look me in the eye while I am telling you this. Is that asking too much?"

Pan got up and walked over, but didn't sit, waiting to see if this was going to be worth his time. Prue sidled up beside him.

"Thank you, Excellencies." The young man inclined his head in a gesture of mock gratitude. "You won't regret listening to what I have to tell you, I promise."

"First tell us your name," Pan demanded.

"I am called Bonnasaint," the other answered immediately.

"From Glensk Wood?"

"Same as you. But I do not live in the village. I live on the far eastern edge, away from other people. You wouldn't have seen me before."

"Why shouldn't we take you to Arborlon, Bonnasaint?" Prue asked him. "Why would you be in danger there?"

"What you should be asking yourselves," the other answered, "is why *you* would be in danger."

"And are you going to give us the answer?"

He nodded. "I was hired by the Queen, Isoeld Severine, to kill her husband. It was done under circumstances that made it appear that the Princess had killed her own father. That way the Queen could ascend the throne and the Princess could be locked away. If you take me back and she finds out, she will not chance that I might say something. She will have me killed. If you were her, wouldn't you?"

Pan guessed he would. He guessed there wasn't much he wouldn't do if he had arranged and carried out a murder of this sort.

"What about us?" Prue asked him. "Why do you keep saying we're not safe, either?"

"The Queen will take no chances. Once she discovers it was you who brought me back, she will wonder how much you know. She will not want to take the risk that I told you anything."

He paused, letting the words sink in. Panterra and Prue looked at each other. Though neither spoke, they were both thinking the same thing.

Bonnasaint said it aloud. "She will have you killed, too."

THIRTEEN

AFTER LOSING THE GIRL HE HAD PURSUED THROUGH the fortress ruins, the demon disguised as a ragpicker had reemerged and turned east toward the mountains from which the now deceased Grosha claimed she had come. He had dismissed the Trolls he'd pressed into his service, sending them back to wherever it was they had come from, bearing the corpse of their unfortunate leader. The demon felt no regrets about killing the latter; in fact, he imagined he had done any number of other humans a great favor. Other than his father, who was undoubtedly blinded by paternal love or perhaps something less noble, there were few who would miss such a creature. A few weeks' time, and hardly anyone would even remember who he was.

But the girl—now, there was someone who deserved further consideration.

The demon was still trying to decide what had occurred at the fortress when he had chased her down and brought her to bay. There shouldn't have been any escape for her; she should have been his to do with as he wanted. Yet someone or something more powerful than he had come to her assistance and spirited her away. Why? Why would anyone bother with this girl? What did she have to offer that mattered so much?

Of course, there was her relationship with the man who bore the black staff. She was important to him, even if she claimed otherwise. Nor was he dead, as she also claimed. That was just a ploy to throw him off, and a bad one at that. He would have known if the bearer of the staff were dead; he would have sensed it in the same way he had sensed the other's presence all those weeks ago when he had first come looking for him. No, the bearer was alive, and the girl knew where he was.

But he didn't think it was the bearer who had saved her. Possession of one of the Word's talismans created a formidable opponent, but it did not invest the user with magic capable of transporting another human from one place to another. No human whom he had ever encountered or even heard about possessed magic that strong. Not even the legends told of anyone with that sort of power. This was something else, he believed. This was a Faerie creature, an ancient one in service to the Word.

Yet why had it bothered with this girl?

He thought about it at length as he walked away from the fortress toward the mountains, climbed the foothills to the lower slopes and then the slopes toward places where he would likely find passage through to whatever valleys lay beyond. He considered the possibilities, but nothing helpful suggested itself. The problem was that he didn't know enough to make an educated guess. There was a background to all of this to which he was not privy. Not yet, anyway. That would change once he found the girl again.

And he *would* find her. He would find her as surely as the sun rose at the beginning and set at the end of the day. He would find her as surely as he would find the bearer of the black staff. However long it took, whatever he had to do to make it happen, he would find them both.

So he walked for several days, taking his time, singing his songs and humming his tunes, at peace with the wasteland around him. He passed through stretches of ruined earth, decimated forests, blackened hills, and scorched grasslands, and he was pleased. This was what he had worked so hard for, what all those who had shed their humanity had sought—a landscape devoid of living things, barren and blasted, empty of nature's troublesome creatures. He could control this sort of world, and control was paramount to his reworked personality. Control was power, and power was sustenance. All the things he had once thought so important—things he could no longer even remember in the specific, but only in the general—had been left by the wayside in favor of the one absolute—power over life and death.

Had he stopped to think it through, he might have asked himself what his world would be like if he and those like him were the only creatures living in it. But such speculations seemed counterproductive to his purpose.

The words to a new tune came unbidden:

Ragpicker, ragpicker, walking through the land.
Make yourself a wish as quick as you can.
Ahead there's a valley where the children play.
But your demon's fire can sweep them away.

He frowned. It wasn't very good, really. Children were of no interest to him. To other demons, yes, those whose lives were dedicated to making human children into a more interesting species. But those demons were gone, swept away in the apocalypse of five centuries earlier. So much had been lost in that time. Demons of all forms, their followers and armies, everything they had been on the verge of achieving. Still, it was never too late to start anew. That was what he told himself every day, and every day he found reason to believe it. Humans were still possessed of the same weaknesses that had brought about their destruction in the old days. Theirs was a race destined to be short-lived. They would find new ways to destroy themselves or to enable the demons and their servants to destroy them. It was inevitable. They just didn't know it.

He wondered how many were living in the valley the girl had come from. He wondered how many more valleys hid similar enclaves. He hoped there were more than a few. He didn't want to end this hunt until his appetite was sated. Surely, there were more bearers of the black staff. Surely there were other talismans and forms of magic to be found and claimed. It was a big world, and you couldn't expect to find everything right away. Not even he could do that.

It took him three days to locate the nearest pass after climbing into the mountains, an undertaking at which he did not work overly hard, acknowledging the limitations of his human body, the ragpicker's body of which he had grown quite fond. He still bore his bundle of rags on his back, a burden he was happy to carry. His trophies, the reminders of his conquests, still meant something to him. He liked to take them out at night when he was alone and look through them, matching each to his memory of its previous owner, remembering who that owner had been and how he or she had died. *At my hands,* the demon always added silently. *All of them, at my hands. Isn't that marvelous?*

Once, during his ascent, he encountered one of the agenahls, a huge tank of a beast lumbering along just above him in the rocks. It spied him quickly enough and swung toward him, sensing the possibility of a quick meal. But then it caught his scent, identified what he was, and backed away quickly. The demon let it go. He appreciated the fact that animals were often much smarter than humans, and he thought that one day they might fill in the gap that would be left when the last of the humans were gone.

He reached the pass leading into the valley shortly before sunset on the third day of searching, when night's gloom was settling in and its shadows were lengthening. He saw the remains of Trolls scattered about outside the pass and then again in the pass itself, the latter mixed with the bodies of humans. The scavengers had gotten to some of them, but not all. Four-footed scavengers were wary of confined spaces like this one, and preferred to do their hunting elsewhere. Mostly, it was the predatory birds that had begun to pick the bodies apart, and these were already gone for the day when he arrived.

A battle of some sort had been fought here, probably by Trolls from the same tribe as those he had encountered at the ruins and residents of the valley into which he was heading. Their numbers were small, but the fighting had been intense. It didn't appear that much of anyone had survived. He wondered if the girl knew about it. He wondered if the bearer of the black staff had been involved.

He threaded the narrow defile, a twisting passageway that widened and narrowed by turns, its walls rising well over two hundred feet. The sky was a narrow strip of gray turning darker as sunset approached. He took note of the numbers of the dead, idly pausing to reconstruct what he thought might have happened and to admire the carnage. Already, he was thinking of what he would do once he was within the valley and had taken the measure of its people. Already, he was considering ways of flushing out of hiding the one who carried the black staff so that he could dispose of him quickly and claim his talisman.

At the far end of the pass, he came upon the abandoned defenses and the larger numbers of dead from both camps. He climbed a ladder to gain the far side, still counting bodies, feeling better now about his prospects. Finding the bearer of the staff could not be all that difficult given the obvious conflict taking place between humans and Trolls. Wherever the fighting was thickest, that was where the bearer would be. The ragpicker needed only to generate the sort of conflict that would bring the bearer out of hiding—something at which he was very good.

"I shall create a little confusion," he said aloud. "I shall cause disturbances great and small. I shall sow dissension and unrest and create mayhem and murder. I shall give the human inhabitants cause for fear and turn them against one another. I shall release the beast that each of them thinks is safely locked within."

It was his intent to decimate the population, and he was already considering how to make this happen. The most obvious way was to bring the Trolls who had already attacked the valley into fresh conflict with the humans who were seeking to keep them out. He did not know the history of these peoples, but history of this sort was pretty much always the same. One side had something that the other wanted. One side sought to take that something away and the other sought to keep it. Both were willing to kill to have their way.

How hard could it be to give them their chance?

He stood amid corpses piled up one upon another and surveyed the killing ground. These few were only the first of those destined to cross over to the land of the dead. These few were just the tip of the iceberg. The demon walked forward until he was at the apex of the descent into the valley. It was just light enough that he could see some of what lay beyond. Far away to the south and east, the lights of a village were barely visible through a thick screen of brume. He would start there, he decided.

Humming to himself, he began his descent.

IT WAS ALMOST DAWN by the time the ragpicker arrived at the outskirts of Glensk Wood, his feet sore and his body weary, but his spirits high. So much to be done, so much to be accomplished. But the rewards were worth the effort, and he felt eager to begin his work.

He walked through the village—strolled, really—greeting people as he passed with a word or a simple nod, an itinerant seller of goods, a harmless old man. Everyone seemed eager to acknowledge him. One or two even offered him food and drink or asked his destination and if they could help him in any way. They saw he was a traveler and might have come far. They extended their kindness without having the slightest clue whom they were extending it to.

It made him laugh inside. It put a smile on his face and a dark satisfaction in his heart.

He found his way to the village council chambers, walked up the steps to the veranda and through the open front door. The cavernous room inside, where the town meetings were clearly held, was empty, and he stood there for a moment imagining what it would look like if it were set afire. He made a promise to himself to find out.

"Help you?" a voice behind him asked.

He turned, smiling. "Perhaps."

He was facing a young man with sandy hair and freckles and an eager face. The young man was wearing working clothes and carrying a wooden box of tools.

"Just happened to be passing by and saw the open door. You looking for Pogue?"

The ragpicker shook his head. "I'm not from here. I just arrived this morning. I sell odds and ends. Who is Pogue?"

"Pogue Kray, the council chairman. He pretty much runs things in Glensk Wood. Which town are you from?"

"Sunny Rise, way to the east. Do you know of it?"

The young man shook his head. "Can't say that I do. I don't get over that way much. Not at all, matter of fact. This is my home." He smiled some more. "Anyway, I just wanted to see if I could help. Pogue is out gathering up men to attend to the defenses up at Declan Reach. Been out since sometime yesterday, making the rounds. So you won't find him, if that's who you're looking for."

The ragpicker cocked his head. "Who I'm really looking for is a man who carries a black staff. Do you know of such a man?"

His new friend nodded eagerly. "Everyone knows about him. That's the one they call the Gray Man. Sider Ament. Patrols the valley rim, checks the passes to see if the wards are still in place. They're not anymore, you know. Down, all of them. The way out—or in—is open to anyone."

He leaned forward conspiratorially. "Word is, there's an army out there. Trolls. They're camped on the flats beyond Aphalion Pass, waiting on something. Word is, they want to take our valley away from us and make a home of it for themselves. Throw us to the wolves or whatever. But we won't stand for that. You heard about this?"

"I did hear something. No details, though. Are there a lot of these Trolls out there? Enough to do what they say they're going to do?" The ragpicker gave the young man his most concerned look. "Do you think our people are in any real danger?"

The young man shrugged. "Could be. I put my faith in the teachings of the Seraphic. I belong to the Children of the Hawk. We believe that we will be saved no matter what the danger, once the valley opens up again. Like it has now. We believe the Hawk will return for us and keep us safe from whatever threatens."

The ragpicker nodded sagely. *Do you, now? Safe from anything at all? Safe from me?* The words burned like a cleansing fire in his heart. "Tell me something of your order," he asked the other. "All of this is new to me. Who are the Children of the Hawk?"

Then he proceeded to listen carefully to everything the young man had to tell him about the sect and its leader, the Seraphic Skeal Eile, who at the moment was gone from the village but was expected back within the next few days. It was a fascinating story, and the demon drank it all in with a rapturous enthusiasm he could barely conceal.

This was so much better than he had hoped. Everything he needed to bring his plans to fruition was right there for the taking. He could hardly believe his luck.

"Well, I will certainly make it a point to speak to your Seraphic upon his return. I think I might be interested in joining your sect. It sounds just right for me. But I want to hear more from the Seraphic himself."

"Oh, he will be glad to speak with you," the young man assured him enthusiastically. He stuck out his hand. "My name is Elson. Yours?"

The ragpicker did not take the other's hand, but only smiled. "My name is of no importance. I am a simple trader in goods and services. A ragpicker, as you can see. But it is a pleasure to make your acquaintance, Elson. I am grateful for your time and your insights."

He started to turn away and then stopped suddenly. "One thing more. You never did say where I could find the man who carries the black staff. What was his name again?"

"Sider Ament," the other replied. "But he's a hard one to find. He comes and goes as he pleases and never with any announcement beforehand. Pogue might know. Or maybe his wife, Aislinne. She has a history with the Gray Man. Knew him when they were both young. He still comes by to visit her now and then. She might know."

The ragpicker repeated the name carefully in his head. "And where will I find her?" he asked.

Minutes later, he was through the door of the council hall and on his way to find Aislinne Kray.

IT WAS A SHORT DISTANCE from the council hall to the residence of Pogue and Aislinne Kray, and the ragpicker found it without any particular difficulty. People helped him navigate the journey, taking time to set him on the right paths, wishing him well as he went. It was early still, but people were up and about, beginning their day, off to work or on errands or whatever pursuits occupied their time. The ragpicker found that everyone knew the Krays and no one questioned why he wanted to visit them at their home. Apparently, it wasn't all that unusual to do so, although one or two people mentioned that the husband was away and the ragpicker might find himself disappointed if that was who he was intending to see.

But the ragpicker was seldom disappointed about anything these days, and the bright promise of finding the bearer of the black staff was a beacon that never dimmed.

It was no different on this day. He arrived at the little cottage to which he had been directed and found the woman he was seeking working in her frontyard flower garden. She was on her knees, digging in the dirt, weeding her beds. But when she heard him call out her name and saw him approaching, she rocked back on her feet and then rose. Tall and slim and centered, she waited on him patiently as he came up the walk, an old man she had never seen before. The demon might have found her pretty—long blond hair gone almost white, brilliant green eyes, fine features—if he had thought that humans in general were the least bit attractive, which he did not. Save for those few who had the use of magic or carried talismans possessed of magic, there was nothing interesting about any of them.

Still, he liked the cool way she appraised him, not in the least afraid, not showing even the smallest deference.

"Good day," he greeted her, giving a smile and a sort of small bow. "Are you Aislinne Kray?"

She nodded. "I am. And you?"

He gave her his patented shrug. "I don't really have a name. Haven't got much use for one. I am a ragpicker, an itinerant, and I never stay long enough in any one place to have need of a name. I had one once, I think, but I have long since forgotten it. I hope that doesn't matter?"

She gave him a look. "It doesn't to me. I can't speak for others. What brings you to my home?"

"A favor." He gave her another smile. "I am looking for a man. His name is Sider Ament. I am told by some of the villagers that you knew him as a girl and that he sometimes comes here. I was wondering if you might know where he is now."

She said nothing, green eyes fixed on his face. Her steady gaze gave him an unexpectedly uncomfortable feeling, and he suddenly wondered if he had said something that gave him away.

Then she shook her head slowly. "You've come too late. Sider

Ament is dead. He was killed last week at Declan Reach. Now, if you will excuse me, I have to get back to work."

The demon was momentarily flummoxed. Dead? That was what the girl in the ruins had said, and he had known at once that she was lying. But this time the words rang true.

"You will pardon me for asking this," he said to Aislinne Kray, "but are you sure? I came a long way to find him, and this news is heart-breaking."

"To me, as well. But there's no mistaking it. The source is unimpeachable. He would not lie. Sider is dead." She hesitated. "Why were you seeking him?"

The ragpicker shrugged. "He did me a great favor once, something of a personal nature, something I don't talk about with anyone. But I never had a chance to thank him. It took me until now to find enough coin and courage to come looking for him." He smiled ruefully. "I waited too long."

The woman nodded. "Would you like some tea?"

The ragpicker nodded. "That would be nice."

She did not invite him inside, but left him waiting on her front stoop while she fetched the tea. While she was gone, he gave thought to what this new information would do to his plans.

"Green tea for a cool morning," she announced, handing him a mug. She sat down beside him. "How long ago was it that you met Sider?"

"Oh, several years. Too long to make excuses." He sipped at the tea. "This is quite good. I can't remember when I've had better." He sipped some more. "I was wondering. When I met him—Sider Ament—he was carrying a black staff carved with symbols. Quite striking. Do you know what became of it?"

For a second time, her green eyes fixed on him, and this time there was no mistake—he had crossed a line that revealed him. She smiled, reached out, and took the mug of tea out of his hand.

"I can't imagine," she said conversationally, "what difference it would make to you, an itinerant ragpicker who met Sider Ament the one time only, what became of the black staff."

He tried a reassuring smile. "It doesn't make a difference so much as it satisfies my curiosity."

She stood up. "I rather doubt that. Just as I am beginning to doubt that you are anything of what you say you are. It was nice meeting you, but I think you had better leave."

He stood up with her but made no move to depart. "You are a perceptive lady. Perhaps you have discerned I seldom leave without gaining possession of what I came for. In this case, it was only information. If I am denied, I might choose to come back for something more."

She gave him a chilly smile. "Others have made the mistake of thinking that way. You can visit their remains in the woods."

She was only a woman holding two mugs of tea and lacking any weapons at all. But there was something about the way she said it that gave him pause.

By then, it was too late.

"Good morning, Brickey," she called to someone behind him.

The ragpicker turned to find a gnarled little man with a shock of unruly black hair and a crooked smile approaching, seemingly out of nowhere. There was something dangerous about him, and the ragpicker sensed it right away. He was certain he could dispose of him, that the little man was no match for him. But there was every chance the effort would draw attention, and he did not want that.

"Can I help with something, Aislinne?" the man called Brickey asked, never taking his eyes off her visitor.

The ragpicker bowed to Aislinne Kray. "I have overstayed my welcome. I apologize. I am sure I can find what I need somewhere else. Good day."

Without a glance for either the little man or Aislinne Kray, the ragpicker turned and walked away. He could feel the woman's eyes on his back, and it made him smile. She might not realize it, but his business with her was far from finished.

He would be back to see her later.

FOURTEEN

S KEAL EILE SAT ON A COUCH IN A TINY RECEIVING room in the Amarantyne Palace, awaiting the appearance of Isoeld Severine, although his patience was growing decidedly thin. He had arrived an hour earlier—coming to a rear door of the building, as instructed—only to find a solitary Home Guard waiting to receive him. Without so much as a word of greeting, the Home Guard had taken him through various corridors to this room, deposited him inside, and left him to whatever solitary pursuits he could manage to invent.

The Seraphic had not expected that the recently widowed Queen of the Elves would greet him with crowds of admirers chanting his name or baskets of flowers strewn on the front walkway as he entered, but he had expected better treatment than this. He had assumed the Queen would be better prepared for the tumult that followed the King's assassination and the incarceration of his daughter for the murder, but it appeared he was mistaken. Isoeld Severine had adopted a fortress mentality right from the start, closing off contact with all but a few trusted advisers and her heavily armed personal guard. Aside from Teonette—though Eile assumed he might be mistaken about this, too—no one had been given access to her.

She had addressed the High Council right after the King's demise, and he was told that she had handled herself well in that situation. She had spoken eloquently of her husband's service and her intention to see to it, no matter if she was proclaimed ruler of the Elves or not, that his legacy endured and his good work continued. Impressed by her dedication to her husband's efforts and memory, they had named her successor on the spot. It was a decision they were all probably regretting by now.

In any case, she had made a bargain with him, and he had yet to see any evidence she intended to keep it. It was his man who had killed the King, done so on his orders and at her request, and the agreement had been plain enough. Once the King was dispatched, his daughter charged with the crime, and Isoeld ascended the throne, he was to be given ready access both to her and the Elven people so he could begin the work of gathering new disciples for the Order of the Hawk. He knew they were there; he had even seen them at gatherings he had held on the outskirts of this part of the kingdom's borders. But they were a minority afraid of condemnation and even retribution for their beliefs, and so they kept a low profile. It was his intention to remove the barriers that forced them to keep silent by making it clear to all that even the Elven throne was accepting of his work.

Yet none of that had happened. The Queen had not so much as mentioned the Children of the Hawk the few times she had addressed either the Council or the Elven people, and for all intents and purposes nothing had changed for the better where he was concerned.

So here he was now, come to find out why this was so, come to advise her that if she didn't act quickly to make things right, she might find out to her regret the consequences of ignoring her promise. He did not intend to back away simply because she had now gotten what she wanted and might feel less beholden to him.

He was considering the nature of the consequences he would impose when the door to the receiving room opened and she stepped through. She gave him only a cursory glance before closing the door behind her and locking it.

"Good day, Seraphic," she greeted, her voice cool.

He nodded, but said nothing in return. She gave him a look and then walked over to the windows that opened into the gardens behind the building and carefully drew together the floor-length curtains, leaving the room in semi-darkness.

"Better if no one sees us just now," she said, turning back to face him.

Even in the dimness of the room's shadowy illumination, she was beautiful to look at. He could understand why Oparion Amarantyne had been so taken with her. He might have been similarly tempted—had been more than once—except he knew what sort of creature lived within that lovely skin.

"I don't mind the secrecy, but I can't say I much care for the treatment otherwise." He walked forward a few steps, putting him close enough to watch her eyes. "You kept me waiting a very long time."

"For which I apologize," she said. "But the High Council has been meeting all day, trying to come to an agreement about how to treat the threat of a Troll invasion. Unfortunately, they lack ideas and backbones in equal measure. It is much easier to debate the matter to death."

She moved into the light more directly, and he saw the deep furrows scratched into the smooth skin of her face.

"Teonette does nothing to help?" he asked, trying to mask his surprise at what he was seeing, wondering who was responsible.

She laughed softly. "Come, Seraphic. A title does not the man make. He may be first minister, but that does not confer on him anything he doesn't already possess. In this situation, he is sadly inadequate. You know what men like Teonette are good for? Of course you do. You must also know, then, that if I relied on him to lend backbone or clear thinking to our efforts, I should already be imprisoned and sentenced."

Skeal Eile felt a chill run up his spine. He could feel it clearly: she was already planning on eliminating her lover, putting one more layer of protection between herself and discovery. Was there any reason to believe she would not seek to eliminate him, as well?

"We had an agreement, as I recall," he said instead. "I was to remove those who stood between you and the throne, and you were to give me free access to the Elven people in order to seek new converts to the

Children of the Hawk. I fulfilled my end of that agreement. Why do you now fail to honor yours?"

"Come, come, Skeal Eile," she soothed, moving right up against him, placing her hands on his shoulders, pressing herself against him. "Don't be like this. Things are more complicated than I imagined. I need a little more time. But consider the rewards of your patience. Teonette might lack backbone and common sense, but you do not. I might have need of a new lover and adviser. The position could open up any day now. Why should you not apply?"

He thought about it for exactly the time it took him to remove her hands and back away. "I think I will stay on the other side of that line, Elven Queen. Tempting though the offer is, I prefer my own company."

She shrugged as if it didn't matter. "Well, if you are that sort, then I understand. Suit yourself."

"But I still intend to hold you to your bargain." He gave her a smile. "Perhaps this would be a good time for you to tell me when and how you intend to honor it—your difficulties with the High Council and the Trolls notwithstanding."

She turned away. "As I said, it will take time. There has been an unexpected setback to our plans. The Princess—dear little Phryne—has escaped. I don't know how she managed it, but she got free. So now I must find her and eliminate her. Her escape does serve a purpose, of course. It suggests she is guilty as charged and might provide the excuse I need to have her killed when she resists being brought back to face her accusers. My men are out hunting her. They will find her sooner or later."

Skeal Eile shook his head. "You let her escape?"

She wheeled on him angrily. "I didn't *let* her do anything. She managed it with help from the outside. Her cousins, the Orullians, perhaps. It doesn't matter. She has nowhere to go that I cannot find her. It won't take long."

"Of course it won't," he chided. "No more than a few hours, I imagine."

She cocked an eyebrow at him. "It might go more quickly if you gave me the use of your assassin again. He seems able enough. Perhaps he could track her down and arrange another accident?"

Skeal Eile shook his head. "He is otherwise engaged." He walked over to the sofa where he had spent his time waiting on her and sat down anew, leaning back into the cushions. "Besides, you haven't finished paying for his previous use. I see no reason to lend him to you again."

"No, I suppose you don't." She stood where she was, studying him. "Very well. I shall arrange for you to be presented to the High Council in a week's time. Afterward, a public forum will be held in which you will be given an opportunity to speak of your work and of the sect. Would that suit you?"

He nodded slowly. "It will do for a beginning. At least, it would show good faith on your part."

She walked over and sat down next to him on the couch. For a moment, he was afraid she would put her hands on him again, perhaps renew her plea for services beyond what he was prepared to offer. But she kept herself at arm's length as she studied his face.

"You and I are more alike than you might care to admit," she said. "We may not be compatible in all of the ways that would make things interesting, but we do share a craving for power and its uses. You would rule the Children of the Hawk and through them, your people. I would rule the Elves. Both of us will not hesitate to remove any obstacles that stand in our way. Both of us use subterfuge, deception, and cunning to advance our interests. Other people are of no importance except insofar as they can help us achieve our goals. I do not fool myself that anything I seek is done with a righteous and noble mind-set. I do not pretend at being honorable or considerate in any way. I was poor and dismissed by everyone for years, and I will not let that happen again."

She paused. "The Trolls that besiege our valley will eventually find a way to get through our defenses—if not those of my Elves, who are skilled fighters, then certainly those of your humans, who are not. When that happens, an escape will be necessary for both of us. We cannot remain if the Trolls seize the valley. We are no match for them."

"Do not presume to speak for me," Skeal Eile warned.

"But I do presume," she said at once. "I know of your small magic. Yet I have something far more powerful. I have magic born of the

Faerie world and brought over into this one. I have Elfstones, Seraphic, and I can stand against anything."

Skeal Eile had heard of Elfstones, though he had never seen any. It was said that no one had seen them in many, many years—that no one even knew where they were at this point.

"You have possession of these?"

She smiled. "They were hidden by Phryne's grandmother, but their hiding place will be revealed to me soon enough, and then they will be mine."

He grimaced. "Will they, now? Then why is it I worry that your expectations might be unrealistic?"

"Because you do not have the faith of your convictions," she said. "And I do. I know how to get what I want. You would do well to keep me as your ally instead of threatening me with reprisals. We are both faced with a dangerous situation that could turn around on us at any moment—if not through the invasion of the Trolls, then through the interference of our own peoples."

He held her gaze for a moment without speaking. "I think that perhaps I am better prepared to face dangerous situations than you are."

Her eyes glittered. "You might do well to hope that you don't have to find out."

She stood abruptly, giving him a dazzling smile. "I think you should go now. We have an understanding. You will hear from me within the week—an official invitation to visit Arborlon and speak to the High Council and the Elven people, as promised."

He started to get up, but she quickly motioned him back again. "Oh, I don't think you should walk out with me, Seraphic. We don't want to create an appearance of impropriety. Let me send someone to escort you out."

"That's very kind," he replied with a smile. He motioned toward her face with a slow, vague gesture. "By the way, I wouldn't let those scratches go unattended. They look rather nasty."

She smiled back. "Accidents happen, Seraphic. You might want to bear that in mind."

Then she turned and was out the door before he could respond. But it didn't stop him from thinking that he would have given anything in that moment to be able to strangle her.

HE WALKED BACK through the city to the small inn at which he was staying, one frequented by non-Elven travelers, and retired to his room to brood. He could not remember the last time he had been this unhappy. What made his situation even worse was he lacked a way to change that. How could he bring Isoeld Severine to heel? He couldn't expose her by revealing her part in the death of the King without revealing his own. He couldn't send Bonnasaint after her because killing her gained him nothing; it just put him further away from his goal of persuading the Elven people to his cause. And threats were pointless. A woman like Isoeld was immune to any threats that he might muster.

He needed something else, another way to get to her, a form of leverage that would force her to do what he wanted. He had believed wrongly that he had gained that leverage by giving her what she wanted—her husband dead and herself poised to gain the throne. Where was her gratitude for that? Nowhere in sight.

What troubled him even more was her failure to take control of things when she'd had the chance. The Elven people were in shock over losing the King; they would have rallied to her at once if she had demanded it. Instead, she had dithered about with her stepdaughter's fate and tried to handle it discreetly. She might have intended to kill the girl, but she had failed to carry out the act. Now it might be too late. In spite of what the Queen thought, the girl would not be easily found. She had family and friends and allies, people who didn't like the baker's daughter who had married their King. They would help her. They would hide her. It could take weeks before anything further happened.

Weeks that none of them had. The Drouj wouldn't sit idle while the Elves worked out their internal problems. They didn't care about the Children of the Hawk or the Seraphic. Both were nothing more than obstacles to be eliminated when they invaded the valley.

Which they would do very soon, be believed. By now, they had probably found one of the passes, and that was all the help they needed. An army of Trolls of the magnitude described by Sider Ament would be more than a match for the people of the valley. They would attack and they would crush any opposition, and that would be the end of everything.

He went down to the tiny dining room and ate dinner at the common table, but spoke to no one. When he was done, he went straight to bed. He would return to Glensk Wood and await word from Bonnasaint on his efforts to eliminate the boy. At least he could count on that much. Bonnasaint wouldn't dare fail him again—not after failing him once already. Kill the boy, take his staff, and tighten his hold on the followers of the Children of the Hawk—that would put him in a better mood. It was bad enough when Sider Ament was still alive and walking the land. It was intolerable that this boy, Panterra Qu—a mere child—had taken his place and was already presuming that simply by virtue of carrying the black staff he could summon, rally, and lead the people of the valley. He had no right to make that assumption. He had no right to anything.

Once he was dead and gone, Skeal Eile would take over and the order of things would be reconfigured.

He slept late in spite of his uneasiness, and it was nearing noon before he left for his village. He borrowed a horse from a family he knew to be committed to his order and rode it hard all day and through the twilight hours. It was dark by the time he reached Glensk Wood, and he still didn't have an answer for Isoeld Severine's defiance.

But I will have that answer before this is done, he promised himself.

He gave the horse to the boy who kept watch over the animals in his small stable and trooped up to the building where he made his home—a large, blocky structure with a meeting hall on the first floor, and his living quarters and offices above. There were no lights on or people about. The door was locked, but he used a key and was inside quickly enough. He stood listening to the silence, a habit he had developed over the years, an exercise in caution he had never quite managed to put aside.

He heard nothing.

He walked through the meeting hall and climbed the stairs to his living quarters. The door leading in was locked. He used another key, pushed the door open, and walked inside.

"I thought perhaps you weren't coming back, Seraphic," a voice greeted him.

He managed not to cry out, but only barely. He looked around, searching the darkness, but couldn't see anything. He wondered for a moment if it might be Bonnasaint, since only he would be this daring, would risk violating his personal quarters by entering uninvited. But it wasn't Bonnasaint's voice.

"I'm over here," the voice said.

A flame appeared, and a candle was lit. The candle sat on a table next to a padded chair, and a man sat in the chair. Skeal Eile could only just make him out—tall, thin, pinch-faced, and craggy. Old, and not in a good way. Weathered and worn down from the inside out. But not weak. Not vulnerable, for all his appearance might suggest. Skeal Eile could tell.

"Who are you?" he asked, managing to put some iron in his voice. "Who let you into my rooms?"

The response was mild. "No one. I let myself in. I needed to speak with you, and I saw no point in waiting outside like one of your supplicants. As for who I am, I leave it to you to determine that. A man possessed of your skills and singular talents should have no trouble recognizing me."

He moved the candle off the tabletop and close to his face. Skeal Eile saw his features clearly, the same features he had made out before in the room's dimness. The candlelight sharpened and defined those features, but did not reveal the identity of the speaker. Some old itinerant dressed in ragged clothes. What was that next to him? A bundle of rags?

"I don't know you," he told the other.

"Look more closely. Look into my eyes."

Skeal Eile almost didn't. Something in the other's voice told him that he wouldn't like what he found there, that he might even be putting himself in danger. But he was still angry at the intrusion, and he wanted to reclaim the high ground in this confrontation, so he looked closely at the other's eyes and watched with terrible fascination as they changed from something human to something that wasn't.

He felt his throat tighten and his mouth go dry. He had some magic at his command and thus some insights into things that weren't known by the average man and woman. He had never seen a demon before, though he had heard about them in stories told of the old world, and he knew he was seeing one now.

"I do know you," he said.

"I thought you might. Men of your sort usually do. They see themselves in me. Or something of what they wish they were."

Skeal Eile swallowed hard. "Why are you here? What do you want with me? I didn't summon you, so you must think I have something you want. But I've got nothing to offer you."

"Perhaps you do," the other said. "But more to the point, I have something to offer you. Would you like to hear what it is?"

Even though he wasn't at all sure that he would, there was only one answer to a question like that. Skeal Eile nodded wordlessly.

"I know something about you," the demon said. "I spent most of the day learning about you, discovering who you are and what you do. I talked to people in the village about you. They were surprisingly willing to tell me things. I know all about the Children of the Hawk. I know all about your place in the community, about your ambitions and hopes, about your small talents. People are in awe of you. They fear and respect you, though not in equal measure."

He paused. "Men like you—ambitious and controlling—want much more than what they have. What is it that you want, Seraphic? Tell me. Tell me about yourself. Tell me everything."

The demon's eyes found and held his, and suddenly Skeal Eile was telling him everything. He simply started talking and found himself unable to stop. The words tumbled out of his mouth with such eagerness that he couldn't even be sure what he was saying. He might have been speaking in tongues for all he could tell. But he could see the demon smiling and nodding, and he knew that whatever he was saying was making the other happy.

"I want to be recognized as undisputed leader of all of the Children of the Hawk," he finished, exhausted. "I want the number of those who believe to increase tenfold. I want to take them from this valley, take them away and find them a new home in which to live. I want them to accept me as their spiritual adviser and mentor. I want no interference of any kind while I accomplish this."

The demon nodded. "Not so much to ask for, considering. Very well. I can give you that. I will give it all to you, if you will help me in return. Repay me for my kindness, you could say. Offer up a trade for my invaluable services. You would be willing to do this, wouldn't you?"

He didn't wait for a reply. "I came here looking for a man who carries a black staff. I caught his scent from a long way off, knew instantly of his presence and tracked him to this village. Now I discover he is dead, killed a few days back at a place called Declan Reach. Sider Ament was his name. What I have not been able to discover is what happened to the staff. The woman Aislinne Kray seems to know, but she refused to tell me. So now I am asking you. Where is it?"

Skeal Eile exhaled the breath he had been holding. Still stunned and frightened by the way in which the demon had forced him to reveal himself, he found in the other's question a glimmer of hope, a chance to turn things around. "Sider Ament gave it to a boy called Panterra Qu. He appointed the boy its new bearer."

"Where is this boy?"

The Seraphic hesitated. "I am in the process of finding that out. I have a man tracking him—a man with instructions to kill the boy and bring the staff to me. I could give it to you when he returns, if you want."

"If you keep your word, I will give you everything you want."

Skeal Eile was confused. "I don't understand. How can you make people follow me?"

The old man smiled crookedly. "You don't want to ask me that. Let me ask you something instead. Is there a girl who travels with this boy? Young, small. Do you know anyone like that?"

Skeal Eile shook his head. "The boy travels alone. There was a girl, but the Trolls have her."

The smile broadened. "Life plays so many tricks on us, Seraphic. So many." The smile died away. "I want that boy, and I want that staff. I am depending on you to produce both. If you fail me, I will abandon you. Is that understood? Do not disappoint me."

Do not disappoint me—the exact words that Skeal Eile had used in his warning to Bonnasaint on dispatching him to hunt down Panterra Qu. Was it coincidence? The demon could not possibly know this. He felt a chill ripple through him. "I won't," he whispered.

The demon got to his feet. "You should go to bed. You look exhausted. I'll be back when you have the staff in hand."

"But how will you . . . ?"

"Know? I just will. Good night."

The demon walked out of the room and disappeared down the stairs. His descent was soundless. Skeal Eile stood looking after him, listening to the silence.

He stood listening for a long time.

FIFTEEN

I

T WAS AFTER MIDNIGHT BY NOW AND TIME FOR HARD-
working men and women to be in bed and asleep, but the ragpicker had an appointment to keep. The one thing he had learned
over the long years of his life—the one thing that had served him well
in his demon work—was that humans were duplicitous. Skeal Eile was
no exception; he might have been worse than most, in fact. So the ragpicker had known better than to trust much of anything he had to say.
The Seraphic might promise he would secure the black staff from its
newest holder—this boy, Panterra Qu—but it was more likely than not
that even if he did so he would not relinquish it once he had hold of it.
A man like the Seraphic was hungry for power, and he would already
know the staff would give him command of magic beyond anything he
possessed.

So Skeal Eile would keep the staff for himself.

Or at least, he would try.

The ragpicker had been careful not to tell the Seraphic either his
suspicions or his real intentions. The other might believe that the rag-

picker trusted him to secure the staff and would simply wait around for that to happen. He might believe the ragpicker wanted the Seraphic to do the work for him. But the ragpicker had learned long ago that if you wanted something done, it was never a good idea to rely on others. Others were never as committed to achieving your goals as you were.

So let Skeal Eile think what he wanted to. Let him believe he had value. Don't reveal the truth about what he was really needed for. Don't tell him that when he provided information, he revealed far more than he knew. So much so he would have been appalled, had his understanding of what was happening not been deflected just enough to cloud his memory. Best if he remembered only certain things. Best if he didn't think too carefully on what was going to happen next.

The ragpicker's plans for the Seraphic, in fact, were complex and far reaching, and they would work best if the latter remained ignorant of true goals. Trusting the truth with such a man was a fool's game. The ragpicker had spent sufficient time during the past few days learning about the Seraphic and his order, about how the people of his village regarded him and how he conducted himself as the self-appointed leader of his sect, to know what to expect. It was enough to enable the ragpicker to take the measure of the man and to determine accurately what was needed to secure his cooperation. Just enough, not too much—that was the key to what the Seraphic needed to know.

That way he wouldn't realize he was doing the ragpicker's work until it was too late.

But first things first. Having made contact with the Seraphic and given him reason to know he was being watched, he could turn his attention to more important things. Let Skeal Eile believe the demon was only interested in the black staff. Let him believe he could manipulate and deceive with impunity. He would learn the truth quickly enough.

The ragpicker was a harsh taskmaster.

He worked his way through the sleeping village to the council hall, intent on paying a visit next to the Drouj prisoner locked away in the building's basement storeroom.

It took him only minutes to reach his destination. Once there, he stood in the shadows, hidden from prying eyes, searching for the guards on duty. There would be two, he had learned—one keeping watch from without and one stationed at the door to the makeshift prison in the basement. A double measure of protection, it was said, against any sort of escape attempt.

When he was satisfied there was no one in the building save the guards and their prisoner, the ragpicker detached himself from the shadows and walked to the main entrance. The first guard was sitting in the shadows against the veranda wall. He waited until the ragpicker had started to climb the steps before calling out to him to stop. The old man gestured vaguely, muttered something about his weary bones, and continued on until he had reached the top riser. He stopped there, stretching his arms and muttering on aimlessly.

When the guard walked over to escort him back down again, the ragpicker seized the man by the front of his tunic and cut his throat with a single swipe of his hunting knife.

Dragging the man inside, the ragpicker left him slumped in a corner of the room, bleeding out his life. It would have been quicker and less messy simply to crush his windpipe and leave him to strangle, but that form of killing wouldn't have suited his purposes in this business.

The ragpicker walked through the hall to the basement stairway and started down the steps. A voice called out to him—the other guard presumably—but he made no response. The second guard met him at the bottom of the stairs and had only just started to ask him his business when the ragpicker swiped his blade across this man's throat, too.

Amateurs, he thought.

Without bothering to move the body, the ragpicker reached down to extract the storeroom keys, stepped carefully around the spreading pools of blood, and walked over to the storeroom door. Two tries with two different keys and he heard the lock give and pulled open the door.

The prisoner was chained to a wall ring in the far corner, sitting on a pallet and looking at him through the gloom. His face, like chiseled wood, was blank and expressionless, but there was a cunning in the gleam of his eyes as he studied this newcomer.

"Arik Siq?" the ragpicker asked.

The prisoner made no reply. The ragpicker crossed the room to stand in front of him. "Are you Arik Siq or no?"

The Drouj stood up, towering over him. Tall and lean, he was so dark he was almost black. "Who are you?"

"Let's have you answer my question first. That would be the polite thing for you to do. Are you Arik Siq?"

"Who else would I be?" the other snarled. "How many prisoners are chained down here besides me?" He paused, studying the old man's face, not liking what he saw. "All right, I'll say it. I'm Arik Siq. What does it matter to you?" He looked past him toward the open door. "Where are the guards?"

"Busy with other things. How would you like to get out of here and go back to your own people?"

The Drouj stared at him. "Who are you, old man? You didn't say."

The ragpicker shrugged. "Just a traveler, come through one of the passes that lead to the outside world. I came looking for a man. He carries a black staff. I'm told he's dead. I'm told you killed him. How did you manage that?"

Arik Siq hesitated, uncertain where this was leading. "Poison darts, from a blowgun."

"Really?" The ragpicker could scarcely believe what he was hearing. "He must have been distracted not to have been able to defend himself. You are a lucky man. Lucky twice over, now that I'm here."

"You're going to set me free?"

"I am."

The Drouj shook his head. "Why would you do that? What do you want from me in return?"

The ragpicker smiled. "I understand that the man you killed gave the black staff to a boy. Apparently the boy tracked you down, captured you, and brought you here. Is that right?"

"He tricked me."

"But here you are nevertheless. If I set you free, I want you to find that staff and bring it to me. You can do what you want with the boy, but the staff is mine. Do you agree to this?"

He watched the Troll give him a quick look and then nod. "Why not? After I kill the boy, I'll bring the staff to you."

He held the old man's gaze for just a second before his eyes shifted away. The ragpicker reached out so swiftly that he had hold of the other's tunic front before there was time to react and had pulled him so close that he was breathing in his face. Arik Siq made a halfhearted attempt to break free, but then the other's free hand closed down on his shoulder, and his features twisted as if daggers had been driven into his body. Groaning, he dropped to his knees, where he remained hunched over and shaking, no longer big and threatening, no longer anything but terrified.

"Do not play games with me," the ragpicker hissed, all pretense of civility gone. "Your life is mine to do with as I choose. You give me little reason to salvage it when you lie to me like that. If you intend not to give me the black staff, then you would be wise not to lie to me about it. I can sense lies, Troll. I can sniff them out!"

"I was just . . . telling you what you . . . wanted to hear!" the other gasped. Then, in a surge of mixed bravado and fury, he added, "Why shouldn't I?"

The urge to break his neck was enormous, but the ragpicker managed to resist the impulse. "Look at me," he ordered, dropping his voice to a whisper. "Look carefully."

Arik Siq did as he was ordered, and the ragpicker let him see just enough of what he was that he could feel the Drouj shiver with recognition. He held him in check a moment longer, letting him feel his strength, giving him time to understand how helpless he was. Then he released him and stepped back.

"If you lie to me again, I will kill you," he said quietly. "Understood?"

The Troll nodded, unable to speak.

"Now tell me again that you will bring me the black staff."

"I will," the other promised, and this time the ragpicker could tell from his voice that he meant it.

"Answer this. Why are they keeping you prisoner here? Why don't they just kill you and be done with it?"

Arik Siq shook his head. "The boy thinks to trade me for the girl we keep as prisoner. Or perhaps for the lives of his people."

"You intend to invade this valley? That's who lays siege to it now, that army to the north? And you spied for them to find a way in?"

"They brought me here of their own free will. They were stupid. They betrayed themselves. They don't deserve to keep this valley. We will take it away from them and make it our new home."

The ragpicker grimaced. *Idiots, all of them.* "But you know the location of the passes now? You know how to bring your army in through either?"

"I know."

"Then bring them. I have removed the guards and opened the door. When we are finished here, you can just walk out. No one will stop you. Go from this village back to your people. Tell them what you know. Advise your father to attack Aphalion Pass because that is where most of those who will resist your invasion will be waiting. The Elves are the real danger. But you will take one hundred of your Drouj and go to Declan Reach. Do not enter the pass. Wait for me outside. Stay hidden. Look for that boy. If you see him, take possession of the staff and do with him whatever you choose. But keep the staff safe and wait for me to come to you."

"All you want is the staff? Nothing more? What if you change your mind and want the valley, as well?"

The ragpicker smiled. "The staff will be sufficient."

"The staff has magic?"

"It does. But not of the sort that would be of any use to you. Don't be foolish. Do what you have promised. Once I have the staff, I will be on my way to other places."

Arik Siq nodded, but the doubt in his eyes was clear. When you were possessed of a deceitful mind, it wasn't difficult to imagine that everyone else was the same. There was nothing the ragpicker could do about that. Not now. But if the Troll failed to do as he was told . . .

He reached down and broke the chain that held the Drouj bound to the iron ring as if it were paper. "Get out of here," he ordered. "Don't let anyone stop you. Don't forget what you are supposed to do. If you fail to follow my instructions, I will find you. Now go."

He stepped back. The Troll climbed to his feet, rubbed his arms and legs where the chain had bound him, looked once more at the old man, pulled up the hood of his cloak so that his face was obscured, and without a word went through the door and up the stairs. The ragpicker listened to the sound of his footsteps receding, staying where he was until everything was silent once more.

Then he walked from the room, satisfied that things were going as he had intended. Setting the Troll free should stir things up nicely.

With luck, he would return with his father's army in tow, which should bring the boy with the black staff running.

After all, that was the only way this matter would be settled. He didn't think for a moment that Arik Siq would manage any better than Skeal Eile to find and claim the staff and bring it to him. He would have to do that for himself. Creating the right conditions for luring the bearer to where he would be waiting was the trick.

He went up the stairs and out the door of the council hall, the night black and empty around him. Sunrise was still hours away; the people of the village still slept.

He allowed himself a small smile. One more task needed doing this night. He was anxious to get it done.

THE DEMON HAD COME into the valley for the express purpose of finding the man and the black staff and destroying both. It was a search that had been ongoing for months, so there was no particular expectation that it would happen quickly. The demon was patient in the way of most demons, and so encountering obstacles and overcoming difficulties was expected. Moreover, it had no special plan for achieving its goals, but simply waited to see what it would find once it got close enough to determine that an end to its search was in sight.

Encountering the girl in the ruins had been the first real indication that the hunt was winding down. Finding his way to this village and speaking with its people had reinforced that hope. But it was Skeal Eile who had provided him with the necessary tools. The Seraphic had given him so much more to work with, information and insights alike, and now it could employ its usual tactics to create the sort of disruption that would bring the bearer of the staff right to him.

He was sowing the seeds that would grow that crop this very night. Not in a way that anyone would suspect—because he needed to go unnoticed among humans if he were to be effective—but by letting the humans themselves do his work for him.

It was so easy. Humans were predictable creatures. They were prisoners of their own emotions, unable to prevent themselves from repeating the same mistakes over and over. They might try to change, but

in the end they always reverted. Their moral codes and need for a sense
of place in the world and dependency on one another doomed them
from the cradle and led them to the grave. They would never change,
and the demon would not have it any other way.

The ragpicker found Aislinne Kray's cottage without difficulty, remembering correctly the paths that led there. The house was dark and
quiet, but he stood outside for a time making sure he was missing
nothing. He had not forgotten the gnarled little man who had appeared out of nowhere on his last visit, an ugly little watchdog clearly
much more dangerous than he appeared. He could see the proprietary
interest in the woman reflected in the little man's eyes, and he suspected that it was not to be taken lightly. He could kill the other easily enough, but once again that might draw attention he was trying to
avoid.

Especially this night.

But eventually, he decided there was no one keeping watch and
whoever was in the house was sleeping soundly. So he made his way
around to the rear of the cottage, opened the simple latch lock with little more than a touch, and stepped inside.

He stood where he was once again, listening. He had known he
would be coming back here from the moment Aislinne Kray had ordered him off the property. Her sense of entitlement grated on him
even now, and he knew he would not be satisfied until he had found
a way to make her pay. His plan for her had solidified while he had
listened to the Seraphic ramble on about his various schemes and
machinations—particularly the one detailing how he had helped the
Queen of the Elves murder her husband.

It was in that dark story that he had found the beginnings of an
idea for his revenge.

It would be particularly fitting given her relationship with the orig-
inal bearer of the black staff, whose unexpected demise had cheated
him of the chance at a killing he would have relished. At least he could
make her suffer in his stead. There was order and symmetry to that.

He finished his vigil, satisfied that nothing was amiss, and began to
move through the cottage. He took his time, pausing often in his
search. He had to be careful not to wake her unexpectedly. He had no
knowledge of where to find her bedroom, or of her sleeping habits. If

he made a hasty or wrong move, he would lose her. She was not some-one he could scare easily or panic into doing something foolish. His best chance was to catch her asleep and dispose of her before she knew what was happening.

When he had gone far enough through the downstairs to eliminate any reasonable possibility that she was there—convinced that the bed-rooms were on the second floor, pretty much as he had expected—he climbed the stairs leading up, his footsteps so silent he might have been a cat. He could move so when it was needed—silent and weight-less. He could slow his breathing and even his heart rate, become little more than a wraith passing through with the night.

He found her asleep and alone in her bed. Her husband had not re-turned from his culling of able-bodied men to defend the pass at Declan Reach. The ragpicker watched her as she slept, wanting to make sure of the deepness of that sleep. Then he crossed the bedroom, bent over carefully, and pinched the nerves of her neck just so, render-ing her unconscious. She never woke, barely moved. He smiled at this. He liked the feeling of power it generated inside him.

Wrapping her in a blanket, he picked her up, slung her effortlessly over one bony shoulder, and carried her back downstairs, her long hair trailing down his back. No one appeared to impede him, although by this time they would be too late in any case. That troublesome little man who protected her was nowhere to be found. Her husband had not returned. She was alone, and she was completely his.

He bore her back through the village to the council hall, encoun-tering no one, entered the hall anew, and trudged down the basement stairs to where he had left the second guard sprawled on the floor. Tak-ing away the blanket, he laid her next to the dead man, making sure she was resting in the still-spreading pool of his blood. He took time to smear some of that blood on her clothing and hands and even her face. Then he stretched out her right arm toward the dead man's throat and curled her fingers around the knife that had killed him.

Rudimentary, but effective. The formula had already worked once for Skeal Eile and the Queen of the Elves when they had killed the King and made it appear as if it was his daughter who had done it. The Seraphic had told him so. It was this story that had given the ragpicker the idea.

He rose and studied his handiwork. It would look as if she had killed both guards and set Arik Siq free. Why she would have done this and what had happened afterward would be anyone's guess. Had he deceived her with false promises? Had she collapsed on discovering the truth? Had he chosen to leave her behind? Speculation would abound and would cause further disruption in the lives of the villagers. That, in turn, would give the rest of his plan a better chance of working out the way he intended.

Whatever the case, by the time things got straightened out—if they ever did—the staff would be in his possession and he would be far away. The whole point of this exercise was to create enough trouble for the inhabitants of the valley that they wouldn't notice what he was about. He didn't really care how any of this turned out for these people.

Because within a matter of weeks, they would all be dead.

SIXTEEN

"WHAT ARE WE GOING TO DO, PAN?" PRUE STARED at him with her strange, empty eyes, but the turbulence of her emotions was clearly revealed by the expression on her face. "Do you think he's telling us the truth?"

They had moved off to one side, safely away from their prisoner's hearing, standing close with heads bent so they were almost touching. The day around them was growing steadily brighter with the rising of the sun, and the meres were shimmering with dampness and shifting mist. Waterbirds called to one another, and in flashes of brightly colored feathers they appeared and then vanished like ghosts in the haze.

"I don't know," Panterra admitted. "But I can't see what lying to us gains him. Why would he make this story up? He knows we're not going to let him go, even if we don't take him to Arborlon."

"He doesn't sound like he's lying," she agreed.

"Even if any part of it is true, we don't want to risk what might happen if we deliver him to the Queen without first knowing the truth. Even if we go before the High Council and let him tell them what he's told us, we could be in a lot of danger. The Queen could find a way to turn the story around on us. She could make it out that we're somehow involved in what's happened. There's no reason the High Council should choose to believe us over her. We don't have any proof about any of this. It's Bonnasaint's word against hers, and that's not enough."

"But we have to do something. We have to help Phryne, no matter what."

He nodded. "Well, we can't help her if we're locked up with her."

As if of the same mind, they glanced over at Bonnasaint, who sat staring off into the distance, distracted. "Too bad we can't leave him here," Pan muttered.

"If we did, he couldn't tell his story. Somehow we have to find a way to let him do that, and we have to make the Elves believe it."

Pan looked at her. "Well, that shouldn't be too difficult, should it?"

They smiled as one. "So what are we going to do?" she repeated.

He thought about it. He was still shaken by the events of the previous night, still rattled by the idea that someone wanted them dead badly enough to send an assassin. Certainly, Skeal Eile had no love for them. But even so, this seemed a bit drastic. What could killing them gain the Seraphic?

"What if," he suggested, "just one of us goes into Arborlon to find Tasha and Tenerife and then brings them back for a meeting? Maybe then we will have a better idea about what we should do."

She cocked her head. "But you swore we wouldn't let ourselves become separated again. No matter what."

He looked at her uncomfortably. "I haven't forgotten. But what choice do we have? We can't leave Bonnasaint alone. We can't even leave him unwatched."

She glanced over at the assassin and then back at Pan. "All right. Just this once. But not again, Pan. Promise me."

He put his hands on her shoulders and squeezed gently. "I promise."

Getting Bonnasaint back on his feet, Pan tied his hands in front of him, then lashed them to his waist and, using a length of cord, fashioned a leash by which he could be led. Bonnasaint grumbled about being trussed up, but the boy and the girl ignored him.

"Where are you taking me?" he asked finally, watching them shoulder their packs in preparation for leaving.

"To Arborlon," Pan advised. "We have friends we can ask for help. They might have a better idea about what to do with you. Don't worry. We won't take you to the Queen."

"You would be wise not to for your own sakes."

Pan walked over. "Don't think for a moment we won't give you to the Queen if we find out you've been lying to us. We don't have any reason to care about what happens to you. We only care about Phryne Amarantyne. To the extent that you can be of help to her, then you are useful to us. Otherwise . . ."

He left the rest unsaid and turned away. Bonnasaint snorted derisively, but otherwise didn't respond.

The boy and the girl shouldered their backpacks, and with Bonnasaint in tow they set out. Both knew the meres well enough to navigate them safely in daylight, but even so they chose a route that kept them close to the northern edges of the lakes, angling their way east toward Arborlon. The sun was fully risen now, and the mists of early morning had begun to diminish, although patches still lingered here and there, thick and smudgy against the mix of daylight and shadows, trapped within thick stands of trees and along the shores of bodies of water that glimmered like mirrors.

"I wish this were all over," Prue whispered to Pan, keeping her voice low and the conversation between the two of them.

He noted the scowl on her face and smiled. "So things could go back to being the way they were? Just you and me and tracking?"

She nodded. "Just you and me and tracking."

He shook his head. "Maybe things won't ever go back to how they were, Prue. Have you thought about that? I mean, after this is over, however it gets resolved, maybe things will have changed so completely that they can't ever be the same. The valley isn't a safe haven like it was. The outside world has found us, and nothing can change that. Like the Drouj, other things will be coming."

"I know." She lowered her voice a notch further. "But that's not what I meant. It can't be the same between you and me. That's the part that really hurts. *We* can't be the same. You've got that black staff, and you'll be just like Sider Ament—a wanderer, a protector of the people of the valley. You won't be a Tracker anymore. Not like you were with me. And I won't be a Tracker because of my eyes. I might not be blind, but I can't tell colors and that's enough of a handicap to keep me from doing my job. I have to do something else with my life."

"It will work itself out. We'll find a way." He wanted to put an arm around her or ruffle her thatch of red hair, but he couldn't do that with Bonnasaint watching. "Besides, we couldn't go back to just being Trackers like we were in any case. The valley, the people living in it, the way we were all once safe here and protected—it will all be different."

She nodded. "It will, and I won't like it, either. I already don't like what's happened. I'm fifteen years old, and I look like I'm blind and you and I are fighting for our lives and the whole valley could be over-run with Trolls at any moment. We have to do something with a man who's tried to kill us, but not something that would let him be killed. We don't have a home anymore because it's too dangerous to go back to the one we had. We have to help Phryne, and we don't have any idea how to do that. We don't even know how to help ourselves. We're just running around in circles, trying to protect each other. Nothing makes sense."

Pan didn't say anything for a moment. "You could do something to help yourself if you left all this up to me and went home."

She glared at him. "You make it sound like that's something I would actually do. Are you deliberately trying to make me ashamed of myself?"

"I'm offering you a way out. Your mother and father might appreciate that. You didn't ask for any of this. I was the one who took the staff from Sider when he was dying. I was the one who made the decision to take on his responsibilities. I didn't expect you to try to help me. I never expected that."

"So now you insult me, too. 'Go home, I don't need you.' What sort of person would I be if I did what you're asking?" She was fuming. "And you want me to believe you didn't expect me to try to help?"

"No. I did, actually. I just didn't want it to happen. I thought you were still a prisoner of the Drouj. I thought I was coming to rescue you, not the other way around."

He paused, collecting himself. "It isn't that I don't want you here with me. I do. I always do. I always will. There's no one I could ever depend upon more than you. But what's happening now is dangerous beyond anything we've ever run up against, Prue. What sort of person would I be if I didn't ask you to think it over before you got yourself any more deeply involved than you already are? What if something happens to you? How would I ever forgive myself?"

"What if something happens to *you*? How would *I* ever forgive *myself*?" she parroted. "It works both ways, Pan."

"But it's not the same thing!"

"Because I'm fifteen and you're seventeen?"

"Because you don't have to do this and I do!"

She gave him a withering look. "If you believe that, you need to have somebody besides me explain to you what friendship is all about!" He started to protest, but she held up one hand quickly. "No, don't say anything more. You'll only make it worse. Keep talking, and you'll eventually sound like a complete idiot instead of just a half-wit. This discussion is over. I am staying with you. Mark it in stone. I'm not changing my mind."

"It could change if you wanted it to." He gave it one last try. "You always have a choice."

"I know that, and I've made it. The King of the Silver River thinks you need my help. He's given me back the use of my instincts to see that you're kept safe. I won't walk away from my responsibility for you any more than you would give up yours for the people of our valley. It's not exactly the same, but it's close enough. You and me, Pan. That's the way it has always been and that's the way it's always going to be. Now shut up and keep walking!"

She said this last so loudly that Bonnasaint, who had been paying scant attention to their whisperings until now, laughed aloud.

"You don't want to cross the line with that one," he observed brightly.

Panterra started to go after him, but Prue wheeled around first, blocking his way, and took five quick steps so that she was standing right in front of their prisoner. "Don't say anything more, Bonnasaint. If you speak even a single word, I will tie you to the nearest tree and leave you for the wolves to find. Pan won't stop me, either."

She held his gaze for a long moment, waiting. He smiled but kept silent. Satisfied, she returned to Pan's side, and they resumed walking.

By midday, they had come in sight of the bluffs on which Arborlon was settled. They could see Elves walking the heights and smell the smoke from the cooking fires. The day had gone warm and the wind still, and there was a sultry feel to the air.

Panterra brought them to a halt. "This is probably close enough," he advised Prue, speaking to her out of Bonnasaint's hearing. "Can you wait here with him while I find the Orullians?"

"I can," she replied. "But I don't think that's the best plan. You should be the one who stays. I'll have a better chance of wandering about as a blind girl. Someone might recognize Sider's staff, and I don't think you want that just yet."

He saw the wisdom in her suggestion and reluctantly agreed. He didn't like letting her out of his sight, now that he had found her again. But that was selfish thinking, so he abandoned it. "Go," he said.

Leaving her backpack behind, she set out for the city. Pan took Bonnasaint into the trees, tethered him to one with the rope, dropped his own backpack beside Prue's, and sat down to wait. The day eased past noontime and into the early afternoon, a slow, lazy passage that made him drowsy as he sat watching his prisoner and thinking of Prue. But he knew how not to fall asleep when on watch, and soon it was the assassin who was sleeping, his head drooping and his snores audible in the silence of the woods. Pan kept an eye out for Elves, as well, but none of them had reason to venture this far afield and none came close to where he waited.

Prue was right about things changing and never going back to the way they were. He hadn't taken time to think about it before, but he did so now. They might not even be living in the valley when this was over. They might be somewhere else entirely. Would they even be together? Could he keep her with him when he carried the black staff and the burden of responsibility that bearing it entailed? He tried to see the future—any future—but it was hazy and out of reach. Too much blocked his vision of what might be. Too many uncertainties made it impossible to think it through clearly.

He was staring into space, seeing nothing, when Bonnasaint spoke.

"This isn't going to end well for you," he said, suddenly awake. "You know that, don't you?"

Maybe he had been faking sleep all along to see if Pan would drop his guard. The boy couldn't tell. "Let me worry about that."

"Oh, I don't worry about it. And I do want you to be the one who does. But I think I should say it aloud, so that you understand. You won't be able to keep me prisoner for long. Others have tried. They're all dead. You're just a boy. You might be a Tracker, but you aren't like me. You can't do what I do. You don't know what I know about staying alive. Sooner or later, you will make a mistake."

Pan nodded. "I already made one. I didn't tape your mouth shut. Should I correct that mistake now?"

Bonnasaint went silent, smiling. But he kept his eyes on Pan and didn't take them off. He was like a cat with a mouse. The boy could feel it. He was aware of the danger of keeping this man close. But he had to try to help Phryne, and this was the only way he could think to do it.

Anyway, by tonight the assassin would be someone else's problem.

It was late afternoon by the time Prue returned, the light failing as the sun slipped west toward the mountains and the mists crept down out of the heights and up from the depths to gather in the woods. She appeared quite suddenly, coming from a different direction than he had anticipated, but walking toward him with purpose. He started to ask what she had found, but she took his arm and led him farther away from Bonnasaint, making it clear that she didn't want their prisoner to hear what she had to say.

"Phryne's escaped," she told him, keeping her back to Bonnasaint. "Or she was rescued, whichever. No one seems to know. It happened sometime last night. The guard was found sleeping, the cell in which she'd been locked up left empty. The Queen is furious. Elven Hunters are searching everywhere, but so far there's been no sign of her."

"What about the Orullians? Maybe she went to them. Maybe they're hiding her."

Prue shook her head. "Not likely. The Orullians are part of a detachment holding down Aphalion Pass. They were already up there when the King was murdered and Phryne imprisoned. Word is, the Queen didn't want them anywhere near their cousin and ordered them kept there. Unless they found a way to sneak out of the pass and away from the other Elves, they're still on watch."

"If they abandoned their post, it would be noticed." Pan thought about it a moment. "But once she escaped, wouldn't Phryne go to them?"

"How would she do that? How would she even get close?" Prue grabbed his arm. "But she might have tried getting word to them that she was free. She might have done that."

"Or she might have gone to her grandmother."

"I thought about that. But they say her grandmother is missing. Some say the Queen had her killed. There are all sorts of rumors float-ing about. No one quite believes that Phryne killed her father. They wonder if the Queen is lying. But she's the Queen, and she has the support of the first minister and the Elven Home Guard. So no one can do much."

"Well, opinions won't change much in Phryne's favor now that she's disappeared. It makes her look guilty. I wonder where she's gone?"

Prue cocked an eyebrow. "I think we need to ask the Orullians."

Pan agreed. "For the moment, we should move farther up the mountain, away from the city. We're too close if they send out search parties."

She started to turn away. "Wait," he said, reaching for her arm. She looked back at him, waiting. "Did anyone recognize you? Or ask who you were?"

"Some asked if they could help me. I played at being blind. A few offered food and coins, but I told them I was one of the Children of the Hawk, come to Arborlon on a pilgrimage. They left me alone then."

"But you're sure about the Orullians not being there?"

She nodded impatiently. "Both up in Aphalion Pass. Come on, Pan. Let's go."

They strapped on their backpacks, released Bonnasaint from the tree to which he was tethered, checked his bonds, took up the leash, and set out anew. When Bonnasaint asked them what they intended to do with him, Pan told him they were going up into the mountains to find someone who would help hide him. Pan could tell from the look on his face that the assassin didn't like the idea. But he didn't care what Bonnasaint liked or didn't like. Bonnasaint would do what he was told and go where he was led. He was lucky they were taking him with them at this point. He was more trouble than he was worth, and he wasn't worth all that much now that Phryne was free. He might still be able to help them prove her innocence, but the boy was growing less and less convinced that the assassin would willingly provide any real help when it came down to it.

He was stunned by the turn of events involving Phryne. Who had freed her if not the Orullians? No one else would dare to defy the Queen and the Home Guard. Nor did he believe that Phryne possessed skills that would have allowed her to escape. The most likely scenario involved a careless guard and a door unwittingly left open— something of that sort.

But he kept his thoughts to himself, and he made it a point to warn Prue not to reveal to their prisoner anything of what had happened. He wasn't sure that it mattered if Bonnasaint knew about Phryne's escape, but he couldn't see any benefit in telling him, either. Better if he were left to wonder what their intentions for him really were.

They climbed into the foothills until it was dark and made camp in a grove of cedars that hid them from view and sheltered them from the wind, which had picked up again. Tethering Bonnasaint to a fresh tree, they set about fixing a meal, building a fire, and warming bread and what was left of the salted meat they had brought. They added some potatoes and carrots—the last of those, as well, because they hoped to be able to get fresh supplies at the Elven camp on the morrow. Originally, Pan had thought they would resupply in Arborlon, but he had abandoned that plan the moment Prue had returned with the news about Phryne.

Sitting by the fire with his food in front of him, he found himself wondering how he had gotten to this point in his life. Not that he didn't understand the choices or the circumstances that had determined the nature of his journey, because he did. He understood them all too well. It was mostly that he had trouble determining at what point his life had changed direction so completely that he had gone down the road that had brought him here. It might have been his decision to follow those strange footprints that he and Prue had discovered all those weeks ago when they had tracked the agenahls. But he couldn't be sure. Looking back, it was all jumbled and blurred, his memories of things no longer as clear as they had been. Or even as important, he conceded. What difference at this point did it make how he had gotten to where he was?

And yet it did. It mattered. He wanted the sense of order and purpose he believed understanding would give him.

He was still pondering this dilemma when Prue said, "I'd better feed our friend."

WHAT HAPPENED NEXT might have been avoided if either she or Pan had been a little more careful or better rested or if her newly revitalized instincts had been able to detect even a hint of what Bonnasaint was so carefully hiding. But the assassin was good at concealing things, and he did so successfully here.

Prue picked up the plate of food that she had left warming by the fire and walked over to where Bonnasaint sat watching. He gave her a smile, which she ignored, and said, almost cheerfully, "I was afraid you were going to let me starve."

"No danger of that," she replied, moving over to kneel beside him. "Just lean forward a little so that I can feed you. There's ale, as well. Here, try this."

She reached out with a spoonful of carrots and potatoes, and in the next instant his arms were around her neck and his fingers were folded across her face. Spoon and plate went flying as she was jerked about and captured in his embrace, arms pinned to her sides. She felt something warm and slick against her skin from where his hands gripped her face and saw patches of red on the sleeves of his tunic.

Blood.

He had rubbed so hard at his bonds that he had torn the skin around his wrists and used his own blood to slip the ropes that bound him.

Panterra was already on his feet and rushing to her aid when Bonnasaint shouted for him to stop. "Don't come any closer, boy. If you do, I'll pop her eyes right out of their sockets. I know how to do it; I've done it before. You might think you can stop me, but you'll never reach me in time. How will you feel if that happens? How would you like it if she were *really* blind? Throw down that staff."

Through gaps in Bonnasaint's fingers where they latticed over her face, Prue saw Pan hesitate. "Do it!" the other screamed. "How blind do you want her to be? More blind than she is? More than she pretends to be? Throw down the staff!"

Pan did as he was told and stood watching. "You don't even have a weapon," he pointed out. "You can't get away."

"I always have weapons—even if they are only the fingers on my hands. I warned you that this would end badly. Now you see. Drop your knives, as well. Then move off to one side."

Some of Bonnasaint's blood had leaked from his wrists and down Prue's face, and she could taste it on her lips, bitter and metallic. She wanted to spit it out, to clean it away, but his fingers were stretched across her mouth. She tried struggling, but his hold on her tightened at once.

"Patience, little one," he purred. "Be good, and I won't harm either of you. I just want to get away. That's all."

She knew without having to think about it that he was lying. He had no intention of leaving them alive. That wasn't who he was. Once he had them under his control, he would kill them both. He wouldn't give it a second thought.

How could I have been so careless? How could I not have noticed that the bonds were loose on his wrists? Even my instincts weren't enough to smell this out! She cursed herself for being such a fool, for leaving herself open to this sort of attack. She was supposed to be protecting Pan, but she couldn't even seem to protect herself.

Bonnasaint lurched to his feet, hauling her up with him. "Now this is what's going to happen," he said to Panterra. "I'm going to leave and I'm taking her with me to make certain you don't do anything foolish. Don't try coming after me or you'll find pieces of her scattered along the way. Just stay right here. I'll let her go when I've gotten far enough away that I feel safe. She can walk back from there."

He paused, and then added, "I'll need to take your knives with me. You don't mind, do you?"

Prue suddenly remembered her own knife, tucked in her belt just under the loose front of her tunic, down beneath where his arms encircled her. She moved her right hand experimentally—just a little—to feel the hilt beneath her fingers.

"I'm not letting you have a weapon," Panterra said at once.

"You aren't in a position to argue about it. Now, don't move."

Bonnasaint began working his way across the clearing toward the discarded knives, dragging Prue with him. The lurching movements allowed her to squirm and shift without drawing his attention. She worked her hand under her tunic front, and her fingers closed about the handle of her knife.

"I might have to take your staff, as well," Bonnasaint added suddenly, flashing Panterra a grin. "Just to make certain you do what you're told. I can leave it behind with the girl when I let her go."

He wouldn't do that, Prue thought. He wouldn't leave anything behind but bodies, not once he had possession of Pan's knives. He was saying one thing, but he was planning something else entirely. He wasn't the kind to leave anything to chance. He had been sent to kill them, tried once already and failed. He would finish the job this time.

They were standing over Pan's discarded weapons. "Just stay calm," Bonnasaint was saying as he loosened his grip on Prue and reached down.

Prue closed her eyes. She had never used a knife on anyone. But she had to do this. She had to make herself do it.

As Bonnasaint's fingers brushed the hilt of Pan's knife, Prue yanked her own from its hiding place, wrenched herself about so that she was looking directly at him—her face so close to his that she could feel the sudden exhalation of his breath and see the frantic recognition in his eyes—and drove the knife into his midsection all the way to the hilt.

Bonnasaint screamed and clutched at her, trying to hold her fast. She fought against him, breaking free as his strength failed and the shock of what was happening paralyzed him. He staggered backward, pushing himself away from her, reaching down for the knife in his stomach. There was blood everywhere, and Prue could not look away. His eyes were locked on hers as he dropped to his knees.

He was still alive when Pan reached her, wrapped his arms about her protectively, and moved her back. Then he toppled over, his eyes empty and fixed, his body rigid.

Strangely, she did not find herself crying. The last few moments were so surreal she could hardly believe they had even happened. She knew what she had done. She had done what she needed to do. She had kept Pan alive. Wasn't that all there was to it?

Then something akin to rage surged through her as the full impact of her actions flattened her momentary calm and everything began to slant sideways.

"We're going to need a new plan," she said to Pan, and then, finally, she managed to look away.

SEVENTEEN

PRUE SPENT THE NIGHT WRAPPED IN PAN'S ARMS, pressed close against him beneath their blankets. She slept a little, although not much, and he stayed awake with her, conscious of the changes in her breathing, of the moments when images of what she had done surfaced and caused her to shiver uncontrollably, and of the dreams that turned to nightmares and made her cry out. She was not handling this well—although he could hardly find reason to think that he would have handled it any better—so he did what he could to help her through it.

They left Bonnasaint pretty much where he had died, Pan taking time to move him out of the open and beneath a huge old cedar where he could be concealed by heavy boughs and hidden from view. He would have done more, even for someone as loathsome as the assassin, but he lacked a digging tool and there were few rocks at this level that he could use to build a cairn. So he did what he could to protect the body, knowing that in the end nature would do the rest.

Sometime during the night he fell asleep, and when he woke the sun was just cresting the mountain peaks, the sky was thick with rain clouds, and Prue was gone.

He panicked, throwing off his blanket and hurriedly pulling on his boots, looking everywhere at once as he did so. Once on his feet, he shouted her name, heedless of who might hear, and was relieved when she called back. He followed the sound of her voice to a break in the trees that allowed a clear view of the valley south and found her sitting on a grassy patch looking out over the countryside.

"Don't do that again!" he snapped irritably. "I didn't know what had happened to you!"

She gave him a wan smile. "Sorry. I just couldn't sleep anymore—or even pretend to sleep—so I got up and came here to think. I forgot that you would be waking up."

She looked so beaten down that he instantly regretted his words. "I just got frightened, that's all. It isn't your fault."

"That's about the only thing that isn't." She looked away again. "I really messed us up, Pan."

The way she spoke the words was troubling. She sounded as if she had given up. "You did what you had to do and there's nothing wrong with that. If you hadn't killed him, he would have killed us. You know that."

"I keep thinking that if I could have wounded him . . . or used the knife on his arms or legs and just . . ."

He put his arm around her and hushed her. "You could have *tried* to do a lot of things. But any one of them would have gotten you killed. You did the one thing that would save us both." He paused, trying to find something more to say, to speak the words that would reassure her. "You did what the King of the Silver River asked you to do. You protected me. And yourself. You didn't mess us up."

She shook her head in denial, but said nothing.

"He was too dangerous to keep around anyway. I should have gotten rid of him earlier. I should have taken him into Arborlon and let the Queen have him. He wasn't going to help us anyway. He was sent to kill us, and he meant to do exactly that."

She nodded, but still said nothing.

"You know he wasn't going to let you go. Or me. You know that, don't you?"

"I do." She looked at him again, and he saw that she was crying. "What I don't know is how I'm going to live with what I did. I killed him. I don't want to be someone who kills people. I know it was necessary and that he was going to kill us and I didn't have a choice. I know all that. Rationally. But in my heart I also know that none of that matters." She caught her breath. "I am breaking apart, Pan. I am all in pieces about this, and I don't know what to do about it."

He watched her silently, unable to think of what else to say. "You didn't have a choice," he repeated finally. "You had to kill him."

"Stop saying that!" She ran her fingers through her red hair as if to pull it all out. "Just stop!"

"What else am I supposed to say? You did the best you could. You can get past this. Give it a little time, Prue. Stop torturing yourself."

She was on her feet then, standing over him as if she might crush him with the weight of her rage. "You stop patronizing me, then! Stop treating me like a child! You want to know what you can do? I don't know! I don't know what *I* can do, so how am I supposed to know what to tell you? Figure it out for yourself. Be my big brother and tell me something that matters. Tell me whatever I need to hear, no matter how unpleasant. Just be honest with me!"

She wheeled away and stalked to the edge of the clearing, hands on her hips, head bent, shoulders shaking. She was crying hard now, but seemed enraged that she was doing so. Or that she was in the place she had found herself. Or that the world had mistreated her so. Or all of the above. In truth, he couldn't say.

"I know one thing I can tell you!" he shouted over to her. "I can tell you that no matter how bad you feel about yourself or me, no matter what happens next or how things turn out, I will be right there with you all the way! I can tell you that!"

She didn't say anything, and she didn't stop crying. He stood up, but he didn't try to go to her. He stayed where he was, waiting her out. If there was anything more to say, she would have to say it. He was all out of words that mattered.

It took a long time, but eventually her body stilled and her head lifted. She stood where she was, looking out across the valley. Then she wiped her eyes, turned around, and came back over to him. Instead of stopping she walked right past him.

"That's more like it," she said. "Let's get our packs and start walking. We don't want to waste any more time reaching Tasha and Tenerife."

He followed her progress as she disappeared into the trees, heading back to their camp. He wanted to tell himself or maybe even her that he would never understand women, but he had a feeling he wasn't the first man to formulate this opinion and very likely wouldn't be the last and that it really didn't matter anyway. So dismissing this useless assessment, he took a deep breath, exhaled loudly, put the entire matter behind him, and tramped after her.

▲ ● ■

WITHIN THIRTY MINUTES, they were hiking through what remained of the foothills heading up into the mountains toward Aphalion Pass.

For the first two hours of their trek, they barely spoke at all, concentrating on the climb, hiding within a shroud of silence where they could think things through. The day remained cloudy and gray, the sun little more than a hazy glow behind the cloud layers, the temperature dropping and the winds growing stronger as they continued their ascent. Once or twice, they saw goats and sheep higher up on the rocky precipices and in patches of meadow only a short distance below the snow line, but nothing of Men or Elves or anything else that walked on two legs. They would have stopped to eat, but there was no food left save for a little bread and water, which they shared as they walked.

More than a few times, Panterra thought to say something further about the events of the previous night, but each time he felt the temptation he resisted it. He knew that nothing he said at this point would help the situation. Prue would talk about it again when she was ready and he had to leave it at that.

So when he finally began talking again, he chose the matter of what they were going to do now that Bonnasaint was no longer with them.

"You said last night we needed a new plan," he opened the conversation, trying to sound relaxed and casual. "I guess the first thing we have to do is pretty much the same as before. We have to find Phryne."

She shrugged. "Except that if Tasha and Tenerife don't know where she is or have some idea of how to find her, we might need to start worrying about that demon. He won't be waiting around for us to finish helping Phryne. He'll already be looking for us."

"First, he has to find his way into the valley."

"He will have already done that."

He glanced at her. "All right. But he would have to find out that we live in Glensk Wood and start looking there."

"He would have found out all about us by now, including that we live in Glensk Wood. You didn't meet him. You can't know what he was like. He isn't human, though he looks it on the surface." She paused. "He'll have found out everything, and he'll be searching already."

Panterra thought about it. "Then maybe we need to find him before he finds us."

She shook her head. "That's a dangerous game. I don't know that finding him at all is the right thing."

"What are we supposed to do? Do you think he will give up looking for us and go away?"

"Don't be smart with me. You know he won't. But maybe something will happen to him in the meantime. Demons can be killed. We know that from our history. The boy Hawk killed one. Kirisin Belloruus killed another. I think his sister killed one, too. Isn't that so?"

He gave her a quick smile. "I don't know that we can count on someone else doing what I think we've been given to do. Think about it. The King of the Silver River sent you back to protect me. That suggests he suspects—maybe knows—that sooner or later I'm going to need you with me to face this demon, because I *am* going to have to face him."

They walked on in silence awhile more, watching the snow line grow steadily closer. It wasn't far now to Aphalion Pass. Ahead, high above the rock-strewn slopes, winged predators circled in slow, steady sweeps. Now and again, one would drop like a stone to snare its prey.

Which are we? Predator or prey?

Pan wondered if they had a choice.

It was past midday when the pass came in sight, its dark split clearly visible even in the diminished light of the cloudy day. When they were still five hundred yards away, an Elf appeared from hiding to challenge them. Pan told him they were friends of Tasha and Tenerife, and the sentry seemed persuaded just by mention of the Orullians and did not ask them anything more, although he did take note of Prue's eyes and gave her more than one close look. Satisfied that they posed no threat, he took them up into the pass where most of the Elven Hunters were still working on building their defenses.

It was an impressive effort. By now the Elven fortifications were more than forty feet high and a dozen feet thick at the narrow point in which they had been established. Ladders and walkways gave the defenders access to the ramparts on the near side; sheer walls with no hand- or footholds confronted attackers on the far. Higher up on the cliffs, crevices in the rocks had been turned into defensive bastions, as well. Any attack force coming down the length of the pass would be vulnerable from three sides and have no cover whatsoever. It seemed as if the Elven position was impregnable.

But Pan didn't like close places, always preferring to be out in the open, and he knew that he wouldn't want to be a defender stationed here in this narrow place, no matter how safe it seemed.

Their guide took them over the wall and then led them ahead through the pass to where Tasha was visible working with other Elves on a set of snares and traps that would serve as perimeter defenses.

"Panterra Qu!" Tasha boomed out with obvious pleasure as he caught sight of the other. "Well met, brother!"

While Tenerife shouted down greetings from his perch high up in the rocks, the big man hurried over to the newcomers. "Little sister, too!" Tasha grinned, but the grin fell away when he got close enough to see the girl's milky eyes. "Shades, what's this? Your eyes, Prue! What's happened here?"

He embraced the boy and then the girl, holding the latter much longer and tighter and whispering softly to her. For a moment, Pan thought the big man was going to cry, which would have been a first for him. But Prue said something back, and from Tasha's reaction—holding her at arm's length for a closer look at her eyes—it could be assumed that she had told him she wasn't as blind as it might seem.

Giving Panterra a puzzled glance, he took them both in tow and led them over to where Tenerife was already climbing down to join them. They went through the same thing with the latter once he saw Prue's eyes, but she quickly calmed him down and then Tasha moved all of them ahead into the pass where they could be alone.

Settled back in a depression in the cliff wall, standing in a loose knot, they gave one another anxious looks.

"Well, here you are," Tenerife began, giving Prue yet another hug. "Safe and sound in spite of our fears. Welcome back."

"Tell us what happened to you," Tasha demanded. "You're not really blind, you said? But you seem so. Your eyes say you are. Tell us everything."

Prue did, mostly. She left out the parts about Bonnasaint, preferring to wait on that, telling the brothers only that after returning from her encounter with the demon and the King of the Silver River and finding Pan, the two had come looking for Phryne to see if there was anything they could do to help free her.

"But when I went into the city looking for information, pretending to be a blind pilgrim, I was told she had escaped," she finished. "So we came here to see if you knew anything."

Tasha grunted. "We know a lot, and we'll tell you if you think you can keep it to yourself. That wild child, Xac Wen, came here some days ago after we found out that Phryne was charged with her father's murder and imprisoned. We knew that wasn't right, and we were afraid for her. The Queen doesn't like Phryne, and we thought she might do her harm. So we sent the boy back with instructions to break her free and bring her here. He's a capable boy; we knew he could do it. He must have done so, since she's gone."

"But we've heard nothing from her since," Tenerife added. "You say she escaped sometime night before last?" He exchanged a glance with his brother. "She might have decided it was too dangerous to try to come to us. She might have gone into hiding. But we haven't seen her or Xac Wen, either."

"Truth is," Tasha continued, "we can't go anywhere just now. We're being kept right where we are on the Queen's own orders. Haren Crayel, our captain of the Home Guard, commands this contingent. He's our friend, so he told us of these orders. Doesn't mean he intends to go against them, you understand, but he thought that at least we ought to know. He doesn't believe the charges against Phryne, either."

He shrugged. "So here we sit, unable to do much of anything."

"Maybe there's nothing anyone can do until we know something more," Pan said quietly.

"Pan and I don't know much about Phryne's whereabouts, but we do know something about the Queen's part in her imprisonment," Prue said finally. She gave Pan a reassuring smile. "It's all right. I'm ready to talk about it."

Then she told Tasha and Tenerife of Bonnasaint's attempt and failure to kill them and of his admission that he was responsible for killing Oparion Amarantyne and that the Queen had arranged it. She also told them of Panterra's plan to bring the assassin here to be held prisoner by the Orullians and their companions until a way could be found to allow him to tell his story to the High Council so that Phryne might be exonerated.

"But late yesterday he got free of his bonds and got his hands on me and told Pan he would kill me if we didn't let him go." She spoke more quickly now, wanting to get through it. "Pan stalled him long enough that I slipped his hold and used my knife."

She stopped, shaking her head. "So now we're starting over on how to prove that Phryne didn't kill her father."

The Orullians stared at her. "Your resilience and determination are admirable," Tenerife said finally. "But I sometimes wonder about your common sense."

"I don't think it bears dwelling on," Tasha said to him, making a dismissive gesture. "Little sister doesn't need to hear this."

"As a matter of fact, I do." Prue looked from one to the other. "I put myself in a position where all this could happen. What kind of common sense does that show? I've never killed anyone before this whole business started, and I hope never to kill anyone again. I'm not made for that. Last night I was so upset with myself that I was blaming Panterra for things that weren't his fault. I was so angry I wasn't able to think about anything else. Now I just wish I could find a way to make things right."

"Prue," Panterra said softly.

Tasha held up one hand, silencing him. "Well, little sister, I can tell you this much. I would rather have things all wrong and you alive than the other way around. Choices are hard to come by when your life is in danger. I don't care how this turned out or what you had to do. It is enough that you are here with us."

"He's right." Tenerife reached out and took her hands in his. "He sees the truth of it. How you reacted and what you were forced to do is terrible enough without trying to assign blame for your choices. Let it go, Prue Liss. We love you, and we don't want you shouldering burdens that aren't yours to bear."

Then he took her in his arms and held her, and for just a moment Panterra Qu was startled to see something in the Elf's eyes and face that told him Prue meant a great deal more to him than anything he had revealed before.

"Thank you," Prue whispered, lifting her head away and kissing his cheek. "You really are my brothers, both Tasha and you."

"Always were," Tenerife added, coloring slightly.

"Wait, now. We haven't been told everything yet." Tasha gestured at Panterra. "You carry the staff that belongs to Sider Ament. How did that come about?"

Pan sighed wearily, as if the effort to speak were too much for him. "Sider was killed by Arik Siq outside Declan Reach maybe ten days ago. I couldn't stop it, even though I tried. When he was dying, he offered me the staff, and I agreed to take it. Now it's mine to use in the defense of the people of the valley."

"We hadn't heard about this," Tenerife said.

"The staff is a great responsibility," Tasha said. "More than you probably want to deal with. But you are like that, Panterra. You always were. You will do as well with it as Sider would have. You will be strong like he was."

"But the demon hunts you because of the staff," Tenerife pressed. "So we'll have to help you keep watch for it. Demons might be mythical in the lore of Men, but Elves know better. We have our histories, and demons have always been part of them. You are at great risk."

"We can speak of that later," Pan said, not comfortable talking about the matter. He knew how things stood without being reminded. "Do you have any idea at all where we can find Phryne?"

They talked about it at length, but neither of the Orullians could help. Normally, if she were in trouble, she would go either to her grandmother or to them. Or, in this instance, Tasha added, she would send Xac Wen in her place. Likely it would be the latter.

"He can't stand not being at the center of things," the big man insisted confidently. "Give it time. He'll show."

TASHA WAS RIGHT. But it didn't happen until evening, long after Panterra and Prue had visited with the Orullians and even pitched in to help them build their snares, having more than a little experience in such matters. The friends had settled into a comfortable reunion, talking of mundane things as the hours rolled on and the daylight began to fade, keeping the more serious matters at bay until later that night when the day's work was done and they could talk alone. They were all eating dinner, gathered about a cooking fire with other Elves, trading stories and sharing experiences, when one of the sentries from inside the valley appeared with Xac Wen in tow. The boy looked as if he had made a hard trek to reach them, his face dirty and sweat-stained, his clothing torn and rumpled.

Tasha rose to meet him, wrinkling his nose. "Stay downwind of me, you muddied little squirrel. No, wait. Don't say anything just yet. Moren will take you out to wash and give you fresh clothes." He turned to the sentry. "Anything close to a near fit will do. Then bring him back. We'll feed and water him and see what he has to say. Go."

The sentry hauled a grumbling Xac Wen off to bathe and change, and by the time the boy returned, looking much better, the four friends had finished eating and moved off to a more isolated place. As promised, they gave him food and drink and waited to hear what he had to say.

What he said first, to Prue Liss, was, "What happened to your eyes?"

"Nothing. It's a disguise." She blinked as if to demonstrate. "Tell us about Phryne."

The boy shrugged. "I got her out, just like Tasha told me to," he said, wolfing down large bites of food between words. But when Tasha cleared his throat and caught his eye, he put his plate aside. "Like I said, I freed her. But then things got strange. First, someone sent her a note saying help was coming. Wasn't me. Wasn't you, was it? No? I didn't think so. Anyway, we never did find out who it was, but Phryne thought it might be the Queen. Since you say you didn't send it, I'd guess she was right. She thought the Queen might be planning to let her escape and then kill her afterward. But that didn't happen. Instead, Phryne said she had to go to her grandmother's house to look around. So we did, even though I thought it was dangerous. There was no reasoning with her. We searched the house, looking for something. I don't know what. Phryne wouldn't say what it was. Then this ghost thing appeared. It looked like her grandmother—like Mistral—but it wasn't real. It talked to Phryne and made this message out of fire that burned in the air and told Phryne to go to the Ashenell. Then some of the Queen's pet guards came looking, and we got out of the house just in time. Phryne was furious. I think she would have done something about them if she could have managed it, but instead she made me go to the Ashenell with her. Well, she didn't make me go exactly. It was more like I made her take me. I couldn't leave her alone. So I went with her and she walked under the Belloruusian Arch and just disappeared!"

He stared at them breathlessly, dark hair tousled and damp, eyes wild and excited. "So what do we do now?"

"You know, if this were anybody else telling this story, I might think they were making it up," Tasha offered.

"I still think he's making it up," Tenerife interjected, his lean face reflecting more than a little doubt. "You are, aren't you, you little water mite?"

"No, it's true—all of it!" The boy looked seriously offended. "How could I make up something like that? Oh, I forgot. At the house, when that ghost thing appeared looking like Mistral, it said something about

Elfstones and that she had them hidden and that Phryne should come and get them. I think that was why we went to the Ashenell, although it might just have been because Phryne wanted to find her grand-mother. She was really worried about her."

"So Phryne disappeared?" Panterra pressed. "She vanished just like that? Didn't say or do anything?"

The boy nodded. "She was right there in front of me one moment, walking under the arch, and then she was gone. I looked all over. I even walked under the arch like she did. Nothing happened. I waited all day for her to come back, and she didn't. So I came here."

Tasha reached out and ruffled his hair. "You did the right thing. Too bad we don't know more about where she's disappeared to, though. Then we would know where to start looking."

"The Ashenell," Prue said at once. "That's where."

"Then why didn't Xac find her?" Tenerife asked in confusion. "He said he was there all day and didn't see her again."

"Not *in* the Ashenell. *Below* the Ashenell. She's gone down into the lower regions, just as Kirisin and Simralin Belloruus did all those years ago. She's gone down there to meet with Mistral. Don't you know the story?"

Blank looks greeted her question, even from Panterra, who had no idea what she was talking about. She gave them an exasperated look.

"All right, then—listen. Five hundred years ago, the Elfstones were in the possession of the dead, specifically Pancea Rolt Gotrin, an Elven sorceress long dead but very powerful even so. Her shade met with Kirisin and struck a bargain with him. If she gave him the blue Elf-stones, the ones they called the seeking-Stones, he would agree to do what he could to persuade the Elven living to seek out and make use of the magic they had lost or forgotten since the days of Faerie. That was how the Elfstones ended up in the hands of the Belloruus family over the years. Mistral must have had them last and told Phryne about them."

"And then sent her underground beneath the Ashenell burial grounds to retrieve them?" Tenerife demanded, clearly disbelieving the whole thing. He shook his head. "Why would she drag her grand-daughter down there? Why not just come back up and give them to

her? What would Mistral Belloruus be doing down there, anyway?
How would she even find the way?"

"The way was hidden before, but Kirisin found it," Prue persisted.
She gave Tenerife a withering look. "Why is it that I know all this and
you don't? No wonder the dead kept the Elfstones from the living for
so long! The living don't even know their own history!"

"Calm down," Tasha hushed her, giving Pan a quick look. "We don't
want to fight among ourselves. We just want to find a way to help
Phryne."

"The Elfstones are a very powerful magic, aren't they?" Prue asked
pointedly. "If they were to come into Phryne's possession, it could
make a huge difference in what happens to her. Doesn't it make sense
that she would take a chance on being able to recover them? Wouldn't
she at least go looking if her grandmother asked her to?"

Both Orullians nodded somewhat reluctantly. "She would," Tasha
said. "She's stubborn that way. She would be seeking a way to get back
at Isoeld Severine and avenge her father's murder. It begins to look
more and more as if the assassin was telling the truth about the Queen.
But how do we get to Phryne to find out?"

"I can show you where she disappeared!" Xac Wen announced,
looking eager to depart immediately. "You just have to come with me!"

Panterra looked at the brothers. "Tasha and Tenerife have to stay
here. They won't be allowed to leave just yet. But Prue and I can come
with you. Maybe we can do something to help find her."

"Because you're really Elves, even though you don't look it?" the
boy deadpanned.

Pan cocked an eyebrow. "Careful, now."

"All right," Tasha agreed. "You take little sister and go with Xac.
And you, squirrel boy, take them where they need to go and make certain nothing happens to them. You didn't do so well with Phryne, so
let's do better with our Tracker friends."

"That wasn't my fault!" the boy exclaimed in dismay. He turned to
Pan and Prue. "It wasn't!"

"No, Xac, it wasn't," Prue agreed, reaching out to touch his cheek.
"It was just something that happened, and assigning blame for it
doesn't help anyone. I should know. Will you take us?"

The boy glanced at the other three as if to make certain of his footing, and then he gave her a firm nod. "I will take you anywhere you want to go, Prue Liss. And I will make sure that nothing bad happens to you."

He looked at Tasha. "We could leave right away."

Tasha rolled his eyes. "Tomorrow will be soon enough for this. Some of us need our rest."

"Not me," said the boy, and went back to eating.

EIGHTEEN

PHRYNE AMARANTYNE EXPERIENCED A MOMENT OF disorientation, a quick change of light to twilight and outside to inside, followed by a loss of balance and a recognition that she wasn't where she had been even a moment earlier. She stopped and tried to regain her sense of place and time, casting about for something familiar. There was nothing she recognized. The Belloruusian Arch, the Ashenell, the tombs and markers, the buildings of the city off in the distance, the day she had walked through only moments before—all gone.

She felt instant panic, fed by the realization that she had lost everything familiar and found in its place nothing she knew. She breathed in and out quickly, and her heart raced wildly. *Be calm*, she told herself. *You're all right. Nothing has hurt you, nothing will.*

Maybe.

How could she know? How could she know anything?

Then her eyes adjusted to the change of light, to this new darkness, and she began to see where she was. She was in a broad cavelike tunnel, its rock walls rugged and rough, bits of roots and vines trailing from its ceiling, broken rocks and pockets of damp littering its floor. Veins of something phosphorescent glowed softly through its length, running on into the distance until they could no longer be seen clearly. From somewhere not too far away, water dripped in slow, steady cadence. When she breathed or scraped her boots on the stone, the sounds echoed loudly.

Otherwise, everything was silent.

She looked around, taking stock of her situation. The passageway in which she stood ran both ways for as far as she could see. There was no sign of how she had gotten here, nothing to indicate the portal that had allowed her to enter. She might have been picked up and deposited by a giant's hand as easily as not. The walls about her offered no doors or alternative passageways. She could either stay where she was or go forward or back, but that was it.

She had retained enough presence of mind to know which was which, so she chose to go forward. But then she stopped herself, turned, and walked back for a short distance. Perhaps she could return to where she had been just by reversing her steps.

But when she'd gone twenty feet and nothing had happened, she realized there was no going back. Not that way, at least.

So she turned around and continued on. She walked for a long time, the sound of her breathing harsh in her ears, her footfalls echoing in the silence. She wished she'd thought to bring food and water, but then realized she hadn't had any to bring in the first place. What she had were the clothes on her back, the long knife Xac Wen had given her, and a desperate need to find her grandmother.

She would have felt better about things if she'd had any clue as to where she was. Sure, she knew she was in a cave passage. She knew she was underground. But where? Somewhere in Arborlon or somewhere else entirely? Magic was at work here—of that much she could be certain. But had it worked to her advantage or not? If it was Mistral's, she was not in danger. But if it were someone else's, how could she be sure of anything? She couldn't even be certain she was still inside the valley. She might have been transported. She might be anywhere.

But who would do this if not Mistral?

She forced herself to think it through logically. Mistral's avatar had come to her to warn her of the danger and of her need to retrieve and take up the Elfstones. Her message, emblazoned in fire across the air inside her little cottage, had summoned Phryne to the Belloruus Arch. So it was reasonable to think it was her grandmother's magic and not someone else's that had brought her to where she was. Otherwise, this was an elaborate trap set by an unknown person or persons, and that just didn't make any sense.

She walked with more confidence now, having decided everything was happening as intended, that her grandmother had arranged all this for a reason. Phryne was where she was supposed to be and doing what she was supposed to do. She wasn't entirely reassured there was no danger, but she did think she was better off than she had first believed.

Time passed, and the tunnel wound on. Not once did it branch or offer any other way to go but forward or back. She felt as if she must have walked miles. But how could an underground passageway—even one as big as this—run so far? Nor was there any suggestion of an end to it. Everything kept looking exactly the same, the walls never changing and the light never altering. She might have been walking in place for all the progress she seemed to be making.

Her thoughts drifted to the events that had brought her to this place and time, beginning with her impulsive decision to go with her cousins and Prue Liss and Panterra Qu to Aphalion Pass and ultimately beyond into the outside world. How different things would be if she had stayed in Arborlon. She was aware of how everything in life could be changed by a single choice, had known it to happen to others, but had never thought she would experience it herself.

Now she wished she could take it all back. Her father might still be alive and her stepmother nothing more than the baker's daughter who had married an Elven King and worked with the sick and injured. But Phryne guessed that she was dreaming. Events would still have turned out somewhere close to where they were. The Drouj would still have found their way to the valley, Isoeld would still have found a way to murder her husband so that she could make herself Queen, and her own sorry state of affairs would still have come to pass.

Of course, there was no way of knowing for sure and nothing to be gained by speculating. You lived the life you were given, good or bad. She let the matter drop.

Ahead, the tunnel began to narrow. She hurried a bit to see what was going to happen and soon found that it tightened into a much smaller passageway that branched in three directions—one each to the left and right and a third between the other two that became a stairway leading down. She hesitated a moment before choosing the middle path. She couldn't have sworn to it, but it seemed to her that something was tugging her that way. Not a voice or a presence or anything quite so substantial; it was more instinct than anything, and she decided to heed it.

The stairway descended in circular fashion, the walls close enough that Phryne could feel the cold radiating off the stone and could see the damp glistening in broad patches. The dripping continued as well, droplets falling on her head or striking her face in icy splashes. The tunnel was windless, the air stale and damp to the taste. She had to duck to avoid low spots in the spiraling underside of the stairs. But she pressed ahead, determined to find an end to her journey.

She found it almost before she was ready. The stairs ended in another tunnel, this one as narrow as the passageway leading down, and she was forced to proceed in a crouch. Water ran all along the floor in tiny rivers and dripped steadily from the ceiling. She was soon very wet about her head and shoulders and shivering with the cold.

Then, suddenly, she heard a faint, dry hissing, a sound flat and empty of life, as if snakes held imprisoned might be pleading for release. It was vast and endless, and it grew in strength the farther down the passageway she went. She tried to make sense of it, but failed. It might have been snakes, but she knew it wasn't. It might have been the sound of water falling in a thin, soft sheen from a great height, but it wasn't that, either. It might even have been a dying breath, the sound of life leaving the body, but she knew that was wrong, too.

Now the passageway was widening out and taking on a different look. Stalactites appeared on the ceiling, each larger than a man, great stone spears on which mineral deposits had found purchase, their encrusted lengths shedding water in slow drippings that stained the tunnel floor. A forest of these formations filled the spaces above her head and left her feeling as if she were in a deadly trap with jaws that might close on her at any moment.

She quit looking up, directed her eyes straight ahead, and pushed on.

When the tunnel finally ended, she was standing at the opening of a massive cavern, a chamber so vast she could not see its far walls and could only barely make out the stalactites clustered on its ceiling. Torches burned through the darkness like tiny fireflies, their glow revealing bits and pieces of the chamber's terrain. A lake at its center dominated everything, broad and sprawling, its waters a strange greenish color, their surface flat and still, mirroring the ceiling and parts of the walls. Massive rocks chiseled into rectangles and pillars rose here and there along the perimeter, remnants of another age.

But what drew Phryne's attention instantly were the tombs clustered around the lake's edge, markers and sepulchers of all sizes and shapes, some with script cut into the stone bold and deep, some with tiny runes she could only barely make out, and some with nothing more than one or two huge letters carved in the ancient Elven language. She had studied that language and learned its characters, and so she could identify what she was looking at, even if she could not interpret its meaning.

She stood for long moments at the cavern entrance, trying to decide what to do next. Then slowly, cautiously, she began to make her way down toward the edge of the lake.

But she had not gone more than a dozen yards before the hissing that had tracked her progress with its steady, insistent buzzing—the hissing she had gotten so used to she had almost forgotten it was there—suddenly increased in intensity. The volume rose abruptly, as if to acknowledge her presence and make known that it recognized her purpose. She stopped where she was, realizing suddenly what she was hearing.

It was the sound of voices whispering—hundreds of them, perhaps thousands, all speaking at once.

She held her ground a moment longer to see if anything else was going to happen, but after a few minutes in which nothing did, she moved ahead once more. Shadows layered the cavern floor in strange shapes, elongated and twisted in the bits and pieces of light, and she could have sworn that some of them moved. But she could find nothing living in the mix of light and dark, and even the sources of the whispering refused to reveal themselves. She walked alone, down through the tombs, down through the shadows, down to the edge of the green, still waters of the lake.

There she stopped, waiting.

Phryne, a voice called out to her.

Even though she had been expecting something to happen, she nearly jumped out of her skin. She wheeled right and left, searching for the speaker, the sound of her name echoing all through the chamber so that it was impossible to trace.

I am here, child.

And there was Mistral. Her grandmother stood next to a huge stone marker not twenty feet away, wrapped in her favorite cloak, the one into which she had woven impressions of the flowers of her gardens. She looked diminished standing in the shadow of the marker, a tiny figure, frail and old, her years a weight upon her shoulders.

She also looked dead. The faint light of the torches passed right through her, revealing her transparency, her changed state of being. She could no longer be seen as one of the living, even by Phryne, who very much wanted her to be. Whatever had happened above-ground, she had crossed over into the spirit world, her life come to an end.

Phryne gave a low moan of dismay and felt tears spring to her eyes. "Oh, Grandmother, no," she whispered.

Her grandmother made a placating gesture. *I know you are disappointed not to find me still among the living. But I am as you see me, my life complete. I was alive when I made the avatar I hoped would bring you to me. I was alive when I made my escape from my home. But there were minions of Isoeld waiting for me, sent to kill me and take from me the Elfstones. She couldn't know for certain I had them, but she certainly suspected. Her creatures would find them on me or find them when they searched the cottage.*

She sighed, a deep exhalation. *My faithful friends, my oldsters from so many years, friends and lovers and servants, fought to save me and died doing so. I escaped because of their sacrifice but was grievously injured.*

Knowing I would die and pass from this world without ever having told you what I must or done what I had promised, I came here, down beneath the Ashenell, down to where the most powerful of the Elven spirit Queens dwells with her people. Here, I could maintain a presence long enough for you to find me.

She made a curiously compelling gesture with one white hand. *And you have found me, child. My trust in you was not misplaced. But your struggle has been every bit as difficult as mine, and for that I am sorry.*

Phryne took a step toward her, wanting to embrace her, to feel the old woman's arms around her one final time. But Mistral held up her hands in warning. *You cannot touch me, Phryne. You must not. We can only talk now, nothing more.*

"Grandmother, I just want—"

No, Phryne! Don't say it! She made a quick, warding gesture. *Things aren't as they seem. We have to hurry. Now talk to me. Tell me what happened to you after your escape.*

The urgency in her voice was unmistakable. It caused Phryne to glance around hurriedly, searching for its source. But she found nothing different than it had been. The tombs were unchanged, the waters of the lake still, the torches casting shadows as before, the cavern vast and silent.

"There's nothing to tell," she answered her grandmother. "I escaped with the help of the Orullian twins and a young boy. The boy brought me to your cottage, which had been searched and abandoned. Your avatar appeared and directed me to the Belloruusian Arch. I fled there when Isoeld's soldiers came to the cottage. At the arch, I passed through into the tunnels that led to this place."

She took a quick breath. "But what am I to do now? I will not let Isoeld blame me for killing my father. Can you help me, Grandmother? Can you do something to help me expose her?"

Mistral Belloruus shook her head. *I am of the dead now, and I can do nothing to aid the living. I lack substance, and I am confined to this place until I am allowed passage to the world of the dead and my final rest. I can do only one thing for you. I can give you the blue Elfstones. I have them with me, and they are meant for you. Take them and use them to help our people. You will find a way. You must.*

She fumbled in her clothing and produced the familiar leather pouch. It was more substantial than the shade who held it and instantly recognizable.

Come closer, she said.

Phryne started toward her, but had taken only a few steps when a sudden wind rose out of nowhere, gusting through the chamber with such force that the torches were nearly extinguished and Phryne was forced to drop to one knee and shield her face. The whispering rose to a new crescendo, filling the immense cavern with a wailing at once so terrible and so sad that it defied belief.

"Grandmother!" Phryne called.

But Mistral Belloruus had shrunk back against the stone marker where she had first appeared, her face twisted with emotions Phryne could not read. She still held the pouch and the Elfstones clutched in her hands, clearly visible through the ephemeral trappings of her diminished body. But no longer was she making any effort at handing them to Phryne.

A voice spoke, harsh and cutting, managing somehow to rise above the wailing of the voices and the wind.

-You are of the living, girl, and do not belong here-

Phryne's throat clenched and her blood turned to ice.

*　*　*

"REMEMBER WHAT I TOLD YOU," Panterra was telling Xac Wen as they neared the Elfitch and the city of Arborlon. "If we're stopped, just say that we're visiting old friends and hope to do some hunting in the eastern wilderness while we're here. You don't have to say anything more."

The boy scowled at him. "I know what to say, Pan. You don't have to worry; I won't make a mistake."

He sounded so fierce about it that Panterra had to smile in spite of himself, but he managed to mask it with a sudden fit of coughing.

Prue, following a pace behind them, stepped forward and placed her hand on Xac's shoulder. "He knows that. He just needs to reassure himself because he's afraid for Phryne. Don't be angry with him."

Xac Wen glanced over at her and scuffed the toe of his boot as
he walked. "I'm not angry at anyone. I just don't want to be treated
like a child. I'm big enough to do what's needed. I rescued Phryne,
after all. I got her out of that storeroom where they were keeping
her."

"Which was a very difficult and dangerous thing to do," Pan said. "I
don't know if any of us could have done it. So I'll tell you what. I'll
stop telling you what to do and just assume you already know."

The boy nodded. "Why don't you tell me what you're doing with
the Gray Man's staff? You could tell me about that, and I wouldn't get
a bit angry."

Panterra rolled his eyes.

While they crossed the meadow to the base of the bluff on which
Arborlon sat and climbed the broad ramp of the Elfitch, Pan repeated
the story of the death of Sider Ament and the passing of the staff to
himself one more time. Xac Wen listened intently, alternately nodding
and grunting until Pan was done.

"Can you do stuff with that staff?" he asked. "Magic stuff? Some say
the bearer can. Is that true?"

"It's true," Pan told him.

"Can you show me?"

"Leave him alone, Xac," Prue interrupted. "He doesn't need to
show you anything."

Elven Hunters doing guard duty looked them over as they ascended the various levels of their climb, but let them pass. One or two
greeted Xac by name, and he responded with a word or a wave but
never anything more. At the top, they left the Elfitch and went into the
Carolan Gardens, working their way along the pathways that crisscrossed the flower beds, trellis vines, and hedgerows to reach the city
proper.

As they passed out of the gardens and crossed a bordering lawn
toward the city roadways, Xac Wen said to Prue, "What happened to
your eyes? And don't tell me that it has anything to do with being in
disguise."

"I lost some of my vision," she said. "Just a part of it. That's why my
eyes look like this."

"What part did you lose?"

"The part that sees colors. I can't see anything but shades of gray anymore."

"How did that happen?"

"Magic. I traded off being able to see colors for having the use of instincts that are valuable in protecting myself and those with me."

"What sort of instincts?"

"Ones that let me sense danger when it is near so that I can be ready for it and maybe avoid it."

The boy studied her for a long moment in silence and then shook his head. "That explanation is worse than the one you gave before. I'll ask you again later."

At one point, they encountered an Elf whom Xac Wen knew, a young woman close to Pan's age. Xac stopped her and asked for word of Phryne. He was told there was no news of the Princess, that since her escape she had not been seen.

"Just wanted to be sure she hadn't returned from wherever she disappeared to," he advised his companions as they left the young woman and walked on.

"She might have returned and not been seen," Prue suggested.

The boy stopped and looked at her. "That's so. But then where would she go? She would have to go into hiding right away."

"She could have found a way to get out of the city and decided to try to reach the Orullians."

He shook his head. "She would stay put for now. She knows I will be searching for her." He stopped suddenly. "There is one place she might go."

He led them hurriedly ahead, moving into a residential section where there were rows of cottages situated on the ground and in the trees overhead. Eventually they reached the tree house that the Orullians had been working on when Pan and Prue had first come to see them weeks ago to discuss the collapse of the protective wall that warded the valley.

"Wait here," he told them.

He scrambled up the stairs onto the platform on which the cottage was situated and disappeared through the door. Pan and Prue waited patiently for his return.

"He certainly doesn't lack for energy," Pan observed quietly.

"He doesn't lack for determination, either," Prue added.

They continued to wait, shifting their gazes every so often to the roads and pathways around them, keeping watch. Neither felt entirely comfortable with the situation, even though there was no reason to think they were in any immediate danger.

Xac Wen reappeared abruptly and scampered down the stairs, his young face grim. "Nothing. She's not been there. We should go to the arch. If she came back through, she will have left me a sign."

It took them less than half an hour to reach the gates of the Ashenell burial grounds. There was little activity in evidence here, the iron gates leading inside open, but the grounds themselves deserted. Xac Wen led his companions ahead without slowing, taking a direct route toward the Belloruusian Arch.

Even before the boy told them they had reached their destination, Pan knew it for what it was. Built of massive stone blocks stacked one atop another, the Belloruusian Arch was fully twenty feet high and almost as wide. The letter *B* was carved into its keystone, signifying the surname of the family and marking the entrance to all the tombs and sepulchers that stretched away within the shadow of its broad span.

"This is where she disappeared," Xac Wen announced, pointing at the arch. "Right there, underneath. She just walked up to it and then vanished."

Panterra studied the arch and the space below for a long time, trying to see if he could discern something that would explain what had happened to Phryne. But he couldn't see anything unusual or revealing about it. Stones and earth—that was all.

"There must be a portal of some sort," Prue said quietly. "There must be magic at work."

Pan nodded. "Definitely magic."

He was resting the black staff butt-downward against the earth, running his fingers slowly up and down its length, feeling the runes respond with a soft tingle. The staff's magic was awake, perhaps responding to something he couldn't see. It was sending him a signal—perhaps a warning—of something waiting.

Yet Prue had said nothing of her instincts responding to any danger. They had been quick enough to warn her when Bonnasaint had lain in wait for them in the meres. So perhaps the staff's response was to the presence of another magic and not necessarily to anything dangerous.

"Do your instincts tell you we are threatened?" he asked her quietly.

She shook her head no.

"Wait here for me," he told her.

He walked forward alone, taking his time, the magic of the black staff fully awake now, coursing up and down its length and into his body. He was prepared to use it if he was attacked, but he couldn't find anything that suggested this might happen. The Belloruusian Arch and the ground about it were empty of movement or sound or life of any sort. He studied the space beneath the arch where Phryne had disappeared, but he couldn't see anything of where she might have gone.

When he was very close, he called up the magic and gave the space directly ahead of him a spray of its bright light. For just an instant, something flickered in response—a sliver of darkness, a splitting of the air that was little more than a vertical shimmer. It was there and then gone again in an instant. Pan blinked in response to its quick, momentary appearance, not certain what it was he had seen.

Slowly, he moved toward it.

⸻

XAC WEN WAS STANDING close enough to Prue Liss that he heard her gasp when Panterra Qu walked up to the exact same spot where Phryne had vanished two days earlier and disappeared himself. The boy couldn't quite believe it, having decided any danger was past and all they were doing at this point was searching for some indication of whether the Princess had come back out again. After all, he had walked beneath the arch, right where the two who had vanished had walked, and nothing had happened to him. So there was no reason to think that anything would happen to either of his companions.

But now something had, and the boy was stunned.

Prue Liss never hesitated. She charged toward the arch the minute Pan disappeared, shouting his name, her voice frantic. Xac chased after her, afraid now for both of them. But when they reached the arch and stood exactly where Panterra had disappeared, nothing happened. The girl felt the air with her hands, waved them as she might to find a spiderweb and clear it away.

"Where is he?" she screamed.

Xac Wen had no answer to offer.

NINETEEN

-Who brought you here, girl-

Phryne did not recognize the voice, but she was able to track its source immediately. It was another shade, an old woman far different in appearance from Mistral. This shade glowed with a malevolent green fire that pulsed at the center of her transparent form with wicked purpose. Bent and withered, her face crumpled like discarded paper, she had a fierce presence as she stood atop the short, flat surface of the pinnacle of a strange triangular stone into which had been carved the letters *P, R,* and G.

-Mistral Belloruus does not rule here. She does not decide who comes and who goes. I do-

Phryne glanced at her grandmother for support, but Mistral was pressed against the stone of the marker, her face turned away.

-Answer my question, girl! Who brought you here? What do the living wish of the dead that you should come to me-

"I don't even know who you are," Phryne answered sharply, recovering herself enough to speak up.

-Little fool! All know my name in the land of the dead! I am Queen Pancea Rolt Gotrin, ruler of those who dwell in this underworld! Now, who brought you here? I will not ask again-

Pancea Rolt Gotrin, who had given the blue Elfstones to Kirisin five hundred years ago in this same spot! Phryne tried frantically to remember the details of the story and failed.

"No one brought me," she lied, determined to do what she could to protect Mistral. "I found my own way here. And I am a Princess in the land of the living!"

The shade hissed as if she had been scalded.

-You lie, Princess of whatever you are. What exactly would you be Princess of? Of the Elves who walk and breathe the air above me? Of the fools who have forgotten their heritage? Of the insects who chose to abandon the teachings of those who made this journey before them? Of what, then? Of nothing! You are Princess of nothing-

"Perhaps it is you who have forgotten!" Phryne snapped in reply, her face coloring. "You were one of us before you came to live with the dead. Perhaps you should remember that the road runs both ways."

-You are arrogant and disrespectful. I should put an end to you-

Phryne took a deep breath and tamped down her anger. "My Queen," she said and dropped to one knee. "I apologize. I spoke out of anger, and for that I am sorry. I did not know it was you until you told me. But your name is not unfamiliar to me. I know how important you were."

-How important I *am*, little fool. More important now, for I am absolute ruler down here. But if you know of me—as you claim—then tell me something specific. Make me believe you speak the truth-

Phryne risked a quick glance at Mistral, who had not moved, save to raise her head and fix her eyes on her granddaughter. "I know that five hundred years ago you met a boy from our family on my mother's side. His name was Kirisin Belloruus. He came to you seeking the blue Elfstones. In exchange for his promise to help persuade the Elven people to resume their study and use of their magic, you gave them to him."

The shade said nothing, waiting for more.

"I know that you have ruled as Queen of this underworld burial ground for centuries, and that you have use of magic still. I know that you can kill me without my being able to stop you. But I hope you will not do that. I am not here to cause trouble. I am here to save our people."

-Very pretty words. You speak them well. You speak them with sincerity and passion. The boy who came before you did likewise, but he betrayed me. He took my gift and failed to keep his word. He did nothing to persuade the Elves to study the old ways, to master the old magic. Would you make me the same promise now if I were to give the Elfstones to you-

It caught Phryne by surprise. She hadn't realized that Pancea Rolt Gotrin had gotten possession of the Stones—and when she remembered the pouch in Mistral's hands, she realized the old woman was baiting her. But why would she do that?

"Kirisin Belloruus did what he could, and some followed him in his studies," she answered. "Most did not and would not be persuaded otherwise. But, yes, I would make the same promise, and I would work hard to keep it."

The old woman laughed, a high cackle that sounded like a wild animal calling out in the darkness of the eastern swamps.

-I know you, girl. You are Phryne Amarantyne. You are Mistral's granddaughter, and she has promised you the Elfstones. That is the reason you are here, isn't it? Come down out of the world of light and living things to this place of darkness and death—what other reason could there be? You needed to find her to gain possession of the Elfstones. Do not suppose that you can dissemble with me-

"It is more than that, my Queen." Phryne decided that addressing the shade with respect was the better choice, and she would stay with it. "I came here to make certain that my grandmother was safe. She disappeared from her home, and I was frightened for her. There are Elves aboveground, among the living, who sought to put her here among the dead. One of them is my stepmother. She killed my father, the King, and she will not be satisfied until the Belloruus line is extinguished."

The shade made a dismissive gesture, hunching her shoulders like a carrion feeder.

-My line was extinguished centuries ago. All of them are dead and gone. All of them live down here to keep me company; all live in the afterlife I have provided for them. What care I for you and yours? Your line is of no importance. Nor are the lines of other families among the living. I care nothing for the living, just as they care nothing for me-

The shade hissed again, softer now and teasing.

-And you are right. I can kill you anytime I choose. I think I will do so now. I grow weary of this talk. You come too late to help your grandmother, Princess of nothing. She is as dead as I am. She died within hours of finding her way to me. She came here injured and I could do nothing to heal her wounds. She carried with her the Elfstones that rightfully belong to me, and so I took pity on her, thinking she had come to give the Elfstones back to me. I did what I could. But she deceived me. She never intended to give the Elfstones back. She intended to give them to you. All along, to you-

"She would have me use the Elfstones to help our people, who are threatened by invasion and extermination. She would have me follow in the footsteps of Kirisin Belloruus and make the magic a part of the lives of Elves once more. She would have me try to help fulfill the promise that Kirisin made all those years ago." Phryne was making it up as she went, desperate to convince this old woman to rethink her position, to remember that she had once been one of the living and so should want to help them. "I will give you that promise you asked for. I will do what you want. I will find a way to make the magic a part of Elven life again. Why not give me the chance?"

-And lose possession of the Elfstones once again? For another five centuries? How stupid do you think I am, Princess of nothing-

Phryne didn't know how stupid Pancea Rolt Gotrin might be, but she had a pretty good idea how bitter she had become. There wasn't a shred of pity left for the living, not a bit of sympathy for their plight, not a care for what happened to them. All she wanted was to regain possession of her precious Elfstones.

But why hadn't she? Why did Mistral still have them?

"If you want the Elfstones so badly, why don't you just take them?" she demanded suddenly. "If you are Queen and ruler of everything, why not take them and be done with it?"

The shade hissed and spat like a cat with its tail in a vise.

-You will give me the Elfstones if you want to get out of here alive! Do you understand me, girl? You will tell Mistral to give them to me-

Phryne saw it then, realized the truth. Pancea Rolt Gotrin, for all

the power that she commanded as Queen of these dead, couldn't take the Elfstones by force. She needed Phryne to get them for her. But why was that? Why couldn't she just take them away? If she had such power, why couldn't she . . . ?

Then she remembered her grandmother telling her that the Elfstones couldn't be taken by force if they were to be of use to the holder. They had to be freely given.

Pancea Rolt Gotrin was waiting for Mistral to break down and do just that, and she would use Phryne as leverage. So if she wanted to make sure that her grandmother's sacrifice in coming here with the Elfstones—in believing, even mistakenly, that this was the only way she could get them into her granddaughter's hands—meant something, Phryne had to act now. She caught Mistral's eye, a quick glance that revealed what she intended to do. She saw the look of dismay in her grandmother's face and realized that there was something else at work here, something she had missed. But it didn't matter. If there was even the smallest chance, Phryne knew she had to take it.

She leapt forward from the water's edge toward the marker against which Mistral was pressed. She had a momentary glimpse of her grandmother's arms raised in warning, stretched out as if to try to stop her. Then Pancea Rolt Gotrin was screaming and something as cold and heavy as frozen iron slammed into Phryne with immense force, knocking her off her feet.

She went down in a heap, gasping for breath, tried to rise, was struck again, and then everything went black.

WHEN SHE WOKE, she was lying on her back, staring up at the stalactite-encrusted ceiling of the cavern. Mistral sat a few yards off, her back against the stone marker, a weary look on her shade's white face.

Child, I did not mean for this to happen.

Phryne took a moment to recall exactly what it was that had happened and failed. "What did she do to me?"

She has magic at her command even here, even in death. She used it to keep you from reaching me, to prevent me from giving you the Elfstones. I came here to ask for her help, trying to stay alive until you reached me. But my wounds were too much for either of us. Once dead, I asked her help again. But she would not give it. She wants the Elfstones for herself. I made the mistake of telling her early on that you would come for me, that I had left a message for you. She was waiting for you to come, knowing what I intended, determined that she would not allow it.

Phryne raised herself up on her elbows, trying to clear her head. Every part of her body ached from whatever the Queen had done to her. "Why can't you just give them to me now? Right now, before she knows what you have done?"

Look behind you.

Phryne did, and she saw Pancea Rolt Gotrin perched atop her triangular marker, watching closely.

If I attempt to pass them to you, she will kill you before you can make use of them.

Phryne studied her grandmother's face, still trying to come to terms with the fact that she was dead, a shade with no physical presence and no place among the living. She remembered so clearly how her grandmother had looked the last time she had seen her—sharp and flushed with the excitement of her intention to give the Elfstones to her granddaughter. She thought of Isoeld and her minions coming to Mistral's cottage to take the Stones by force, and her sadness turned to icy rage.

"Won't she grow tired of watching us?" she demanded. "Won't she eventually leave us alone?"

The dead do not sleep. They are patient. They are good at waiting. Besides, she has no choice. To be of use, even to the dead, the Elfstones must be freely given. They cannot be taken by force. You know this already, child. She will keep us here until one of us gives her the Stones. In the end, if she must, she will destroy us both.

"But what more can she do to you? I am the only one she can hurt."

She can use you to hurt me. She can even use her magic to take away what little remains of me. She has that power.

Phryne felt whatever small hope remained draining away. "What can we do?" she asked.

We can wait. We must. At some point, she may become distracted, and we will have our chance. When that happens, we will have to act swiftly. I cannot touch you. I must set the Elfstones on the ground, and you must snatch them up instantly. If she sees what we are doing, she will kill you in the blink of an eye. The dead are quick; do not think otherwise. If we are slow or careless, whatever we attempt will end in failure.

Her grandmother paused, her voice become a whisper.

Pancea is a monster, child. She keeps you safe now so that you can persuade me to give the Elfstones to her so that you can go free. But once she convinces you to do this, she will take your life.

"And waiting is our only choice?" Phryne's voice was a low hiss of dismay. "I can't wait! Isn't there something else we can do?"

Her grandmother shook her head as if the answer to that question was more than she could bear. One withered hand lifted and gestured. Phryne's eyes closed in response, and she fell fast asleep.

PANTERRA QU FELT A CHANGE in the temperature of the air and in the brightness of the light, and then all at once he was in a different place entirely. He stopped where he was and looked around, discovering that the portal through which he had entered was nowhere to be found and that instead of standing beneath the Belloruusian Arch, he was in a tunnel. For a moment he was confused; he tried to get his bearings and at the same time figure out what had caused this to happen. He knew at once that magic was at work, and that in all likelihood his own had responded to it. He glanced briefly at the black staff, but its rune carvings were dark. Whatever help it had given him was finished. He thought briefly of Prue, knowing how frantic she would be, watching him disappear and not being able to reach him—it was a safe assumption she couldn't or she would have been there beside him by now—or know where he had gone.

Then he put it aside. There was nothing he could do about any of it, and for the moment none of it mattered. What mattered was finding Phryne. Wherever he was, it was entirely possible that she was there, too. According to Xac Wen, she'd done exactly what he'd done almost two days earlier when she disappeared. It was reasonable to assume that whatever had happened to him had happened to her, too. If he was lucky, he might be able to find her.

He started walking down the tunnel in the direction he had been facing on passing through the portal. The passageway looked the same both ways, but he had to assume Phryne would have made the same choice he was making. Veins of phosphorescent minerals embedded in the walls gave off enough light to let him find his way. Starting slowly, he scanned the rocky surface of the tunnel floor for signs of other footprints and after a short time found what he was looking for—scuff marks and small pieces of debris knocked free of the stone. Reassured, he kept going.

He walked for a very long way, wondering as time passed if he had made a mistake in reading the signs. It was unlikely, he told himself. His tracking skills wouldn't allow for it. But the distance seemed great for an underground tunnel with no branches. Still, he pushed ahead, determined to see this through.

In the end, he reached a place where the passageway branched either right or left or continued ahead, angling downward. He took a long time to study the rocky floor at this point, searching for fresh sign. He found what he was looking for when he had followed the middle passageway to where a set of stone steps began a steep descent. There he discovered a clear boot marking and knew this was the way Phryne had gone.

Shouldering his pack and taking a fresh grip on his staff, he started down the stairway.

He descended many steps, winding his way downward in circular fashion, water dripping, splashing on his face and hands and soaking his clothing. He listened carefully for voices, but the only sound he heard was a strange hissing, something that resembled the breathing of a huge creature. He recalled the dragon in Aphalion Pass and wondered if it were possible that it made its home this far under the earth. He wondered what he would do if he found it.

At the bottom, he found another passageway, this one with its ceiling clustered with stalactites, puddled below with small pools of the mineral-infused water they had shed. He continued on, moving carefully, quietly through the near-darkness. The hissing sound was growing louder; whatever its source, it lay not too far ahead. A snake? He didn't care much for the thoughts that image conjured, imagining how large the snake would have to be to make a sound of that size. No, it was something else. More like a waterfall. Or steam escaping from a vent.

Finally, he arrived at a massive cavern dominated by a lake that was ringed by hundreds of tombs and markers stretching away for as far as the eye could see. Phosphorescence infused the walls here, too, illuminating the stone garden and casting shadows in strange shapes and forms.

He walked forward cautiously, wending his way into the burial ground, through the clusters of tombs and markers, down toward the edge of the lake. The hissing grew louder, and suddenly he could discern voices. He recognized now what he was hearing. It was whispering, a vast collection of hushed voices all speaking at once. He could catch snatches of words and phrases, but not enough so that any of it made sense. He wondered where the voices were coming from, and an instant later knew the answer.

He was listening to the dead speaking to one another.

A moment after that, he saw Phryne.

PHRYNE. WAKE UP.

She heard her grandmother's voice from a long way off, from far down in a warm drowsiness that wrapped her like a blanket. She tried to ignore it, anxious to be left alone, content in her sleepy world. But the voice became more insistent, a barrage of words that prodded like sharp sticks.

He is here. The boy you hoped would come. I have brought him to you.

Phryne responded, knowing at once that her grandmother was speaking of Panterra Qu. She had told her grandmother of him, tested her command of the Elfstone magic by finding him, and Mistral Belloruus would have been quick to recognize the attraction. But why would she bring Pan here? He would want to help, but he was no match for a creature like Pancea Rolt Gotrin.

Struggling to wake up all the way and frightened now for Pan, she forced herself into a sitting position and cast about. Her grandmother was seated right where she had been sitting when Phryne had fallen asleep—hadn't her grandmother done something to make that happen?—still holding the pouch with the Elfstones clasped in her hands. Time had passed—it must have passed—but there was no way Phryne could know how long she had been sleeping.

"Why is Pan here?" she demanded. "Why did you bring him?"

Her grandmother's face had assumed a stronger look.

Watch and see.

Pancea's shade had reappeared atop the triangular marker, all gnarled and bent, radiating its sickly green light, ghostly in the darkness of the cavern. She was turned away from them, looking back over the clusters of markers and tombs to where Panterra was walking toward her. It took a moment for Phryne to realize that the black staff he was carrying was the same one she had last seen in the hands of Sider Ament.

"Phryne!" he called out to her.

She started to reply, but Mistral quickly hushed her. Atop her perch, Pancea was shrieking as if scalded, her rage directed at the boy. In response, the dead who followed her were rising from their resting places and filling the empty spaces between markers and tombs with their ghostly forms, all white and transparent and ephemeral as mist. Their whispers were wild and excited as they drifted into view and formed clusters, all of them massing and then coming together about their leader.

Mistral Belloruus had gone into a crouch, fingers pressed to her lips.

Watch.

Pancea Rolt Gotrin's hands swept up and wicked green fire flashed at her fingertips, driving into Panterra Qu. But his black staff responded more quickly still, blocking the attack and shattering its thrust. The boy held the staff before him, sweeping away shards of flame, but the attack had staggered him, and Phryne could see him falter.

"Phryne!" he called again, but his voice was weaker.

Now.

Her grandmother tossed the pouch with the Elfstones toward Phryne, but it landed short and lay halfway between them, unprotected. The Elven girl flung herself across the space that separated them, fingers closing on the little bag. She heard Pancea scream again, saw another flash of green fire that flared all around her and everywhere at once. Curling herself into a ball around the bag and its contents, she tore the leather bindings apart and dropped the blue Elfstones into her hand. A moment later, she was on her feet, the Stones clutched tightly in her hand as she turned to face the malevolent shade.

But Pancea was no longer atop the triangular marker. Instead, she was right in front of Phryne.

-Give them to me-

The words had the force of a curse laid upon her, but Phryne only clutched the Elfstones tighter, fingers wrapped around them as she raised her arms defensively.

-Little fool-

Green fire lashed at the girl, tearing at her with such force that she felt as though her arms had been pulled from their sockets and her legs shattered. She was flung backward onto the cavern floor, pain ratcheting through her unprotected body. But even though she felt she might lose consciousness, she was determined not to let go of the Elfstones. Fighting through her weakness and nausea, she rolled away from the shade and struggled to her knees, still trying to bring the Elven magic to life, to focus her efforts on making it hers. She could feel the immediate connection, the magic of the Stones filling her body, white-hot as it surged into her, but she could not bring it to bear.

Pancea screamed at her.

-Give them to me now, Princess of nothing-

She started toward Phryne, fingers extended like claws, face twisted into something more animal than human, less shade and more ghoul. Phryne, still trying to recover from the damage that had been done to her, scrabbled backward toward the lake, blinking rapidly, shaking her head. There was no sign of Panterra, nothing to tell her what had happened to him, nothing to show that he was even still upright.

"Pan," she managed to whisper.

Then Mistral Belloruus threw herself on top of Pancea Rolt Gotrin and bore her to the ground. The Queen shrieked in fury and thrashed wildly, trying to break free. But Mistral would not release her grip, pinning the other shade's arms to her sides, holding her fast. Locked together, they rolled over and over on the cavern floor, a strange jumble of diaphanous whites and greens. Jets of fire rocketed from Pancea's arms, but did nothing more than sear the stone and foul the cavern air.

"Grandmother!" Phryne howled, trying to focus the magic of the Elfstones, desperate to help, dancing this way and that around the combatants.

Run, Phryne!

Her grandmother's words were quick and certain and pregnant with emotion that brooked no argument and left no room for doubt about what she was doing. Phryne saw it at once.

Mistral was giving whatever life she had left to save her granddaughter.

Run.

Phryne broke and ran, propelled by the force of her grandmother's words, knowing that this was the only chance she was going to get. It was there in her act of sacrifice and in the force of her words. It was unmistakable and inexorable. Phryne ran as fast as she could toward the place where she had last seen Panterra, ignoring her pain and fear, fighting through her clouded vision and diminished strength. Something exploded behind her, and a huge boom filled the cavern with light as bright as the sun's. The shades of the dead disappeared. The whispering died. All that remained were echoes and wisps of something that looked like smoke and might have been souls.

Phryne, one tiny scrap wailed as it flew past, and then it was gone.

TWENTY

WHEN MISTRAL CALLED HER NAME THAT FINAL time, her grandmother reduced to a scrap of smoke, Phryne lost all control. Wailing in despair, she tore ahead faster than ever—faster than common sense dictated or reason allowed—through clouds of spirit smoke and shrill echoes that resonated off the cavern walls. She didn't think about where she was going and what she was doing; she just ran. She caromed off the walls of the tombs and sepulchers, dodged through the forests of stone markers, a rat trapped in a maze, and fled from both what she could see and what she could not. She heard Pan call her name—heard him call it more than once—but she did not slow.

Behind her, the shades of the dead faded along with the smoke that marked the passing of their remains, and the echoes of the struggle between Mistral Belloruus and Pancea Rolt Gotrin subsided. The dark and the silence closed about her, wrapping her with the ragged rasping of her breathing and the pounding of her footsteps.

"Phryne, stop!"

Pan's voice. Again. No mistake. But she didn't slow, couldn't stop running, continued her uncontrolled flight.

Had to get out of there. Had to escape.

Then she was clear of the cavern and into the tunnel beyond, still running, her lungs burning, her body aching, her vision beginning to fail as small white dots filled the blackness right in front of her eyes. She caught glimpses of the phosphorescent veins of minerals buried in the rock as she sped on and so was not entirely blind to where she was going. But the blindness was coming on as stress and exhaustion threatened, and now she was running from that, as well.

She might have kept running forever had she the strength to match her intent. But she was tiring so quickly, she was beginning to stumble. She fought to keep going, blinded to everything, even to Panterra, who had caught up and was yelling at her to stop.

Then she felt him slam into her, tackling her and bringing her down in a crumpled heap. He crawled on top of her, holding her fast even as she struggled to get up again. His arms encircled her, and he held her to him, lying close, telling her it was all right, they were safe, it was over.

She shook her head violently, sobbing. "It's not all right! She's gone! Mistral's gone! That other woman, that shade, Pancea . . . Did you see? My grandmother's just . . ."

Words failed her, turned to mush, a jumble of sounds that lost coherence. She lapsed into crying jags so deep and long that she was shaking all over and gasping for breath. She couldn't stop. She tried and couldn't. Panterra continued to hold her, even when she begged him to let her go. He held on, all the while hushing her, telling her he was there, that he would stay no matter what, that he wouldn't leave her.

She cried herself out. She couldn't remember ever crying so hard, not even for her father after he was killed. But for her grandmother, she gave up everything she had, sobbing until she was exhausted and was left lying inert and all but lost to herself in Panterra's arms on the cold and the damp of the tunnel floor.

"She did it for you," she heard him say in her ear. "She did it to save you, to give you a chance."

Was that what had happened? It had ended so quickly, so abruptly, the thrusting of the Elfstones into her hands, her grandmother's attack on the Queen of the Dead, the battle between them as the magic exploded out of them both and Mistral yelling at her to run . . .

Run to where?

Where had she run?

"Let go of me, Pan," she told the boy. "I'm all right now. I need to sit up. Please, let me go."

He did so, albeit reluctantly, and she drew herself up and looked around. She had no idea where she was. Except she didn't think she was in the same tunnel that had brought her to the cavern and her grandmother.

She turned to him, taking a deep, steadying breath. "Do you know where we are? Did you come in this way? I don't think I did. I don't recognize anything. Pan?"

He shook his head. "You ran so fast. I just ran after you. I didn't pay attention to where we were going. But I think you're right. This isn't the same tunnel. I came in the same way you did. I just followed your trail until I found you."

"Through the Belloruusian Arch? You followed me?" She was incredulous. "How did you do that? How did you even know to come here?"

So he told her everything that had happened to him since he had left her all those weeks ago, leaving Arborlon with Sider Ament and going in search of help from the cities and villages to the south. She listened with a mix of awe and disbelief as he related the story of Sider's death, the passing of the staff, and his own part in taking up the Gray Man's work and of his efforts at hunting down Arik Siq in order to bring him to Glensk Wood. She was filled with relief at the news that Prue Liss was alive, even though her relief was tempered as she learned further of Prue's encounter with the King of the Silver River and the burden she had been given to bear as protector of Pan. She found herself wondering how a girl no older than fifteen and no bigger than a minute could possibly do anything to keep a bearer of the black staff safe from the demon that hunted him.

When he finished telling her how Xac Wen had found him and brought him to the Belloruusian Arch, where he had used the magic of the staff to force his way through a gap in the door that led down

below the Ashenell, she put a hand on his cheek and began to cry
again. "I hoped you would come for me. I prayed for it. I didn't think
anyone else would—Tasha and Tenerife confined to Aphalion Pass, my
whole family dead or missing, Isoeld and her creatures taking control
of everything. I didn't know what to do. I thought if I could find Mistral, she would tell me . . ."

She caught her breath, stopped talking, and shook her head. "And
now Grandmother's dead, too. I didn't think anything would ever happen to her. She was so strong. It still doesn't seem possible."

She closed her eyes, lips tightened into a thin line. She was dirty
and ragged and worn to the bone, and she couldn't imagine that things
had come to this. When she opened her eyes again, the look she gave
Panterra was hard and brittle. "If I get out of this alive, if I live to see
Isoeld again, she will be the sorriest thing that ever walked."

"We'll get out of this. We'll find a way. Do you still have the Elfstones?"

She had forgotten about them completely. In her panic and desperation, she had lost track of what had become of them. But when she
glanced down at her tightly clenched fist she realized she was still gripping the Elfstones.

"We can use them to find our way out," she said, her voice tired but
hopeful. "These are seeking-Stones. Mistral told me what they could
do. I can make the magic show us where to go."

She climbed to her feet, and Pan rose with her. He didn't look
much better than she did, but she was so happy he was there she
wouldn't have cared if he had looked twice as bad. She saw the way he
gripped the black staff. It suggested an inner confidence that she had
not seen the last time they were together. It suggested that whatever
they faced, he was equal to the task.

She gave him a smile. "All right. Let's see what the Elfstones tell us.
Let's see where we should go."

When she opened her fingers, the Stones lay glittering in the faint
light of the tunnel, their deep blue color alive with an inner glow. She
could already feel the magic responding to her, as if it recognized that
she was their new owner, their caretaker. She felt its soft heat penetrate her skin and fill her with warmth she remembered from when
she'd used the Stones last.

Last, and once only, she reminded herself. She had no real experience with this magic. She would be testing herself when she called on it now. She must be wary.

She must be respectful of their power.

Mistral had intended the Elfstones for her, had died to give them to her so that she might use them to help the Elves. Phryne still couldn't imagine how she would do this. But none of that mattered now. What mattered was finding a way out of the underground. Nothing she did would help the Elves until she was back in Arborlon.

She cupped the Stones in her hand, wrapping her fingers about them, feeling them press against her flesh as she closed her eyes and began to picture where it was she wanted to be. She thought of Arborlon first, of its buildings and trees and gardens, of its people old and young. She thought of Tasha and Tenerife. Nothing happened. She shifted her thinking to blue sky and green grasses, to trees and rivers, to the fresh smells she knew from home. She tried to keep her thoughts straight and focused, but she had difficulty doing so. Her mind kept playing tricks on her, shifting from one picture to the next, from people to creatures to plants to places, back and forth. Everything seemed to morph into something else.

But finally the Elfstones responded, their warmth increasing, their magic abruptly surging into her. She opened her eyes as the blue light exploded out of the Stones and flashed down the tunnel's length, ripping through the darkness for unimaginable distances, piercing a barrier of something that looked to be a thin sheet of clear water, and flashing onward from there to an opening that led out into a forest she did not recognize—the trees old and huge and hoary—before winking out.

"What was that?" Pan asked softly. He'd seen it, too. He looked at her in wonder. "I've been everywhere in the valley and never seen a forest like that one. Are you sure about this?"

She almost laughed. "I'm not sure about anything. I'm not sure where we are or where we're going or how we will get there. I'm not sure that what we just saw is where I asked to go. But the Elfstones say this is what we're supposed to do."

"That isn't how we got here," he pointed out. "This tunnel, the one the Elfstones showed us? That's a different way out entirely. Why is that? Why not take us back the way we came?"

"There's no point in asking me, Pan. I only got to use the Elfstones one time, when I asked them to find . . ." She hesitated, realizing what she was about to say. Then she shook her head and dismissed her reticence. "When I asked them to find you—a test Mistral insisted on—they worked fine. But this time, I don't know."

She felt a flush creeping up her neck as she admitted she had spied on him, and quickly said, "Maybe they don't work as well down here, so far underground, so close to the tombs of the Gotrins and their magic. Maybe they don't respond the same. Or maybe I didn't ask them in the right way. I don't know."

He reached out and closed her fingers back around the Stones. "I think we'll be all right. Let's see where this tunnel leads."

She shoved the Elfstones back into the pouch and the pouch into her pocket, and they set out once more. Movement seemed to help ease her grief. She was still thinking of Mistral, of the way she had just evaporated into nothing, of the loss of the last member of her family. But she was past her shock and despair now, beginning to accept what had happened. She wasn't sure how strong she was, but she knew that she could function again, that her panic was banished and her common sense restored.

She knew, as well, that while Panterra Qu was with her, she would be stronger still. But she was ambivalent about how that made her feel. She didn't want to be dependent on anyone at this juncture; she felt she needed to be strong in her own right, able to face up to and respond to the dangerous challenges that threatened without having to rely on someone else. But there was something about the Tracker's presence—something in his demeanor and attitude—that was reassuring and comforting. She knew she liked him; she had known that from the first time she saw him. But now she was beginning to wonder if what she felt was something more.

Maybe something *much* more.

The thought tweaked at her as they walked, nudging this way and that inside her head, giving rise to possibilities that went way beyond anything she had ever imagined. Some of those possibilities made her blush, but the darkness hid that from the boy. Some gave her pause in a way nothing had for years. She let it all take hold and then released it and washed it away.

It didn't hurt to consider things that might one day be. Or even things that might never be.

When they had walked for so long that she was almost falling down with fatigue, Pan had them stop. He produced food from the backpack he had carried down from the Ashenell, sharing what he had, giving them both a long rest. While they recovered themselves, he talked of the changes to Prue and the fears he had for her.

"She said she was willing to give up her sight in order to help me, but I don't know. Not being able to see colors anymore doesn't sound so bad, but I think it is. Especially for a Tracker, for someone who spends her entire life outdoors. Seeing colors is important to what we do. It helps identify things. It blends with smell and taste and feeling and hearing. They all work together to tell us what we need to know. She doesn't have that now. Not like she did."

"She would do anything for you, Pan." She gave him a long look as she took the last bite of the bread he had given her. "You know that. You shouldn't be surprised by her sacrifice."

"I'm not surprised, but I don't like it. She wasn't aware of what she was giving up. She doesn't even know for sure if it will make a difference. She doesn't know how to help me. No one in the valley has ever come up against a demon. No one knows anything useful—how to defend against them or what it would take to kill one. How can she know what to do?"

Phryne shrugged. "You can never really know, can you? Not even if you know that it's coming and when it will come. Not even if it's something you've faced before. You go on instinct. That's what she'll do here. That's what you'll do, too." She paused. "I don't think the King of the Silver River would have given her this . . . this burden if he didn't think she was able to carry it. He must have some reason for thinking she can make a difference. Otherwise, the whole exercise is pointless."

"I know. I know that's so. Rationally, I know. But emotionally?" He shook his head. "The King of the Silver River is a spirit creature, a being out of the old world of Faerie, and who knows what he's thinking or what he has planned? It might not be what we think."

She gave him a smile. "So it's good that everything else that's been shoved on us is so well sorted out, isn't it? You with your black staff and its magic and me with my Elfstones and their magic, all of it so perfectly understandable and easily managed—no troublesome uncertainties at all."

She watched her smile transfer itself to his face. "Well, when you put it that way . . ." He got to his feet. "When you put it that way, I guess it's time to start walking again."

They set out shortly afterward, leaving further discussion for later. They both knew how hard this was going to be, and they knew as well how the odds were stacked against them in a way that did not offer a great deal of hope. But sharing the uncertainty and danger made it more manageable than it would have been otherwise, and that was something that Phryne was clinging to.

After what seemed like hours—though it was impossible to tell how much time had passed—they reached the place shown them by the Elfstones and found the way forward blocked by what appeared to be a transparent curtain of water spread across the entire width of the passageway. Except that, on closer inspection, they discovered it was not water at all. It was something else, more like spiderwebbing, more fibrous than liquid. It rippled gently, fastened to the rock all the way around at the edges, no gaps at all, its membrane clear enough that they could see colors and shapes on the other side.

They could see the end of the tunnel.

"Isn't that a forest out there?" Phryne asked.

Panterra nodded wordlessly. He stepped forward and touched the curtain experimentally with the end of his staff. The membrane shivered, and then the staff passed through, as if the surface were liquid after all. He drew the staff back again, looked at it, touched it where it had penetrated and shook his head.

"Nothing. No film, no dampness, nothing." He looked at her. "Want to try just walking through?"

She nodded. "I think we have to."

She took his hand. Together, they stepped toward the strange transparency and passed through.

There was a moment of dislocation, of being in one place and then another. The temperature warmed, the light brightened, and the smells that filled the air freshened. All of a sudden they were no longer underground, the passageway and the cavern they had fled as distant as yesterday. Instead, they stood at the mouth of a cave that opened out onto the forest they had seen while still on the other side of the strange transparency.

Phryne looked back the way they had come. The curtain and the passageway it had barred were gone. She was looking at a solid rock wall that formed the back of the cave in which they now found themselves. It was clear that magic had allowed them to leave, but would not allow them to reenter.

"I didn't want to go back, anyway," Phryne said softly, knowing there was no longer any reason even to consider it.

Leaving the cave and its sealed entrance to the underground tombs of the Gotrins behind them, they set out anew, emerging into the light of day and a forest of tall, multi-limbed trees that looked like oaks, but were something else entirely. Huge, hoary old growth, they formed a forest that stretched away from the cave and the hillside into which it burrowed for as far as they could see. Moss and lichen formed an eerie second skin over trunks and branches, the colors a mix of contrasting greens that allowed only bits and pieces of the graying bark beneath to show through.

"What are these?" Phryne asked.

Panterra shook his head. "Whatever they are, they're dead. Look at the branches. Lichen and moss everywhere, but no sign of buds or leaves. The whole forest is dead, probably a long time for this much covering to spread. This doesn't look like anyplace I've ever—"

He stopped in midsentence and looked at her, and she knew at once what he was thinking. "We're not inside the valley anymore, are we?" she said. "We're outside again."

"I think so. I don't understand it. The time and distances are all wrong. It must be the magic that made it possible for us to come this far in such a short time. We couldn't have walked it in less than a day or two." He paused. "But why would the Elfstones bring us this way? Why didn't they keep us inside the valley? Phryne, did you do something . . . I don't know, something that . . . something different . . ."

She gave him a look that silenced him at once. "I did exactly what I was told to do by Mistral. I did the same thing I did when she told me to test it the first time by trying to find you!" This time she didn't blush. She was too angry. "Don't you try to put this on me!"

"I was just . . ."

"You were just suggesting I did something wrong!"

"But I wasn't . . ."

"Wait a minute." She held up one hand, palm out, to silence him. She stood frozen in place for long moments, thinking. "Just wait. Maybe this *is* my fault. I was supposed to focus on where I wanted us to go. But I didn't use just one image. I used images of Arborlon and Tasha and Tenerife and trees and sky and a lot of other things. I couldn't seem to keep one thought steady. I didn't know what image I should use."

She paused once more, shaking her head in frustration. "Except that nothing I pictured in my head was this. Everything was the valley. So why are we out here?"

Pan's voice softened. "Maybe the Elfstones made a decision of their own on where they wanted us to be. All magic is unpredictable. We know that much. So maybe . . ."

She moved close to him, taking his wrists in her hands, gripping tightly. "This is my fault, isn't it? I'm the one who uses the Elfstones, so it has to be my fault." Fresh tears filled her eyes, and her composure broke. "I'm sorry, Pan. I did the best I could, but I don't think it was enough. I let myself be distracted. I didn't prepare. I was still thinking of Mistral and what she . . ."

She was sobbing and rambling both at once, shaking her head and jerking at his arms as she held on to him, unable to stop herself. Pan stood motionless before her, looking distraught, and then all at once he freed himself with a quick twist of his wrists, put his arms around her, and pulled her against him. "That's enough, Phryne," he whispered, his face pressed against her hair. "Don't say any more. You don't have to apologize to me."

He held her for a long time, even after she had gone quiet and was holding him as tightly as he was holding her. She had her face buried in his shoulder and she was content to stay there, happy just to be held and comforted by the warmth of his body and his words and to not let anything disturb the moment.

But then he eased her away from him, and she looked up to meet his steady gaze. "Wherever we are, we'll find our way back to where we need to be. It doesn't matter how this happened. It only matters that we're safe now, that we're free of the Gotrin shades and the under-ground tombs. That's enough for us."

She nodded, swallowing hard. "I don't know what's happening to me. I never behave like this. I never fall apart." She shook her head in dismay. "It's losing Mistral or using the magic or . . ."

"Or both and the fact that you're exhausted." His eyes fixed on hers. "How long since you've slept for more than a few hours?"

She shook her head, unable to remember. "I don't know. A long time. Days, I guess."

"You'll sleep tonight, I promise you. Come on. Let's start walking. We have to get out of this forest in order to see where we are."

They set out through the maze of moss-and-lichen-covered trees, through the skeletal remains of the dead hardwoods, the remnants of the old world and reminders of what had been lost. Once, this forest must have been beautiful, so many huge old giants clustered together, their interlocking boughs covered with leaves, sunlight filtering to the earthen floor. There would have been clusters of wildflowers and ferns and flashes of small animals and birds. That was all gone now, the forest dead and deserted of life, a graveyard every bit as empty and bereft as the one they had just escaped.

"This is taking too long," Phryne declared not long after, drawing up short. She was recovered by then from her breakdown and better able to think about what was needed. "I should try using the Elfstones again."

Pan stopped and faced her. He looked unconvinced. "I don't know," he said carefully. "Using their magic might call attention to our presence. We don't know what might be attracted."

"But how much more trouble are we likely to get into if we just wander around in here? We could be going in the exact wrong direction."

"I don't know," he repeated.

She took his hand and squeezed it. "Please, Pan. Let me try. I know I can do this. I'll be careful."

He squeezed her hand back, persuaded. "All right. Do it."

Once more, she produced the Elfstones, dumping them out of their pouch and into her open palm. This time, she formed a steady image of Arborlon, dismissing all other choices as she closed her eyes. The familiar warmth rose from the Stones into her fist and arm and from there into her entire body. She felt the magic strengthen as it surged through her, and her eyes snapped open.

Blue light lanced from her closed fingers in a different direction from the one they had been taking, angling off to their left and cutting through the trees until it found open country, blasted and barren, where clusters of rocks and dead trees dominated ravines that crisscrossed to foothills that bordered mountains she recognized immediately.

The flow of the magic dissipated, and the blue light died away. "Did you see?" she asked him excitedly. "Did you see those mountains? Aphalion Pass cuts right through them into the valley. Arborlon is just beyond!"

"I saw," he answered. "Now we know. Everything is all right. We know where to go. Thanks to you, we know."

For a moment, they stared at each other without speaking, both of them smiling and giddy. Then at the same moment he reached for her, she moved into his arms and kissed him on the mouth. She kissed him for a long time, hungry for it, for him, wanting the closeness, the feel of him. She didn't care what it meant or how it had happened or even what it would lead to. She just wanted to do this—something she had secretly considered for longer than she could remember—without having to give it thought or measure its consequences.

She liked it that she was the one who broke the kiss. She stepped back from him, still holding his arms, and she saw at once the confusion in his eyes. "I didn't mean . . . it was just . . ."

"I wanted to kiss you," she said, cutting him short. "I did it because I wanted to, and I'm glad I did."

He nodded quickly. "Me, too. I wanted to kiss you, too."

She took his hand and began walking in the direction that the Elfstones had showed them. "I might want to kiss you some more," she told him after a moment, giving him a wicked smile. "Maybe a lot."

He took a long time to respond. "I might want that, too," he said.

TWENTY-ONE

THEY HAD WALKED A LONG WAY INTO THE SKELETAL bones of the forest, the fecund smells of decay and ancient earth assailing their senses—already spinning from the kiss—before Pan made himself let go of Phryne's hand. He did so reluctantly, but with a sense of relief, as well. He couldn't seem to think straight when she was holding on to him like that. His memory of the kiss kept crowding out everything else, and in country like this he couldn't afford the distraction.

Breaking contact seemed to help. She moved away from him a few steps once he let her go, and when he glanced over she gave him a neutral look. He couldn't help wondering why she had done it. Not that he wasn't happy she had; he most assuredly was. He didn't think he would ever have a kiss like that again. Not so deeply passionate and not under such desperate, almost frantic conditions. But he didn't understand the reason for it. She could have chosen another way to express her euphoria. She could have just held him, and he wouldn't have given it a second thought.

Of course, he had embraced the kiss—had wanted to share it—every bit as much as she had wanted to give it to him. He hadn't done anything to stop it. In retrospect, he knew that even if he had the chance to go back and change things, he wouldn't.

But having the memory embedded in his consciousness—a memory he knew he would never lose—was bittersweet. After all, where could kissing Phryne lead that would serve any purpose? Phryne's life and his own were going in different directions. Now that he had assumed possession of and responsibility for the black staff and she had done the same with the Elfstones, it might seem as if their shared involvement with magic would actually bring them closer together. It might also seem that being from different Races wouldn't matter, either, since neither of them had shown the slightest inclination to let that be a barrier between them. He had witnessed the reluctance of people from the various Races to intermarry or to form attachments that would cause difficulties for them later, but he didn't think that was an issue here.

What was a problem and why they could never be together was that once she was absolved of the accusations against her, then in accordance with Elven law Phryne was going to become Queen of the Elves. With her father gone and her stepmother holding the throne under false pretenses, she was the logical choice. When that happened, she could never become involved with someone from another Race, especially someone like him. Trackers were rangers and scouts; they were seldom settled for more than a few days in one place. A Queen must be settled in one place forever and her mate or consort must remain at her side.

He didn't know why he was thinking about this, and he cut himself off angrily. One kiss did not create a lifetime relationship. One moment did not define everything that would happen in the future.

And yet . . .

Phryne and he. Together.

He couldn't stop thinking about it. There was no question that he liked her. Or even that she liked him. It wasn't something he could mistake. It was there in her eyes and voice, in the way she talked to him, in the way she responded. He couldn't say he didn't find her fascinating in a way he had never found anyone else. He felt so different when he was with her, more so even than with Prue—who, after all, was his best friend. But this was something else. He had never thought it mattered that his brother–sister relationship with Prue was all he had. He had never wanted anything more, not with her or anyone. He liked his wilderness life. He liked sharing that life with Prue, the two of them companions on the road to new experiences and new discoveries every day they were together. Other men might settle down and marry. Other men might find a life in the villages and towns. He had never wanted that.

Until now. Until Phryne Amarantyne.

He took a deep breath to steady himself, deciding as he did so that breaking contact with her physically hadn't solved the problem. He was still distracted, still thinking about her, still wondering what was going to happen to them. He knew, and at the same time he didn't know. Not for sure. Wouldn't know for sure, in fact, until their fate in the business at hand was settled.

Still tasting her mouth on his, still visualizing the moment in his head, he forced himself both to push a few levels deeper in his thinking and to pay attention to what was around them.

Their surroundings didn't change much in the few hours that were left to them before darkness. The forest went on much as before, the mossy, lichen-striped trees stretching on in a seemingly endless maze, their shadows beginning to lengthen as the sun faded west. All this time, they saw nothing but the trees. Not even birds found homes here; not even the smallest creature. He guessed there must be insects, but they weren't in evidence. It was a graveyard as stark and empty as the underground burial site of the Gotrins. While still daylight, it was easy enough to see what lay around them, what might prove dangerous. But as twilight approached and the last of the light began to fade, it became more difficult to be certain—even for Panterra, whose eyesight was excellent and who was trained to navigate in the dark.

"We have to find shelter," he told her.

These were the first words he had spoken to her since the kiss, and they felt forced and awkward. Panterra did his best to pretend that they weren't, that what had happened was relegated to the past and everything was back to the way it had been. But he didn't think he was fooling her, and he certainly wasn't fooling himself.

He cast about as they walked, looking for a likely campsite. After they had walked another fifteen or twenty minutes, he found a tangle of fallen trees that formed a makeshift shelter on three sides. While it would not conceal them entirely, it would give them some protection. He didn't really think there was anything in these funereal woods that would cause them problems—or even bother to show itself—but there was no point in taking chances.

Placing Phryne inside the weave of limbs and trunks, he found several loose branches not far away and dragged them over to close off the entry, as well. When he was almost done, he stepped inside the shelter with her and dragged the last branch into place, sealing them off.

"Now we should be safe," he declared, giving her his most reassuring smile.

"We'd better be," she replied, giving him a look. "Because now we're trapped in here."

She sat back against the heavy branches, watching for his reaction. Then, seeing his confusion, she laughed. "Don't look so serious, Pan. It's all right. I know you did it to keep us safe. Come here. Sit with me."

He moved over and leaned back against the branches next to her. He could feel the heat of her shoulder and arm press up against him, and he felt her looking at him.

"Did you ever imagine that your life would change all at once like this?" she asked him.

He shook his head. "I didn't think it would ever change. I thought it was all settled. I would be a Tracker, working with Prue, for as long as I lived. I guess I still see things that way, even though I know they aren't."

"Well, think about it. You didn't want it to change. You didn't ask for it to change; it just happened. No one asked you what you wanted. No one asked me, either. We're here, sitting together in this mass of brambles and branches, because of other people's actions rather than our own."

He thought about it, glancing over at her now. "We could have refused to do what was asked of us. Me, more easily than you, I guess. But we could have said no to what we saw happening. We could have left it to someone else."

"Not and be the people we are. But I just think it's so odd. I had my life planned out, too. I wasn't going to be anything other than what I was—not for a very long time—because my father was going to live out his life. It would be years before anyone came to me and said it was time for me to be Queen." She laughed softly. "Even saying it sounds odd. I never thought of myself that way. I never wanted it. I wanted something . . ."

She paused a long time. "Just something different, I guess."

"But your father must have spoken about it with you. He must have told you that you'd be ruler of the Elves after him."

She leaned against him, resting her head on his shoulder. "We never talked about it. We never talked about much of anything after my mother died. He just went away from me. In his head, anyway. He left, and I was mostly alone after that, and the idea of being Queen was never in my thoughts. Even after Isoeld became his wife, it was never there. Not like I'm sure it was in hers." She paused. "I was stupid!"

"I don't think so. I think you were just being yourself. I would have done the same thing. Anyone would have."

She looked up at him, tears in her blue eyes. "Sometimes, you say just the right thing, Panterra Qu."

They rifled through his backpack, pulling out what little was left of their food, which was pretty much a reprise of the meal they had eaten earlier. They still had some water, so they were able to make do for the moment. But Pan knew they would have to find more of both soon, and that might not be easy outside the familiar confines of the valley. The old world had been poisoned and depleted in so many ways that it was impossible to guess at what might be safe to eat and drink.

As they consumed their meal, he found himself studying her between bites, trying to do so without drawing her attention. He liked how she looked, how everything about her seemed just right. Her chestnut hair, blue eyes, the slant of her brows and narrow cheekbones, the upsweep of her Elven ears, the slender parts that were smooth and soft and still so strong—everything that had always been there and to which he had paid so little attention. Or which he had failed to look at in quite the same way, he amended. After all, he had found her intriguing right from the first, when she had walked with him during their climb out of Arborlon to Aphalion Pass, asking him questions, teasing him slyly, showing so much interest. Then, he hadn't given it a lot of thought. Now he couldn't seem to give it enough.

When they had finished eating and had cleaned up their little den, they leaned back once more against the tree limbs and stared out at the darkness. It was so deep and black they could see almost nothing beyond the branches that enclosed them.

"I would like to see more of our new world," she told him after they had been silent for a time. "I know it's dangerous and unfamiliar, but I want to know about it."

"I think you might get your chance," he replied.

She looked at him. "You do? Why do you say that?"

"Because I think we're all going to get to know more of it as time goes on. The valley won't be our home anymore. We'll do what our ancestors did before they were closed away. We'll go exploring. Haven't the Elves been talking about that for a long time now? At least since there were signs the protective wall was coming down?"

She nodded. "That's so."

"I don't think we can stay in the valley much longer, even after the Drouj leave. We have to go out and see what's there. We have to learn what survived and how to deal with it. We have to educate ourselves. Trackers understand this. Whenever something new is discovered, we go to study it right away. A new place, a new creature, a new plant. We build on our knowledge of things that way. It won't be any different for us now that we have the world outside the valley to study."

"Well, I want to be someone who does that. I want to be like you. I want to travel to places and see things and learn about it all. I don't want to sit around a palace and be Queen. I never wanted it before, and I don't want it now. What use is it? Some people like making decisions and giving orders and controlling other people's lives. Even Father liked it, I think. But I don't. I don't want any of it."

"Who will take the throne if you don't?" he asked. "Aren't you the last of your family?"

She shrugged. "There are cousins, other families related to the Amarantynes. Or to the Belloruus line. Let one of them take the job. Once we're safe again and I've dealt with Isoeld and her creatures, I'll give up the Elfstones and leave."

She made it sound simple enough, but he wondered if someone in line for the Elven throne could simply walk away. Would it even be allowed? He hadn't heard of anyone ever doing so.

"We don't have to spend time thinking about it just yet," he said finally. "We've got to find a way to stay alive long enough to make worrying about it necessary."

"I know." She made a dismissive gesture. "You don't have to tell me that. I know what we're up against."

She seemed to go away then, looking off into the darkness, easing away from him just enough to let him know she didn't want to think about the present, and talking about the future, about its possibilities and her dreams, was her way of escaping. He heard her exhale slowly and felt her lean forward, head lowered as if the weight of all that had been laid upon her shoulders was suddenly a burden too great for her to bear.

"It's just so unfair. For all this to happen at once—the Drouj invasion, the death of my father and grandmother, being given responsibility for the Elfstones, and finding myself trapped outside the valley and hunted like a fugitive. I just feel beaten down by it."

He leaned forward, placing his head next to hers. "It isn't easy now and it won't be easy later, but we'll get through it, Phryne. You and I. We'll look out for each other. We'll take care of each other and things will work out."

He didn't know if he believed that or not, but he said it because it seemed that it needed saying. If they weren't committed to that much, then he didn't see any hope for all the rest of it—for the larger threats of the loss of their homelands and the destruction of their peoples, for a failure of any form of magic to survive if theirs was lost, for a collapse of what remained of civilization and a quick descent into anarchy.

She inclined her head sideways until it was touching his own. "I could go with you when it's time, Pan. When you decide to go out into the larger world, to leave the valley and go exploring, I could go with you. I would like that. I could learn to be a Tracker. You know I could. You've seen what I can do. I'm strong enough."

He put his arm around her and hugged her against him. "I don't think there's anything you can't do."

"Will you take me with you, then?"

Her voice was so plaintive that it almost broke his heart. She was asking so much more than what the words suggested. He could tell it from the tone of her voice and in the hesitancy of the way she spoke. He could feel it ripple through her where they touched heads and shoulders. She wasn't just asking if he might consider her request; she was begging.

"Please, Pan. Will you take me?"

He took a deep breath, his arm tightening about her. He knew what he should say, what it made sense to say, what everything that was practical and right suggested he say. But he also knew what she needed to hear. He knew how close she was to coming apart. As strong as she was, as steady as he had seen her on so many occasions when there was every reason for her to crumble, it was different now. Here, in this place and time, she was right on the edge.

"I'll take you," he promised.

She didn't say anything in response, didn't do anything. She went as still as the air in their forest of dead trees, staring down at her feet, keeping the contact with him that she had formed, but not increasing the pressure.

"Promise?"

"Promise."

"You're not just saying it?"

"What do you think?"

"I think maybe I love you."

His eyes, lowered before, snapped up at these words, and suddenly he was staring out into the darkness, which was nearly complete, and finding in the space directly outside their makeshift shelter a pair of huge yellow eyes staring back.

It required massive willpower not to jerk away and leap up and instead to remain as still as she was, but somehow he managed it. The eyes were bright and their gaze intense, reflecting the glow of distant stars that peeked through the heavy clouds and filtered through the trees. Steady and unblinking, they seemed to float in the darkness like giant orbs.

"Phryne," he said softly.

"What?"

"I want you to do something for me. I want you to lift your head just a little and look outside the shelter. But don't say or do anything else. Don't make any other movement at all. Don't be frightened."

She did what he asked, raising her head and staring out, and he felt the shiver that ran through her when she saw the eyes. But she kept herself from moving or speaking; she kept from panicking.

After a few long moments, she said, her voice very small, "What is it?"

As she said it, the eyes suddenly shifted, sliding to the right, and suddenly the body they occupied became partially visible, bits and pieces of it revealed by the ambient light. It was a massive cat, bigger than anything Pan had ever heard of and certainly bigger than anything he had ever seen. Its coat was a mottled gray and black, its head broad and flat with small ears, and its neck encircled by a thick ruff. When it shifted again, all the time studying them, he could see the muscles of its long, sleek body clearly defined beneath the sheen of its hide.

A massive paw lifted and pulled experimentally at the branches, which gave way easily to the immense pressure. Pan heard Phryne gasp and felt his own heart begin to race in fear of what might be coming.

But then the cat lowered its paw and circled away, gone as quickly as wind-blown smoke. Phryne clung to Pan, as if somehow she could find protection by doing so. He couldn't imagine what he would do against something that huge. He had the staff and its magic to protect them, but he wondered how useful they would be. It was one thing to stand against something as bulky and slow as an agenahl, but something else again to face a creature like this.

The cat reappeared suddenly, materializing back in front of them in almost the exact same spot as before, eyes first and then bits and pieces of its body coming into view. The darkness was a perfect cover for it; when it blinked and the eyes disappeared, the rest of it seemed to vanish, as well. It watched them with renewed interest for a few long seconds more, and then casually yawned. Its mouth opened and kept opening until Pan had to look away to avoid staring any longer at those huge, sharp teeth gleaming in the dark. He could barely breathe, and he was pretty sure that Phryne was beyond even that.

When he looked up again, the cat was gone.

Phryne exhaled sharply, and then whispered, "That was the biggest, scariest . . ."

She trailed off. "I know," he whispered back.

They sat close together in the darkness without moving for a very long time, waiting for the cat to return. But it did not reappear, and when he couldn't stand the silence any longer, Pan said, "I think it was just curious."

She nodded. "I think so, too. But I wouldn't want to take the chance of being wrong."

"Did you see what it was doing? It was studying us. It didn't look hungry. Just . . . interested."

"I guess it could have gotten to us if it wanted to. These branches wouldn't have stopped it."

"I don't know *what* would have stopped it."

"I don't think we ever want to be in a position where we have to find out. How big was it? What do you think it weighed?"

"A cat that size? Five hundred pounds easily. Probably eight or nine hundred. All muscle. A hunter."

"But not hunting us."

"Not tonight, anyway."

His arm was getting stiff from being wrapped about her shoulders all this time, and he started to take it away. "No, don't do that," she said at once. "I'm freezing. Can't you feel it?"

She scooted over farther and pressed against him. He couldn't tell from that alone, but when she put her hands over his, they were ice cold. He put both arms around her at once. "Are you feeling all right? You're not sick, are you?"

"Not yet. But I don't want to risk it. Can you put the blanket around me, too?"

He loosened the straps that bound the travel blanket to his backpack and carefully wrapped it about her shoulders. "Now get inside it with me," she said. "Like before. Put your arm around me again."

He did as she asked, pulling her against him and covering them both with the blanket. It would have helped if the blanket was bigger, but there was no help for that. They were lucky to have anything at all to warm themselves. "Better?"

She shifted her head until she was looking at him. He could feel her gaze more than see it, could feel strands of her hair brush up against his face as she leaned forward until her forehead was resting against his. "A little."

He felt her adjust her position slightly, turning toward him. Then her fingers were fumbling at the front of his shirt, working at the buttons, loosening them. He felt a moment of panic, thinking that he needed to stop this, but not wanting to. He tried to think what to say. "Phryne, I don't . . ."

"Shhhh," she said at once. "Don't say anything. Keep watch for that cat and let me do this."

When she had all the buttons undone, she slipped her hands inside and pressed them against his skin. They were so cold that he jumped in spite of himself, shivering as they moved from one warm place to the next.

"Much better," she murmured. "Am I too cold for you?"

He didn't trust himself to answer, so he simply shook his head no. He closed his eyes as her hands moved around to his back. Pressing harder.

"I'm getting warmer already," she said, and kissed him lightly on the cheek. "Here, let's try this."

Her hands slipped out again, and he could feel her moving against him once more. Cocooned by the darkness, he waited to see what she was doing. Then, abruptly, she took hold of his wrists and pulled his hands inside her now open blouse and held them there.

He gasped in shock. "Phryne, this isn't . . ."

"Don't talk," she said again. "Don't say anything. Just leave your hands where they are."

Then she slipped her own hands back inside his shirtfront and moved them up and down his sides.

"Listen to me, Pan. I don't know what tomorrow or the next day or the next is going to be like, but I know about tonight. So just do what I tell you. I promise it won't hurt."

He was not surprised at all when he discovered that she was right.

TWENTY-TWO

WHEN PANTERRA QU WOKE THE FOLLOWING morning, it took him a minute to realize that he was alone. He was still rolled up in the blanket, cradling his head on one arm as he looked out from his prone position at the shadowy forms of the trees in the predawn light. Everything was very still, but he could smell the woods and the damp in the air, and when he glanced at the slowly lightening sky he saw a mix of heavy clouds and mist dropped down so low they scraped the treetops. He was warm and drowsy and filled with a sense of happiness and contentment he found hard to believe.

But when he reached back for Phryne, he discovered she was gone and jerked upright at once, the mood broken. He didn't see her anywhere at first and cast this way and that, trying to make her out through the dimness and the shadows. He dropped the blanket, crawled from beneath their makeshift shelter, and climbed to his feet, ready to go looking.

Then he spied her, well off to one side, sitting quietly on a fallen trunk and looking off into the distance toward which they had been traveling the day before, so still she might have been a part of the forest. He watched her for a moment, waiting to see if she would notice him. When she didn't, he looked down at himself and, feeling foolish, quickly pulled on his boots and clothing. When that was done and she still didn't seem to have noticed him, he began rolling up the rumpled blanket so he could strap it to his backpack.

"I thought you might be planning to sleep the day away," she said suddenly.

He glanced up from his work and saw her looking at him. By now, he was vaguely irritated with her—first, for leaving him alone, and second, for acting so nonchalant about everything. The way she was speaking to him made it sound as if nothing at all of what he so vividly remembered had even happened.

"I didn't know you were awake. In fact, when I didn't find you next to me, I thought you might have gone somewhere."

"Gone somewhere?" She laughed and brushed back her hair with both hands. "Where would I go?"

She rose from her log, walked over to him, and knelt close. "Did you think I might leave you? Is that what you're saying?"

He shrugged. "No, I guess I didn't think that."

She reached up and touched his cheek and then leaned in to kiss him. "You are a terrible liar, Panterra Qu. That is exactly what you thought. But I forgive you."

She was so beautiful in that moment, so bright and fresh and wonderful to look at, that he was pleased beyond words to be forgiven, even if he didn't think for a moment he needed it. "I was just worried about you."

"Just hold that thought. I might have need of it later. Do we have anything to eat?"

They didn't, of course. They had eaten the last of their food the night before and drunk all but the last few swallows of their water. Until now, it hadn't seemed all that important. But their hunger was real and pressing, and suddenly they could think of little else. Bereft of breakfast and anxious to do something about it, they packed up the last of their things in preparation for setting out. There would be little chance for food until they got back inside the valley, and nothing that happened before then was going to make things any easier.

They began walking once more, still heading in the same general direction they had been going earlier, still looking for an end to the lichen-and-moss-shrouded forest. The sun rose above the eastern horizon, but the day remained overcast and gray while the air grew thick and sultry. Around them, the trees formed the walls of a maze that hemmed them in and held them prisoner. They could tell themselves there was an end to this, a way out, but it didn't feel like it.

Neither of them spoke for a long time as they traveled, lapsed into an uncomfortable silence. Pan didn't know what was wrong, but something definitely was. Still clinging to the tattered remnants of his euphoria and anxious to share what he was feeling, he finally grew impatient. "What were you thinking about back there, sitting off by yourself?"

She glanced over. "Maybe I was thinking about you. Would you like it if I was?"

He grinned in spite of his uncertainty. "You know the answer to that."

"I know the answer. But it isn't what I was doing. I was thinking about something else."

When she didn't offer an explanation, he said, "Tell me."

"It doesn't matter."

"Yes, it does. Tell me."

"You don't have to know everything about me."

"I have to know this. Tell me."

She shrugged. "I was thinking about choices and how we make them. About how some are so easy and some so hard. I was thinking how we make some because we want to and some because we have to. Does that help?"

He smiled. "Well, I hope last night's choice was one you wanted to make and not one you felt you had to."

"Actually, it was both."

"Because it was something you'd been thinking about and . . ."

She wheeled on him suddenly, bringing them both to a stop. "Pan, let it go. I don't want to talk about it right now."

He could hear the irritation in her voice, and he was suddenly confused and hurt. "Don't talk about it? What does that mean? I thought . . ."

"Last night was last night, and it's over with. Don't try to make more of it than what it was."

"Don't make more . . ." He glared at her. "That's a little difficult at this point. Besides, didn't you tell me you loved me? Are you saying I shouldn't make anything of that?"

She studied him a moment, biting her lip. "That's not what I said. I said, 'I *think* I love you.' There's a big difference. Besides, there are other things that . . ." She left the sentence hanging and sighed. "Let's walk while we discuss this."

Side by side, they went on. Pan stared at the ground in front of him, caught up in a whirl of emotions, chief of which was a mounting sense of doubt that only moments ago hadn't been there.

"When you lose a father and a grandmother, and they are the last of your family, you see things a little differently," Phryne said finally. Her voice was softer now. "You think about how fragile life is, about how quickly it goes by, how quickly things become lost. You take life for granted most of the time. You live it in the moment and you don't think a lot about the future because the future seems a long way off. But when people you love die, suddenly the future seems a whole lot closer and very uncertain."

She glanced at him quickly and looked away again. "But it's every-thing, really. The Drouj threatening to invade our home, my step-mother murdering my father so that she could be Queen, being imprisoned and escaping and going down into the tombs of the Gotrins to find my grandmother, being given the Elfstones to use to protect the Elves when I don't really know how to do that . . ."

She trailed off, shaking her head.

"It's not so different with me," he interjected quickly, trying to find common ground. "Losing Sider, losing Prue and then getting her back only partially whole, being hunted by this demon I didn't even know existed, and now running away with you. It's not so different."

"Then you should understand what I'm feeling. Time is something precious, especially now. We might not have all that much of it. So there is a temptation to do things because you don't want to lose the chance. You don't want to let those things slip away and never know what they might have been like."

"Last night," he said.

"Last night," she agreed.

"But that doesn't mean—"

"It doesn't mean a lot of things," she interrupted him. "Especially in the way I thought it would. But it does mean a few. Last night was a small moment in whatever time we have left. I did it because I didn't want to miss out on something wonderful. I did it because I was frightened. I felt alone and vulnerable, and I wanted to feel something. I wanted to be close to someone, and you were there. I like you, Pan. Maybe I even love you. But last night was a small part of everything else that's happening to us. That's what I was thinking about this morning. I was thinking about what I have to do if I can stay alive long enough to do it. First of all, I have to discover what I am supposed to do with the Elfstones. Mistral gave them to me because she felt that using them would let me help my people. But how will they do that? How am I supposed to use them?"

She held up one hand quickly to stop him from saying anything. "Just let me finish this," she said, stepping closer to him now, putting one hand on his cheek. "Let me say everything I have to say."

He could feel her affection for him in the touch of her hand, and all of his anger and growing sense of loss were suddenly gone, and he was ready to do anything for her.

"I have to go home again and face Isoeld. I have to find a way to prove that she had my father killed and should not be Queen of the Elves. I have to stand up with my people—with Tasha and Tenerife and Haren Crayel and all the others—against the Drouj. I have to find out if I can do what Mistral believed I could do. The choice is already made for me in all these things. I didn't make it; it was made for me. It isn't something I can walk away from. I know that now."

Her hand dropped away. "Then, Pan, when that's done, maybe I can think about us. In the right way, the way I would like to—not just because of last night or some other night but because there might be a whole lot of nights, maybe even a lifetime. I can think about it because then there will be a future that isn't measured in hours or days."

"It isn't measured that way now," he insisted.

She gave him a sad smile. "Of course it is. You don't have to pretend this is all going to turn out right. I know the odds of that happening. I know what we are up against. But I need you to acknowledge that I do. Don't pretend with me. Don't try to shelter me. I needed that yesterday, but today I'm someone else. I'm who I was always supposed to be, I hope. I'm strong enough to do what I have to do. I need you to be strong with me."

He nodded slowly. "I just worry we've lost something since last night, and I don't like how it makes me feel. I don't like that you don't think last night means something more—that maybe it doesn't mean as much to you as it does to me. It makes me sad."

She stepped up to him and kissed him hard on the mouth and held the kiss for a very long time. "There," she said, stepping back. "That's what it means to me." She smiled at the look on his face. "But it's over and done with, and we have to think about what's coming. We have to leave last night behind."

He didn't want to leave last night behind. He wanted to build his life around it. He wanted to make it the beginning of everything. But he nodded slowly and forced himself to smile back.

"All right," he agreed.

But it wasn't all right and he wasn't done with it, either, not now and not ever. That was what he promised himself as he let the matter drop.

THE DAY PASSED SLOWLY after that. Neither felt much like talking so mostly they were silent. The only exchange of words came when Panterra—assiduously studying his surroundings in an effort to stop himself from thinking about Phryne—felt it necessary to pass along information on what his instincts and tracking skills were telling him. Twice they crossed the prints of what he believed to be the cat they had seen the previous night. Although the tracks were several days old, he was taking no chances and made it a point to direct them a different way. Once, they caught sight of a solitary agenahl, huge and ponderous as it threaded the gaps between the forest trees. Seemingly out of place in such confines, it nevertheless managed its way. It did not detect their presence, and they stood perfectly still until it was well out of sight.

Several times, they saw huge birds overhead, great wings outstretched, soaring through the cloud cover and gloom. It reminded Pan of the dragon, though these were clearly species of a different sort and nowhere near as large. But he knew that life had evolved outside the valley and much of it was larger and stronger and more dangerous than anything living inside. When the two merged, the Races were going to have to find a way to equalize the unequal struggle that was inevitable.

A handful of small rodents with sharp teeth came at them threateningly at one point, but Pan used a quick burst of magic from his staff to turn them away. Insects bit and stung them when given half a chance, and something far up in the mossy trees hurled sticks and nuts at them. But at least they were seeing signs of life now, an indication that their woodsy graveyard was beginning to change into something less barren and empty. Pan picked up a handful of the discarded nuts and broke open the shells. Edible. He gathered more and shared them with Phryne, and they ate hungrily. Then they pushed on, shrugging off their discomfort, keeping their direction fixed in their minds, watching out for each other.

All the while, they searched diligently for a source of fresh water. A few times, they crossed streams that were fouled and smelled as bad as they looked. Once, they found a pool that appeared to be clean but then saw animal bones and half-eaten carcasses scattered about it. The longer they traveled, the more convinced Panterra became that they were not going to find drinkable water until they were safely away from this forest.

It took them almost until sunset to achieve their goal, emerging into a series of barren, empty hills that stretched away father than they could see, folding into lowlands and clumps of heavy brush to their right and abutting a broad plateau to their left. But finally they could see the mountain ranges that were their destination, though the peaks were little more than a ragged line against the horizon and miles away from where they stood.

Phryne glanced left and right. "Which way should we go?"

Pan took a moment to study the choices and shook his head. "Nowhere just now. It's too late to travel any farther today. We'll find a place to spend the night and take this up again in the morning."

He could see that she wanted to object, that she was anxious to press on. But to her credit she didn't argue the matter, deciding perhaps that he was right about trying to cross those hills in darkness. So she simply nodded and joined him in searching for that night's shelter. There was not much to be found without going back into the woods, and neither of them wanted to do that. They ended up settling on a fold in the hills that would keep them mostly hidden and hunkered down in its lee. There was nothing to eat or drink, so they soon rolled up under Pan's blanket, huddled close together, and drifted into an uneasy sleep.

Nothing disturbed them that night, although had anything threatened them Pan would have known. He was awake almost the entire time, unable to sleep, unwilling even to try, his thoughts on Phryne as she pressed close to him, wondering at how things could change so quickly and wishing he could have done something to stop it. At least, he told himself, she wasn't trying to avoid him altogether, sleeping so close to him. At least she wasn't signaling that she no longer wanted him near.

But this alone provided scant comfort, and his thoughts of her were dark and despairing. The hours passed and sleep eluded him as surely as his hopes for the future he had once imagined possible.

When dawn broke and she woke, he kissed her once on the cheek, quick and purposeful, and rose to see what the new day had to tell him. He was hungry and thirsty and tired, as he knew she also was, and he wondered how long they could go on this way.

"I don't know where we are," he admitted as they stood together and looked out across the empty terrain. "I don't recognize any of this. I don't know where we are or which way the passes lie."

She nodded, as if expecting him to say as much. "Then I'll use the Elfstones to find out."

He looked at her doubtfully. "There's a risk in that, as you already know."

"But if we don't use them, we'll continue traveling blindly ahead, and that's every bit as dangerous. I think we have to."

She waited, looking at him. "I think so, too," he agreed finally.

He moved a few steps away from her and took up a protective stance as she prepared to use the Elfstones, reaching into her pocket to produce them and pouring them out of their pouch and into her hand. She stood there a moment studying them, as if not quite sure what it was she was holding, as if weighing what it meant to summon the magic. Then she folded her fingers about the Stones, faced off toward the mountains, and closed her eyes.

Long moments went by. Pan waited impatiently, eyes scanning the surrounding countryside. He didn't like it that they were so out in the open, unprotected even by the trees. If anything attacked, it would be on top of them almost before he could react to it.

But there wasn't any choice if they wanted to get a bearing on where they needed to go.

He glanced at Phryne. Nothing was happening.

After a long time, she opened her eyes and looked at him in bewilderment. "It isn't working. The magic isn't working. I can't make it do anything!"

She sounded almost stricken, suddenly in doubt again. He went to her at once and put his hands on her shoulders. "Yes, you can. I've seen you do it before, and you can do it again. Just remember that you are still new at this, so it might take a while before you can make it work right away."

He took his hands away. "Tell me what you were envisioning, what you were focusing on in your mind?"

"Aphalion Pass," she told him.

"All right. Maybe that's too vague an image. The passes all tend to look somewhat the same. Try picturing Arborlon instead. That's a more specific image. Wherever the Elfstones take us, we will have to go through one of the passes. That's good enough."

She studied his face silently. Then she turned away again, folded both hands about the Elfstones, closed her eyes, and went still as stone.

Again, Panterra waited.

This time she had a better response. The Elfstones flared to life, their bright blue fire quickly building strength. It lanced out across the barren hills toward the mountains, illuminating everything, rendering the whole of the landscape clear and close, revealing miles of rough, blasted terrain before closing on the massive rock walls. Once there, the light angled into a split that had been invisible just seconds before, careening down canyon walls, through a narrow defile, past a defensive wall constructed at a narrows with dozens of bodies scattered on either side, and finally down into the valley they both knew so well and to Arborlon's familiar cottages and gardens.

Then the light flared and died away, and the images vanished.

The boy and the girl exchanged glances. "That wasn't Aphalion Pass," she declared.

"No," he agreed. "It was Declan Reach. Those were the defenses I worked on with the men from Glensk Wood. But those men are all dead, and the defenses are still abandoned. I don't understand it."

"I don't, either. Why aren't others from the village guarding that wall? Something bad has happened, Pan."

He looked back out across the hills, unwilling to speculate. "If Declan Reach is the closest entrance into the valley, we're way south of Aphalion. We need to start walking."

They set out anew, fresh purpose driving them beyond thirst and hunger and exhaustion, revitalizing their determination. They entered the hill country and began the arduous task of countless ascents and descents, of navigating ravines and gullies while making sure they kept in sight the destination shown them by the Elfstones. It was not hard to do so since three clearly recognizable peaks formed a sharp row of spikes right where the pass at Declan Reach awaited. The trick was in minimizing the amount of time wasted in finding their way over the uneven terrain, a task they were not in the best shape to undertake.

They did what they could, but much of the time they were below the horizon and could not see clearly where they were going until they scaled the next rise and could measure the direction to their destination anew. It was slow, monotonous work, and they found their strength rapidly draining away. The day was overcast once again, and the clouds had trapped a layer of heat and dust beneath their covering, making the boy and the girl thirstier still.

Soon both were sweating as they plodded along with unmistakable looks of resignation and despair on their faces.

Several hours later, when they finally stopped to rest, it seemed they were no closer than before.

"I don't know if we can do this," Phryne groaned, lowering her head between her knees and running her fingers through her tangled hair. "I'm so tired."

Pan knew that she was just voicing the same frustration he was feeling, so he didn't reply. They sat where they were, not speaking, waiting for their strength to return.

Then Pan looked up suddenly. "Do you hear something?"

Phryne didn't even bother to look up, let alone answer. She just shook her head.

But Pan got to his feet at once. "Shouting, screams—somewhere over there." He pointed north, beyond Declan Reach. "There's a battle being fought."

Phryne rose quickly then, looking where he was pointing. "I don't see anything."

"I don't, either," he said. "But I can hear it clearly enough. Do you?"

"I do now. Who do you think it is?"

He looked over at her. "Find out. Use the Elfstones."

She didn't even bother to argue. She produced the Stones and held them out before her in the direction of the fighting. She kept her eyes open this time, watching and waiting, her concentration complete.

The Elfstone magic flared to life, exploded out of her hand, and shot away into the distance. Over miles of hills and gullies, over barren ground and jagged rock, out across the broad expanse of grasslands beyond, the magic traveled, opening a window into everything that lay between them and its final destination.

Then the battle was right in front of them, and they could see the armies clashing at the head of a pass that was undoubtedly Aphalion. Elves and Drouj were locked in a terrible struggle, and bodies already lay scattered across a landscape where blood ran in bright crimson streams.

The magic flared once more and died, leaving Panterra and Phryne openmouthed with horror.

"I have to go there!" she said at once, turning toward him, despair and shock twisting her features. "I have to help them!"

She was already moving away in a swift walk as she dropped the Elfstones in their pouch. "Hurry, Pan!"

He rushed to catch up, taking a quick look about as he did so, an automatic response to a sudden decision that took them ahead so recklessly. It was a pivotal moment. As he scanned earth and sky in all directions, sharp-eyed and suspicious, he saw the black dot. It was so far away that for a moment he almost missed it. But within seconds it had grown much larger against the blue of the sky. It was moving toward them, and it was coming quickly.

"Phryne!" he called out in warning.

She swung back, slowing but not stopping, confusion replacing determination on her face. "What is it? Pan, why are you . . ."

Then she saw it. It was much closer now, close enough that it was taking shape, the particulars of its fierce features revealed. Phryne stood where she was, whether in shock or awe, Pan couldn't tell. He thought to run to her, to pull her back, to try to find a place for them to hide. But there was no point. They were standing in open country devoid of hiding places. They were exposed on the crest of a hill, visible for miles to anything with good eyes, and Pan was certain beyond any doubt that the eyesight of the creature coming toward them was excellent.

"Pan!"

He heard her call out his name in something of a gasp, but he could not tell if it was a summons or an exclamation of some emotion he could not fathom.

Then, its great wings spread, its long neck angled forward, and its huge clawed feet outstretched, the dragon reached them and began to descend.

TWENTY-THREE

"I DON'T THINK THEY'RE RETURNING THIS WAY," XAC Wen said.

Prue, sitting off to one side, her back resting against the stones of the Belloruusian Arch, did not reply. She was ragged and dirty, her clothes stained and rumpled, her face smudged with dust and streaked with tears of rage and frustration. It was nearing dawn, and she had been sitting there all night with the boy, waiting for Pan to reappear.

"I mean, this is exactly what happened to Phryne," the boy continued, repeating an observation he had already made a dozen times before. "She walked beneath the arch, disappeared, and didn't come out again. I waited then just like I'm waiting now, and it was a waste of time."

"Don't talk anymore," she told him.

But he did, of course. If there was one thing Xac Wen was good at, she had discovered over the past fifteen or so hours, it was talking. He talked incessantly, anxious to share his thoughts—all of his thoughts—

making no distinction between those that had purpose and those that did not and doing nothing to keep the number of repetitions to anything remotely resembling a reasonable count.

"I'm not saying anything bad has happened to them—that they're dead or anything. I'm not saying that. I just think they might have found another way out, that's all. I'm just saying I think we have to consider the possibility."

She didn't care what he thought they should do, and she didn't want to hear his views on the subject of Pan's well-being. Mostly, she just wanted him to go away. She was a solitary person by habit and occupation, and the only company she had ever really enjoyed was Panterra's. What little respite she'd gotten from Xac Wen's incessant chatter came when she sent him away to find food and drink, back when yesterday was ending and night was coming on. Eating and drinking were necessary if she was to maintain her energy, and the boy had agreed to scrounge up a meal for them both.

Most of that precious energy, so far, had been used up listening to Xac Wen talk and working hard not to think about how much she would like to cut out his vocal cords.

But attacking the boy wouldn't help the situation, and she wasn't entirely sorry he was there. Notwithstanding his inability to keep silent for more than a few minutes at a time, he provided her with much-needed companionship, a chance to sleep, and a fresh set of eyes to make sure the wrong people didn't discover them. She had no idea who else she could trust, but she guessed not much of anyone besides the boy.

Really, there was no help for it. It was settled, as far as she was concerned, that she was not leaving the Ashenell without Pan. She had been told that she would be able to protect him, to help keep him safe from the things he couldn't keep safe from by himself—from the demon certainly, but probably more than that. She knew she hadn't done much to help him so far, but that didn't change her belief in what the King of the Silver River had told her. Even with Pan missing and perhaps lost, she would not give up. Sooner or later, he would resurface. When that happened, she would be there waiting and afterward would stick to him like a second skin.

Even so, she continued to remain uncomfortable with the fact that she had no idea at all how she was going to do that. Thinking of it made her feel helpless. Especially right now. She didn't know where Pan had gone or what to do to find him. She didn't know if she could protect him from the demon hunting them. She didn't even know what she should do about Xac Wen, although with her patience almost exhausted, she knew she was going to have to do something soon.

"Maybe we ought to take a walk through the Ashenell and see if there isn't another place in the tombs where Pan might have come out," Xac said, breaking into her musings. "He might even be looking for us right now."

She didn't think so, but she knew an opportunity when she saw one. Sending the boy out to search for Pan would at least keep him from sitting around and driving her crazy with his babbling. "That's a good idea. Why don't you make a careful search of the burial grounds while I stay here and keep watch."

Xac headed out with a wave and a smile, and it almost made her feel bad about what she was doing. Almost, but not quite enough to call him back. Who knew? Maybe he *would* find something. Maybe Pan had come out somewhere else besides the way he had gone in. They couldn't be sure if no one looked, after all.

She watched him until he was out of sight, wondering briefly if he would be all right and almost immediately deciding that if anyone could be safe in the Ashenell it would be Xac Wen, and she resumed her position in front of the arch. No one had gone past them the entire time they were there, from yesterday afternoon until now. As far as she was able to tell, no one had even come into the Ashenell. She felt like she was the last person alive in the city. The sounds beyond the cemetery boundaries were muffled and indistinct; mostly there was only the silence and the rustle of the wind in the trees and the singing of the birds.

She felt newly discouraged. She wasn't going to be able to keep this up much longer. It didn't matter what she hoped might happen if she stayed where she was, the end result was the same. She wasn't doing anything and she knew she needed to, even if she didn't know what it was. She just couldn't continue to sit here like this.

She allowed herself a few minutes to pout and grumble in a whisper that didn't reach beyond her own ears. She was entitled. Pan should have taken her with him. He shouldn't have gone under that arch alone, leaving her behind. He knew how vulnerable he was if she wasn't with him. She had made it clear enough.

Unless he hadn't believed her. Unless he thought the King of the Silver River had lied to her or tricked her and she was being used in some secret way she didn't understand. The thought paralyzed her momentarily. Then she gave a mental shake of her head. She didn't believe this; of course she didn't. The problem was that no matter what she believed, Pan might believe the exact opposite. It was difficult to accept that he wouldn't tell her so, but no one was acting or thinking in the usual ways since the protective wall had failed and the Drouj had appeared.

"Just look at me," she whispered.

Have faith in yourself.

The voice was in her head, but all around her, too. She cast about in surprise, but not in fear. She recognized the voice.

Panterra Qu cannot come to you. You must go to him.

"But where am I supposed to go?" she demanded, coming to her feet, continuing to look for him in vain. The King of the Silver River was there, but invisible to her. "Tell me what to do!"

She sounded more desperate than she wanted to, but she couldn't help herself.

Go where you are led, Prue Liss. Do what your heart tells you.

"Who is going to lead me? Where will I be taken? What do you mean, 'Do what my heart tells me?' My heart isn't telling me anything!"

The words exploded out of her as she wheeled this way and that, searching for the source of the voice.

"Tell me what to do!" she repeated, her voice becoming a scream.

But this time there was no response. She waited, but there was nothing more. She circled the arch, as if by doing so she might find some sign of him. There was nothing to find. He was gone. Having said what he had come to say—those few small words she clung to like a lifeline—he had left her.

She was suddenly enraged. Was he watching everything? Did he see her from some distant vantage point that allowed him to measure what it was she was doing and how successful she was in doing it? She hated the idea. She had been given a quest and deprived of a part of her eyesight in order to fulfill it, and yet now it seemed she was not to be trusted in spite of her sacrifice.

For a few minutes, she was caught up in the white-hot heat of her anger, unable to see past a raft of imagined betrayals and deceptions. Then, finally, she calmed down enough to regain her perspective. A Faerie creature like the King of the Silver River would have sufficient magic to be able to track her movements; she was foolish to think anything else. If he saw something that troubled him, he would certainly consider speaking to her about it. Pan was missing and she was lost as to how to find him. So he was telling her what to do.

Sort of.

But not exactly.

After all, he hadn't answered any of her questions directly. He could have told her something more specific about where Pan was. He had chosen not to do that, and she supposed he must have had a reason for making that choice. But he had also implied she was still under an obligation to protect Pan. Otherwise, why had he bothered to tell her Pan wasn't coming back and she must go to him?

She was marching about, trying to think it through, when Xac Wen appeared on the run, shouting her name.

"Prue! Are you all right? I heard you scream!"

He had his long knife out, prepared to defend her against whatever danger threatened. A brave little boy, she thought. Now she really was ashamed.

She held out her hands to hold him back. "It isn't anything. I just got frightened. I thought I saw something, but I was wrong. I'm sorry."

He looked at her doubtfully. "Well, I just wanted to be sure you weren't in any . . . I don't know. What was it you thought you saw, anyway?"

"A ghost. A shade. Forget it. Any luck finding Pan?"

He shook his head. "Why don't you go look for a while and I'll stay here. Go that way." He pointed. "I haven't searched over there yet."

Because she didn't want to talk to him anymore about the scream and needed uninterrupted time by herself to think about the words of the King of the Silver River, she nodded her agreement and started off.

She didn't think she would accomplish anything by doing so, but she was anxious to be alone again.

She moved through the tombstones and sepulchers at a steady pace, casting about idly as she walked. The day was gray and overcast, the smell of rain in the air, sweet and slightly metallic. The dawn had left a layer of dew on the grasses and leaves, and moisture stained the stones of the graveyard in dark patches. She kicked at the earth in frustration, her thoughts scattered by Xac Wen's abrupt appearance and an ensuing rush of doubts about what she should do or even if she were going to be given a chance to do it.

Birdsong rippled through the stillness in small chirps and long cries, and she found herself staring through the shades of gray that colored her new world, trying to find the birds themselves while at the same time attempting not to think of how bleak everything looked. She blinked a few times, as if by doing so she might improve her ability to see colors. But nothing changed. She realized that her sight impairment was beginning to depress her in a way that was pervasive and crippling. She couldn't quite escape the sense of loss that grew out of having everything she saw reduced to grays and blacks. She could remember other colors so clearly, could still picture them in her mind. But it wasn't the same when she couldn't actually see them. The loss diminished her world, and by doing so it diminished her, as well.

Tears filled her eyes. Suddenly she wanted to cry.

Then she saw the scarlet dove. It was soaring high above the oak trees that were clustered all through the cemetery, a splash of brilliant red against the moody gray backdrop of her vision, a thing so beautiful that she could no longer hold back her tears. That something so wonderful could exist was a cause for celebration and the giving of thanks. She watched it swoop and dart, winging this way and that, riding on the back of the wind.

When it changed course abruptly and came flying directly toward her, she uttered an exclamation of delight and hugged herself. The dove flew at her with fierce determination, then banked away at the last minute and came to roost on a tree branch not thirty feet away.

Prue stared at it in disbelief. She had thought she would never see it again. Yet here it was, returned out of nowhere. It perched quietly on the branch, its sharp little eyes fixed on her as if watching to see what she would do. Prue was afraid to move, worried she might frighten it away. She badly wanted it to stay where it was so she could look at it, the only color she was allowed in her sight-impaired world. She wanted to look at it forever.

But at the same time she was admiring it, she could not help wondering why it was there. Why had it come back? Why now? She had thought it lost to her forever, once she found Pan.

Once she found Pan, she repeated.

And now she needed to find him again.

Go where you are led . . .

She heard the words of the King of the Silver River whispering in her mind, her memory of them clear and sharp. She stifled a gasp of recognition, still staring at the bird. It was the scarlet dove that had appeared to her when she was alone in the wilderness and had first discovered her sight was diminished. It was the dove that had shown her the way home—and to Pan.

She knew at once it wasn't a coincidence that the dove had returned.

She couldn't help herself. "Do you know where he is?" she whispered. "Beautiful thing, have you come to help me?"

The bird lifted off, flew a short distance away, and landed on a different branch. Prue walked toward it slowly, trying hard not to hurry, not to frighten it. "Are you taking me to him?"

When she was close, the dove flew to another branch, this one a little farther away, and landed once more. Prue stopped questioning whether the bird might be leading her to Pan. She knew that was exactly what it was doing. She rushed after it, no longer trying to hold back.

The bird flew swiftly, and soon she was running to catch up to it. She had gone all the way to the boundaries of the Ashenell when she realized she was being taken a different way than she had come. If she continued, she would leave the cemetery without passing Xac Wen.

Which would mean, of course, he would not know where she had gone, only that she had disappeared like Panterra and Phryne before her.

She almost turned back, but the fear of losing sight of the scarlet dove kept her from doing so. It was more important to find Pan than to explain herself.

Once she had passed through the south gates, she knew there was no going back, only forward. She hesitated one final time, still debating about taking time to find the boy. After all, when she had followed the dove back to the valley from wherever the King of the Silver River had left her, it had waited on her when she faltered to make certain she could follow it. Wouldn't it be the same here? But watching as the scarlet dove circled back and then flew on and out of sight, she experienced doubts she could not banish. Finally, she gave up thinking she could do anything else but follow it and ran on.

As she did so, the Elves she passed gave her second looks, apparently noticing her eyes and wondering how a blind girl could run as quickly and unerringly as she did. She slowed, tiring anyway, still not recovered from her journey coming up from Glensk Wood to Aphalion Pass and then back down to Arborlon. She had slept little and eaten less. She was already wondering how far she would get before thirst and hunger knocked her down.

She was still struggling with the guilt she felt for running out on Xac when she passed a boy who was about his age. She gave him a quick glance, then wheeled back and called him over.

"Do you know a boy called Xac Wen?" she asked him.

"Everyone does," the boy answered, trying hard not to look at her milky eyes. His narrow face and severely downward slanted eyes gave him a feral look. "What's he done now?"

"Nothing. But he's sitting at the Belloruusian Arch waiting for me, and I need someone to tell him I'm not coming. Can you do that? Do you know the arch?"

The boy nodded. "I know it. But I'm not going there."

She glanced over her shoulder, searching for the dove. She saw a flash of scarlet far in the distance, high in the trees. "I'll give you something if you do." She rifled through her pockets and produced a small metal bracelet Pan had made for her years ago. It was one of her most treasured possessions. "I'll give you this," she said, holding it out.

The boy took it from her, looked it over carefully, and nodded. "Bargain. I'll tell him what you said. Who are you?"

"My name is Prue. Tell him I think I know where Panterra is, and I have to go there right away. Can you remember to tell him that?"

He nodded, gave her a kind of salute, and dashed off, heading in the general direction of the Ashenell. She had to hope for the best now. She had to pray he would do what he had promised.

She wheeled back and began running again. Ahead, the scarlet dove swept across the trees, just barely staying in view. She followed it out of the city and down the Elfitch and back toward Glensk Wood. She found that odd. It wouldn't be going there, would it? Would Pan have gone home?

Even when she was well beyond Arborlon and continuing south, the scarlet dove leading her on, she was still trying to decide.

THE OTHER BOY'S NAME WAS ALIF, and Xac Wen had seen him around, but didn't know him otherwise. He listened to what Alif had to tell him, questioned the boy's memory, and dismissed him.

That Prue Liss.

Girls were strange anyway, but she was stranger than most. First she screamed like she was under attack when she wasn't and said she saw a ghost. Then she went looking for Panterra Qu and claimed she'd found him and was going off to join him. Alone. Without coming back to tell any of it to Xac and without asking for his help—which she almost certainly would need—but instead sending Alif in her place.

No explanation for any of it.

How did she find out where Panterra was if all she was doing was searching for him in the Ashenell? She was already leaving the cemetery when she encountered Alif, so she hadn't found him there. But where had she found him?

He started off in the direction she had taken—the one she must have taken to have encountered Alif where she did, not too far outside the south gates. Maybe it was too late to catch up to her, but he intended to try. He didn't like being left behind like this. She owed him an explanation, and if he could find her he would demand one. Hadn't he done an awful lot for her? Hadn't he stayed with her when he could just as easily have left?

But instead, she had left him! That was the thanks he had been given for all he had done!

He passed through the south gates and began walking toward the edge of the city and the Elfitch. Along the way, he stopped Elves he knew and asked if they had seen a young girl, describing her. A few had noticed such a girl, a strange one who was half running, half walking, staring off into the distance as if she were seeing something they weren't. Xac Wen didn't know about this last part, but the "strange" label certainly fit. He picked up his pace, thinking he might still catch up to her.

But when he reached the Elfitch, he discovered she had passed the guards stationed there some time ago and no one had seen which way she went after that.

He stood at the top of the ramps, staring off into the distance. There were only two choices, really. She could have gone south and home to Glensk Wood or she could have gone north to Aphalion Pass. He couldn't imagine why she would choose the former; Panterra Qu would hardly go back to his village after coming all the way to Arborlon to help Phryne. There was no imaginable reason for it.

He looked over his shoulder and back at the city. Of course, she might still be somewhere close by if she thought that was where Panterra might have surfaced.

What was he supposed to do?

Having no better plan, he backtracked into the city to gather together supplies before heading out to Aphalion Pass to relate what had happened to the Orullian brothers.

TWENTY-FOUR

LOCKED AWAY IN THE BASEMENT STOREROOM OF the council chambers at Glensk Wood—the very same storeroom that had once imprisoned Arik Siq—Aislinne Kray wondered if everyone had forgotten her. She had been imprisoned for so long now that she no longer even knew if it was day or night. They had given her a box of candles so she wouldn't be left in the dark, a pitcher of water and bowl with which to wash herself, a pallet and blanket so she would have a place to sleep, a chamber pot, and nothing else. They came now and then with food and to empty the pot—guards who had been given the task of keeping watch over her—but they never spoke to her, not even when she asked them questions, and they never responded to her requests for sewing materials or books to read or even implements with which to draw.

Even now, she had no real idea what had happened to bring her to this sorry state.

What she did know, and even this was by way of an educated guess, was that she was being blamed for Arik Siq's escape. She could not imagine why that was. That she would do anything to help one of the Drouj—especially the one responsible for the death of Sider Ament—was preposterous. She had no reason to want to help such a man and nothing to gain by doing something that would harm her own people.

Yet here she sat, accused of a gross betrayal and consigned to this room for what it seemed might be the rest of her life.

Rationally, she knew it wouldn't really be that long, but it was beginning to feel like it. When you couldn't see outside and know whether it was dark or light, when you couldn't speak with anyone about what was happening in the larger world, it felt as if time had stopped completely.

That even Pogue had not come to see her was particularly hurtful. She knew their relationship had been suffering, especially since Sider Ament had appeared in the village with his news of the collapse of the protective wall. But she hadn't thought he would abandon her completely. She had assumed he would at least want to hear her explanation of the charges her accusers—whoever they were—had placed against her. She had thought he would be willing to let her offer a defense. But apparently she was wrong. He had not come once, had not sent word, had done nothing to contact her since her imprisonment.

She bent to the bowl and splashed water on her face. She did this more often than she liked to admit, trying to wash off the grit and dust that seemed to attach itself to her body even though she mostly just sat in one place. It was becoming a habit she couldn't seem to break, a response to the way her skin was tightening and her nerves were always on edge. Being shut away like this was beginning to affect her in unpleasant ways. Washing herself seemed to help, but in the end, she knew, it might not be enough to keep her sane.

Finished with her ritual, she sat thinking about the world outside the walls of her prison, about sunlight and fresh air, about the sound of children's voices, and all at once she was crying. She didn't try to stop, letting it go, wanting to try to get it out of her system. At some point, she was going to need to be strong enough to deal with whatever her jailors had planned for her. Because if there was one thing she was sure about, it was that she wasn't going to escape further punishment.

Even so, she was surprised when the lock to the storeroom door released, the door swung open, and Pogue Kray walked in.

She rose to meet him. She had given up expecting anyone other than the guards who kept watch on her, least of all her husband. To her surprise, she was pleased to see him, relieved that he had come to her at last. Better late than never, and maybe now he could be made to see the wrong that had been done to her.

Although nothing in the hard set of his face suggested that this would be the way things went.

"Aislinne."

He spoke her name not as a greeting but as an expression of distaste. He did not approach her, made no attempt to embrace her. Instead, he moved off to one side, allowing the guard to pull the door closed behind him. He stood in the shadows, just barely at the edge of the candlelight, arms folded over his chest.

Suddenly angry, she said, "Why have you waited so long to come to see me? Am I that loathsome to you?"

He nodded slowly. "Worse, Aislinne. You have betrayed me as a husband and as leader of this village and its council. You have shamed me with your actions—not only now, but before, over and over again."

"You speak of Sider Ament. I never betrayed you with him, not ever. Nor did I do anything to help free the Drouj. He is no friend of mine."

Her husband turned away from her and spat. "He was your lover. Most likely, they both were."

Aislinne was astonished. "That is not true! That doesn't even make any sense! I can understand your suspicions about Sider, unfounded though they are. But the Drouj? Why would you think something like that?"

"Because you were seen!" he roared, causing her to flinch in spite of herself. "Because it was reported, and now everyone knows!"

"Seen? Seen by whom?"

He made a dismissive motion with one hand. "What does it matter? You were seen, your actions reported, your betrayal revealed. You must have thought I wouldn't care, since our marriage flounders and our time together no longer means anything. You must have been attracted to the Drouj and acted in your impulsive way."

"Pogue, this is nonsense . . ."

"But setting him free?" Her husband ignored her efforts to interrupt. "Letting him loose knowing he will go back to his people and bring them through the passes and into the valley to kill us all? Did he promise he would come back to save you if you helped him? Did you believe him?"

He was almost in tears, this big, burly man who could crush her with barely a thought. He stopped abruptly, putting his hands over his face in an effort to hide it from her.

"Pogue, no."

With complete disregard for what he might do to her, she walked to him and put her hands on his shoulders and held fast to him. "These accusations are all lies," she said quietly. "I don't care who spoke them or who repeated them afterward. I have never even spoken with the Drouj. I have never been in the same room with him. I have not betrayed you in any way. I did not set him free. I would never do anything like that, not for any reason. Certainly not because of an attraction to him. Look at me, Pogue."

He dropped his hands and faced her.

"I will say it again. I did not set him free. My word on this as your wife. My most sacred word."

"I don't know what to believe," he said finally. "Not anymore."

"Look at me," she said again. He had shifted his gaze downward, but now he lifted it and stared into her eyes once more. "Believe in me. Just on this, if nothing else. Believe what I am telling you. Do not abandon me. Do not let them do this to me. Let me face my accusers. Make them bring my accusers forward to condemn me to my face. I ask nothing more. Just that."

He shook his head, signifying the impossibility of her request. "Skeal Eile says there is no doubt. You were seen."

Skeal Eile. She had thought as much. "Skeal Eile hates me. You know that. If he were looking to place the blame on anyone, he would think of me first. If he has witnesses, let him produce them. Let me face them. This is wrong, Pogue. You know it is."

He ran his big hands through his coarse, dark hair and down over his face, wiping away the tears that streaked his cheeks. "I want to believe that. I want to believe what you tell me. But something . . . something keeps me from doing so. Doubts I cannot shake. They haunt me. I see you with him. Then I see you with Sider." He shook his head once more. "It drives me half mad. I can barely function. That's why I didn't come sooner. I couldn't make myself."

She put her arms around him and held him. "Something is very wrong here. Something more than what has happened to me. Something has infected the whole village. It hasn't felt right here for days, but I had dismissed it until I was imprisoned. We have to find out what it is. You and I. We have to remember who we are and what we mean to each other. You are my husband, and I love you. Sider Ament is dead and gone, and the past is gone with him. You and I are the present. But we are threatened, Pogue. Our home is threatened. Glensk Wood and our friends and neighbors, too. Can't you feel it?"

He nodded slowly. "I've wondered."

"Have you sent anyone to defend Declan Reach yet? Has there been any word from Esselline?"

He shook his head. "I haven't even thought about Esselline or the passes. Skeal Eile said . . ."

He trailed off. She looked in his eyes and saw the confusion and uncertainty mirrored there. This wasn't like Pogue—nothing like him at all. He was strong and firm and decisive. He would never equivocate as he was doing now.

"Go to the council and ask that I be brought before them to answer to the charges lodged against me," she begged. "Ask that I be given a chance to defend myself. Please."

He nodded slowly. "I will, Aislinne. I will do that." He sounded stronger now, less uncertain. "I should have done it before. I'm sorry. I didn't want any of this to happen to you."

He bent forward, this big man, and kissed her softly on the forehead. The gesture was hesitant, almost as if he thought she might break under the weight of his touch.

Then he turned and went over to the door, calling loudly for the guard to come let him out.

THE RAGPICKER, who had been listening outside, stepped away quickly and headed back up the stairs to the council chambers. The guard hadn't noticed him; the ragpicker had used magic to make certain of that. He had suspected that it would be wise to listen in on Pogue Kray and his wife when he had heard the latter announce to Skeal Eile his plan to visit her. The council leader wasn't a strong man when it came to his wife. Even as subverted as he was by the ragpicker's magic and as convinced by Skeal Eile's insistence on his wife's infidelity, he was influenced more by his love for her than by anything else. The ragpicker had known that at some point his hold over the big man would weaken and his plans would have to change.

As he departed the building and went out into the midday sunlight, he was already considering his choices in the matter.

First, he could kill the woman. He could make it look like suicide, and once she was dead she wouldn't be able to dispute anything. On the other hand, it would likely mean the end of any hold he had over Pogue Kray and a possible collapse of his larger plan for the village and ultimately the boy who carried the black staff.

Second, he could let the woman have her chance to dispute the charges and rely upon his own "witnesses"—compelled to say what he wanted them to say—to convince the council she was lying. That was a big gamble. The woman was strong-willed and well respected in the community, and there were already those who were questioning the decision to lock her away.

Third, he could put his larger plan into action right away and remove all possibility of disruption.

Deciding which choice to select was surprisingly easy. The ragpicker already knew which one it would be.

He walked on through the village to the home of Skeal Eile and without bothering to knock walked through the door. The Seraphic would be home. He had given him instructions to stay there until he returned from spying on Pogue Kray. These days, enmeshed as he was in the machinations of the demon and convinced that his participation would eventually yield results favorable to his own ambitions, Skeal Eile always did what he was told.

The Seraphic came down the stairs from his second-floor lodgings and looked past the ragpicker quickly, checking to see if someone had followed him. The ragpicker smiled. Skeal Eile was still worried about appearances when appearances were the last thing he should be thinking about.

"Was he persuaded by her?" the other asked quickly. His sharp-featured face looked troubled. "Did he listen to her?"

"He will ask the council to allow her to speak in her defense. He will ask that she be allowed to confront her accusers. We will have to produce the witnesses we claim we have. Unfortunate, but it can be done."

The Seraphic stepped away, shaking his head. "I don't like this. Aislinne Kray is dangerous. It would be better if we simply killed her."

"Would it?" The ragpicker frowned. "I notice you haven't done so before this. What makes it any wiser to kill her now?"

"We have her charged with a crime and imprisoned. It would be a simple matter to arrange her death. Suicide. Guilt and the ensuing depression over her betrayal led her to take her life, we would say." He shrugged. "Pogue would be upset, but he would get over it. He doesn't love her all that much."

The ragpicker shook his head. *Idiot. He loves her more than you think.* "It creates problems we don't need. It would be easier if everyone simply forgot about this woman. It would be better if they had their attention focused elsewhere."

The Seraphic looked at him with renewed interest. "You have something in mind?"

The ragpicker paused, thinking how best to word what he wanted to say so as not to alert the man to what was coming. It was time to end this charade, but he wanted things to go smoothly.

"I think we need to consider moving ahead more quickly with our plan for you to take control of your followers—as well as those who might be persuaded to become your followers. A demonstration of your strength is needed. An example must be made. The woman is an obstacle that needs removing, but first you need for all the people of

Glensk Wood to recognize that you are the proper person to lead them. That as Seraphic of the Children of the Hawk, you are the logical choice—not Pogue Kray."

Skeal Eile nodded eagerly. "I agree. But the people will not choose me over Pogue. They accept me as leader of the sect, but not of the entire village. How am I to change that?"

"Can you not simply persuade them?" The ragpicker's voice was sly and insinuating. "Can you not use your oratorical skills and your nascent magic? How can you lead if you cannot command?"

The Seraphic flushed. "This is your idea," he said petulantly. "Instead of questioning my abilities, shouldn't you be advising me? You have the experience and the magic. You are the demon!"

The words were out of his mouth before he could stop them, and terror filled his eyes. "I didn't mean . . . I was just making a point that . . ."

Whatever he intended, it came too late to save him. He must have seen it in the ragpicker's eyes because he tried to turn and flee. But he was an ordinary man and no more, while the ragpicker was exactly what the other had called him and much too quick to be denied. The demon seized the Seraphic's wrists and locked his fingers about them. Skeal Eile's face twisted in pain, and he struggled desperately to escape, flailing wildly and hauling back with all the strength he could muster to break the ragpicker's grip. But strength of the sort the ragpicker possessed far surpassed that of the Seraphic, and the latter's attempts were in vain.

Slowly, inexorably, the ragpicker dragged his prisoner close—so close that they were soon eye-to-eye with almost no distance between them.

"I fear you are losing control of yourself, Skeal Eile," the ragpicker whispered. "I fear you are incapable of holding your tongue. You seem content to let your emotions rule your common sense, even when you should know better."

"No, please!" The Seraphic was still fighting, but the fear in his eyes told his captor he was already beaten. "Let me go! I won't say another word to anyone! I'll leave! I'll go away! Far away! You won't ever see me again!" Tears began streaming down his hatchet face. "I'll do anything you say! Anything!"

The ragpicker smiled. "All true. Every word of it, Seraphic. Even if not in the way you intended."

Skeal Eile tried to scream, but the ragpicker's bony hand flashed to his neck and pressed against a bundle of nerves and muscle buried beneath his skin. There was a sharp pain, and suddenly he could no longer speak. He resumed fighting, but it was a weaker, resigned effort. His spirit was broken, and he saw his own end.

"Hold steady, now," the ragpicker whispered, eyes bright and predatory as he leaned close. "This will only take a moment."

SKEAL EILE TRIED to fight against what was happening, but he was powerless against the creature that held him. He knew it was a demon he fought against, and he understood what that meant. He even understood in general terms the nature of his inevitable fate. He was going to die. He had crossed a line, and he was going to pay the price. At some point, he had lost his perspective completely by allowing this creature into his life, by embracing its cause as his own, by accepting it as an ally. Always so careful before, always making certain that he was the master and not the slave, this time he had forgotten himself.

He thought suddenly of Bonnasaint, whom he had not heard from since the other left on his hunt for Panterra Qu. What had become of him? No word at all, and nothing to suggest whether he had done what he was supposed to do.

He thought of the Drouj, Arik Siq, and found a sudden, perverse satisfaction in the fact that he would return with his people, and they would decimate the valley. What difference if he died now? The end was decided for all of them.

He thought of Isoeld—vain and ambitious and foolish—now Queen of the Elves and thinking herself safe. Perhaps she was, for the moment. Perhaps her stepdaughter would come to a bad end, just as her husband had. Perhaps she would find a way to make that happen. Perhaps she would even find a way to escape the Drouj. But sooner or later, she would find herself on the receiving end of a long knife, dying in the same way her husband had, an expendable pawn in someone else's schemes.

Then, suddenly, something was happening to him. He could feel himself being turned about so that he was facing away from the demon. He could feel the other pressing against him from behind. The pressure was intense, and then it was excruciating. He was being crushed. He tried to scream, but his vocal cords had been silenced and no sound came from his open mouth. He gasped and panted and drooled as the pressure increased to a point beyond bearable, and all he wanted to do was to make it stop.

"Good-bye, Seraphic," he heard the demon whisper.

He experienced a strange sense of invasion, as if the other were reaching inside him to make room for himself. His body seemed to widen and stretch to allow for this, his organs pushed aside and his bones broken and shattered. He shrieked silently, but he could only hear the sounds he was making in his head. He begged for it to stop, to be over. He fought to keep himself together, but he was already beginning to disappear. His thoughts scattered and his mind lost focus. Everything began to close down and turn fuzzy. The pain eased slightly, and a strange sense of listlessness replaced it. There was nothing left for him. Nothing.

At some point, he could feel the demon's thoughts begin to intermingle with his own, as if the demon had gotten inside his head. In a few brief seconds, all of the demon's dark memories were revealed to him. All the years spent hunting down humans, all the killings and destruction witnessed and perpetrated, all the terrible ravages that had led to the destruction of the old world—they were there in his mind.

He thought he would go insane, but before that happened his brain simply quit working and his world went dark.

*   *   *

WHEN IT WAS FINISHED, the ragpicker gave himself a moment to adjust to his new look. He hunched his shoulders and stretched his arms, testing the fit of his new skin, adapting to his new appearance. He walked over to the window and looked at his reflection in the glass. What he saw pleased him.

He was no longer the ragpicker. He was Skeal Eile.

But a better, stronger, more capable Skeal Eile, freed from the other's mortal weaknesses and limitations.

The demon smiled. The Seraphic had served his purpose, but his usefulness was ended. What was needed now he could best accomplish on his own.

What was needed was an event so shocking it would bring the bearer of the black staff running right to him.

TWENTY-FIVE

WORD TRAVELED QUICKLY, AND BY THE END OF the day people were flocking to the village square in Glensk Wood to gather for the address that the Seraphic of the Children of the Hawk had announced he would deliver. They came not just from within the village proper, but from miles away, traveling by whatever means they could. It would be an announcement of cataclysmic proportions, it was rumored—one that promised to be life changing. No details were offered, not even to Pogue Kray and the members of the village council. The Seraphic had declared that all present would hear the announcement together so that there could be no mistaking its meaning. Those who could not come at once might hear of it later, but by then it would almost certainly be too late.

But too late for what? No one knew. They pondered those words, every last one of them, and then each determined individually to be in attendance and began making their plans on how they would do so.

Although curiosity brought some of them, mention of the Hawk brought many more. For the fate of the Children of the Hawk and of the sect itself was at the center of what the Seraphic would reveal, the rumors continued, and all those who believed must be present when that fate was announced.

By sundown, the village was filled with people who had come from everywhere, all of them crammed together in the village square and spilling out from there into the side streets and pathways. There was never any question of attempting to get all of them under one roof; there was no building large enough to house so many. The Seraphic would address them out of doors—outside, where the Hawk had always wanted them to make their homes. All in attendance would be able to hear the Seraphic's words, no matter how far away they stood, no matter how much noise interfered with their hearing. It was a promise given by the head of the order, and as such it was a promise that would be kept.

When the sun had sunk to just above the western horizon, fleeing quickly now from the dark shadow of night's approach, the Seraphic ordered the torches lit. As the darkness engulfed the last of the sun's fading light and the pitch fires of the burning brands were all they had by which to see, he mounted the wooden steps to the platform he had ordered constructed and faced the crowd.

The demon that had cloaked itself in the skin of Skeal Eile would have laughed aloud had it been possible to safely do so. They were like sheep, these humans—ready to follow, eager to be led, happy to be told what was needed. He could see it in their faces and hear it in their hushed voices as the crowd noise slowly diminished. He could feel it in the vibration of the night air.

They were primed and ready for something magical. They expected no less. And he would give it to them, while they, in turn, would give him readily and willingly what he would otherwise take by force.

Seated just behind him on a row of wooden benches, the village council sat watching. Centered in their midst was Pogue Kray. He had tried to talk to the man who appeared to be Skeal Eile earlier in the day, wanting to tell him that he intended to release his wife and allow her to face her accusers. The power of the magic that the demon had used to hold him in thrall had dissipated. He was a different man, no longer distrusting, believing now that his wife had been wronged. But his change of heart came too late. His fate was sealed. The demon had put him off with cautionary words, suggesting this was not the time, hinting that all of his concerns would be addressed before the night was over and those who had transgressed or been accused of transgressions would find a lasting peace. For tonight, he promised, the Children of the Hawk would come into their own, and the village of Glensk Wood and all its people, believers or not, would be the better for it.

He kept it vague, but purposeful, and the leader of the council was turned aside.

Which was necessary, the demon knew. The council leader's patience was waning, and the demon knew that if he did not like what he heard this night, he would stand and object. He would repudiate Skeal Eile and his sect in front of the people. He would try to turn those gathered against the Seraphic.

Oh, yes, he would try, even though it was a foregone conclusion that he would fail. Still, by failing he would serve a larger purpose.

The demon stepped forward, outwardly Skeal Eile to those gathered, the Seraphic of the Children of the Hawk. Heads turned and the din of conversation stilled.

"Friends! Neighbors! Believers in the Way of the Hawk! Fellow citizens of this valley home!"

His voice rose, echoing out across the square and down the side streets and pathways, amplified a dozen times over. There was no one who could not hear him, no one whose attention was not immediately commanded. All fell silent in the wake of his call to order and its reverberations through the branches of the trees. He lifted his arms high and then slowly lowered them, as if drawing those gathered to him, a shepherd summoning his flock.

"Today we begin the reclamation of our heritage. Today we commit to putting an end to the threats we have endured these past few weeks from those heathen that occupy the old world and would occupy ours, as well. They camp just without the walls of our valley. They seek to find a way to come inside. They would kill us and enslave us and put an end to all we have been promised."

His hands lowered, but he kept them lifted slightly, palms up, still gathering them to him. "Five centuries have we waited for a sign. Our teachings tell us the Hawk promised he would send us that sign when the protective wall fell. He would tell us when it was right and proper for us to go out into the larger world and reclaim what was once ours. He would return to lead us, to take us to our new home, to give us back what was stolen from us. Do you believe this, brethren? Do you?"

The murmur grew to a low rumble punctuated by shouts of affirmation. The Seraphic's arms lifted anew, a gesture that brought the crowd instantly to silence.

"Hear me! I am Seraphic to the Children of the Hawk, but I am also to all of you as a shepherd is to his flock. I am caretaker and caregiver. I am the link between the now and the yet to come—between what has been and what will be. I am that, but more than that, I am an instrument of service for the one who brought us here and made us safe. I did not seek this role; it was given to me. It was given, and I accepted that gift because I knew the source and could do no less. I am humbled by what that means, no more so than now, as I stand before you.

"I have called you to me to speak words that will change your lives. Not just the lives of some, but of all—believers and nonbelievers, men and women and children, the descendants of those who came first to this valley. I am overwhelmed by what I must tell you and by what I have been asked to do on your behalf. I am a simple man who has been given an awesome responsibility. I do not think I can do it alone. I will need you to help me. But before you can help, I will need you to listen closely to what I have to say and to find a way to believe that it is so."

Again, the arms lowered, and this time the head bowed. "I have had a vision." His voice was a deep rumble in the stillness. "In my dreams, in my sleep, the Hawk came to me."

A fresh murmur rose from the assembled. The demon spoke right over it. "He came to me as a boy—the boy he must have been when he brought our ancestors here. He was as real as you and I. He was flesh and blood and yet he was something more. He was brilliant with light and fiery of purpose. He told me the time had come to leave the valley. He told me I was to lead you on your journey to a new place he has found for you."

He paused. "He told me he waits for you just without the walls of this valley home, and you are to go to him."

Now the murmurs turned to shouts, and not all of them were favorable. There were catcalls thrown out and vile names hurled, cries of "Madness!" and "The man's insane!" and much worse. But there were shouts of support, as well, and the demon was heartened.

"He told me this!" he roared, his voice becoming like thunder. "He gave me power I did not ask for, but which he said I would need if I was to make believers of you! Watch!"

One hand lifted and pointed toward a torch. The torch flared with new life. He found another, and again the torch flame gained strength. He found another and another. The crowd roared with fresh emotion, people turning this way and that to watch the torches burn higher and brighter. They screamed his name—"Skeal Eile, Skeal Eile!"—though that was not who he was and only who he appeared to be. But they shouted in wonder and awe, and they kept shouting as he dimmed the torches with the pointing of a finger and then brought them to life renewed.

It was a dramatic moment, but it wasn't nearly enough for what was needed. The demon gave them just enough, and then turned to face those who sat on the benches behind him. Pogue Kray was already on his feet, his face dark, his big fists clenched.

"What sorcery is this?" he demanded, his own voice loud and challenging. "What is its purpose, Seraphic? What is it you are asking of these people?"

"Only what I was told to ask," the demon replied at once. "That they should follow me out of the valley to their new home! That I should bring them to where the Hawk waits."

Pogue Kray exploded. "Are you mad? Take the people of Glensk Wood from this valley where they are safe and secure out into a country filled with monsters? Where the Drouj are waiting for us, an entire army of them? This is what you claim you were told to do?"

"I claim it, and I stand behind it! All are free to do as they choose, but those who believe will come with me!"

"No one will go with you while I am council leader!" Pogue Kray was incensed. "You claim to have spoken to the Hawk? Where is your proof of this? Where is the evidence of this bestowal of leadership? Why should you expect anyone to believe that you are chosen for this mission? Because you say it is so? Because you are the Seraphic? You expect people to risk their lives on nothing more than your word?"

The demon turned away from him and pointed again at the torches. This time they exploded instantly into ash and were gone, plunging the assemblage into darkness lit only by the faint light of moon and stars. Murmurs and shouts turned to screams.

The demon turned back to Pogue Kray. "Do you doubt me still?" He turned to the frightened people around him, to the vast crowd that had begun to shrink away from him. "Do any of you doubt me? Would you test me further?"

He saw doubt flicker in the big man's eyes as he turned back, but then Pogue Kray took another step toward him. "It will take more than fire tricks and charlatan magic to make anyone follow you, Skeal Eile. I should have put an end to your games a long time ago. But it is never too late to correct an obvious mistake. Stand down from this plat-form!"

"It is you who should stand down," the demon hissed at him.

Pogue Kray reached for the Seraphic, but the other caught his wrists and held them fast. The members of the village council backed away in fear as they saw their leader rendered helpless in a grip Skeal Eile should not have been capable of maintaining against a man who was ten times his better in any test of strength.

The demon bent close to his captive and let him look into his eyes. Pogue Kray thrashed helplessly, his face twisting with frustration. "You are a fool," the demon whispered. "But you will serve as an example of what happens to those who doubt my calling!"

The eyes burned into those of the village leader, and suddenly Pogue Kray could not make even the tiniest sound. Even though he tried to scream aloud his rage, he was rendered silent.

"This man has blasphemed against the Hawk!" the demon screamed to the assembled, who were milling like frightened cattle and trying to find somewhere to go but were packed so tightly to-gether they could barely move. "This man would pretend to be your leader, but he is weak and helpless in the face of the power given to me. Which would you rather have to protect you against the things that wait without the walls of this valley? Upon which would you rather depend? Speak, now! Say it quickly and clearly! Which path will you follow when this is done?"

Then he picked up Pogue Kray as if he were a child and held him aloft, dangling over his head. The feat seemed effortless, and suddenly everyone was staring at him, standing there with the village leader hoisted like a doll stuffed with straw.

"I am the right hand of the Hawk!" the demon screamed. "I am charged with the responsibility of saving you, and unbelievers will not be allowed to obstruct my efforts!"

Then, letting out a terrifying roar, he threw Pogue Kray from the platform and across the clearing, over the heads of the people assembled, into an oak tree's massive trunk. The council leader struck with an audible crunching of bones and dropped in a heap to the ground. Blood leaked from his ears, nose, and mouth and from a dozen other places where his body had been torn open.

He lay still, his eyes open and his gaze fixed, and he did not move.

"Pogue Kray failed to believe in the power of the Hawk and in my duty to save you, his people. So he died for his sin. If there are others who choose to follow his path, they will die, too. Not by my hand, but by those heathen who wait without and seek to come in. They will die by tooth and claw and hunger and disease because they failed to heed. Death comes calling, my brethren. It comes to consume us."

He straightened, completely at ease. "But I will not let it touch you. I will not let it even get close. Do you believe me? Shout it out, if you do! Make your belief in the Hawk a clarion call to action!"

Scattered shouts rang out amid a larger number of uncertain murmurs and cries.

"Louder!" the demon screamed at them. "If I can't hear you, I can't help you! Tell me you believe!"

Then, suddenly, everyone was shouting and howling their support, all of them joined in the wild rawness of the moment, caught up in the demon's demonstration of strength and their need to be reassured that there was someone who could help them. Their shouts rose to wails and screams, and at the demon's beckoning they pressed forward toward the platform, begging him to help them, to stand with them, to give them the benefit of his protection.

Of the Hawk's protection.

Even the council members were with him now, coming close enough that they could be heard above the crowd's roar, but not close

enough that he could touch them. He smiled benevolently and nodded his approval. They were his now, all of them.

They were his to do with as he chose.

Except for one, who quickly melted away into the darkness.

* * *

AISLINNE KRAY SAT QUIETLY in the near-darkness of her prison,
listening to the sounds echoing without. Even from underground in
the basement storeroom and from behind thick walls and the heavy
wooden door, she could hear the tumult. She had become aware of
something happening earlier, perhaps as long as several hours ago,
voices drifting down to where she sat, growing steadily stronger as
time passed, both in numbers and in volume. Some sort of gathering
was taking place right outside the building in which she was locked
away. She wondered if it had anything to do with her imprisonment.
Had Pogue called for her release? Were people gathering to hear his
decision and to make a judgment of their own on her fate?

It was impossible to tell. Because the sounds did not come from
overhead—there was no creaking of floorboards or thudding of
boots—she knew that everything was taking place outside the building. Time passed as the sounds rose and fell in regular cadence until
just a little while ago they had erupted in a series of sharp bursts.

Something unexpected and wild had happened, for all at once
the collective voice of the crowd exploded with such a roar that she
came to her feet in response. She hurried to the door and tried to
listen through the cracks in the jamb. She pounded on the door and
called the guards to tell her what was happening, but no one came.
She shouted a long time, but to no avail. Defeated, she walked
back across the room and resumed her seat. She was at the mercy
of her captors, and she was not sure that even her husband could
save her.

Pogue, please help me, she whispered silently. *Do not abandon me.*

As if in answer to her prayer, she heard movement on the other
side of the door. The scrape of a boot, a fumbling at the door, the release of the lock, and a soft squeal of wood and metal as the door
swung open.

She moved back quickly, suddenly uncertain who it was. "Pogue?" she asked softly.

"Aislinne?" a voice whispered.

"Brickey!"

She felt a surge of relief. He had departed several days ago for Hold-Fast-Crossing, not long after her encounter with the ragpicker, to find out what had become of Hadrian Esselline, and many were the times since—especially after they had locked her away in this storeroom—that she had wished she had never let him go.

The little man stepped quickly through the door and closed it behind him. He was dust-covered and his black hair was sticking up like the quills on a porcupine. "Shhh, softly now. I gave the guard something to make him fall asleep, but he might have friends nearby. Are you all right?"

"Now that you're here, I am. When did you get back?"

"Not more than two hours ago. Soon enough to see the villagers charging about like headless chickens and to hear of the madness that's taken hold. What are they thinking, shutting you away like this, blaming you for the Troll's escape?"

She shook her head. "If I knew, I would tell you. I was asleep in my bed one minute and thrown into this room and charged with all sorts of things the next. I only just last night met with Pogue. He waited until then to come to me, telling me I had betrayed him. But he's not himself. Wasn't until we talked, anyway. He might be more so now. He's promised to see to it that I have a chance to face my accusers."

"I wouldn't count on that happening, Aislinne." The little man glanced back at the door as if expecting someone. "Things have gotten much worse since you spoke with him. Bad enough that I decided right away I had to get you out of here."

"But I have to give Pogue a chance to see if—"

"Pogue Kray's chances are all used up. He lies dead in the village square, his bones broken by something that looks like the Seraphic but very likely isn't."

"Skeal Eile killed him?"

"A Skeal Eile made over or just a creature that looks like Skeal Eile. I saw him pick up your husband as if he were made of straw and throw him twenty feet through the air into the trunk of a tree. The Seraphic might have use of some small magic, but nothing this powerful."

"Who, then?"

"The ragpicker, I would guess."

"That old man?"

"He's more than an old man or even a simple ragpicker. I sensed something strange about him the moment we met. He's something more than he seems and nothing good. He's found a way to make Skeal Eile his own, a willing tool in his plans, whatever they are. Now Eile claims to have spoken to the ghost of the Hawk. He says the boy has returned and wants everyone to march out of the valley so they can be taken to some new, faraway place to live. Madness."

"Out of the valley! We have to stop this!"

"A fine sentiment, but devoid of anything resembling common sense. What we have to do, Aislinne, is get away from here and find help somewhere else. I have news of another sort that suggests a further reason we can't stay. Esselline isn't coming. Apparently, he had second thoughts about the advisability of getting involved in our struggle. That's the way he sees it, I am told—as *our struggle*. He's a proud man with a modicum of courage, but he's a fool for public opinion, as well. With Sider dead, he feels he is released from his promise. He thinks it best to stay home and defend his own ground rather than to rush to our aid. He doesn't see us as worth saving, I guess. I had thought better of him once, as I suppose Sider had. We were both mistaken."

Aislinne was stunned. "He's just abandoning us? He's not even sending some of his soldiers?"

Brickey shook his head. "Time to go. We need to get out of here before the new and improved Skeal Eile thinks to send someone to dispose of you. He has no reason to keep you alive now. The people are with him, howling at the moon like wild animals, infused with the spirit of their new leader's words. With Pogue dead, he commands them all, and you haven't much protection against whatever he might decide to do with you. Come."

He took her arm and steered her toward the door. She did not speak against what he was doing or resist the pull in his hand. She could barely make herself think straight in the face of this latest news—Pogue dead, Esselline not coming, the people of her village—people she had known all her life—driven to a desperation and madness that could only end badly for everyone involved.

And Skeal Eile—that hateful, venomous snake, feeding the resultant frenzy with his poisonous words—was at the forefront of it all.

"Hurry, Aislinne," Brickey urged, pulling open the door.

She was right behind him as he went through the opening and came face-to-face with Skeal Eile.

TWENTY-SIX

THE SUDDEN ENCOUNTER CAUGHT ALL THREE BY surprise. For one endless second they froze, locked in place as if they had turned to stone. Even the sounds of wildness and passion from without seemed to go silent.

Then Aislinne Kray, staring directly into Skeal Eile's face, saw his eyes change from a soft brown to blood red, and she recoiled.

What are you?

The Seraphic's features were unmistakable, but there was something else, too: something that peered through those red eyes and shadowed that twisted face.

"Going somewhere?" he whispered.

Brickey reacted instantly, launching himself at Skeal Eile and propelling the Seraphic backward into the hallway. Tough and tenacious, he attacked with the ferocity of a wild animal, driving into the other's midsection until both were off their feet and tumbling onto the hard earthen floor in a tangle of arms and legs.

"Run, Aislinne!" the little man shouted.

She did as she was told, charging past the combatants as they thrashed, catching just a flash of Brickey's knife as it rose and fell, burying itself over and over again in the Seraphic's body. She could hear the latter's grunts as the blade struck, could hear the sound of his breathing change. But his efforts to free himself did not cease, and she had a terrible, unshakable premonition that the knife wasn't doing any damage.

By then she was past them and racing up the stairs, taking the steps two at a time until she reached the hallway, the entry, the door, and finally the world outside where the night was soft and velvet and welcoming. A crowd was still milling about in the aftermath of the earlier gathering, but she pushed through them without stopping, breaking clear of the hands that reached for her. She breathed deeply the forest air as she burst into the open, a sense of freedom filling her with hope for the possibility of escape. She never slowed. She kept running, down forest paths, down lesser byways, heading for her house. She might not have been thinking as clearly as she should, but at least she was thinking. She knew where she was going. She knew what she needed to find. She realized the importance of not being seen and recognized.

What she couldn't seem to fix on was where she would go once she was clear of Glensk Wood.

She allowed herself a moment to think one last time of Brickey, whom she already knew she would never see again. Brave friend, she thought. He had given his life for hers.

Abruptly, she changed her mind. It had been her intention to go to her home, retrieve a travel cloak and weapons, and flee south to one of the other villages. But there was no time for the former and the latter was the obvious choice—and she could not afford to make a mistake. Instead, she veered north toward the deep woods and the high country. Sider's country. She would go there. She knew it well enough to find her way. She would go to his childhood home, abandoned now, fallen into disrepair, and find what she needed.

She ran hard, and soon her breath was ragged and her muscles aching. She had left the village behind, the madness and chaos consuming it. But even escape could not free her from her sense of disbelief and shock.

That—that *thing*—inhabiting Skeal Eile's body wasn't the Seraphic.

Old stories recalled themselves—stories of the time when the Hawk led his people into the valley. They had been pursued by many evils, but chief among them were the demons.

And now one was in their midst, disguised as Skeal Eile. She had no doubt this was what she and Brickey had faced. And suddenly she stopped where she was, appalled.

That old man, the ragpicker, trying to charm her into revealing what she knew about Sider and his talisman. That old man, who had threatened her in his chillingly soft-voiced, terrifyingly confident way, letting her know that if she crossed him she would live to regret it. She could still feel herself wilting under the force of his words, only just managing to hold on.

Skeal Eile was only a pawn in this, not the instigator she had thought him to be. The eyes gave away the demon within; there was no mistaking it. But the demon had not always been there; if it had, she would have noticed. Sider would have noticed. The demon was new, and it had taken the Seraphic's form, which was why it had been able to kill her husband so easily, why it could charm the people of her village as the real Seraphic had never been able to do, why it had up-ended everyone's lives in a single night with false promises and twisted dreams. He was the reason Arik Siq was free and she was made to appear responsible. He was the cause of everything twisted and bad that had happened.

She almost collapsed with the weight of her revelation. It was a struggle even to continue to walk, to put one foot in front of the other.

She forced herself to start moving faster. She could not afford to be recaptured.

She reached a stretch of deep woods just outside the village and plunged in without slowing, intent on getting through quickly and making her way to higher ground. She was tiring now, no longer able to run, to find the reserves of strength she knew she would need if she were pursued. Once, when she was younger, she could have run all day. Once, when she was with Sider, she had done so, matching him stride for stride, as strong and able as he was, a match for him in every way. What she had lost was a pain she had carried with her ever since. But now, fleeing from the demon, it surfaced with fresh intensity and made her weep.

She staggered to a halt finally, stopping to listen to the stillness. Though she tried, she heard nothing. The night was deep and empty of sound; not even the night birds called out. She took deep breaths to steady herself, thinking that perhaps she had lost him, had left him behind—the demon that pretended at being Skeal Eile, the monster she had feared would continue to track her.

But maybe not. Maybe not.

She swallowed hard and started out again, setting a fresh pace, slow but steady. She was in thick woods and heavy grasses, and she could not go any faster. But perhaps this was fast enough.

"Aislinne? Are you there? You are, aren't you? I can smell you."

She felt herself tighten with fear, but she kept going.

"There's no point in running from me. There's nowhere you can go that I can't find you. Why not just put an end to this?"

Somehow, it had managed to find her trail. Somehow, it had closed the gap she thought she had opened between them. She had run so hard, so fast, and yet here it was, almost on top of her. She felt fresh tears run down her cheeks, but she stayed silent, working her way through the trees.

"I will make it quick, if you simply wait for me to come to you. Just give me a word or a sign to let me know you prefer it that way. Your little friend isn't here to help you anymore. Nor is your foolish husband. Nor the man who carried the black staff until he died at the hands of the Drouj. They're all gone. You're all alone."

She wanted to scream, to shatter his bones with the force of her rage. But she could do nothing to him. She wasn't even carrying a weapon.

"Aislinne, are you listening? I know you can hear me."

There was no escaping this creature, yet she must find a way. She tightened her resolve and pressed on, sliding ghostlike through the trees, stepping carefully, silently. *Leave no trace of your passing. Leave no footprint or sign. Stay focused on what is needed. Do not let yourself be swayed by his words. They are only words, and they cannot hurt you.*

Yet they did. They cut like knives.

She was deep in the woods now, so far in that she could only barely find her way from one sliver of moonlight to the next, everything gone stifling and dark, layered with shadows. She was infused with a sense of need for haste that she knew she must resist. One step at a time, she told herself. The demon had gone silent, but she knew it was back there, following doggedly, determined to catch her and put an end to her.

If she was lucky. Much worse, if she was not.

Then a shadow crossed her path just ahead, a glimmer of something unlike real shadows, something not wholly dark but lit from within. She gasped in spite of herself and almost gave way to the fear pressing down on her. But then the shadow disappeared, and she turned away from it.

She blinked uncertainly. She must have imagined it. It wasn't there now, had barely been there before. Yet something about it—something in the way it moved—was familiar.

"Aislinne?"

The demon again, but farther off now, its voice more distant.

She moved ahead carefully, waiting for something more. Abruptly, the shadow was there in front of her again, a faint glimmer, a forest wraith come out of nowhere to intercept her. She veered away once more, hurrying just a little faster now to get clear of it. It was there before her only an instant and then gone. Just as before, it seemed no more than a vision her imagination had conjured.

But this time she had the odd impression that it mimicked something of Sider Ament.

On she went, working her way through a tangle of trunks and grasses, ruts and gnarled roots, the shadow appearing and fading again at regular intervals, each time causing her to veer in a new direction, each time reminding her in faint ways of Sider.

She only heard the demon once more. It called her name from what seemed like a great distance, and then she didn't hear it again.

It was nearing dawn when she found her way clear of the forest and started upcountry toward Sider's old home. The night air was cold on her skin; she wore only the clothes she'd had on while imprisoned, not having had time to find anything more, and she shivered in the predawn chill. But she kept moving to keep warm, to reach her destination, and after a time she didn't notice the cold so much.

She thought about the ghost in the woods, the shadowy form with the inner-burning light, and she decided that it wasn't her imagination or a hallucination. It was something else entirely. It was Sider reaching out to her, keeping her safe, even after death. She didn't know if she believed such a thing was possible, but that was what she felt.

She trekked out of the forested valley floor and began to climb toward the scattering of homes on the upper slopes. Although Sider's home was abandoned, another farmer had taken over management of his parents' fields and farmed them as part of his own. Sider had never said anything to the man and his wife about wanting compensation, but had simply let it go. The farmer and his wife already lived nearby when Sider departed with the former bearer of the black staff. After his parents died, the house was left vacant—already beginning to fall into ruin. Sider had never returned, so far as anyone knew. But that was like him, she thought. He had never come back to anything. The past was never his concern.

But on this occasion, it would be hers.

If she could be safe anywhere, it would be here.

Still keeping a sharp eye out for the demon, still afraid it might find her, she worked her way steadily upslope to the beginnings of Sider's old homestead and from there around the early plantings in the fields to where the remains of his house stood abandoned. She approached cautiously, aware that she was unarmed and woefully deficient in fighting skills. But the building was dark and silent and, in the end, empty. Mice and rats and a few nesting birds had made a home within, but nothing more dangerous was in evidence.

She stepped inside through the open doorway, the door itself long since gone, and stood looking into the darkness as her eyes adjusted. She listened to the sounds of wings beating and paws scurrying, and then she moved through the tiny living area, past the little kitchen space, and into the room at the back of the house that had been Sider's.

Once within that room, she stopped again. Moonlight flooded through the open window, illuminating a bed, a chest at its foot, and a small table and chair. There was nothing else, and what remained was splintered and broken and empty of anything useful. Bones from another life, the skeleton of better times—it made her cry all over again.

But then she wiped the tears away, took a deep breath, and moved to one corner. The boards that hid the concealing compartment Sider had built with his own hands were still in place. She found the cleverly designed fingerholds, released the small wooden slide latches, and lifted the boards away.

Beneath she found what she was looking for, a bundle fully six feet long wrapped in canvas and lashed with leather ties, right where Sider had left it all those years ago. She removed it from its hiding place, laid it on the floor, and loosened the ties.

She caught her breath. They were still there.

Before her lay an ash bow and a quiver of steel-tipped arrows. Sider had made them himself, choosing the woods, carving the bow and each shaft, weaving the heavy string, forging the metal tips at the village smithy, sewing the quiver and sheath. He had done it not long after he met her and had taught her how to use it. He was good with the bow, but she was better. *One day*, he had told her, *after we are married, these will belong to you. They will be a wedding present.*

He had tried to give them to her anyway, when it was clear there would be no marriage, but she had refused. Even so, she had never forgotten them. She knew where he hid them, how he had fashioned this hiding place to keep them safe. She hadn't been sure she would find them here, but she knew he had never carried any other weapon after he had received the black staff.

As she knelt on the cottage floor looking down at the bow and arrows, memories she had thought forgotten flooding through her, she wondered what had made her come here. If she had wanted a weapon to protect herself, she could have made other choices.

Why had she made this one?

With so much lost, with so much stolen away, perhaps she had wanted to take something back. Sider, Pogue, Brickey, her friends, her home, and her place in the world were all gone. Everything she had been able to count on over the years—vanished. She sensed that she would never get any of it back, that she must start over again and find a new life.

But the bow and arrows were something she could take with her. They would give her a sense of security if the demon came after her. They were Sider's, and she believed now that he would always be with her.

Exhausted, she took the bow and arrows and moved back out into the front room of the ruins. Except for the bowstring, which was in shreds, the weapon was still in perfect shape. She would find a replacement for the string from one of the surrounding farms or hunting shacks in the morning. If needed, she would weave one herself. For now, she had to rest. She propped herself up in one corner where she was hidden from view but could peer out through cracks in the boards at the countryside leading up from the valley. If the demon still pursued her, she could see it coming.

She knew it was wishful thinking to suppose that she could stop the demon if it found her. She knew, as well, that escape was unlikely. But her belief was all she had, and so she clung to it.

Outside her little shelter, dawn was breaking.

She fell asleep watching it unfold.

"CITIZENS OF GLENSK WOOD! Pay close heed to me!"

The demon that appeared to be Skeal Eile scanned the anxious faces of the crowd. The sun had risen, a blood-red sphere in the eastern sky, a promise of something unspoken.

"A new day begins, a day that shall see us all on our journey to join hearts and minds and hands with the one who brought us here so many years ago and has now come to gather us up again, sheep into the fold!"

The demon stood on the steps of the council hall building facing the multitudes he had called together, the men and women of the village still flush with the wildness and fever of the previous night, remembering what had been promised them, hungry to witness its coming. He held them all spellbound, captivated by the dark magic of his voice as it layered the air infusing their senses, drawing them in when reason—had there been even a shred of it left—would have warned them to back away.

"You were promised that this day would come. From the time of your ancestors, you were assured of it. The Hawk brought you safely into this valley and gave you this home. But one day, you were told, the protective wall of magic that he had created would fall away, and he would return for you. You were told this, and you believed. Now is that day. The wall is down, the magic is gone, and the old world crouches like a beast on your doorstep. But you are not forsaken. You are not abandoned. The Hawk has come to lead you to safety."

There were scattered shouts and cheers, and even in the eyes of those who said nothing, but only listened, trust and blind faith were reflected, conjured by the demon's magic. There was no hint of doubt, and no one questioned the words of the speaker.

This was so easy, the demon thought as he lifted his arms in an embracing gesture, drawing them further in. They were sheep then—they were sheep now. Pitifully willing to believe the wildest, most improbable of myths—myths they themselves had created and nurtured as they would the flowers of a garden, fragile and beautiful and ephemeral. They wanted so badly for someone to assure them that the bright and shiny promise was faithful to the dreams they so readily embraced. Make us safe. Keep us well. Take us to where nothing threatens, to where all is peaceful and can be kept so.

Such sheep.

If not for Aislinne Kray, he could be truly content. But after tracking her to the deep woods he had lost her, and that was troubling. It was impossible that such a thing could happen once he had gotten the smell of his quarry, but in this case it had. It bothered him even now, hours later, after he had returned empty-handed. Still, it was not important in the larger scheme of things, he reasoned. She was nothing to him but an irritant, and she played no role in his plans for the bearer of the staff and the staff's magic. He would have both, and he would have them soon.

"We must trust in the promise that the place we seek awaits us and the Hawk will lead us there. I have seen him. I have spoken with him. He will take us one village at a time to where no dangers will ever reach us again. He begins with us, with this village, with the people of Glensk Wood, because we stand nearest the danger and require the quickest response. Others will see him, as well, when he returns for them, but we are the first."

He paused meaningfully. "But only if you believe! Only if you act on your faith! Only if you are true to your commitment to his teachings and to your sect and to your Seraphic!"

He had made himself larger and more dramatic in appearance than the real Seraphic had looked when he was alive. He had changed his features and his voice, and the overall impression he had created was one of power and majesty. Those assembled saw him as enhanced by the power invested in him as their spiritual leader; they had witnessed firsthand how easily he could dispose of those who challenged his authority. Though the body had been removed during the night, no one had forgotten the fate of Pogue Kray. Such power commanded respect and discouraged doubts. It was so now as the Seraphic revealed what was required of them.

"Do you believe?" Skeal Eile demanded suddenly, his voice booming out across the square and down the paths and roads that were crammed with the people of the village. "Do you believe enough to come with me? Do you believe enough to do whatever is needed to find your way? Do you commit to what your faith asks of you? Will you put aside your doubts and fears and march boldly out of this valley to your new home? Who among you is with me?"

The roar of commitment was vast and deafening. Voices rose as a single bellow of affirmation and trust.

"Let me hear you!" the demon shouted over the roar. "Let the whole world hear your song of faith!"

The crowd had gone wild, arms raised and fists clenched in gestures that matched the cacophony of their voices. They were his now, committed to his cause—a cause as thin and transparent as the air they breathed and every bit as necessary to their desperation. They would go with him, and they would find what he had promised.

But they would not find it in the way they believed. They would find that even a new world was full of surprises.

"Gather your children and old people together! Take up your weapons and collect food and water! We leave at once!"

He watched them scatter to their homes to do as he had commanded of them, and he felt a great sense of satisfaction. His power over them was complete, the dark magic he wielded irresistible. With no one to stand against him, with no voice to be raised in protest, there was nothing to sway them from the course he had set. They gave no thought to what would be demanded of them. They would follow him to wherever he led them, no matter the destination, no matter the cost.

They would follow him, and they would pay the price for doing so.

IT WAS NEARING MIDDAY when Prue Liss reached the slopes of the valley leading down into Glensk Wood. She had been following the scarlet dove all night and throughout the morning without stopping for more than a few minutes at a time to rest, calling on reserves of strength she hadn't known she possessed. She was driven in large part by her need to find Pan, to reach his side before anything worse could happen. She had no idea if this was possible. Even now, the path she followed was seemingly taking her back to the village of Glensk Wood where she was certain he would not go. She struggled with her doubts as she traveled, more than once thinking to turn aside in favor of a more likely destination. Yet the dove drew her now as it had when it had brought her to Pan the first time, and she could not make herself forsake it.

But with the sunrise her strength had begun to fail, and now she wondered if she would be worth anything even when she found him.

Ahead stood the ruins of a house sitting silent and deserted amid fields freshly plowed and awaiting spring plantings. The dove had flown toward it and now sat upon its blackened eaves, awaiting her. She trudged ahead to catch up, the muscles of her legs operating on memory and not much else. She had to sleep soon, she knew. Even if the dove went on, she could not. She was too tired to keep going. She had to rest.

She had almost reached the ruins when she heard a stirring inside the broken walls and saw a shadow of movement pass across the timbers of the far wall.

"Hello?" she called out.

When Aislinne Kray—dirty and bedraggled and grim—came around the corner of the doorway with a steel-tipped arrow and unstrung longbow gripped in one hand, she was shocked into complete silence.

"Prue?" the other asked in disbelief. "Is it you?"

They rushed to each other in mutual relief and hugged long and hard. "I didn't know what had become of you after the Trolls took you," Aislinne said. "How did you get free? What brought you here? Where is Pan?"

She backed away from Prue and gasped. "Your eyes! You're blind!"

"Not so blind that I can't see you!" Prue laughed. "Mostly, I just can't see colors now. I can still see everything else. I'll explain. But what are you doing so far from home? You don't look as if you've eaten or drunk anything in days, and your clothes . . . Aislinne, what's happened?"

They sat down together at the edge of the fields and began to trade stories, a process that took them much time. They had not seen each other since Aislinne had been imprisoned and Prue had escaped the Drouj and encountered the King of the Silver River. When they had caught each other up on everything that had transpired and what it was that had brought them to this time and place, they stopped talking altogether for long moments, locked in an awkward silence that discouraged either from saying anything more.

"What will you do now?" Prue asked the other finally. "Where will you go, if you can't go back to Glensk Wood? Is there family that will take you in?"

Aislinne shook her head. "Distant family, people I know about who live in other villages but that I haven't seen in years. Or in some cases, ever. There is no one else. Not even Brickey now. Not you or Pan, either, it seems. I came here because I could think of nowhere else and because I felt Sider calling me here. It's silly, I know. Irrational. But I thought I saw him when I was fleeing, and I was so afraid of that creature—"

"When he came for me in the ruins," Prue interrupted, "I could barely breathe. All I could think about was getting away. I don't ever want to see him again, and yet I know I must. The King of the Silver River made it clear that sooner or later Pan would have to face him. When that happens, I have to be there to try to protect him."

"But what will you do? How can you help?"

Prue shrugged. "I don't know. I will do whatever I can. But I was sent back for that express purpose, Aislinne. My sight is diminished, but I was given back my ability to sense danger so that I could aid him. I must try."

"You have greater courage than I do." Aislinne brushed back locks of her graying hair, her face suddenly old and worn. "I could never have done what you are doing if it were asked of me. I couldn't even make myself go with Sider when he chose to take up the black staff."

"He never asked it of you." The girl smiled. "Besides, you don't know what you can or can't do until you are forced to find out. I discovered that among the Drouj."

Aislinne nodded, sighed. "So this scarlet dove? Do you intend to follow it farther?"

Prue nodded. "I think I must. It came to me so that I would. Like before, it will lead me to Pan. But I think that maybe this time, given what you've told me, the demon might be waiting. The dove leads me toward Glensk Wood, and that is where the demon is. And even if Pan isn't there now, he might be coming soon. I have to hurry."

Aislinne considered. "The demon intends to lead the people of the village out of the valley, so he won't be there long. But wherever Pan is, that's where the demon might be going, too." Aislinne shook her head. "I think I should go with you."

"But this isn't your . . ."

"It isn't my fight? My problem? My responsibility?" Aislinne smiled. "I think it is all of that and more, Prue. Besides, what else would I do? Hide out here in the ruins of Sider's past? What sort of coward would that make me? No, I want to come with you."

She picked up the ash bow and looked at it. "I don't know what made me decide to come here and find this, but I think maybe it was Sider. He's gone, but it feels like he is still looking out for me. He meant this bow for me, you know. It was to be a gift. But I wouldn't take it. Not if he wasn't going to stay with me. But I was good with it once, and I have used a bow since and think I am good with it still. I don't know how much help it will be, but it might be some. Please let me come with you."

"You've done more than enough for us . . ."

"Please, Prue. Let me come."

Prue had never seen Aislinne like this. Always so self-assured, so much in command of every situation, so much the leader when others were lost—now she seemed none of these. She was a woman searching for a reason to go on, trying to find a way to heal the damage that had been done to her. She had lost so much. Maybe she was entitled to get something back.

"All right," she said to the older woman. "We will go together."

"And look out for and take care of each other."

"And find Pan."

Aislinne reached out and gave the girl a hug. "You're all grown up, Prue Liss. Whatever you've lost of your sight, you've made up for with your courage. I am proud of you."

Prue blushed. Final smiles were exchanged; no further words were needed. Then Prue caught sight of the scarlet dove lifting away from the ruins of Sider Ament's abandoned home, and the girl and the woman rose together and set out to follow it.

TWENTY-SEVEN

THE DAY WAS BRIGHT AND CLEAR AND FILLED WITH sunshine all the way from the valley floor to the mountain heights, and it seemed on such a day as if anything was possible. The demon, caring nothing for the day itself but understanding the impact of its false promise on those foolish creatures he led, was pleased. Stretched out behind him for almost half a mile, the people of Glensk Wood marched forth at his beckoning to fulfill the destiny he had arranged for them. The men bore weapons, most of them crude and ancient, not concerned they might be needed, secure in the knowledge that their faith in their leader would sustain and protect them.

Just as he had intended, the demon thought, turning back suddenly to give those who pressed closest a dazzling smile of reassurance.

"Sing for me!" he cried out to them. "Lift your voices and fill the world with joyful sounds!"

Someone began to sing, a woman, her voice high and clear. Her song must have been a familiar one, an old favorite, for almost instantly others joined in. The song was of planting and harvesting a crop and knowing it would keep their stomachs full and their families safe and well.

"Sing!" he encouraged, walking back to where the next group was bunched together, urging them to take up the song. After he had heard the verses repeated, he joined in, making himself one of them, caught up in the euphoria of the moment.

So they went, passing through the forests and climbing toward the peaks north and west, to where Declan Reach waited. The pass would be empty, the defenses abandoned. No one had gone up there to replace those the Drouj had killed; Pogue Kray had begun the job of gathering fresh defenders but had failed to dispatch them before his untimely end. Nor would the Drouj summoned by Arik Siq have replaced them. The demon had made it clear when he set the other free what it was that he intended. Arik Siq would not go against him; he would do as he was told.

Such a wonderful day! So filled with promise, so rich with possibilities! The demon was pleased.

The march continued, although after a while the singing faded. It became obvious that conserving energy was necessary because the climb to the pass was a long one. Few had made it recently; some had never gone. Those who knew warned those who didn't, and soon everyone had lapsed into a resigned, somewhat worried silence. The demon heard the muttering. No one liked the idea that there would be no rest, but they knew the Seraphic was a hard man with deep convictions in the purpose he had set himself. It was another test of faith, they whispered. It was a proving of devotion to the cause, and all of them were being measured.

The demon moved among them freely, cheerfully urging them on, asking them to hold on to their faith and each other. He let the lines spread out, the stronger outdistancing the weaker, the young moving well ahead of the elderly and the women and children. Morning passed into afternoon, and still he kept them moving. When the weak faltered, he sent the strong back to help them, thereby depleting the energy of those who had charged ahead, wearing them down, as well. The whole procession continued at a halting, determined pace, and the demon worked hard at shaping its look and feel. What had started out so positively quickly degenerated into a slog that wore at the body and mind.

By midafternoon, people were dropping by the wayside.

They started giving up one at a time, the old fading first, followed by mothers with children. Their numbers were small at first, one or two here and there. Others stopped to help, sometimes picking up the children and carrying them, sometimes giving the old people an arm or shoulder for support.

But even that wasn't enough, as the demon knew it wouldn't be. A steady ten-hour march would test even a seasoned hunter. So, eventually, the numbers of those failing increased and of those helping declined. The march pushed on, and in its wake bodies lay scattered across the landscape, collapsed and spent or simply abandoned. Some families left their weaker members behind simply because they didn't want to be burdened by them. Some left them out of a selfish desire not to be left out of what waited ahead, when their destination was reached. Some left them because their own strength was so badly eroded that they could barely keep going themselves.

All the while, the demon kept them moving, moving, moving. He ordered, demanded, cajoled, and threatened. He made promises of help to those left behind, never intending to keep them. In a few instances, he lent his own strength to those begging for it, demonstrating his commitment to them. He was everywhere, a steady, dependable presence, infusing the air with his words and his magic, keeping them all on the path he had set.

"No stopping!" he shouted to them. "No resting! Eat and drink of your food and water as you walk! We have a goal and we must attain it this day! We must reach our destination! We must sacrifice the few for the greater good! Press on!"

Amazingly, they did. Though he was using his magic and his oratory, those would not have been enough without a blind willingness to be misled. They were tough and strong, these people, but they were like sheep. They believed without question that what waited was worth any sacrifice. Years of expectancy, generations of stories told about their arrival and eventual departure from this valley, made them blind to the truth.

By sunset, they had reached the opening to the pass at Declan

Reach. It rose ahead of them, a black gap in the mountains, empty and shadowed. Behind them, the valley was already cloaked in twilight and the first stars were beginning to appear. People hurried now, throwing aside whatever caution remained, anxious to gain the opening, to pass through and reach the outside world and the safety that had been promised them. They went forward in large knots, following the Seraphic, keeping him in sight as he beckoned, showing them the way.

They did not look back at what they had left behind. They did not see those still limping or crawling to catch up. They did not see those who could not do so. They barely noticed the desiccated corpses of those who had died defending the pass days earlier.

They did not see the truth of things.

"I WISH I COULD SEE what you see," Aislinne said at one point, walking side by side with Prue Liss. "This scarlet dove you follow—it's frustrating watching you search for it while I'm not able to see it at all. It might as well be invisible."

Prue smiled. "Then you have a small sense of what it's like for me. I can't see colors, except for the dove, and it only lets me see it in small glimpses as it flies away and waits for me to catch up to it. I see only grays and blacks and nothing else. I search for the things that you can see without even trying, but they are lost to me."

She glanced over. "Like you, I want to see them for myself."

Aislinne nodded. "I suppose it's the same thing. But it's worse for you than it is for me, isn't it? All those beautiful colors turned to shadows. How were you able to adapt, Prue? Are you getting used to it at all?"

"I didn't have a choice. I had to get used to it. And you're right—it's not easy. I haven't really managed it yet. Maybe I never will. I miss some things so much. The different blues of the sky and the greens of the trees and grasses and plants, just for starters. And I think sometimes that not seeing colors is affecting my emotional state. I cry a lot just thinking about it."

"That doesn't seem so strange," Aislinne said quietly. "I find myself crying a lot, too, lately."

She was thinking of Sider. But there was Brickey, too. There was Pogue, a loss she felt far more keenly than she was willing to admit. She was wondering what it would be like to live without all those people she had been close to. Prue could read it in her face as she turned away and pretended to study the countryside. She could see it in the tears that ran down her cheeks before she quickly wiped them away.

"We don't seem to be going toward Glensk Wood anymore," Aislinne said suddenly, trying to mask her discomfort. "For a while, I thought that was where we were being led—back to the village. But the dove doesn't seem to be flying that way anymore, if I read the course of our passage right."

"You read it right," Prue said. "I thought the same until the dove brought me to you. I thought it was taking me back to the village, and I would find Panterra there. But we're heading for the mountains."

She paused, considering. "For Declan Reach, in fact. Look." She pointed. "That notch in the peaks. Do you see it? That marks the way to the pass, and we're traveling straight toward it."

"Then what we're looking for is somewhere up there," Aislinne said.

Prue nodded. She'd been keeping close watch on their direction, worried as well that the scarlet dove might be taking them back to Glensk Wood, back to where Aislinne had seen the demon last. That old man frightened her more than anyone or anything she had ever encountered, and she did not relish a further confrontation, even knowing that one was coming. Better that she find Pan first, if it was meant to happen. Better that she have him standing next to her so they could face the demon together.

Now she was wondering if the flight of the scarlet dove meant she was to leave the valley entirely. Was it possible that when Pan disappeared below the Ashenell he somehow ended up outside their safe haven once more?

She watched the dove fly into view ahead of her, a quick flash of crimson against the grays and blacks, before disappearing. It was still traveling toward the mountains.

Toward Pan.

She wondered suddenly if she were taking something for granted that she shouldn't. There was nothing to say that even though the dove had led her to Pan once it would do so a second time. It was a creature of the King of the Silver River and perhaps of her own magically altered condition, and it might well be serving more than one purpose. She couldn't really be sure. She couldn't know until she had arrived at wherever she was being taken.

But something odd was happening through all this. She was experiencing a strange new connection with the dove. When she had first seen it, when it had revealed to her that she had lost the ability to see colors, she had felt an immediate closeness to it. Then the dove had disappeared, and she had not thought she would see it again and the connection felt broken. But when it had returned and ever since, their bond, built on little else than its presence and her unmistakable sense of emotional attachment, had grown steadily stronger. The scarlet dove had come to mean something more to her than a symbol of what had been lost or what might be found. It had evolved into a companion, a living reassurance that there was purpose in what together they were doing. It represented their shared connection to Panterra, their commitment to protect him so he could fulfill his obligations as the new bearer of the black staff.

It was a strange way to look at it, as if it were a belief carved out of air and faith and promises. Yet it felt real and tangible. When she saw the dove, flying on ahead in search of Pan—which she believed deep down it was doing—she was filled with unmistakable hope.

It was midafternoon and they were ascending the slopes through the forests toward the mountain peaks, the air cool and brisk with the steady retreat of the sun west, when they began to find the stragglers from the Glensk Wood evacuation. There were a few old people at first, limping back down the hillside, holding one another up, heads down, bodies bent. Their faces were stricken as they spoke, and their voices were infused with bitterness.

"Left us, they did. Just left us like trash thrown away."

"Abandoned us without a word."

"Went on ahead, even our children. Couldn't find it in their hearts to stay with us, even when we begged them."

"Friends, neighbors, everyone. All they could talk about was the Seraphic, and how he was leading them to something wonderful, something waiting just ahead."

"Time slipping away, they said. Time running out."

Heads shaking, they moved on. Prue exchanged a glance with Aislinne. It was the demon's work in his guise as Seraphic, taking the villagers to some imaginary safehold where the boy who had saved their ancestors would be waiting for them.

Soon, there were others—small groups and then more. Old people, women, and children. Some younger men, as well, who had been injured sufficiently that going on became impossible and going back difficult. They were helping one another now, which seemed to Prue a good thing, but there was no disguising the disappointment and sadness that marked them all. They felt they had missed out. They had been cheated of what had been promised them. They had been left behind, and perhaps no one would ever come back for them.

"Just go home," Aislinne told each of them, trying to offer reassurance. "Help anyone you find, but go home and stay there. This isn't what it seems. It isn't anything of what you believe."

The girl and the woman walked on, stopping only long enough to offer encouragement to those they found along the way. They could not stay to help and could not turn back. There was no time for that. They had something else that needed doing, something more important and necessary.

They had to find a way to save the entire valley.

"How are we going to do that?" Aislinne said at one point. "What can we do that will make a difference?"

Prue shook her head. "I don't know. Whatever we can, I guess. But we have to try. There's no one else to help Pan, and I won't let him face this alone."

It was well after midnight before they reached the pass at Declan Reach, the half-moon risen and the stars shining brightly in a cloudless night sky, bathing the valley in brilliant white light. They were no longer encountering stragglers or abandoned villagers; those who felt themselves faltering at this point must have found fresh reserves of strength that allowed them to go on. The split into the pass gaped dark and empty before them as they neared, and there was no sign of movement or hint of sound from within. They came upon the bodies of the dead, those men killed days earlier in the Drouj surprise attack, ruined and decaying. The smell wafted through the darkness, and carrion-eaters tore at the remains.

Prue and Aislinne skirted the edges, the latter with an arrow notched in her bow and held ready. The dove had flown on ahead into the pass, still leading them onward. Neither of them spoke as they followed after. Rather, they listened and watched.

Prue kept her eyes on the flashes of scarlet that appeared and vanished in the shadowy depths of the pass, making sure she did not lose contact. At her side, Aislinne's eyes flicked right and left, searching for what was hidden. But Prue knew that when danger was close, she would sense it first. By now, she was certain her instincts were working as the King of the Silver River had promised they would. She did not know if this would be enough to keep them safe, but it was the best she could hope for.

What troubled her most was what she was expected to do once they found either Pan or the demon in their search. Wherever the scarlet dove was leading Aislinne and herself, one or the other or both would be waiting. She could feel it in her bones. The promised confrontation would take place at the end of this hunt.

Aislinne touched her arm. Something was moving in the shadows ahead. She stopped where she was, Aislinne with her, and they watched as a form shambled out of the darkness, slowly taking shape. It lurched from side to side, and stumbled frequently, as if drink or exhaustion had dulled its reflexes and eroded its sense of balance.

The girl and the woman exchanged an uncertain glance, and then Aislinne pulled Prue to one side of the passageway, flattening them both against the rock wall.

Then the shadowy form emerged from the darkness into a broad patch of moonlight, lifting its head as if in shock at the brightness of the light, and there was just enough time to recognize that it was one of the villagers from Glensk Wood before its legs gave way and it tumbled to the ground.

*   *   *

FIVE HOURS EARLIER, those who followed the Seraphic had passed this way. Weary and footsore and anxious, they found renewed strength in their leader's words, spoken to them as they entered the pass.

"We are almost there!" he shouted out. "The long trek is almost

over, and the Hawk awaits us. Just through this pass and a little way beyond. When we reach him, he will tell us where we are to be taken and
what we will find waiting when they get there. He will soothe our
aches and pains; he will heal our hearts and minds. And remember
this! Those left behind are not lost, only delayed. They, too, will find
their way to us and be joined anew to families and friends. All will be
together."

Buoyed by the words of the Seraphic, they marched through the
pass, closely bunched now, for they had been allowed to wait until the
stragglers who could manage to do so had caught up to the main body.
More than two thousand strong, the bulk of those men and women
who made their homes in Glensk Wood were joined as one in their
common effort to reach the newer, safer home that had been promised
to them. A few still doubted. A few still voiced their concerns. But others shouted them down, proclaiming themselves true believers in the
teachings of the Hawk and the promise of his return. All would soon
be revealed, and they would be reunited with their spiritual leader and
never leave his side again.

When they reached the far end of the pass, the Seraphic brought
them to a halt. They were to wait for him here, he advised, while he
went on ahead to make certain the Hawk was ready to receive them.
Then he would return. Be patient, he urged them. Be worthy of the
gift that was about to be bestowed on them.

His own little joke, he thought as he walked away.

Because while they were being patient, the demon went out from
the pass and straight to where he sensed Arik Siq and his Drouj soldiers were waiting. One hundred strong, armed and ready, they hid in
the rocks just north of the pass entrance, as he had instructed they
must do.

"They are weak and foolish people," he told Arik Siq, once the
other had appeared. "You may kill them all at your leisure."

"Will they not resist?" the other asked, doubtful of this claim. "Will
they not fight for their lives?"

"There are not enough of them for that," the demon lied. "Besides,
they are too exhausted to give you much of a struggle. Kill them, and
then we will wait for the boy to come."

"You are sure he will do that?" The Drouj was watching him

closely, intense and anxious. "Why would he come if they are already dead?"

The demon smiled. "He will come *because* they are already dead. He will want to see for himself. To find out what killed them. To exact revenge. Isn't that what you would do?"

Arik Siq nodded. "Bring these people to me, and I will put a quick enough end to them."

The demon turned away. Such bravado. But it was dust in the wind, and the end of things would be something far different from what Arik Siq expected. The demon misled him as he misled the people of Glensk Wood and everyone else he had ever encountered, and the result was always the same.

It only remained for them to play out the roles he had assigned, and then to die.

He went back into the pass, brought the faithful to their feet, and marched them forth into the brave new world beyond. They were singing again—a nice touch—songs of hope and promise, of overcoming obstacles and realizing dreams. Fools, all. He saw them looking about hopefully as they caught their first glimpses of the old world, a world they had never seen. He saw their smiles as he took them onto the slopes canting downward from the mouth of the pass to begin their descent.

And then the Drouj fell on them like wolves. Weapons drawn, blades glinting in the moonlight, the Trolls waited until their victims were clear of the pass, then slipped in behind them to block the way back, and with howls of wild animals began slashing their victims to pieces from the rear. They made no distinctions among men, women, and children, between young and old, between brave hearts and cowards. They tore into them with terrible ferocity, hacking and cutting, pushing them downhill, away from safety, away from any hope. In droves, they slaughtered them.

But some fought back, using weapons they had brought with them or had torn from the hands of their attackers. Because there were so many more villagers than the demon had led them to believe and they were so few themselves, they began suffering losses that steadily diminished their ranks and hampered their ability to complete the slaughter. Soon the dead on both sides had eroded the number of fit combatants, and it was uncertain who would prevail. The demon aided in this, now and then selectively cutting down a Troll here and a human there, whittling at them like a knife at a piece of wood. He did it surreptitiously, his acts unseen by others, his efforts covert and stealthy.

In the end, almost everyone lay dead. Of the Drouj, only Arik Siq and another five remained. A handful of survivors of the Glensk Wood party had managed to regain the mouth of the pass and disappear into its black maw, most of them badly injured and a couple of those dying.

It was the strongest of those who would survive that made it far enough to find Prue Liss and Aislinne Kray before collapsing.

TWENTY-EIGHT

XAC WEN WAS NOT FEELING GOOD ABOUT THINGS as he climbed toward Aphalion Pass, leaving Arborlon and the Elves behind. First Panterra Qu had vanished beneath the Belloruusian Arch in exactly the same way that Phryne Amarantyne had disappeared a few days earlier, and no amount of searching the Ashenell with Prue Liss or waiting patiently for a miracle to bring Pan back yielded any sort of useful result. Then Prue disappeared, as well—not as Pan had done, walking beneath the arch, but by simply abandoning him and departing the cemetery and the city entirely. No reason, no explanation, and apparently no thought for Xac, save the cryptic message she had left with that other boy, Alif or whatever his name was. Up and gone, running off as if she knew where she was going but was not about to share that information with him.

So now that everyone he had been entrusted with helping had vanished, he was beginning to regard himself as fairly useless. As much as he prided himself on always being ready to deal with trouble, he had failed miserably here. But rather than stew about it, he had accepted his failure and set out for Aphalion, intending to give a report to Tasha and Tenerife, hoping they might have a suggestion about what to do next.

Certainly, he didn't.

Of course, there was still a chance that Prue had gone north instead of south, intending to seek help from the Orullians, just as he was doing. She was determined to find Pan, so whatever she did would be governed accordingly. If she thought she could get what she needed from the brothers, she would go to them. It was a long shot at best, but he kept an eye out for any sign of her footprints.

He found nothing.

Not that this was much of a surprise to him. His tracking skills were rudimentary, and the trails leading up to Aphalion were so thoroughly covered with boot prints by Elven Hunters coming and going that it would have been virtually impossible for anyone—except perhaps Pan—to separate out a single set.

So he pushed on as quickly as he could, knowing that the best thing he could do at this point was to get to where he was going and give his report. Afternoon passed into evening and evening into night. He stopped to sleep for several hours before continuing on, the way clear enough with moonlight flooding out of a cloudless sky.

It was almost midday of the following day when he neared the pass and caught sight of a solitary Elven Hunter coming down off the slope ahead of him. They were on course to intersect, so the boy drew to a halt and waited for the other to reach him.

By then, Xac Wen could tell from the man's face that something was dreadfully wrong.

"What's happened?" he asked.

"The Trolls have attacked the pass!" The Elf blurted it out in a series of gasps that suggested he had been doing more than sitting around while this was going on. "We need more fighters or we'll be overrun. I'm on my way to tell the Queen."

As if that will do any good, the boy thought. Then he changed his mind; the Queen was as much at risk as any of them. Surely, she would send reinforcements, if only to protect her throne.

"You have to turn around and go back," the messenger insisted. "It's too dangerous up there for a boy."

"I can't," Xac Wen said, quickly conjuring up an excuse. "I have a message of my own for Haren Crayel. I'll go back after I deliver it."

The Elven Hunter gave him a long look, then shrugged and trotted away. It wasn't his concern.

Xac gave him a final glance before continuing on, picking up his pace as he did so, anxious now to discover what was happening. With Arik Siq a prisoner at Glensk Wood, he wondered how the Drouj had learned the location of the passes. But there might have been someone else—another Drouj—who had escaped the struggle with Sider Ament.

Whatever the case, the result was the same. Defensive walls and bulwarks notwithstanding, the Elves were in trouble.

As he reached the entrance to the pass, he saw the first indications of how serious that trouble was. Elves were running back and forth in front of him, and some were carrying litters bearing wounded. A makeshift shelter had been created out of canvas stretched across a timber frame, and it was already filling up. Elven Hunters manned the ramparts, but the fighting didn't seem to have reached them yet. They were facing forward down the pass, watching whatever was happening farther on, but not doing much of anything other than that.

The boy decided immediately that he was going over the wall and out to where the fighting was taking place. He would find the Orullians there.

Because he had been up in the pass not too long before, he knew where to go to find what he needed. He rushed over to the supply racks, snatched up a chain-mail vest and a bow and arrows. He had his hunting knife with him already, but it was a poor weapon in a fight like this. In point of fact, not much of anything was of use if he got himself into a hand-to-hand-combat situation. He was too small and slight to stand up to even the weakest Troll. He remembered how dwarfed he felt when Arik Siq had come hunting for him on the Carolan heights. If he were brought to bay, he would be dispatched with little effort. The best thing for him to do was to stay out of reach and use the bow.

Of course, the best thing would be to find Tasha and Tenerife, give his report, and get out of there. But he was astute enough to realize that it might not be simple to do that. Unless he was badly mistaken, the Orullians would be right in the thick of the fighting.

Donning his gear, shouldering the bow and arrows, and pulling the visor of his helmet down over his face to conceal his youthful features, he set out for the defensive wall. Mingling with a couple of other Elven Hunters, he went up behind them on one of the ladders and then followed them down the other side. No one said anything. He was tall enough to pass for one of them with the vest and helmet in place. He kept his head down and his feet moving, acting as if he had someplace to go and no time to stop and talk.

Luck was with him. He cleared the wall and the chaos he encountered just beyond and continued up the defile with a handful of others. The clash of weapons and the shouts and screams of combatants rose from somewhere ahead, beyond what he could see. Streams of Elven Hunters passed one another coming from and going toward the fighting, and the ferocity of the sounds made Xac Wen turn cold inside. He knew he was in over his head, that he had never fought in a real battle and had no training for doing so. He might have imagined what it would be like, but already he could tell that the reality would be something else entirely.

Just stay calm, he told himself. *Don't panic.*

But when he was through all the twists and turns, facing toward the far end of the pass from atop a narrow ridge of high ground and listening to the sounds of the madness that lay beyond, all his resolve turned to water.

The Elves had built defenses across the mouth of the pass, elevated bulwarks and shields staggered at twenty-foot intervals to provide a broken, jagged wall that could not be scaled by a large attacking force without first breaking it up into smaller units. Defenders could stand at these walls and contain a much stronger force because there was no good way to physically muscle through without facing withering crossfire from bows and arrows and spears, darts and slings and javelins, with every step.

Beyond, on slopes that fell away from Aphalion's narrow entrance to the plains and hills of the old world, the Elves were fighting to keep the Trolls from gaining even that much of a foothold, arranged in lines across the approaches, their numbers three and four deep, with spears at the forefront, bowmen and slingers behind, and swordsmen to back them up. They occupied all the best defensive positions, deeply entrenched in clusters of boulders and behind shallow ridgelines.

But Xac Wen, with no formal training or tactical experience in the art of war, could already tell that none of this was going to be enough to stop the Drouj.

To begin with, there were thousands of them, outnumbering the Elves defending Aphalion Pass, and they were armored and bearing huge axes and eight-foot spears. They had battering rams and covered wooden shelters that rolled along on wheels to protect against attacks from the Elven longbows. They were formed up in squares and wedges, shields linked together, their attack fronts bristling with steep tips and long oak shafts to keep their enemies at bay while they skewered them. The foremost of these formations were already heavily engaged with Elf skirmishers, and their relentless, steady advance was pushing back the Elves and trampling them underfoot. Bodies lay everywhere across the slopes, and even though the uphill march was a struggle requiring enormous strength and endurance, many more Elves lay dead than Trolls.

Xac Wen watched as bowmen sent fire arrows into the battering rams, but the fires were quickly quenched with buckets of water and heavy pieces of canvas. Ravines and tangled clumps of deadwood stopped some of the siege machines, and sustained volleys from the Elven longbows slowed others. But overall, the attack was pressing ahead and gaining ground.

Before much longer, it would reach the defenders in the pass. On their right flank, the attackers were nearly to the first of the shields that stretched across the Aphalion's heavily defended mouth.

Pushing forward to the wall itself, the boy crowded in beside Elven Hunters already in place and scanned the lines of attacking Trolls and the Elves resisting them.

That was when he caught sight of the Orullian brothers.

Mounting a counterattack, Tasha and Tenerife were leading a heavily armed contingent of Elven swordsmen from a split in the rocks perhaps a hundred yards downslope from the pass into the teeth of the nearest square. Where they had come from was anybody's guess, but the boy supposed they must have found their way there by scaling the cliff walls inside the mouth of the pass and then descending again somewhere outside. What mattered was that they had managed it and were making a desperate effort to block the Drouj advance.

Xac Wen almost went over the wall in response to the rush of excitement that momentarily pushed aside his fear and fed him with a sudden, impetuous courage. But the realization that he lacked any weapon for close-in fighting stopped him from what would have been a foolish decision, and instead he drew back and held his position.

On the right flank, the Elves had reached the Troll square, and working in pairs just at the edge of the extended lances they used thin metal shields on which to impale the deadly steel points. Once the iron tips were caught on the shields, they could not be withdrawn without pulling back the shafts, and the Elves rushed forward between the clusters of useless wooden spear shafts in a sustained charge that took them right up against the Troll front. Tasha led the way, as big as any Troll and twice as fierce, howling the Elven battle cry, his great sword cutting into the vulnerable front line of the attack. Some of the Elves died in the attempt, but most got close enough that they were able to use Trolls at the forefront of the square as shields against those coming from behind. Shoving them backward in a dramatic show of sheer strength, the Elves broke down the attack and went right into the heart of the square.

But the victory was short-lived. Almost as soon as the first square disintegrated, two more appeared to take its place, positioned in a pincer movement so as to trap the Elves between them. Tasha saw what was happening and sounded a warning. The Elves withdrew, taking their wounded with them, leaving the Trolls with nothing but open ground and empty air. Longbows covered their retreat, and for a moment the attack stalled out.

Tasha and Tenerife came over the wall, bloodied and sweating and cursing in the worst language Xac Wen had ever heard—and that was saying something. The Elven Hunters at the wall moved aside to let the returning fighters get past and into the cool shadows of the pass, where most collapsed, throwing down their helmets and weapons and taking long drinks of water from a bucket and ladle being passed around.

The boy started over, and then hesitated, not certain that he wanted to face the Orullians when they looked so angry. But by then, it was too late. Tenerife had seen him.

"Xac Wen, you wolf's pup!" he yelled at the boy. "What are you doing here? Haven't we trouble enough without you adding to it? Where are Pan and Prue?"

Tasha was on his feet and on top of Xac Wen with a single leap. He took hold of the boy's tunic and lifted him up to eye level. "You haven't a brain in your head, you little lizard! Now, what's this about? How did you get past the wall?"

Xac, sputtering and cursing some himself, demanded to be put down before he would answer. Only then, when Tasha had complied and both brothers were standing right in front of him, did the boy fill them in on what had happened to their friends.

"I didn't know what to do when Prue disappeared, so I came here. I can go look for them some more, but I don't know where to start. Tasha, it's not my fault that this happened!"

Tasha nodded grimly. "No one said it was." He looked at his brother. "I don't think we can help them just now. And I don't want to send this boy off on his own searching."

"No, this will have to wait," Tenerife agreed.

Shouts came from the defenses. The Trolls had broken through the last defenders stationed outside the mouth of the pass and were advancing in force.

Tasha glanced over his shoulder at the dark forms closing on their position. "Too many for us to stop. We have to draw back to the larger wall and hope that holds. Come, Tenerife. Let's do what we can. Xac Wen, you get out of here right now. All the way out. Back behind the walls at the head of the pass. Now, you little guttersnipe!"

The boy took off at a run, not daring to challenge Tasha face-to-face. But as soon as he had gone a short distance, he stopped and looked back. The Elven Hunters at the defenses, Tasha and Tenerife among them, had formed up in a defensive line to stop the Drouj advance. Already, the boy could see the dark armored forms advancing on the pass, coming through the last of the outer defenses, scrambling over them and through the ravines and gullies, forming up their attack lines for a final surge. Already the boy could tell that when that surge came, it would sweep the Elven defenders away like dead leaves.

But the Elves had realized this as well and were prepared for it. Forming ranks three men deep, they notched arrows to their longbows, lined themselves across the width of the pass, and in sustained volleys fired into the Troll lines. The pull required to draw an Elven longbow was immense, and the velocity and force of the shaft once released massive. Xac Wen had seen Tasha put an arrow all the way through a tree trunk a foot in diameter. So when the arrows were released into the armored ranks of the Trolls, they went right through the protective metal to the flesh beneath. The Trolls died in clusters, impaled repeatedly. The Elves fell back, formed up, and fired into the enemy ranks again.

But the Trolls kept coming, using shields to absorb or deflect some of the arrows, keeping their ranks filled with new bodies as dead and wounded fell by the wayside. They had seen most of what there was in the way of defensive tactics in their time as soldiers, and they were not about to let the Elven bowmen stop them now.

On they came, and slowly but steadily, the Elves gave ground.

Xac Wen gave ground with them, retreating amid a cluster of others who were not at the forefront of the fighting, making his way back through the twists and turns of Aphalion Pass toward the defensive walls at the far end. He held his bow and arrows ready, prepared to fight if it became necessary, aware of how fragile the line of fighters ahead of him would become if a sustained rush were mounted.

Shouts and the brittle clang of metal weapons echoed through the defile walls, a din so cacophonous that it threatened to overwhelm the boy's courage.

He lost track of where he was, moving back in fits and starts, jostled by those about him who were doing the same, trying hard to concentrate on not stumbling and falling. He was afraid if he fell that the crush might stop him from rising again in time to avoid the wave of fighters coming after.

Then, suddenly, he was bathed in an unexpected wash of sunlight, the walls parting abruptly to form a huge arena space within the center of the passageway. It was here, he realized, that Tasha and Tenerife, leading the little company of friends from Arborlon and Glensk Wood, had come looking all those weeks ago to discover if the protective walls of the valley were really down.

It was here they had encountered the dragon.

Without even thinking about it, he lifted his gaze toward the gap in the cliffs that opened to the sky.

And thereby witnessed a miracle.

AT DECLAN REACH, earlier that same day, the sun rose with a bright glow behind the wall of the mountains, bathing the lands west in a faint sheen of silvery light that just managed to chase back the last of the night's shadows and illuminate the features of the battlefield where the dead lay in heaps. The demon, still wrapped in his Skeal Eile disguise, took a moment to look about at the carnage he had created. Acres of bodies spread away before him, stretching from the mouth of the pass for hundreds of yards downslope toward the empty flats and rough hill country beyond. The last of the Drouj survivors picked through the remains in search of spoils, gathering up bits and pieces of lives gone dark, carrion in search of an unspecified sustenance. Only Arik Siq stood apart, his gaze shifting between the Seraphic on the one hand and the dark mouth of the pass on the other. What he was looking for was difficult to say. Perhaps he was trying to make sense of things, realizing that in some way he had transgressed beyond even what he had thought himself capable of doing. Perhaps he was just trying to stay alert to whatever else might be coming his way.

Whatever he was doing, the demon thought, it wouldn't save him from his fate. In the end, he was just another sacrifice waiting to be led to the altar and butchered.

The demon sat off to one side, away from the mangled corpses and the stench of death, consciously separating himself from these creatures he despised so thoroughly. Even dead, they were an abomination. But he suffered them because they were the food on which he feasted and, in this instance, the lure that would bring to him the bearer of the black staff. The demon would suffer anything to get his hands on the bearer's magic, and he would suffer it for as long as was necessary. The entire focus of his life, for the moment at least, was on waiting for that to happen.

It won't take long. The bearer will hear of this. He will hear of it and he will come. And I will be waiting to put an end to him and to take from his lifeless hands the black staff he carries. And then the magic will be mine.

He believed himself a simple creature with simple needs. There was nothing complicated about him. He was single-minded, and he was driven. He craved power and immortality—insofar as such things might be attained—and dominance over all living things. He understood this about himself, and he believed that what he craved was only what he deserved. He had made the pact required long ago so that this could come about when he shed his human skin. He thought nothing of the exchange in retrospect; he barely remembered making it. Travel down that road far enough and you forget entirely where you came from. The journey becomes the destination in a twisted sort of way. The need to acquire more of everything, to possess as much as there was to possess, was insatiable.

He watched the Drouj some more, moving through the dead, gathering their precious trophies. Stupid creatures. Beasts of low cunning. Some were bleeding from wounds they had not even bothered to tend, so eager were they to gain possession of something they could point to as a remembrance of this day.

Arik Siq walked over to him, the flat, featureless face in sharp contrast with his own disgust-etched countenance. He saw the Troll hesitate and quickly smoothed away the offending wrinkles. Even so, he gave the other a cold, impatient look. "What is it?"

"We are done here," the other said. "We should go, my Drouj and I. We're too few to hold the pass, too few to do anything that matters. We need my father's help."

The demon brushed the demand aside with a wave of his hand. "You need nothing you don't already have. You need only me."

"But what is there to be accomplished . . . ?"

The demon rose, standing so close to him that even though he was much bigger he took a quick step back.

"Are you questioning me?"

Arik Siq shook his head. "No. But I don't see . . ."

"You don't need to *see*. You just need to do what you're told."

The Troll stared at him and then shook his head. "I grow tired of this."

The demon smiled. "Do you?"

"What game are you playing? Whatever game that is, I want no further part. The Drouj are strong enough without you. If you care nothing for the valley and only for the black staff, then there is little we can do to help each other more. You will gain the staff quick enough without my help."

"But I like keeping you close," said the demon, "so that I don't have to worry about you. I've heard you are fond of poisoned darts fired from blowguns—that you favor long-distance killing weapons that allow the user to stay safely hidden."

"I've had enough of you!" Arik Siq snapped. "I don't care what you claim to be. Maybe you are a demon and maybe not. Whichever it is, I waste my time here. If you want the black staff, go out and find it yourself! I am going back to my father. Find someone else to do your killing for you!"

He started to turn away, but the demon reached out and touched his arm. Just the brush of those fingers against the fabric of his tunic was enough to cause Arik Siq to stop and turn. "Let me go."

The demon nodded. "I intend to. But I want to tell you something important first."

The Droùj gave him a look. "What is it?"

The demon crooked one finger, beckoning him to come closer. Warily, Arik Siq leaned in. One hand held a dagger not ten inches from the demon's throat. "Be careful that you don't cause my blade to slip."

The demon smiled. "I am always careful."

His hand whipped out, and he disarmed Arik Siq so quickly that the other barely knew what was happening. In the next second that same hand was closed about the Troll's neck, squeezing. Arik Siq tried to free himself, but all of his strength had gone out of his body, leached away like water from a dry streambed.

The demon brought his face—Skeal Eile's face—close to Arik Siq's. "I am tired of you. There was little enough reason to keep you alive in the first place and no reason at all now. You asked me to let you go? Very well. I will fulfill your wish. Good-bye."

He brought his other hand up and placed it on the Troll's head, fingers tightening. A jolt went through Arik Siq's strong body and his arms and legs began to shake. He thrashed momentarily, and then steam began to leak from his eyes and nose and mouth and ears. A terrible look of anguish crossed his rigid features, twisting them into a grotesque mask. The demon kept smiling at him, increasing the pressure. The Troll's thick skin resisted his efforts far better than the soft skin of humans, but in the end it only prolonged the agony.

He took a long time to die, but in the end his heart gave out and he collapsed at the demon's feet. The demon looked up and saw the other

Drouj watching him in shock, either unwilling or unable to intervene in what they had just witnessed.

He shouted at them. "Get out of here! Go back to his father and tell him what has happened to his son!" He used his boot to roll the body away from him. A strange sense of rage filled him. "Tell him I've decided I will keep for myself the valley he wants so desperately!"

The Trolls hesitated and then quickly began moving away, glancing back at him in fear and loathing, causing him to smile. Stupid creatures, like all their kind. Beasts.

He surveyed the carnage anew, and then he sat down to wait.

TWENTY-NINE

THERE WERE MOMENTS OF PANTERRA QU'S LIFE THAT were frozen in his memory, perfect crystalline pictures made bright and clear, capable of recall as if they had happened just seconds ago. He never planned on keeping them. He didn't even choose them. They chose themselves, embedding in his consciousness and reappearing and fading on a whim. Some lingered because of their emotional impact, and some found a home for reasons he knew he would never fully understand.

But a special few were there simply because it was impossible to forget them, and he would not have chosen to do so if he could.

Such was the case with that singular moment in time in which the dragon descended from out of the bright blue of the afternoon sky and settled to the earth directly in front of him.

The weight of the creature surprised him. The dragon caused the ground to shake and clouds of dust to rise not only from the beating of his huge wings, but from the broad splay of his feet, as well. Pan took uncomfortable note of the size of the hooked claws, each as big as one of his legs. He watched awestruck at the complex way the leathery wings folded in on themselves and then a second time against the armored body. His eyes roamed across the staggered blankets of scales that covered the great body, aware of how they grew uniformly smaller toward the ends of its forelegs where they joined to the great claws and to the places where the neck joined to the head. The dragon's skull was encrusted with knobs and horns, his eyes buried deep beneath jagged brows, and its massive jaws studded with clusters of broken teeth that protruded from blackened gums.

But it was the sheer size of the beast that overwhelmed him. The dragon was too big to take in all at once, and he could not seem to bring himself to believe that such a massive creature was possible. Even though Pan had seen him once already. Even though he was standing right there in front of him, looming over him like some great cliff. Even so.

The dragon held himself perfectly still for long moments, his eyes shifting between Panterra and Phryne Amarantyne, as if deciding which to eat first. It was a terrifying thought, but an inescapable one. Dragons ate meat, the legends said. So why wouldn't he think about eating them? Yet he didn't seem interested in doing that. He studied them in a way that suggested he was looking for something else.

"Oh, you beautiful thing!" Phryne said softly.

They were the first words she had spoken since the dragon had landed, the first indication she had given that she wasn't in total shock. The tremor in her voice caused Pan to look over at her in surprise. She wasn't shocked; she was excited.

To Pan's horror, she took a tentative step toward the beast, her hand outstretched. "Phryne!" he gasped.

"Stay where you are, Pan," she said at once. "Don't move. Don't alarm him. I think I know what's happening. Just stay still."

No part of him thought that this was a good idea, but it was too late to do anything but what she asked. She was too far away from him to stop.

"Beautiful creature, are you the last of your kind? Are you all that is left? The only one?" Phryne was cooing at the dragon, no longer advancing, but still holding out her hand. To his shock, Pan realized she was holding out the Elfstones.

The dragon, watching intently until now, suddenly dropped his head so that his nose was only inches from Phryne's outstretched hand. He could hear the rough sound of his breathing, then a sharp snuffle and a grunt that came from deep inside his belly.

"Do you see, Pan? Do you see how he's reacting? He senses the Elfstones! He smells their magic! That's what drew him to us! I knew it!"

Certainly, something had brought the dragon to them, Pan thought. He had flown a long enough distance to reach them, flying so straight to where they crossed the foothills that backed up against the mountains and passes leading into their valley home that he couldn't possibly have arrived by chance alone. Phryne had just finished using the magic to reveal the details of the battle they had heard raging in the distance, and moments later the dragon had appeared.

"What does he want with the magic?" he pressed.

She shook her head. "I don't know. He wants something, though." She shifted her focus back to the dragon. "Oh, you lovely, wonderful creature, tell me what it is!"

The dragon lifted and dipped his head again, almost as if acknowledging her question. He positioned his nose just above the Elfstones, waiting to see what she would do. The yellow eyes lidded to slits and his long, black tongue licked out.

Impulsively, Phryne opened her clenched fist, palm up, to reveal the Stones cradled in her fingers.

The dragon shifted his head so that he could better see what she was doing, and when he caught sight of the Elfstones, he emitted a sudden violent sound that fell somewhere between a cough and a bellow. This caused the girl to flinch, but she held her ground as he sniffed into the cup of her palm, and then shook his head as if to acknowledge what she had done.

"It's the magic that drew you to us, isn't it?" she whispered. "What is it that you want with it? Do you want me to call it up for you? Is that what you want? Is that what made you come? To see how the magic is made?"

"Phryne . . ."

Panterra spoke her name softly, wanting to warn her that summoning the magic might have exactly the wrong effect on the creature. He might react in an entirely different way than she expected. If he thought the magic dangerous, a threat to his safety, he could end her life with one snap of his great jaws.

But Phryne was no longer paying attention to him. She was focused exclusively on the dragon, staring into his eyes, watching the way he reacted to her every move. She was enraptured with him, compelled by him. There was a bond between them, Pan realized, one that had begun to form the moment she had revealed the Elfstones and now held them fast.

Then Phryne closed her eyes and went down inside herself in the way she had learned to do when summoning the magic. Pan felt a shock of dismay go through him at the realization that she intended to do exactly what he had feared she might. She was responding to what she believed the dragon wanted of her, but by doing so she was taking a terrible risk.

The magic flared to life, the blue light leaking through the cracks between her fingers, sharp and clear. Instantly the dragon responded, making strange sounds deep in his throat, his eyes no longer lidded but wide open, his nostrils flaring. He snapped his long tail, causing Pan to jump back in spite of his resolve, clouds of dust and clots of earth flying as the spikes raked the ground. Phryne's eyes snapped open at the sounds of the dragon's agitation, and she let a little more of the magic escape her fingers. The dragon gave a deep growl, almost a wail, and bobbed his head toward her fist.

"Look, Pan! He wants the magic! He's entranced!" She was so excited that she was almost hopping as she watched the dragon's movements, a huge smile spreading across her face. "Oh, he's so wonderful, isn't he? He's perfect!"

She released a short burst of the blue light—just a momentary flash. The dragon lunged toward it, tongue licking out, as if trying to taste it. He snapped at the light as Phryne moved it around experimentally, fascinated with its elusiveness.

"Phryne! Stop playing with him!" Pan was beside himself. "He's going to get angry!"

She actually laughed then, not in a derisive way, but gleefully. "No, he likes this! He likes being teased! Look at him! He's having such fun!"

Indeed, it seemed that way. The dragon was shifting this way and that, yellow eyes following the movement of the light, trying to keep up with its quickness. He huffed and snorted and sometimes actually whined like a house pet.

But finally Phryne closed off the light, bringing the magic back inside, and the Elfstones went dark again.

The dragon went very still, waiting. When nothing happened, when the light failed to reappear, he began casting about, searching for it. When that failed to produce results, he looked at Phryne and then spread his great wings and rose into the sky. He soared away, spiraling across the vast blue, and for a moment Pan thought he might be leaving. But then down he came anew, settling right back into the space he had occupied earlier.

Phryne looked over her shoulder at Pan, who was still standing rooted in place, not certain what to do. "You see? He wants to play some more! He wants the light!"

Panterra wasn't sure about that. The dragon might not be thinking that way. Who knew how dragons thought? But Phryne wasn't about to listen. She'd captivated the beast, and now she was looking to do something more. Already, she was advancing on him, fearless and confident, holding out the hand with the Elfstones, the light dimmed but the scent of the magic clearly recognizable to the dragon. He sniffed the air, and then as Phryne stopped while still a dozen feet away, the great beast lowered himself to the ground and dropped his head until it was resting against the earth with his horned snout almost touching her.

She walked forward once more, stopping when she was right in front of him. Reaching out the hand that held the Elfstones, she caressed the scales of his great muzzle. Immediately, the dragon lidded his eyes and went very still.

"Phryne?" Pan kept his voice quiet. "What are you doing?"

"Testing a theory," she answered, not looking at him. "Finding out if something is possible, something . . . wonderful. Can you hand me your cloak?"

"What?"

"Your cloak. Can you hand it to me?"

He didn't argue. He removed his travel cloak, folded it over his arm, and walked up beside her. He could see one of the dragon's eyes fix on him, opening slightly, sharp and baleful. Without looking away from the dragon, he handed Phryne his cloak.

"Step back," she said quietly. "You're making him nervous."

He almost laughed. *He* was making the *dragon* nervous? But he did as he was told, backing away slowly, trying not to show how frightened he was, determined not to do anything that would antagonize the beast. Phryne held her ground. It seemed that she felt no fear, that nothing of this business troubled her in the least. Rather, with her face glowing and her smile bright, she seemed eager and excited.

"I can't believe I'm doing this!" he heard her whisper. "Pan, stay where you are. Don't move."

He watched as she moved around to stand right in front of the dragon's left eye, where he could see her clearly. Stripping off her own cloak, she bound it to Pan's using the clasps that fastened each about the neck of the wearer. Then she walked to a place just behind the great head, to where the dragon could still see what she was doing, and carefully flipped the joined cloaks across the beast's neck where it joined to his head and the spikes separated to form a narrow . . .

He froze with the word on his lips.

Saddle.

"No, Phryne!" he cried out, starting forward.

Instantly the dragon's head lifted and swung toward him, his jaws parting, and Pan got a very clear and unobstructed view of rows of jagged teeth starting at the tip of the snout and running all the way back into the darkness of the throat. The dragon's tongue licked out, and he hissed in warning.

Phryne whirled on him. "Stay still, Pan, or he will kill you! You don't command the magic he craves. I do. He will do what I say. I can feel it. But I can't protect you!"

"You can't protect yourself!" Pan snapped back.

"That remains to be seen. That's what we're going to find out!" She was moving toward the makeshift saddle, the hand with the Elfstones held out toward the dragon, holding his attention. She had summoned the magic anew, and it was flaring within her fist, shards of it clearly discernible. The dragon watched her carefully.

"Don't do this!" he said, angry now and afraid. "You can't ride a dragon!"

"I think I can. I think I've found my way back to the Elves. I think this is how I can reach them and how I can help them." She was standing right next to the dragon, looking up at the layer of cloaks, unable to reach them from the ground. She looked back at him. "Will you help me up?"

He shook his head. "I can't do that."

"Can't or won't, Pan?"

"Either one. This is crazy!"

"Please!"

"Phryne, forget this."

"No. I won't do that. I know I'm right." She saw what was in his eyes. "You don't believe me? Then, watch this."

She must have known in her heart, in some way he would never understand, what would happen when she let the blue light escape in a thin stream that spilled to the ground right beneath the dragon's jaws. At once the great head lowered, eyes fixing on the light. When she lifted the light skyward, the dragon looked up, head leaving its resting place, wings beginning to spread.

Quickly, she canted the Elfstone magic down again. "I can control him with the light. I can make him move the way I want. I can guide him."

"You can't know what will happen once you get up in the air!" Pan was frantic, trying to find a way to make her rethink what she was about to do. "How will you even hold on once you're flying?"

"Help me up, and I'll show you."

She looked at him, waiting. For a moment, they faced each other in silence, and he saw her remarkable features clearly—the upsweep of her eyebrows and ears; the lean, narrow face with its delicate bones; the eyes that could be blue one moment and hazel the next; the honey-colored hair, tousled and lank from their travels; and the sleek, beautiful shape of her body.

"Pan," she said, "my people are dying. I have to try to help them. I can't reach them in time to do anything that matters if I can't get the dragon to fly me there. I think he came to me for that reason. Not intentionally, but because of fate or chance or something beyond what we understand. He's a gift. Please, let me use him."

Pan took a quick breath and exhaled. Without a word—so deeply in love in that moment he could barely stand it—he walked over to her. He formed a cup with his hands and bent to offer her a foothold. She leaned down and kissed him on the face, then put her foot in his clasped hands and boosted herself onto the dragon's neck.

Pan stepped back. The dragon did not react to the sudden change in weight. He stayed where he was, watching the play of the Elfstone magic against the earth in front of him. He seemed almost oblivious to the presence of his rider.

"Now tie the ends of the cloaks together beneath his neck," she said.

Again, Pan did what was asked, his efforts painstakingly cautious, the heat of the dragon's breath raw and sharp against his skin as the beast bent close to watch.

"Let me go with you," he said.

But Phryne Amarantyne shook her head. "He won't allow it. He won't permit anyone to ride him but me. I can sense it, Pan. This gift is mine and mine alone. I have to do this by myself. You have to let me."

He started to protest and then stopped himself. He knew it was useless, that she wouldn't relent.

"Take the staff and go back to Glensk Wood and Prue," she told him. "Find out what has happened there. You have to help your people, too."

Her hands stripped off the belt she was wearing, and she hooked it to a cluster of knobs and horns directly in front of her, cinching it tight. She placed her free hand on the belt, securing her grip.

"You see, Pan?" She smiled. "I won't fall off."

She raised the blue light to eye level, and the dragon's head swept up. The huge body shifted and the beast came to his feet, wings spread wide. Pan moved back, giving him more space, his eyes still on Phryne. But she wasn't looking at him anymore, her gaze shifting between the dragon and the distant north.

Then she swept the Elfstone light skyward in a blaze of bright azure, and the dragon lifted away, his great wings flapping, his body stretching out, and his spiked tail whipping sideways.

"Good-bye, Pan!" Phryne called back to him.

Unable to take his eyes away, helpless to prevent what was happening, Panterra Qu watched as she dwindled to a tiny speck. He could not believe she had done this. Impulsive, unpredictable, and even self-ish, she was nevertheless intelligent enough to know when she was placing herself in danger, and yet she seemed not to have realized that here. In a single rash and impulsive act, she had thrown away all caution and placed herself in the hands of a fate that could easily betray her.

And she had abandoned him.

He stood there, stunned and hurt. He watched until she had disappeared into the aether, and then he knew he had lost her.

THIRTY

PHRYNE AMARANTYNE WAS CRYING, TEARS STREAM-
ing down her cheeks, blurring her vision.

It might have been the heartbreak she was feeling at having left Panterra Qu, who had risked his life for her, had come to save
her when no one else could, and whom she had now abandoned,
choosing instead to go to her people.

It might have been the joy that flooded through her as she flew
astride the dragon, soaring into the blue, becoming one with clouds
and mist and distant places that maybe no one else would ever see, free
and filled with wonder and a deep, abiding sense of pleasure.

Or it might simply have been the wind, whipping past her face,
chilly and raw and stinging.

But she wouldn't have traded her blurry, damp eyes and discomfort for anything in those moments. She had never felt anything like
this—never even imagined it was possible. In truth, though driven to
ride the dragon, though convinced she could, she had doubted herself.
Dragons, after all, did not exist. Riding a dragon was a dream. But now

she was living that dream, doing the impossible, and the exhilaration she was experiencing was overwhelming.

Her discomfort and tears did not last. Even after only a short time, she felt as if she had been doing this all her life. The dragon's huge body undulated as it flew, and soon she was anticipating its rhythm. She began to feel comfortable with the steady motion. Her hands explored the huge scales just in front of where she sat, her fingers tracing their rough surfaces. They felt like flat stones, but they were warm to the touch. She could hear them creaking as they rubbed against one another. Her perch began to feel safe and secure, and the fears she'd had at the beginning that she might lose her balance and fall disappeared.

North, the first shadings of twilight crept into the heights of the mountains that ringed her valley home, spilling over the rocky cliff edges to begin their downward slide toward the foothills and the mouth of Aphalion Pass. She could neither see nor hear the battle being fought there, but she knew from the vision shown her by the Elfstones that its outcome hung in the balance. She urged the dragon on by force of will, the pressure of her legs against its scaly neck, and judicious use of the Elfstone magic that directed her toward her destination. Torn between emotions, riddled with guilt and need, she knew one thing and one thing only.

She had to reach the Elves in time to save them.

She had to fulfill the task she had set herself so that all she had gone through and all she had risked would mean something.

The dragon flew on, his efforts swift and steady, and the mountains began to come into sharper focus. Phryne worried that the beast would lose interest in chasing after the Elfstone magic, and to prevent that from happening she shifted the blue light just enough to make sure she was keeping his attention. Once or twice, she even maneuvered the light close enough for the long tongue to lick out and touch it. Maybe that helped, or maybe the dragon just liked the idea of the pursuit. Whatever the case, he showed no signs of becoming distracted. Nothing else seemed to be competing for his attention. He was content just to sail along, tracking what amounted to little more than colored air.

Still, she reminded herself, it was Elven magic; it would have properties of its own, ones that Phryne could neither see nor understand, yet perhaps the dragon could.

She thought of Panterra often, remembering the night she had given herself to him. Why had she done that? It was a spur-of-the-moment decision, made when her emotional pain demanded that comfort of some sort be found. It was difficult to explain. She didn't love him. Or maybe she did love him, in her own way; certainly he was in love with her. But what was the point? Even if she had wanted something more with him, she couldn't have it. Everything prevented it: from her father's murder and Isoeld's treachery to the invading Drouj and their efforts to overcome the Elven defenses to the possibility that she might soon become Queen of the Elves. And Pan's own situation was no less difficult. Pursued by a demon, saddled with the responsibilities of a black staff bearer, searching once again for Prue, and trying to help keep Glensk Wood and its people safe from the Drouj—it all stood in the way of anything that either Pan or she might wish would happen.

She felt herself growing tired, the energy and excitement she had felt earlier sapped by time's passage and her emotional and physical exhaustion. She wondered how long she had been flying. She wondered how much farther she had to go.

Once, she found herself falling asleep, rocked by the motion of the dragon's body, lulled into a dangerous drowsiness, and she jerked awake just in time to keep from sliding off the dragon's neck. It scared her enough that she vowed angrily she wouldn't allow it to happen again.

Ahead, the sun was dropping toward the horizon, and its rays were bathing the slopes of the mountains and the rippled surface of the foothills in shimmering gold.

Then she heard the first faint sounds of the battle she had come to find and, shouting into the wind, she urged the dragon to go faster.

SQUINTING INTO THE BLAZE of sunlight west from out of the blackness of the shadowed corridors of Aphalion Pass, Xac Wen stared in disbelief. He had seen what was flying toward him, and he still couldn't believe it. He *knew* it was the dragon—that it *had* to be the dragon—yet he still kept waiting for it to be something else.

Then it screamed, and right then and there Xac Wen quit trying to find reasons not to believe. That was a dragon, all right! He began yelling wildly for Tasha and Tenerife. He didn't know where they were or even where he was at this point. Around him, the battle had come to a standstill while the participants stared at the phenomenon overhead.

Then, abruptly, impossibly, Xac Wen saw something else.

"Shades!" he whispered to himself.

He looked again, harder this time, making certain of what he was seeing.

"Tasha!" he cried out anew, repeating the name over and over until all at once the larger of the Orullian brothers was yanking him about by the front of his tunic.

"Quiet down, you little banshee!" The big man was streaked with dirt and blood and his face was a mask of rage. He shook the boy for good measure. "What's wrong with you?"

"Look!" He pointed skyward. "Do you see it?"

"I see it. It's that dragon again. As if we needed something else to deal with."

"No, not the dragon! Look closer. Up by its head!"

Tasha squinted into the glare of the sunset, his hand slowly loosening its grip on the boy's tunic.

"Phryne," he breathed softly. "That's Phryne!"

* * *

THE ELVEN PRINCESS WAS PLASTERED against the dragon's neck, one hand gripping the leather belt, the other using the Elfstones to guide the beast. But now that she had reached her destination, she wasn't sure what she should do. The near end of the pass was clogged with Trolls marching forward in tight ranks and rolling up Elven defensive lines that were already shredded. Farther into the pass, all the way back to the wide place where she had first seen the dragon, the Elves were forming up anew. Why they were doing that and not making for the safety of the defensive wall at the far end of the pass where they would find some measure of protection was a mystery. She watched other Elven Hunters rush forward to reinforce those already engaged and realized they meant to make a stand. It was a futile, hopeless effort against what was coming at them. They would all be massacred.

Then someone below saw the dragon and everyone stopped and stared at it. Arms lifted, fingers pointed, and shouts and cries rose in confusion and wonder. This was her chance. If she could separate Drouj and Elves, if she could force their armies to back away from each other, the battle might be broken off and the attack halted.

She directed the dragon downward, seeking Tasha and Tenerife, and found them. She flew toward them, and as she did so the dragon screamed. She couldn't tell at first why he did that after being silent all this time, her concentration on controlling the dragon's dive and holding on to her perch. Then arrows began whizzing past, and she realized they were being fired on.

Momentarily frightened for her mount, she shifted the blue light skyward once more, and the dragon wheeled back toward the outland end of the pass. She could see Troll bowmen and slingers firing their missiles at her, trying to bring the dragon down. She almost laughed, it was such a futile effort.

Ignoring them, she flew the dragon back the way she had come and out over the open foothills beyond, then swung him around, her decision about what to do made. When she had the beast flying in the right direction, she quit using the Elfstones for guidance and summoned the magic for an attack.

It was a new experience. She had not tried this before, although Mistral had said it was possible. But she imagined the effort required would be the same. So she gathered her thoughts, set her mind to accomplishing what was needed, and conjured the Elfstone magic. Prepared, she waited until she was almost on top of the front ranks of the Drouj army and then commanded the Elfstone fire to strike.

Except that the result was not what she had hoped. She had thought she'd mastered the magic and could command it now. But while the Drouj ranks split apart and scattered at the dragon's approach, the Elfstone fire failed to materialize. She tried summoning it again and again, keeping up her efforts for as long as she could manage. But after only a few minutes she could feel her strength failing.

Seconds later, the few shards of Elven fire she had managed to conjure died out completely.

She experienced a rush of dismay and anger. She was too weak! She was too unpracticed! She hadn't used the Elfstones enough to learn how to master their power, and so now she had nothing left to call upon to use against the Drouj.

Then she remembered from Mistral's teachings that the Elfstone magic could only be used to protect against other magic, and the Drouj commanded none.

That might have been the end of things if not for the dragon. Having reached his own conclusions about what was needed, he took control. He might have been responding to her commands earlier, guided by the Elfstones, but she no longer had use of the blue light to rein him in. Screaming as if he had gone mad, he dived almost vertically toward the opening of the pass, body stretched out and wings folded close. Phryne felt her heart go straight to her throat. The dragon was attacking. She might have wanted to stop him, but there was nothing she could do now but hang on and hope.

The dragon reached the opening to the pass and breathed fire into the Trolls gathered there—a fire that was a hundred times more devastating than what Phryne had been able to conjure with the Elfstones— incinerating dozens before lifting away at the last minute to soar back into the sky. But he wasn't finished. Flying ahead between the peaks and cliffs, he found his way down the defile to where the front ranks of the Drouj had re-formed almost on top of the Elven defensive lines and attacked a second time. Fire sprayed everywhere, making no distinction between Elf and Troll. Phryne was screaming at the dragon, trying to stop him from including the Elves in his assault. But the dragon saw only enemies, all of them trying to hurt him (or perhaps her), and he burned them all.

As the beast broke off his attack and swept skyward again, she had just a moment to glance down and see that before the dragon struck the Troll ranks had already driven the Elves from the wide spot in the pass back into the narrows so that most of those caught out in the open were Drouj.

Most, but not all.

She wondered suddenly about Tasha and Tenerife, always at the forefront of every effort.

She closed her eyes in dismay, and then quickly opened them again. She had to stop this. She had to take back control of the dragon before any more Elves died. What had seemed like a good idea was turning out to be a bad one. If she couldn't make the dragon confine his attack to the Trolls, she had to find another way.

Panterra was right. She had assumed things she had no right assuming. She had believed she could make the dragon bring her to Aphalion and do her bidding solely because she had possession of the Elfstones. But no magic could do everything, and none of it was predictable. She had been told as much by Mistral. Yet in her haste and in her determination to do something, she had ignored her grandmother's words.

Now her people were paying the price for her foolish and reckless disregard.

And suddenly, just like that, she knew what she had to do.

She steeled herself for what was needed, calling up the Elfstone magic one more time, conjuring an image that was dim and not fully formed because she had never seen what she was looking for. She forsook any further attempts at using the magic to strike back at the Trolls; she knew she didn't have the strength or skills for it. Something less demanding and overt would have to do.

The blue light flared and lanced away, and the dragon immediately went after it. Back down the length of the pass the great beast flew, the Elfstone magic showing him the way. Phryne held the light steady and stayed focused, beating back her weariness and fear and shame, giving herself over to the singular purpose she had embraced. Onward they flew, dragon and Elven Princess, over the lines of milling Trolls, through the cliffs and drops, and back out into the old world where the bulk of the Drouj army was held in check, waiting for the order to attack.

Let me just do this one thing, she thought. *Let me do this, and I will ask nothing more.*

She was searching for Taureq Siq, and with the aid of the Elfstone magic she found him at the rear of the Drouj lines, surrounded by his command staff and bodyguards. The blue light revealed him even though she had never seen him before. The makeshift images she had formed out of what others had described was enough. She had mastered the Elfstone magic sufficiently to be able to make it do that much, and it did not fail her now.

She took the dragon down at once, telling herself that what happened next would depend entirely on the Drouj Maturen—a cold denial of responsibility for what she already knew he would bring down upon his own head.

Taureq Siq did not disappoint her. Upon catching sight of the dragon, he ordered his bodyguards to attack. It was a death sentence. Arrows and slings and even spears, when the dragon got close enough that they could be employed, were useless. The metal tips bounced harmlessly off the beast's armored plates, and within seconds the Drouj gave up their efforts and tried to flee, scattering in all directions. It made no difference. The dragon was enraged, and he turned his deadly fire on them, sweeping the hilltop on which they had been clustered, burning them all to smoke and ash.

Phryne saw Taureq Siq in his final moments, his features so clear she could even make out his look of amazement that this was happening. He had chosen to stand his ground, one arm wrapped about the neck of an aide, holding the unfortunate in front of him like a shield. It did little good. The dragon fire burned through the luckless aide as if he were made of paper and then consumed the Maturen, as well.

Taureq Siq burned as if the weight of all his terrible deeds could be measured by the intensity of the flames.

All across the foothills and into Aphalion Pass, the cry went up that Taureq Siq was dead. The Trolls of the Drouj army were immediately thrown into disarray, no longer certain of what they should do. Leaderless and confused, they began to withdraw, backing out of the pass, their unit commanders pulling back with them. Soon the retreat was a complete rout as even those who had advanced deepest of all into the defile felt their courage give way.

His rage sated, the dragon broke off the attack, lifting away in a long, slow spiral. Phryne, who still clung to his neck, suddenly realized that something was wrong with her. Glancing down, she saw that arrows and darts sprouted from her body, her skin was burned by fire, and her clothes were smoking and blackened. She had failed to notice any of this until now, consumed by her struggle to help the Elves. She slumped in the makeshift saddle in response, dizzy and weak at the sight of the damage she had suffered. Parts of her body felt strangely numb, and she was having trouble breathing. For a second, she considered forcing the dragon to land, just so that she could get off.

But she couldn't do that—not out here where the Drouj were still everywhere and there was no protection for her. So she mustered what strength she could and sent the Elfstone magic in search of Tasha and Tenerife. The blue light found them quickly enough, and the dragon responded by taking her to them. He went willingly, his eagerness to pursue the blue light renewed, flying back into the mountains, tacking across the deep split of the pass below until he had reached the wide spot where she had left the Orullians what now seemed like hours ago.

There were Elves clustered below, but they scattered into the narrower parts of the pass the moment they saw the dragon returning. This time they did not try to use their weapons, alerted perhaps by the brothers that she was aboard. The dragon spiraled downward in a slow, winding descent that brought him to the floor of the pass, where he settled in place, his wings folding against his body.

Closing her fingers tightly about the Elfstones, Phryne caused the magic to diminish to a soft pulse.

No one tried to approach as she slid down the great neck and dropped to the ground in a heap. With the last of her strength, she directed the Elfstone magic skyward. The dragon spread his wings and rose into the air, gathered himself when he was above the peaks, and flew until the coming night had swallowed him.

When she could no longer see him, when he had disappeared for good, still chasing after the magic he so desperately wanted, she closed her fingers around the Elfstones until the blue light had faded, then tucked the Stones into a pocket. She struggled to rise, to drag herself to someplace where the dragon couldn't see her if he chose to return, but her body wouldn't obey her. Then Tasha was there, only steps ahead of Tenerife and dozens more. Voices assaulted her, shouts of greeting and cries of "Queen" and "Amarantyne." She saw faces she recognized, among them Xac Wen's, his boyish features bright with excitement and wonder. Tasha and Tenerife held everyone back, calling for a healer, directing traffic. Tasha lifted her into his strong arms and bore her through the crowd.

"Make way, Elven Hunters!" he roared at them, his voice booming out. "Make way for our real Queen!"

She let the waves of sound wash over her, unable to respond to them, unwilling to make the effort. She had no strength left to do so. Her head was spinning and her thoughts were scattered. Her body felt numb all over and she was very cold.

"Thank you, Tasha," she whispered up to him.

The big man dipped his head. A drop of something wet splashed on her face. "You saved us all, Phryne. Now just hold on. A healer is coming."

"Can you imagine the stories they will tell about this?" Tenerife bent close to kiss her forehead. She could see the warmth reflected in his eyes. "You were so brave, Princess."

"I feel so cold."

"Tasha, we're losing her! Hurry."

Phryne closed her eyes as they entered the narrows of the defile and passed out of the fading daylight and into the darkness beyond.

IN HER DREAMS, she was flying again, borne on the back of the dragon, his great wings spread out beneath her, his body undulating as it soared over acres of countryside all lush and green with new growth amid blue rivers that tangled and twisted like silken threads. She felt the wind in her face and the sun on her skin, and the world was fresh and clean once more.

Beautiful creature, she called to the dragon, and he glanced at her with his lidded reptilian eyes and she felt his love for her.

You will always be mine, she told him. And I will always belong to you.

She lay forward against the rough plates of the beast's scales, feeling them press against her face, and she rode the air currents toward a peaceful sleep.

HAREN CRAYEL, captain of the Elven Home Guard and commander of the Elven Hunters warding Aphalion Pass, stood apart with Tasha and Tenerife in the aftermath, their heads bent close, their hard eyes fixed not on one another but on the ground at their feet.

"What do you want to do about this?" he asked quietly.

Tenerife looked at him. "You already know the answer to that."

"Do we have your support?"

"Would it matter? Has it ever mattered? Just tell me how much time you need."

"We could leave at once. Be there by dawn."

Tasha shook his head. "No, I want to be certain that it happens in the right way. I don't want any mistakes. Give us until tomorrow night."

Tenerife hugged himself, kicking at the earth. "That should be time enough."

The captain of the Home Guard nodded. "Someone may get there ahead of you, tell them what's happened here. It won't be so easy then."

Tasha grunted. "It won't be so easy, anyway."

He glanced over to where Xac Wen knelt beside the carefully wrapped body of Phryne Amarantyne. His brother and Haren Crayel followed his gaze, and then looked at each other.

"What we need," Tasha said softly, "is an experienced trickster."

THIRTY-ONE

A WEARY, FOOTSORE PANTERRA QU STOOD ON A
rise that gave him a clear view of the mountains west and
the first hints of the opening into Declan Reach. He had
walked east through the remainder of the day and most of the night,
stopping only once to sleep for several hours before rising and continuing on. He had determined some time back that he could make the
entrance to the pass by daybreak and be back in Glensk Wood by midday. He hoped he would hear some news of Prue once he got there,
but if there were no news to be had he would rest again and then continue to Arborlon.

Of course, there were potential complications he did not like to
dwell on. The Drouj might have dispatched an invasion force to Declan
Reach as well as to Aphalion. If they had discovered the location of the
one, there was a good chance they had discovered the location of
the other, as well. The Elfstones had revealed no indications of a battle
being fought there, so either the Drouj had not yet attacked or they
had attacked and were already through and inside the valley. If the lat-

ter were true, they now held the pass, which would prevent him from reaching his home without going north to Aphalion. That, in turn, would mean that instead of letting Phryne go on alone, he should have insisted on going with her.

He didn't like thinking of that possibility. It was painful enough already just accepting that she was gone.

He took a moment to look north, peering through the moonlit darkness as if he might learn what had become of her and the dragon. There was nothing to see, of course, but he couldn't help wondering what had happened to them. He no longer heard the sounds of a battle being fought, the sounds he had heard yesterday long since gone and replaced by a deep, abiding silence. Whatever conclusion had been reached, it was over and done now. Her part in the outcome of things was decided; his was still to be played out.

He experienced a fresh pang of disappointment thinking back once more on how they had separated. The fact was she had left him behind, and he did not like how it made him feel. She had said the dragon would not take them both, but he had wondered about that from the moment she had said it. He had helped her leave him, knowing she genuinely believed her people needed her more than he did. It wasn't his place to second-guess her choice. Not even if his doubts proved to be valid.

He looked east again. He could argue this with himself all night, and had pretty much done so. But his own problems were more pressing than his wounded pride and damaged heart. He might love her; he might even one day see something come of that love. But just now, it didn't really matter. Just now, it was a small thing.

Putting any further debate aside, he started walking. It was still dark, dawn an hour or so away, but he would reach the pass by then and discover how things stood. Phryne Amarantyne had troubled him from that first day when they had climbed out of the valley toward Aphalion Pass, and he expected she would continue to do so for some time to come. Prue would have known what to say to him, had she been there. Prue always knew what to say.

But Prue wasn't there, of course, and the best he could hope for was that he would find her again before another day passed.

He trekked on, wending his way over rough hills and down twisty gullies, stirring up dust as he walked through country that felt as dead as his hopes for remaining a Tracker. That dream was over—for both Prue and himself. Things would never be the same for them again, and that was a pain he felt more keenly than anything related to Phryne Amarantyne. He wished there was something he could do to change what had happened to Prue, but he knew there wasn't. She had made the choice that had diminished her sight; it had never been his to make. She'd had a chance to help keep him safe, and he understood it was a chance she would take every time it was offered regardless of the price extracted. Prue was like that. Loyalty and sacrifice were qualities she valued and understood. Particularly where it involved those she was close to and especially with him.

He wondered where she was.

He wondered what had happened to her.

Moonlight shone out of a cloudless sky, the barren world about him as silent and lifeless as a cemetery, he continued walking, searching for a way he could find out.

* * *

PRUE LISS AND AISLINNE KRAY CROUCHED in the concealment of a cluster of rocks at the head of the pass leading out from Declan Reach, as silent as shadows. The man they had left behind had whispered of killing and madness, his voice hoarse and barely audible, his wounds grievous enough that he could not continue farther, and they had left him there for others to find. And eventually others had come, though only a handful, stumbling out from the killing field in ones and twos, ragged figures in the darkness, bloodied and despairing, the last of those who had gone with Skeal Eile to die on the flats beyond.

"All dead," one woman had gasped as she came up to them and they caught her in their arms. "Killed, every one of them. Killed by him, by the Seraphic! He lied to us. He deceived us all."

Another had repeated the words, bitter and enraged and devastated by what had happened. That one, too, had gone on. Aislinne had given each of them water to drink and a bit of food and told them to wait inside the pass for help to come. Where it would come from, she had no idea. But it was all Prue or she could do. The scarlet dove flew on, and they were committed to following it to where they would find Panterra Qu and whatever fate awaited them all.

Now they were in hiding at the far end of the pass and had seen for themselves the source of the horrific stories related by the ragged people they had encountered earlier. Not a hundred yards from where they crouched the killing field began, a span of several acres covered by the mingled corpses of Drouj and people from Glensk Wood alike sprawled everywhere across the slopes. Neither she nor Aislinne had ever seen so many dead people before, and the enormity of it was appalling. Human men, women, and children and Drouj soldiers, their blood dark and stiff on their skin and clothing, their limbs twisted and fixed, their eyes blank and staring. Many of these were people they had known; some had been friends and neighbors. None had deserved this.

In the midst of this carnage, Skeal Eile sat waiting, his back to them and his eyes on the countryside beyond. They had seen his features clearly when they had crept through the shadows of the defile to their hiding place, not daring to come any closer than they were. He had been moving about then, glancing this way and that, his nose lifting as if he were testing the air for scent. They knew he wasn't who he seemed—he wasn't Skeal Eile at all, but the demon that had tracked them both. They could feel what he was in their bones—Prue in particular, her instincts screaming at her, shivers running up and down her spine. They looked at each other, their breathing labored and harsh in their throats, and they knew.

But they had not spoken of it. Not once. At first, it had been too risky with the demon threading his way through the dead, turning this way and that, searching. It was dangerous enough being this close to him. Later, when he had settled down and taken up his current place of watch, they had still kept silent, an unspoken agreement. Once, Aislinne had gestured to suggest that perhaps they should retreat farther back into the pass. But Prue had pointed to where the scarlet dove had come to roost in the rocks overhead. It was no longer leading them, she indicated. It had found what it was looking for. It was waiting here for Panterra Qu, and she and Aislinne must wait with it.

By gesturing and mouthing words, she made her point, and even though Aislinne could not see the dove, she had understood, nodded in agreement, and settled back with her bow and arrows clutched close.

If this was where the matter was to be decided, Aislinne Kray would take a stand, as well. Prue knew what she was thinking, how she had made up her mind that it would all end here. Both of them had come searching for a resolution to the madness that had been threatening all of them ever since the demon had found his way into the valley, and now both believed that no resolution could be found without Panterra Qu. He was coming, and the demon was waiting for him. There was no other explanation for what was happening. The dead were meant to draw the bearer of the black staff, and the demon would wait for as long as it took for that to happen.

But Prue and Aislinne would wait with him. They could be patient, too.

Aislinne shifted closer to Prue and put her lips to the girl's ear.

I could kill him from here.

Prue looked at her.

One shot, through the heart. A second to join it, if I am lucky. It might be worth trying. We could end it all.

Prue shook her head. *You can't kill him that way.*

We don't know that.

I know it. The King of the Silver River said Pan must confront the demon to put an end to him. We must wait for that.

Aislinne studied her face for a long time, and then nodded and settled back once more.

On the slopes leading up to the pass where the demon sat amid the dead, the darkness was beginning to draw back.

THE DEMON WAS A PATIENT CREATURE. Waiting did not trouble it. Even waiting days or weeks did not distress it. It had learned how to wait, helped in part because its life span was so long and time was so unimportant. It was easy to wait in this instance, where it would yield such rich rewards. There were many things not worth waiting for and times when patience was wasted, but it was not the case here. The demon had already been waiting centuries. It had not even come close to laying hands upon one of the black staffs since the collapse of the old world and the destruction of the last of the Knights of the Word.

The possibility of it happening now was exciting and compelling, and his need for it was overwhelming. Possession of power drew the demon now as always—power over life and death. That power would soon be his, and the satisfaction he would feel when it was his to wield was worth any wait.

So he sat there in the killing field, the smell of death all around him, sharp and pungent in the night air. He drank it in out of habit, but barely gave it a thought as he did so. He had drunk it in so often, been surrounded by it so endlessly, that it no longer held much interest. The dead that lay at his feet were worth nothing in any case. It was the bearer's life that had real value.

It was his anticipation of what it would feel like to take that life that mattered.

Had he been less immersed in the intoxicating smell and taste of death and less obsessed by his craving for the power of the black staff, he might have sensed the presence of Prue Liss, who was hidden little more than a hundred yards away. He might have caught a whiff of her strange magic or a whisper of her companion's soft breathing. But on this night, in this place, and with his thoughts directed on other matters, he failed to do so.

Time slipped away, and once or twice he thought he heard stirrings from within the shadows of the entrance to the pass. But he gave it almost no thought, assuming it was one of those unfortunates who had managed to crawl from the heaps of dead in a futile effort to reach safety in Glensk Wood. Such safety was an illusion, given what he had planned for those who lived within the valley. And even if it was something or someone who thought to do him harm, he didn't care because nothing that humans and their like possessed could threaten him. He had already seen the best of what they had, and it was nothing.

Only the bearer of the staff could do him harm, and he would make swift work of that one, once he surfaced. A newly endowed bearer of magic was no match for someone like him, a practiced wielder, a skilled user, and a creature comfortable with death.

He watched the darkness slowly fade, watched dawn's light surface from behind the mountains east, watched the shadows draw back and begin, one by one, to vanish. The new day had arrived, and it held the promise of something wonderful.

Then suddenly he saw the solitary figure moving across the foothills west, slowly taking shape as it emerged from the gloom. A man carrying a black staff. He could hardly believe his good fortune.

Anticipation coursing through him, he watched the man draw closer.

PANTERRA SMELLED THE DEAD long before he saw them; the breeze wafting down out of the mountains carried the stench to where he trudged through the early-morning light. The slopes ahead were crumpled and riven by gullies and ravines, and the shadows hid the bodies until he was no more than a hundred yards off. He was struck at once by their numbers. Hundreds littered the landscape—perhaps thousands—twisted and layered in death, intertwined in a complicated weaving of limbs and bodies. He couldn't tell who they were and couldn't begin to guess what had brought them there, so close to the mouth of the pass at Declan Reach that they almost certainly must have come from within the valley. Refugees, perhaps, fleeing some horror that had taken place in his absence.

Or was this something else?

As he got closer, he realized that the dead were both human and Troll, and that in all likelihood, they had killed one another. Some were still locked in death grips, weapons in hand, arms clasped about each other. The Trolls were armored and the humans were not, but there were so many more of the latter that he knew what they had lacked in arms and armor they had made up for in numbers. The struggle had been bitter and quarter had not been given. The dead included women and children, as well as men; it included young and old. Apparently, the Trolls had been waiting for this exodus and had fallen on the travelers as they started downslope from the pass entrance.

He ventured closer and peered down at the faces. Two he recognized right away. They were from Glensk Wood. The man had been a carpenter, the woman his wife. They had lived not far from him when he was growing up. He glanced about in disbelief and found more familiar faces. They were all from his village.

Then he saw the solitary figure sitting in the midst of the dead back toward the cliff wall, still almost entirely hidden in shadow. He straightened and took a closer look, trying to make out who it was. He took a step forward, took another, and then a few more.

The figure rose suddenly and stepped·toward him, coming out of the shadows and into the dawn light. It was Skeal Eile.

Right away, Pan knew the Seraphic was responsible for what had happened. He knew it instinctively, the way he knew how to read sign and sense the way a trail would go just from a single scrape of a boot on a rock. This was Skeal Eile's doing, all these people dead, people from Glensk Wood who had followed and trusted him. The boy flushed with rage, wondering if the Seraphic had managed to find a way to kill everyone in the village. Were Prue's parents among the dead? Was Prue herself? Aislinne? How many others he had known all his life? How many lay dead at his feet, all because of this one hateful man?

He started forward in a white-hot rage, and he might have kept going except that suddenly the runes carved into his black staff began to burn fiercely. Their light was sudden and brilliant, and he stopped where he was. It was an unmistakable warning. He knew that much from what Sider had told him. When there was extreme danger close at hand, the runes would glow. But what sort of danger was it that threatened here? Not Skeal Eile. He was treacherous and manipulative, but Pan was his match even without the staff. This was something else.

Then he remembered the demon that Prue had said was hunting him, and he cast about for some sign of it. But nothing moved on the killing field. There was only Skeal Eile and himself. He stayed where he was, thinking it through. The demon might be hiding in the pass, but why would it do that when he was close enough for it to attack? Was it counting on the Seraphic to somehow distract him?

He had too many questions and not enough answers. He had to act on what he could see.

"What's happened here?" he called out.

Skeal Eile shook his head, coming a few steps closer. "The villagers were set upon by the Trolls when they emerged from the pass last night. They killed each other. Even Arik Siq is dead. He lies here." He gestured at a body sprawled close by. "Would you like to see for yourself?"

"Where were these people going?" Pan asked, ignoring the offer.

"To find a new home outside the valley. To go somewhere safe. I was leading them there. I was sent a dream by the boy Hawk, telling me where to go." He shook his head. "But I only led them to this. My own people."

He sounded genuinely stricken, but Pan didn't trust it. "Yet you survived while they all died?"

"A cruel trick of fate. I was knocked down early and pinned beneath the bodies. I lay there until it was over, stunned and bleeding, unable to move."

"Your vaunted magic? Your skills with oratory? Nothing would have helped?"

"Do not mock me, boy. I did what I could. I don't have to explain myself to you or anyone else."

This was the Skeal Eile Pan knew, arrogant and dismissive. The boy began to advance on him anew, enraged. But once again the runes of his staff blazed and a fresh uneasiness washed through him.

He stopped once more, trying to decide what was wrong. The demon was here. It had to be. Close by. It felt as if it were right in front of him.

His gaze fastened on Skeal Eile. *Right in front of him.* Skeal Eile, for all intents and purposes, but yet not quite as Pan remembered him. Something was different—enough so that he realized the truth. He took a quick breath. He had almost missed it, almost given himself over to his worst enemy. This wasn't the Seraphic he was dealing with, even if that was how it appeared. It wasn't the Seraphic who was standing there, speaking to him.

It was the demon.

The confrontation that Prue had warned him about was happening right now, and he hadn't even been aware of it.

He had just enough time to whip the staff around in front of him like a shield, the magic flowing through its length and into his body, his startled recognition changing to steely determination as the demon attacked. It must have seen something in his eyes or read it in his body language, but it acted quickly, arms extending in a billowing of black robes, fire lancing out in a wicked green wave. The magic slammed into Panterra and threw him backward, knocking him off his feet to sprawl among the dead. It washed over him like a blanket that would smother him, sucking away all the air, its heat intensifying as it pressed downward. Pan fought back with his own magic, using the staff to keep the flames at bay, fighting to gain space and time.

When the attack broke off, a sudden cessation of sustained effort, Pan rolled away from the place to which he had been pinned and surged back to his feet. But at once the attack began anew, this time in a series of sharp bursts that struck with such force his bones rattled. He fought this attack off, too, but it drained his energy and left him shaking. The demon was giving him no chance to react to what was happening. He was fighting a defensive battle, and the effort he was expending kept him from mounting any sort of counteroffensive.

"Put down the staff, Panterra!" the demon shouted at him, striking out once more, using blades of fire this time, spear points that lanced and cut like steel edges. "You can't harm me. You can't defeat me. Don't be foolish. Lay down the staff, and I will let you live. The staff is all I care about."

He kept coming toward Pan as he attacked, getting steadily closer. Pan was being wrenched about, knocked over each time he sought to gain his feet, pressed backward as if by a great wind. He managed to keep the staff between himself and the demon, fending off each punishing blow it delivered, but he could do little else.

"Are you listening?" the demon called out. "Time isn't something you have to waste, boy. Better that you do as I say before I am forced to turn you to dust. What a shame it would be if you failed to protect that little girl who thinks so much of you."

Pan clenched his teeth, trying to respond. But he couldn't speak.

"Your friends are all dead, Panterra. Did you know that? The girl is all that's left. If you want to keep her safe, lay down the staff. Don't be a fool. Do it now."

Whatever else he did, it would not be that. His hands tightened on the length of black wood, feeling the steady pulse of the runes against his skin, and he fought his way back to his feet once more.

PRUE LISS WAS STILL CROUCHED behind the rocks at the entrance to the pass when Panterra Qu appeared from out of the fading night.

She watched him approach the killing field and the waiting demon. She had thought to go to him right away when she saw him, but Aislinne had pulled her down again, shaking her head. *Wait,* she had mouthed silently.

When Pan had begun speaking with the demon, assuming it was Skeal Eile, Prue almost went to him again. But then the demon did something to give himself away, and Pan summoned the magic of the black staff just in time to save himself. From there, the battle had escalated quickly until now the mountain air was thick with smoky residue from expended magic, the smell bitter and strong in her nostrils, the taste metallic on her tongue.

I have to do something to help him, she thought.

It was what she had been charged with by the King of the Silver River. It was what she had been given to do, and even if she wasn't certain how to go about it, she had to try something. She had been struggling with her sense of inadequacy from the moment the King of the Silver River had told her what she must do, but there was no time left to think about it. The battle was raging back and forth in front of her, the combatants fighting their way across the killing field, the dead lying all around them, the earth bloodstained and scarred. Panterra was being pushed back, slowly and steadily, by the demon's attack. He was still protecting himself, but she could tell that it was only a matter of time until the attack broke down his defenses and left him helpless.

She felt a wave of despair sweep through her. Pan still wasn't experienced enough for a battle of this sort. He wasn't trained to fight it. The black staff was still too unfamiliar and the magic too strange. He was wielding it the way he would any new weapon—tentatively, defensively, uncertainly. Though he did his best, it was already clear that his best might not be good enough to save him. If she didn't intervene in a way that would shift the momentum in his favor, he would die.

But still something held her back, preventing her from intervening. *Do something!*

Then abruptly the scarlet dove left its roost and began to soar through the skies above the fighters, spiraling blood red against the grays and blacks that colored Prue's world. Prue's gaze shifted instantly to track its flight. It had taken on a distinctly different look now, more fierce and warlike, more hawk than dove. She watched it bank and straighten, gain altitude and then descend. What was it doing? She could feel its fluid movements in the beating of her heart. She could feel them tugging at her, the bond between them stretching.

She came to her feet in response, left her place of hiding and strode out through the shadows into the early-morning light. "Stay where you are," she whispered to Aislinne as she did so. "Don't let him see you."

She kept walking until she was clear of the pass and standing fully exposed in a patch of sunlight. She saw Pan glance her way—a moment only, because that was all he was allowed before being forced to return his attention to the demon. But it was enough. He knew she was there. He was frightened for her, she could tell, but he was uplifted, too. It reflected in his eyes before he was forced to turn away again.

She lifted her face to the morning sky and watched the scarlet dove sweep toward her, the most beautiful thing she had ever seen and the last of any real color. She wanted to reach out and touch it, to feel its soft body and silky feathers in her hands. She could almost feel them now, but it was only the morning breeze caressing her skin.

The demon had thrown Panterra down yet again, and this time the boy did not seem able to rise. Sprawled on the ground, he held the black staff protectively before him, struggling to sit up as the demon's magic forced him back down. The demon approached in a leisurely fashion, taking his time, using a steady flow of magic to pin the boy in place. He was speaking to Pan, but Prue couldn't hear what he was saying. Pan thrashed and fought against the bonds being layered atop him, but he could not break free.

Prue knew it was the end for him, and that almost certainly meant the end of her. She tightened her resolve. She would not allow it. She would not stand aside and watch it happen. If it were to end for them, it would not end without a fight.

"Ragpicker!" she screamed at the demon.

The demon turned at the sound of her voice, surprise reflected in its strange red eyes.

Then the scarlet dove dropped straight out of the sky and onto its face.

PANTERRA WAS FIGHTING for his life, staggered by the onslaught of demon magic, when Prue appeared suddenly out of the entrance of the pass. He had only a moment to decide that it was really her, and then he was forced to turn away again as the demon's attack intensified.

When he went down for the final time and found himself pinned to the ground by his attacker's magic, he was hoping for only one thing—for Prue to get away, to flee what was happening before the demon saw she was there. But then she called to it, using a name he did not recognize, drawing its immediate attention, and his hopes faded. He tried again to rise, to take advantage of the momentary distraction. But the demon's focus was back on him almost instantly, the magic lashing him, holding him down, squeezing the air from his lungs and sapping the strength from his body.

It drew closer, talking to him all the while in an almost casual fashion, speaking as if to an old friend, as if nothing odd were happening. It reached out its hand as if intending to help him to his feet, even as its fingers were stretching toward his head.

Then for no discernible reason that Pan could determine, the demon went completely mad. It threw up its hands, clawed at its face, twisted its body this way and that, and screamed in a voice that was filled with pain and rage. It spun about like a scarecrow blown loose in a great windstorm; it thrashed as if a thousand bees were stinging it all at once. Its attack on Pan ceased altogether, and although weakened and battered by the demon magic the boy managed to scramble back to his feet.

Once righted, he acted quickly to refocus the magic of the black staff, gathering it to him, feeling its power surge and twist from the wood into his limbs and down into his body before reversing and then flowing back out again in a white-hot heat.

But in those few moments that it took Pan to pull himself together, the demon caught hold of whatever had been causing it such pain and flung it aside. There was a scarlet explosion on the morning air, as if something made of flesh and blood had been ripped apart. He heard Prue scream. Then one clawed hand, dripping with gore, gestured toward her, and the demon fire struck her a hammer blow and collapsed her like a rag doll.

Panterra Qu intervened a second too late to prevent it from happening, but fury fueled his effort and the black staff's magic exploded into the demon. Yet somehow, even though it was staggered by the attack, the demon managed to remain upright. Face ripped to shreds, blood everywhere, the horror it had become twisted in a ghastly smile as it wheeled back on Pan, hands lifting for another assault.

Then Pan heard a bowstring release, and a black arrow struck the demon with such force that the steel tip sprouted from his chest. The creature gasped, staggered, and turned partway around as a second arrow buried itself in its throat.

Aislinne Kray stood at the entrance to the pass, a third arrow readied for use.

Pan struck out at their enemy again, and this time the staff's magic caught the demon completely unprepared, striking him a massive blow and throwing him backward. This time, he couldn't seem to recover before Pan had struck him again. Then struck him once again. Pan didn't know if it was the aftershock of whatever had clawed the demon's face or the damage caused by Aislinne's arrows or the power of his own magic, but the cumulative effect was devastating.

The demon screamed, thrashing as the third arrow struck it. It staggered away in a futile effort to escape further injuries, but it was too late. Broken and battered, it dropped to its hands and knees, head hanging down, blood dripping from every part of it.

Panterra limped toward it, suddenly aware that he had been injured, that not everything was working right. But his concentration was intense enough to push aside the pain and confusion, and he summoned the staff's magic one more time. Centering it on the stricken demon, he burned it from the head down until nothing remained but the thin, bitter taste of ashes wafting on the mountain air.

ABANDONING THE CHARRED OUTLINE of the demon, Pan limped hurriedly over to where Prue sprawled on the ground, watching Aislinne approach from the other direction, abandoning her bow as she ran to join him. Even injured as he was, he reached the girl first and dropped beside her, lifting her into his arms and cradling her limp body. The demon fire had seared the skin of her face and arms, but maybe not badly enough to do permanent damage. Her eyes were closed, and she was breathing in shallow gasps.

"Panterra!" Aislinne said, kneeling beside him. "Is she alive?"

Pan nodded. He reached out and smoothed back damp strands of red hair from her face. Aislinne brought out her water skin and held it to Prue's mouth, letting a little of the water trickle onto her lips. The water ran down her face, but she did not respond.

Aislinne placed her head against the girl's chest, listening. "Her heart's beating. I think it's just the shock of what happened to her." She looked over. "But I don't know exactly what that was. Did you know about her eyes? About the scarlet dove? I think that was what distracted the demon when it was after you. I can't explain why, but it just seemed as if she was following it when she showed herself."

Pan didn't care about the dove. He didn't even care about the demon now that it was dead. "She has to be all right," he said, the words tight and hot in his throat. "She can't be hurt. Not after all this."

Aislinne reached out and touched his arm. "What about you, Panterra? Have you looked at yourself yet? You are bleeding through your clothes."

He looked down and saw that she was right. As well, his skin was blistered and blackened, and he thought he might have cracked some ribs and maybe broken several fingers on one hand. But none of that mattered. Prue was his only concern, and he would not think of himself until he had been reassured about her.

Suddenly she gasped, coughed roughly, and jerked sharply in his arms. He helped her sit up, feeling her body tense as he did so. "Pan?" she whispered, her voice hoarse and thick.

"Right here. Right beside you."

"The demon?"

"Dead. It's over, Prue. We won."

She shook her head. "Did we?"

Her eyes blinked open, and he saw the cloudy look directed straight in front of her, empty of sight. Her seemingly sightless eyes still bothered him, even knowing she actually could see, if only in black and white. "We did, Prue."

"All the people from the village dead, all of them gone forever. It doesn't feel as if we won."

"Drink this," Aislinne interrupted, holding out the water skin.

Prue groped for it in a way that suggested she was struggling with her muscle control. "Put it in my hand, Pan."

"What's wrong?" he asked, doing as she requested and watching her take a long, slow drink. "Are you hurt?"

She finished drinking and held out the skin for him to take. Aislinne took it instead, giving Pan a worried look.

Prue's laugh was soft and unpleasant. "The King of the Silver River warned me there might be something more taken away. He as much as told me to plan on it if I did what he asked of me. I didn't pay enough attention to what that might mean. I didn't want to. I only wanted to help you."

"You did help me," he told her.

"Attacking the demon to distract him long enough for you to fight back cost the scarlet dove its life—if it possessed any real life in the first place. I don't think it did. I don't think it was real. I think it was a part of me. So when it was destroyed, another part of me was destroyed with it."

Pan shook his head, bending close to look in her milky eyes. "What are you talking about? What's been destroyed?"

She gave him a small smile, and her hand found his cheek. "It doesn't matter, Pan. It isn't your fault."

"Prue, you have to tell me. What's been destroyed?"

Her eyes filled with tears. "My sight, Pan. When the demon tore the scarlet dove off its face and smashed it, I lost the rest of my sight. Now I really am blind. Completely. I can't see a thing."

THIRTY-TWO

B Y MIDDAY, FOLLOWING THE MORNING THAT WIT-
nessed the end of the Drouj threat, the news of the Elven
victory at Aphalion Pass had reached Arborlon. A messenger
dispatched by Haren Crayel, captain of the Home Guard and commanding officer, had spread the word freely on his way to give his report to the Queen, and the city had erupted in cheers of jubilation and
relief. Impromptu gatherings quickly escalated into full-scale celebra-
tions that spread throughout the entire city, and by noon there was virtually no one who hadn't heard the details.

Among those who had heard were Isoeld Severine and First Minister Teonette. The messenger had made certain they both knew all the
details of the struggle that had resulted in the death of Taureq Siq and
the wholesale flight of his Troll army. He had also advised them of the
incredible appearance of Phryne Amarantyne riding astride a dragon
and bearing the missing blue Elfstones, the magic of both beast and talismans combining to put a decisive halt to the Drouj invasion. He
closed by adding that the Princess was on her way now to the home

city to meet with the High Council, where she intended to set right the matters of who had killed her father and who was entitled to sit upon the throne.

All true, of course, save for that last part. But that was what the Orullian brothers had instructed him to say to the Queen, and Xac Wen knew how to tell a lie when it was needed and a greater good would be served. He had done it before, and he would do it again—though never with half the satisfaction he felt this time.

By midafternoon, he had completed his task, departed the palace and the chambers of the Queen, where she had received him with frosty silence, and headed straight to the north gates of the Ashenell where Tasha had told him they would rendezvous. The day was warm and overcast, and the skies suggested rain by nightfall. But in his present good mood, it felt decidedly bright and warm.

He found Tasha and Tenerife right where they had said they would be, just past the cemetery gates, hiding out of sight behind a scattering of ancient tombs in a small copse of evergreens.

"How was it?" Tasha asked at once. "Did you do as I asked, little monkey?"

"If you stop calling me names, Tasha, I might find myself more willing to carry out requests of the sort you keep making of me!" the boy snapped in reply. "Yes, of course I did as you asked."

"How did she respond?"

The boy shrugged. "She didn't like hearing any of it; you could tell that much by what she didn't say. She just listened and stared at me and then sent me away."

"Teonette?"

"He wasn't there. I didn't see him until I was leaving and repeated everything again. He gave me the same treatment." He paused. "Why are we doing all this? Why not just march right in there and haul her off to the prisons? Why not take it before the High Council and expose her for what she is? Why are we messing around with this?"

"Because we have to be careful here," Tenerife advised. "Putting her in prison isn't even a possibility. She is a Queen, and the Elves don't put their rulers in prison. They banish them or confine them to their quarters in some out-of-the-way place."

"More to the point, we don't have the proof we need that she killed Oparion Amarantyne. If Phryne had lived . . ."

Tasha couldn't finish. He shook his head, his lips tight. "We need her to confess. If she thinks Phryne is coming for her, we might find a way to get her to do that."

"Well, I made sure that's what she thinks," the boy declared. "But what good does telling her a lie do us?"

Tasha leaned over and grasped him by his shoulder, one great hand taking hold almost gently. "Let's wait a bit and see."

Tenerife left them then, and the big man and the boy sat together at the foot of one of the tombs and shared a lunch the former had packed down out of the pass. They visited quietly after that, talking of yesterday and what Phryne Amarantyne had done and how it would change everything that had happened since the Drouj had appeared.

"Have you heard any more from Panterra or Prue?" Xac asked at one point. "Did they find each other? Do you know what has happened to them?"

Tasha Orullian shook his head, looking sad. "I don't, young Xac. They seem set upon a course that could take them away from us entirely. I do think Panterra must have found Phryne or she wouldn't have been able to come back to us at Aphalion. I can't guess what might have happened to him since. Of little sister, I know nothing at all. But we'll keep searching until we find them both."

"I want to help," the boy declared grimly. "I don't want them to end up like . . ." He cut short what he was going to say and stared at the tops of his boots. "Poor Phryne. At least she found the Elfstones she was searching for." He managed a faint smile. "She seemed to know how to use them well enough on those Trolls, didn't she? But it was the dragon that was so . . . well, you saw it, too. She not only rode it, she managed to control it. She had it flying where she wanted and made it use its fire to break apart the Drouj attack. Imagine how it would feel to be able to do that—to fly on a dragon and turn it against your enemies."

Tasha shook his head. "Some things you're not supposed to do. Riding a dragon is one of them. She crossed a line when she did that, and I think she paid the price for it."

Xac Wen nodded. "Maybe. Doesn't matter. It was still wonderful. I won't ever forget it."

The big man clasped his hands and sighed. "None of us will, little man. None of us will."

They were silent after that, lost in thought. The sun drifted west, the light faded to dusk, and the world slowed and stilled around them. The clouds that had begun to form earlier had massed and darkened further, and the first few drops of rain began to dampen their faces.

It was fully dark and raining hard when Tenerife reappeared. "They're off," he announced, giving Tasha a look.

"Then so are we." The big man was on his feet at once. He turned to Xac Wen, who had scrambled up after him. "It might be better if you wait here."

The boy was incensed. "I'm not waiting here! I did everything you asked of me, and I'm coming with you to see how this ends. You can't stop me!"

Tenerife gave a short laugh. "Who would be foolish enough to try?"

Tasha bent close, his features taut and expressionless. "Listen to me, then. If you come, you can only watch. You can do nothing else. Agreed?"

"Agreed."

"You will also have to keep to yourself everything you see. Maybe forever. That might be hard for a wild jaybird like you. Can you do it? Do you promise? No matter what?"

"I promise. Not a word."

They set out at a trot, Tenerife leading the way. As they went, he quickly explained that he had kept watch on the palace near its rear entry until well after dark before seeing Isoeld surface from out of a small cottage at the rear of the grounds that he knew to be connected to the palace by an underground tunnel and through which Elven rulers had been slipping away to clandestine meetings since long before he was born. Teonette had been waiting just at the edge of the grounds, and together they had set out on foot traveling eastward.

"The rats flee the sinking ship," Tasha observed. "Just as I thought they would."

"They will have horses and a carriage waiting, but not until they are safely outside the city," he finished.

"Then we can catch them before they escape," Tasha responded, and picked up the pace.

They raced through the city in a line, Tenerife leading, Xac Wen trailing, down roads and pathways, through small stands of trees and between houses, three shadows lost in the darkness and the rain. At times, even Xac found it hard to tell where it was they were going, but Tenerife seemed completely certain and never hesitated.

"Stay well behind us and out of sight," Tasha told Xac at one point. "Don't let her see you. We don't want her to know that you're with us."

Xac Wen wasn't entirely certain what they intended to do, but he understood well enough that the Queen would recognize him if he showed himself and the brothers didn't want that.

Damp all the way through and winded when they finally slowed, the boy peered through the gloom and mist at the eastern edge of the city amid scattered woods and tall grasses to watch the distant flicker of a light bobbing and swaying not too far ahead. Tenerife turned and pointed, nodding back at his brother and Xac, and all three dropped into a crouch as they continued forward. The boy knew how to move without making noise much better than most, a street kid of his own choosing for most of his life, his home life untroubled but boring when compared with the adventure he had always found in the larger world. So he kept pace with the Orullians and did so silently, hanging back so as not to be in the way, watching the figures ahead grow steadily larger and more distinct until at last he could see their faces.

Isoeld Severine and Teonette.

They were following a narrow path, each of them carrying a bundle, wrapped in heavy-weather cloaks with hoods pulled up so that the only view he had of their faces was when they looked back now and then and the light caught their features. It was clear they had a destination in mind and were hurrying to reach it. Xac guessed the news had unsettled them enough that they had decided to get away before Phryne arrived to confront them. Given that the Princess knew the truth about them and now possessed the magic of the Elfstones, neither Queen nor first minister saw much future in Arborlon. Better to slip away and start over somewhere else in the valley—a self-imposed exile that would not be challenged once they were gone.

Of course, they wouldn't be traveling without something to trade for what they needed. What would they have taken that would be valuable enough to give them the means to attempt a fresh start?

The boy couldn't think of anything, and in any event there was no further time to consider the matter. The pair had reached the carriage that Tasha had foreseen they would have arranged, a team of horses already hitched in place and a minder waiting. A few words were exchanged, and the minder took something from Teonette and disappeared into the night. The first minister watched him go, then opened the carriage door and helped the Queen inside. As she glanced back once, Xac Wen saw her face clearly. Even at his young age and with his limited experience, he thought her the most beautiful woman he had ever seen.

"Now," Tenerife said to his brother.

They sprang to their feet and sprinted for the carriage, tearing through the thin screen of trees and breaking out into the open not fifty feet from the carriage. Teonette saw them coming and vaulted into the driver's seat, a more agile man than Xac would have believed, given his size. But Tenerife was quicker and caught hold of the reins on the lead horses, swinging the team about to prevent it from bolting. Tasha was a few steps behind, and he gained the first step of the carriage just as Isoeld bolted out the door on the other side and began to run.

For a moment everything was swallowed in rain, darkness, and confusion. Xac did as he had been told and stayed well back from where the struggle was taking place around the carriage. But he saw everything that happened. Teonette had produced a short sword and was hacking down at Tasha. Tenerife was still struggling with the traces and the team, trying to hold them in place. But he lost his grip and was thrown down, and the team bolted ahead with Teonette still in the driver's seat urging them on. Tasha hung on to the carriage for a few seconds longer and then let go, staggering ahead for a few steps before dropping on all fours, muddied and soaked.

The carriage thundered through the darkness and disappeared from view, the first minister urging it on.

Tenerife ran past his brother to give chase, but Tasha called out sharply, "Let him go! The Queen is the one we want!"

Tenerife drew up and turned back, panting. "You're right. We can find him anytime."

The brothers trudged back to where Xac Wen waited. Without being asked, the boy pointed in the direction he had seen Isoeld Severine go. "Good eyes, eagle boy," Tenerife said, giving him a grin.

They began tracking the Queen. It wasn't all that difficult. She was leaving a trail so easy to follow that even the darkness and rain failed to mask it. Even Xac was able to pick it out with no trouble. Tenerife led once more, and the three picked their way ahead through the trees at a steady pace, watching for any sign of their quarry. Her cloak was found discarded a hundred yards off, apparently too cumbersome for her to be bothered with. A scarf was discovered farther on, then the bundle she had been carrying.

They hurried ahead, slowly closing the gap between themselves and their quarry. After thirty minutes of hard pursuit, they caught up to her. By then, she had run herself out and was collapsed on the ground beneath a towering hickory, her clothes muddied and torn, her face twisted in fury.

"You have no right to treat me so!" she spat at them.

"We have every right," Tenerife replied. "We are here at the command of the Princess. She insists you be present when she arrives."

"I don't answer to her! She isn't anything to me!"

"So it would appear, given your efforts to have her imprisoned and killed." Tasha gave her a smile. "Do you think she doesn't intend to see you pay for your treachery? What will you tell the members of the High Council when she confronts you with the truth? Do you think your lies will count for anything then? She's a hero now, Isoeld. She saved the Elven nation with her acts of courage at Aphalion Pass."

Hiding back in the trees, remaining perfectly still, Xac Wen could still see clearly the look of mingled fury and despair on the Queen's face.

"I will deny everything! No one will challenge me!"

Tasha shrugged. "Perhaps. We're going to find out, at any rate. Too bad your first minister won't be there to support you in your efforts. I've never seen anyone run away so fast."

He reached for her arm, but she jerked away quickly, her haunted eyes shifting this way and that. "Teonette is a coward. If not for me, he would have crawled back to the High Council begging for mercy long ago. Let him go. I didn't need him then, and I don't need him now."

"You can tell all that to the High Council when we bring you before them," Tenerife said brightly. "It should be interesting to see their reaction."

She sneered at him. "You are such a fool. You and your brother both. You think this matter all done and over already, don't you? The little Princess returns, the conquering heroine, and the evil Queen is deposed and sent into exile. So simple. Except that isn't how it's going to happen. The Princess will make her case, but I will make mine, as well. She is young and wild and often confused—everyone knows that. I'll convince the High Council that she misread what she heard and saw. I was there, but it was an assassin that killed the King. I was trying to save him, and I did manage to save her. But she was so out of her mind with grief that she had to be restrained and locked away for her own protection."

Tasha and Tenerife exchanged a quick glance.

"It won't work," the former declared. "They won't believe you."

"No? Why don't we find out? Take me back and let me face them. Running away was never a good idea in the first place. Teonette's solution—a coward's way. In fact, he forced me to go with him. He threatened to kill me if I didn't. The assassin was his doing, not mine. I discovered it only tonight. He admitted it. He wanted me for himself. He's always wanted me."

"You had nothing to do with the killing? Is that what you plan to say?"

"Of course! Look at me! Do I appear dangerous to you? Do you think the High Council will see me as dangerous? Or as a beautiful woman coveted and manipulated by strong men!"

The brothers stared at her in silence. She looked from one to the other, and then walked right up to Tasha and cupped his face in her hands. "You can't win this, Tasha. Not this way. But there is another. You could support me. You could tell them that what I say is the truth. If you did that, I would make you my new first minister. And your brother could have a place on the High Council, too. There's no reason you shouldn't both be there to help me govern as Queen. We share the same concerns; we both want to see things set right. Phryne is young and untrained; she needs time to grow and mature. When I am gone, she can be Queen after me. There's plenty of time yet for her. We can make her understand."

She was touching his face all over. "In the meantime, you can hunt down Teonette and silence him! We both want to see him punished. We could share so much, you and I."

Her voice was seductive and compelling, and she stroked the big man's arms and shoulders, casting glances at Tenerife as she did so, commanding attention as only beautiful women can, demanding they consider what in a different time and place they never would.

Tasha nodded slowly. "We could do that. Couldn't we, Tenerife?"

"We could," his brother agreed.

"Be your consorts together?" Tasha pressed. "Act as your protectors and advisers?"

"All of that! Anything you want!"

Xac Wen, still in hiding, was so horrified at what was happening that for a moment he almost left his hiding place to try to stop it.

Tasha was caressing Isoeld in response to her advances. "You are a beautiful creature, Isoeld," he told her. "What man wouldn't want to do what you asked of him?"

"Only a fool," Tenerife said.

Tasha placed his hands on either side of her face and drew her to him. "But then we've never been particularly bright," he whispered.

Then he tightened his grip, wrenched her head sharply to one side, and broke her neck.

THIRTY-THREE

ON THE DAY PANTERRA QU HAD CHOSEN FOR HIS departure, almost a month after his battle with the demon at Declan Reach, Prue Liss walked to the edge of the village with him to say good-bye. Aislinne Kray went with them, mostly because she wanted to say good-bye, too, but also to make sure Prue was able to return home safely. By now, Prue had learned to make her way about the village unaided, able to find her way from Aislinne's home, where she was living and studying, to visit with her parents and others and to run small errands. Every day she became more capable, less hindered by her blindness. Her instincts, still strong in spite of the death of the scarlet dove, seemed to provide her with a fresh way of seeing things; much of the time it was as if she could actually see with her other senses. Aislinne was teaching her to become self-reliant, working with her on counting steps and marking obstacles, tracking her movements to familiar places until she was able to go to them alone.

"Gray out here today," Pan said to her. He was holding her hand as if they were children again. He was not guiding her; he knew better than to do that. She thought that mostly he just wanted to be close to her until it was time. "Rain clouds everywhere."

She could smell the air, damp and metallic. For some, it might seem a reflection of the dark mood of the people of the valley, almost all of whom had found their lives upended in one way or another since the Drouj invasion had been turned back. Even in the farthest corners south, where no hint of the danger had manifested itself and life had gone on pretty much as always during the time of the threat, the confidence and certainty of earlier times had evaporated. No longer could anyone afford to feel safe behind the protective walls that had offered sanctuary for so long. No longer could they rely on the valley to protect them. Those days were gone forever, and no one knew what life would be like in the aftermath.

Nor were the peoples of the valley united in even the smallest of ways now that both the Elves and the people of Glensk Wood had been left to defend the valley on their own. None of the resident Trolls or Spiders had come forward to help. None of the other villages or towns or city fortresses south had chosen to stand with them. Not even Hadrian Esselline, after making his vaunted promises of assistance personally to Sider Ament, had materialized. In the end, no one had come, and those who had been betrayed were not about to forget it.

This had more than a little to do with Panterra's leaving, Prue believed, although he would never admit it to her.

"You understand why I'm doing this, don't you?" he asked her suddenly, as if reading her mind. "Why I'm going?"

"I do," she assured him.

"I don't want to leave you," he added. An uncomfortable silence settled in place between then. He squeezed her hand gently. "If there were another way, I wouldn't."

She looked up at him with her milky eyes and smiled. "Stop apologizing, Pan. You don't have to keep reassuring me about this. I know I can't go with you. Not like this. You can't be out there worrying about me. You have to do this without me, and I am at peace with that."

"I just feel bad about it."

She would have felt bad, as well, in other circumstances. Terrible, in fact, if not for what she had been told by the King of the Silver River. If Pan survived his battle with the demon hunting him, his destiny was to guide the people of the valley to a new safehold in a new country in much the same way as their ancestors were guided here five hundred years earlier. She believed it was so, and if it were to happen Pan must return from his search. It might take him months, but eventually he would come back. When he did, he would take her with him to wherever he was going. She was certain that was how it would happen.

"Where are we meeting them?" Aislinne asked suddenly, walking a discreet distance behind the couple.

The Orullians. They were coming down out of Arborlon to make the journey with Pan. It had been their idea, in fact. With the people of the valley now fully aware of the dangers lurking without and splintered in ways that might never be repaired, thoughts had turned anew to striking out for distant territories. The Elves had always wanted to go, foremost of all the races to wander and resettle, and now they had both their incentive and their chance.

Tasha and Tenerife had made the decision weeks ago, not long after Phryne's death. With the old order wiped out, the Amarantynes forever gone, they had little connection to those who now struggled to determine how the new order would be shaped. Better to be elsewhere while things were being sorted out, Tasha argued. To be among the first to find another place where those who might be dissatisfied with life in the valley could resettle, Tenerife added.

They had asked Panterra to come with them, and he had agreed.

Prue wasn't entirely sure why. It might have been for much the same reasons that the Orullians were leaving. Or perhaps he already had an inkling that the best use of his newly established responsibility as a bearer of the black staff meant discovering what was out there instead of trying to imitate his predecessors. Whatever his thinking, he was unwittingly fulfilling the destiny that the King of the Silver River had said would be his.

They reached the western edge of the village, and as they did so Tasha and Tenerife stepped out of the trees. "Late again," the former chided Pan. "You'll have to do better if you intend to travel with us."

They hugged, all of them sharing a warm greeting, even Aislinne, and then stood awkwardly, looking for a way to avoid what was coming next.

"You look well enough for someone who fought and killed a demon," Tenerife observed, mostly to Pan, but taking in Prue and Aislinne with a sideways glance.

"We're hardy folk down here in the valley," Pan replied. "Are you both healed, as well?"

The brothers shared a shrug and an exchange of glances. "Mostly. On the outside, at least. I think we're still a little bruised in here." Tenerife touched his heart. "When we think of Phryne."

Pan felt a sudden tightening in his throat, and he had to fight to hold himself steady so that no more tears would be shed when so many already had been. "We all miss her," he said.

It was all he could manage. It didn't begin to express what he was really feeling, the intense pain her loss had caused him, the dark emotions he was keeping closed away. But Phryne was gone, and there was nothing he could do about it. In truth, he didn't think there ever had been anything.

"Did they ever catch the Queen?" Prue asked.

"Neither her nor her consort. Both disappeared without a trace."

"But they'll be found sooner or later," Tasha insisted.

The way he said it told her more than he had intended. Prue could read things into the way people spoke, her instincts telling her what wasn't said as surely as what was. Tasha was telling them what they wanted to hear. She wondered what that meant about the fate of Isoeld Severine.

Aislinne cleared her throat. "Have the Elves chosen a new leader yet?"

Tasha shook his head. "They debate endlessly, each faction trying to persuade the other of the rightness of their own choice. All are suitable, if your standards are minimal. None is outstanding. I think the discussion will go on awhile longer."

"In the meantime, the High Council rules the Kingdom and no one seems entirely displeased that this is so. Perhaps the days of a monarchy are coming to a close."

Tasha gave him a look. "Well, we'll know soon enough on our return. Are you ready, Panterra Qu?"

Prue heard Pan hesitate. "I need a moment to speak with Prue. Alone."

She felt him take her arm and guide her some distance away from the others. When she could sense that they were far enough removed that their conversation would not be overheard, he stopped and faced her.

"I have some things to say before I go. Some things I need to say. I want to begin with this: I will never forget what you did for me. Not ever. I owe you my life, and I will dedicate that life to doing the things I think you would want me to do. You gave up so much for me, Prue. Your sight, but more than that. Your whole life was settled. We were to be together, partners and Trackers. Now that won't happen. But maybe some other things will."

"Pan, you don't have to—"

"Just listen," he interrupted. "Just let me get this out. I'm going with the Orullians because I believe that at the end of the day we will all have to go. We will have to leave this valley and find new homes. We won't leave together or stay together. Trolls, humans, Spiders, Elves, whatever names we give ourselves, we won't stay together. Different paths will be taken and different futures found. What I want to do is find our future, yours and mine."

She felt tears spring to her eyes. "I would like that."

"I can't imagine my life without you, Prue. You are my best friend; you always will be. You are another part of me, a part that when missing leaves me feeling incomplete. I want us to be together again. I want us to get back what we can of our old life, even if it's not here. Will you wait for me so that we can try to do that?"

She put her arms around him. "You know I will, Pan. I will always wait for you."

His hand came up to cup the back of her head, his fingers tangling in her red hair. "I won't make you wait long, I promise."

He held her and for a long moment neither of them spoke. Then Prue broke away, stepping back, pushing at him. "You have to leave now. Go on. Tasha and Tenerife are waiting."

He stayed where he was for a moment longer, and then she heard him walk away. She followed, taking her time, listening to the voices of the others greeting him as he returned.

Then they were all hugging one another a final time, exchanging good-byes and good lucks and promises to be careful and to meet again soon.

When it came Tasha's turn to hug her, Prue felt his hand press something into hers. "These are for you," he said. "Keep them safe until you find the right person to give them to. It isn't me or Tenerife, and just now I can't say who it is. But I know they will be safe with you."

She realized from the size and shape of what she held that he had given her the blue Elfstones. "I can't take these," she said. "They belong to the Elves."

"They do," the big man agreed. "To all the Elves, in point of fact. But only one can wield them, and it shouldn't be just anyone. It should be someone who thinks less of himself than of his people. Or her people, perhaps. For now, they should be put away somewhere safe. Phryne gave them to me . . . there, at the end, when I was carrying her from the pass. She told me to keep them safe. You may be blind, little sister, but you see things much more clearly than most people."

Prue shook her head. "This just doesn't feel right. I'm not even an Elf."

"Ah, but you are. We've already established that, haven't we, Tenerife?"

"Some time back," his brother replied. "In fact, you yourself told Xac Wen you were an Elf, if I remember right."

"So keep them safe until the Elves are ready for them again. You'll know when the time is right."

Then they were moving away, the brothers and Pan, calling back to them, their voices fading out as they passed through the trees and down the pathways and beyond her hearing.

She felt Aislinne put her arm around her shoulders. "They will be back before you know it," she whispered. "Safe and sound."

Prue nodded wordlessly. She knew without question that what Aislinne said was true.

ABOUT THE AUTHOR

TERRY BROOKS is the *New York Times* bestselling author of more than thirty books, including the Legends of Shannara novels *Bearers of the Black Staff* and *The Measue of the Magic;* the Genesis of Shannara novels *Armageddon's Children, The Elves of Cintra,* and *The Gypsy Morph; The Sword of Shannara;* the Voyage of the Jerle Shannara trilogy: *Ilse Witch, Antrax,* and *Morgawr;* the High Druid of Shannara trilogy: *Jarka Ruus, Tanequil,* and *Straken;* the nonfiction book *Sometimes the Magic Works: Lessons from a Writing Life;* and the novel based upon the screenplay and story by George Lucas, *Star Wars:*® *Episode I The Phantom Menace.*™ His novels *Running with the Demon* and *A Knight of the Word* were selected by the *Rocky Mountain News* as two of the best science fiction/fantasy novels of the twentieth century. The author was a practicing attorney for many years but now writes full-time. He lives with his wife, Judine, in the Pacific Northwest.

ABOUT THE TYPE

This book was set in Berling. Designed in 1951 by Karl Erik Forsberg for the Typefoundry Berlingska Stilgjuteri AB in Lund, Sweden, it was released the same year in foundry type by H. Berthold AG. A classic old-face design, its generous proportions and inclined serifs make it highly legible.